Within an Inch
Life

Emile Gaboriau

Alpha Editions

Contents

P 169, 174
P 173
P 179
P 181
P 303
P 313
P 336
P 339
P 379

FIRST PART

FIRE AT VALPINSON

These were the facts:—

I.

In the night from the 22nd to the 23rd of June, 1871, towards one o'clock in the morning, the Paris suburb of Sauveterre, the principal and most densely populated suburb of that pretty town, was startled by the furious gallop of a horse on its ill-paved streets.

A number of peaceful citizens rushed to the windows.

The dark night allowed these only to see a peasant in his shirt sleeves, and bareheaded, who belabored a large gray mare, on which he rode bareback, with his heels and a huge stick.

This man, after having passed the suburbs, turned into National Street, formerly Imperial Street, crossed New-Market Square, and stopped at last before the fine house which stands at the corner of Castle Street.

This was the house of the mayor of Sauveterre, M. Seneschal, a former lawyer, and now a member of the general council.

Having alighted, the peasant seized the bell-knob, and began to ring so furiously, that, in a few moments, the whole house was in an uproar.

A minute later, a big, stout servant-man, his eyes heavy with sleep, came and opened the door, and then cried out in an angry voice,—

"Who are you, my man? What do you want? Have you taken too much wine? Don't you know at whose house you are making such a row?"

"I wish to see the mayor," replied the peasant instantly. "Wake him up!"

M. Seneschal was wide awake.

Dressed in a large dressing-gown of gray flannel, a candlestick in his hand, troubled, and unable to disguise his trouble, he had just come down into the hall, and heard all that was said.

"Here is the mayor," he said in an ill-satisfied tone. "What do you want of him at this hour, when all honest people are in bed?"

Pushing the servant aside, the peasant came up to him, and said, making not the slightest attempt at politeness,—

"I come to tell you to send the fire-engine."

"The engine!"

"Yes; at once. Make haste!"

The mayor shook his head.

"Hm!" he said, according to a habit he had when he was at a loss what to do; "hm, hm!"

And who would not have been embarrassed in his place?

To get the engine out, and to assemble the firemen, he had to rouse the whole town; and to do this in the middle of the night was nothing less than to frighten the poor people of Sauveterre, who had heard the drums beating the alarm but too often during the war with the Germans, and then again during the reign of the Commune. Therefore M. Seneschal asked,—

"Is it a serious fire?"

"Serious!" exclaimed the peasant. "How could it be otherwise with such a wind as this,—a wind that would blow off the horns of our oxen."

"Hm!" uttered the mayor again. "Hm, hm!"

It was not exactly the first time, since he was mayor of Sauveterre, that he was thus roused by a peasant, who came and cried under his window, "Help! Fire, fire!"

At first, filled with compassion, he had hastily called out the firemen, put himself at their head, and hurried to the fire.

And when they reached it, out of breath, and perspiring, after having made two or three miles at double-quick, they found what? A wretched heap of straw, worth about ten dollars, and almost consumed by the fire. They had had their trouble for nothing.

The peasants in the neighborhood had cried, "Wolf!" so often, when there was no reason for it, that, even when the wolf really was there, the townspeople were slow in believing it.

"Let us see," said M. Seneschal: "what is burning?"

The peasant seemed to be furious at all these delays, and bit his long whip.

"Must I tell you again and again," he said, "that every thing is on fire,—barns, outhouses, haystacks, the houses, the old castle, and every thing? If you wait much longer, you won't find one stone upon another in Valpinson."

The effect produced by this name was prodigious.

"What?" asked the mayor in a half-stifled voice, "Valpinson is on fire?"

"Yes."

"At Count Claudieuse's?"

"Of course."

"Fool! Why did you not say so at once?" exclaimed the mayor.

He hesitated no longer.

"Quick!" he said to his servant, "go and get me my clothes. Wait, no! my wife can help me. There is no time to be lost. You run to Bolton, the drummer, you know, and tell him from me to beat the alarm instantly all over town. Then you run to Capt. Parenteau's, and explain to him what you have heard. Ask him to get the keys of the engine-house.—Wait!—when you have done that, come back and put the horse in.—Fire at Valpinson! I shall go with the engine. Go, run, knock at every door, cry, 'Fire! Fire!' Tell everybody to come to the New-Market Square."

When the servant had run off as fast as he could, the mayor turned to the peasant, and said,—

"And you, my good man, you get on your horse, and reassure the count. Tell them all to take courage, not to give up; we are coming to help them."

But the peasant did not move.

"Before going back to Valpinson," he said, "I have another commission to attend to in town."

"Why? What is it?"

"I am to get the doctor to go back with me."

"The doctor! Why? Has anybody been hurt?"

"Yes, master, Count Claudieuse."

"How imprudent! I suppose he rushed into danger as usual."

"Oh, no! He has been shot twice!"

The mayor of Sauveterre nearly dropped his candlestick.

"Shot! Twice!" he said. "Where? When? By whom?"

"Ah! I don't know."

"But"—

"All I can tell you is this. They have carried him into a little barn that was not on fire yet. There I saw him myself lying on the straw, pale like a linen sheet, his eyes closed, and bloody all over."

"Great God! They have not killed him?"

"He was not dead when I left."

"And the countess?"

"Our lady," replied the peasant with an accent of profound veneration, "was in the barn on her knees by the count's side, washing his wounds with fresh water. The two little ladies were there too."

M. Seneschal trembled with excitement.

"It is a crime that has been committed, I suppose."

"Why, of course!"

"But who did it? What was the motive?"

"Ah! that is the question."

"The count is very passionate, to be sure, quite violent, in fact; but still he is the best and fairest of men, everybody knows that."

"Everybody knows it."

"He never did any harm to anybody."

"That is what all say."

"As for the countess"—

"Oh!" said the peasant eagerly, "she is the saint of saints."

The mayor tried to come to some conclusion.

"The criminal, therefore, must be a stranger. We are overrun with vagabonds and beggars on the tramp. There is not a day on which a lot of ill-looking fellows do not appear at my office, asking for help to get away."

The peasant nodded his head, and said,—

"That is what I think. And the proof of it is, that, as I came along, I made up my mind I would first get the doctor, and then report the crime at the police office."

"Never mind," said the mayor. "I will do that myself. In ten minutes I shall see the attorney of the Commonwealth. Now go. Don't spare your horse, and tell your mistress that we are all coming after you."

In his whole official career M. Seneschal had never been so terribly shocked. He lost his head, just as he did on that unlucky day, when, all of a sudden, nine hundred militia-men fell upon him, and asked to be fed and lodged. Without his wife's help he would never have been able to dress himself. Still he was ready when his servant returned.

The good fellow had done all he had been told to do, and at that moment the beat of the drum was heard in the upper part of the town.

"Now, put the horse in," said M. Seneschal: "let me find the carriage at the door when I come back."

In the streets he found all in an uproar. At every window a head popped out, full of curiosity or terror; on all sides house doors were opened, and promptly closed again.

"Great God!" he thought, "I hope I shall find Daubigeon at home!" M. Daubigeon, who had been first in the service of the empire, and then in the service of the republic, was one of M. Seneschal's best friends. He was a man of about forty years, with a cunning look in his eye, a permanent smile on his face, and a confirmed bachelor, with no small pride in his consistency. The good people of Sauveterre thought he did not look stern and solemn enough for his profession. To be sure he was very highly esteemed; but his optimism was not popular; they reproached him for being too kind-hearted, too reluctant to press criminals whom he had to prosecute, and thus prone to encourage evil-doers.

He accused himself of not being inspired with the "holy fire," and, as he expressed it in his own way, "of robbing Themis of all the time he could, to devote it to the friendly Muses." He was a passionate lover of fine books, rare editions, costly bindings, and fine illustrations; and much the larger part of his annual income of about ten thousand francs went to buying books. A scholar of the old-fashioned type, he professed boundless admiration for Virgil and Juvenal, but, above all, for Horace, and proved his devotion by constant quotations.

Roused, like everybody else in the midst of his slumbers, this excellent man hastened to put on his clothes, when his old housekeeper came in, quite excited, and told him that M. Seneschal was there, and wanted to see him.

"Show him in!" he said, "show him in!"

And, as soon as the mayor entered, he continued:—

"For you will be able to tell me the meaning of all this noise, this beating of drums,—

"'Clamorque, virum, clangorque tubarum.'"

"A terrible misfortune has happened," answered the mayor. From the tone of his voice one might have imagined it was he

- 6 -

himself who had been afflicted; and the lawyer was so strongly impressed in this way, that he said,—

"My dear friend, what is the matter? *Quid?* Courage, my friend, keep cool! Remember that the poet advises us, in misfortune never to lose our balance of mind:—

> *"'Æquam, memento, rebus in arduis,*
>
> *Sevare mentem.'"*

"Incendiaries have set Valpinson on fire!" broke in the mayor.

"You do not say so? Great God!

> *"'Jupiter,*
>
> *Quod verbum audio.'"*

"More than that. Count Claudieuse has been shot, and by this time he is probably dead."

"Oh!"

"You hear the drummer is beating the alarm. I am going to the fire; and I have only come here to report the matter officially to you, and to ask you to see to it that justice be done promptly and energetically."

There was no need of such a serious appeal to stop at once all the lawyer's quotations.

"Enough!" he said eagerly. "Come, let us take measures to catch the wretches."

When they reached National Street, it was as full as at mid-day; for Sauveterre is one of those rare provincial towns in which an excitement is too rare a treat to be neglected. The sad event had by this time become fully known everywhere. At first the news had been doubted; but when the doctor's cab had passed the crowd at full speed, escorted by a peasant on horseback, the reports were believed. Nor had the firemen lost time. As soon as the mayor and M. Daubigeon appeared on New-Market Square, Capt. Parenteau rushed up to them, and, touching his helmet with a military salute, said,—

"My men are ready."

"All?"

"There are hardly ten absentees. When they heard that Count and Countess Claudieuse were in need—great heavens!—you know, they all were ready in a moment."

"Well, then, start and make haste," commanded M. Seneschal. "We shall overtake you on the way: M. Daubigeon and I are going to pick up M. Galpin, the magistrate."

They had not far to go.

The magistrate had already been looking for them all over town: he was just appearing on the Square, and saw them at once.

In striking contrast with the commonwealth attorney, M. Galpin was a professional man in the full sense of the word, and perhaps a little more. He was the magistrate all over, from head to foot, and from the gaiters on his ankles to the light blonde whiskers on his face. Although he was quite young, yet no one had ever seen him smile, or heard him make a joke. He was so very stiff that M. Daubigeon suggested he had been impaled alive on the sword of justice.

At Sauveterre M. Galpin was looked upon as a superior man. He certainly believed it himself: hence he was very impatient at being confined to so narrow a sphere of action, and thought his brilliant ability wasted upon the prosecution of a chicken-thief or a poacher. But his almost desperate efforts to secure a better office had always been unsuccessful. In vain he had enlisted a host of friends in his behalf. In vain he had thrown himself into politics, ready to serve any party that would serve him.

But M. Galpin's ambition was not easily discouraged, and lately after a journey to Paris, he had thrown out hints at a great match, which would shortly procure him that influence in high places which so far he had been unable to obtain. When he joined M. Daubigeon and the mayor, he said,—

"Well, this is a horrible affair! It will make a tremendous noise." The mayor began to give him the details, but he said,—

"Don't trouble yourself. I know all you know. I met the peasant who had been sent in, and I have examined him."

Then, turning to the commonwealth attorney, he added,—

"I think we ought to proceed at once to the place where the crime has been committed."

"I was going to suggest it to you," replied M. Daubigeon.

"The gendarmes ought to be notified."

"M. Seneschal has just sent them word."

The magistrate was so much excited, that his cold impassiveness actually threatened to give way for once.

"There has been an attempt at murder."

"Evidently."

"Then we can act in concert, and side by side, each one in his own line of duty, you examining, and I preparing for the trial."

An ironical smile passed over the lips of the commonwealth attorney.

"You ought to know me well enough," he said, "to be sure that I have never interfered with your duties and privileges. I am nothing but a good old fellow, a friend of peace and of studies.

"'Sum piger et senior, Pieridumque comes.'"

"Then," exclaimed M. Seneschal, "nothing keeps us here any longer. I am impatient to be off; my carriage is ready; let us go!"

II.

In a straight line it is only a mile from Sauveterre to Valpinson; but that mile is as long as two elsewhere. M. Seneschal, however, had a good horse, "the best perhaps in the county," he said, as he got into his carriage. In ten minutes they had overtaken the firemen, who had left some time before them. And yet these good people, all of them master workmen of Sauveterre, masons, carpenters, and tilers, hurried along as fast as they could. They had half a dozen smoking torches with them to light them on the way: they walked, puffing and groaning, on the bad road, and pulling the two engines, together with the heavy cart on which they had piled up their ladders and other tools.

"Keep up, my friends!" said the mayor as he passed them,— "keep up!" Three minutes farther on, a peasant on horseback appeared in the dark, riding along like a forlorn knight in a romance. M. Daubigeon ordered him to halt. He stopped.

"You come from Valpinson?" asked M. Seneschal.

"Yes," replied the peasant.

"How is the count?"

"He has come to at last."

"What does the doctor say?"

"He says he will live. I am going to the druggist to get some medicines." M. Galpin, to hear better, was leaning out of the carriage. He asked,—

"Do they accuse any one?"

"No."

"And the fire?"

"They have water enough," replied the peasant, "but no engines: so what can they do? And the wind is rising again! Oh, what a misfortune!"

He rode off as fast as he could, while M. Seneschal was whipping his poor horse, which, unaccustomed as it was to such treatment, instead of going any faster, only reared, and jumped from side to side. The excellent man was in despair. He looked upon this crime as if it had been committed on purpose to disgrace him, and to do the greatest possible injury to his administration.

"For after all," he said, for the tenth time to his companions, "is it natural, I ask you, is it sensible, that a man should think of attacking the Count and the Countess Claudieuse, the most distinguished and the most esteemed people in the whole county, and especially a lady whose name is synonymous with virtue and charity?"

And, without minding the ruts and the stones in the road, M. Seneschal went on repeating all he knew about the owners of Valpinson.

Count Trivulce Claudieuse was the last scion of one of the oldest families of the county. At sixteen, about 1829, he had entered the navy as an ensign, and for many years he had appeared at Sauveterre only rarely, and at long intervals. In 1859 he had become a captain, and was on the point of being made admiral, when he had all of a sudden sent in his resignation, and taken up his residence at the Castle of Valpinson, although the house had nothing to show of its former splendor but two towers falling to pieces, and an immense mass of ruin and rubbish. For two years he had lived here alone, busy with building up the old house as well as it could be done, and by great energy and incessant labor restoring it to some of its former splendor. It was thought he would finish his days in this way, when one day the report arose that he was going to be married. The report, for once, proved true.

One fine day Count Claudieuse had left for Paris; and, a few days later, his friends had been informed by letter that he had married the daughter of one of his former colleagues, Miss Genevieve de Tassar. The amazement had been universal. The count looked like a gentleman, and was very well preserved; but he was at least forty-seven years old, and Miss Genevieve was hardly twenty. Now, if the bride had been poor, they would have understood the match, and approved it: it is but natural that a poor girl should sacrifice her heart to her daily bread. But here it was not so. The Marquis de Tassar was considered wealthy; and report said that his daughter had brought her husband fifty thousand dollars.

Next they had it that the bride was fearfully ugly, infirm, or at least hunchback, perhaps idiotic, or, at all events, of frightful temper.

By no means. She had come down; and everybody was amazed at her noble, quiet beauty. She had conversed with them, and charmed everybody.

Was it really a love-match, as people called it at Sauveterre? Perhaps so. Nevertheless there was no lack of old ladies who shook their heads, and said twenty-seven years difference between husband and wife was too much, and such a match could not turn out well.

All these dark forebodings came to nought. The fact was, that, for miles and miles around, there was not a happier couple to be found than the Count and the Countess Claudieuse; and two children, girls, who had appeared at an interval of four years, seemed to have secured the happiness of the house forever.

It is true the count retained somewhat of the haughty manners, the reserve, and the imperious tone, which he had acquired during the time that he controlled the destinies of certain important colonies. He was, moreover, naturally so passionate, that the slightest excitement made him turn purple in his face. But the countess was as gentle and as sweet as he was violent; and as she never failed to step in between her husband and the object of his wrath, as both he and she were naturally just, kind to excess, and generous to all, they were beloved by everybody. There was only one point on which the count was rather unmanageable, and that was the game laws. He was passionately fond of hunting, and watched all the year round with almost painful restlessness over his preserves, employing a number of keepers, and prosecuting poachers with such energy, that people said he would rather miss a hundred napoleons than a single bird.

The count and the countess lived quite retired, and gave their whole time, he to agricultural pursuits, and she to the education of her children. They entertained but little, and did not come to Sauveterre more than four times a year, to visit the Misses Lavarande, or the old Baron de Chandore. Every summer, towards the end of July, they went to Royan, where they had a cottage. When the season opened, and the count went hunting, the countess paid a visit to her relatives in Paris, with whom she usually stayed a few weeks.

It required a storm like that of 1870 to overthrow so peaceful an existence. When the old captain heard that the Prussians were on French soil, he felt all the instincts of the soldier and the Frenchman awake in his heart. He could not be kept at home, and went to headquarters. Although a royalist at heart, he did not hesitate a moment to offer his sword to Gambetta, whom he detested. They made him colonel of a regiment; and he fought like a lion, from the first day to the last, when he was thrown down and trod under foot in one of those fearful routs in which a part of Chanzy's army was utterly destroyed. When the armistice was signed, he returned to Valpinson; but no one except his wife ever succeeded in making him say a word about the campaign. He was asked to become a candidate for the assembly, and would have certainly been elected; but he refused, saying that he knew how to fight, but not how to talk.

The commonwealth attorney and the magistrate listened but very carelessly to these details, with which they were perfectly familiar. Suddenly M. Galpin asked,—

"Are we not getting near? I look and look; but I see no trace of a fire."

"We are in a deep valley," replied the mayor. "But we are quite near now, and, at the top of that hill before us, you will see enough."

This hill is well known in the whole province, and is frequently called the Sauveterre Mountain. It is so steep, and consists of such hard granite, that the engineers who laid out the great turnpike turned miles out of their way to avoid it. It overlooks the whole country; and, when M. Seneschal and his companions had reached the top, they could not control their excitement.

"Horresco!" murmured the attorney.

The burning house itself was hid by high trees; but columns of fire rose high above the tops, and illumined the whole region with their sombre light. The whole country was in a state of excitement. The short, square tower of Brechy sent the alarm from its big bell; and in the deep shade on all sides was heard the strange sound of the huge shells which the people here use for signals, and for the summoning of laborers at mealtimes. Hurried steps were heard on all the high-roads and by-roads; and peasants were continuously rushing by, with a bucket in each hand.

"It is too late for help," said M. Galpin.

"Such a fine property!" said the mayor, "and so well managed!" And regardless of danger, he dashed forward, down the hill; for Valpinson lies in a deep valley, half a mile from the river. Here all was terror, disorder, and confusion; and yet there was no lack of hands or of good-will. At the first alarm, all the people of the neighborhood had hurried up, and there were more coming every moment; but there was no one there to assume the command. They were mainly engaged in saving the furniture. The boldest tried to get into the rooms, and in a kind of rage, threw every thing they could lay hold on out of the window. Thus the courtyard was already half full of beds and mattresses, chairs and tables, books, linen, and clothes.

An immense clamor greeted the mayor and his companions.

"Here comes the mayor!" cried the peasants, encouraged by his presence, and all ready to obey him.

M. Seneschal took in the whole situation at a glance.

"Yes, here I am, my friends," he said, "and I thank you for your zeal. Now we must try not to waste our efforts. The farm buildings and the workshops are lost: we must give them up. Let us try to save the dwelling-house. The river is not far. We must form a chain. Everybody in line,—men and women! And now for water, water! Here come the engines!"

They really came thundering up: the firemen appeared on the scene. Capt. Parenteau took the command. At last the mayor was at leisure to inquire after Count Claudieuse.

"Master is down there," replied an old woman, pointing at a little cottage with a thatched roof. "The doctor has had him carried there."

"Let us go and see how he is," said the mayor to his two companions. They stopped at the door of the only room of the cottage. It was a large room with a floor of beaten clay; while overhead the blackened beams were full of working tools and parcels of seeds. Two beds with twisted columns and yellow curtains filled one side: on that on the left hand lay a little girl, four years old, fast asleep, and rolled up in a blanket, watched over by her sister, who was two or three years older. On the other bed, Count Claudieuse was lying, or rather sitting; for they had supported his back by all the pillows that had been saved from the fire. His chest was bare, and covered with blood; and a man, Dr. Seignebos, with his coat off, and his sleeves rolled up above the

- 14 -

elbows, was bending over him, and holding a sponge in one hand and a probe in the other, seemed to be engaged in a delicate and dangerous operation.

The countess, in a light muslin dress, was standing at the foot of her husband's bed, pale but admirably composed and resigned. She was holding a lamp, and moved it to and fro as the doctor directed. In a corner two servant-women were sitting on a box, and crying, their aprons turned over their heads.

At last the mayor of Sauveterre overcame his painful impressions, and entered the room. Count Claudieuse was the first to perceive him, and said,—

"Ah, here is our good M. Seneschal. Come nearer, my friend; come nearer. You see the year 1871 is a fatal year. It will soon leave me nothing but a few handfuls of ashes of all I possessed."

"It is a great misfortune," replied the excellent mayor; "but, after all, it is less than we apprehended. God be thanked, you are safe!"

"Who knows? I am suffering terribly."

The countess trembled.

"Trivulce!" she whispered in a tone of entreaty. "Trivulce!"

Never did lover glance at his beloved with more tenderness than Count Claudieuse did at his wife.

"Pardon me, my dear Genevieve, pardon me, if I show any want of courage."

A sudden nervous spasm seized him; and then he exclaimed in a loud voice, which sounded like a trumpet,—

"Sir! But sir! Thunder and lightning! You kill me!"

"I have some chloroform here," replied the physician coldly.

"I do not want any."

"Then you must make up your mind to suffer, and keep quiet now; for every motion adds to your pain."

Then sponging a jet of blood which spurted out from under his knife, he added,—

"However, you shall have a few minutes rest now. My eyes and my hand are exhausted. I see I am no longer young."

Dr. Seignebos was sixty years old. He was a small, thin man, with a bald head and a bilious complexion, carelessly dressed, and spending his life in taking off, wiping, and putting back again his large gold spectacles. His reputation was widespread; and they told of wonderful cures which he had accomplished. Still he had not many friends. The common people disliked his bitterness; the peasants, his strictness in demanding his fees; and the townspeople, his political views.

There was a story that one evening, at a public dinner, he had gotten up and said, "I drink to the memory of the only physician of whose pure and chaste renown I am envious,—the memory of my countryman, Dr. Guillotin of Saintes!"

Had he really offered such a toast? The fact is, he pretended to be a fierce radical, and was certainly the soul and the oracle of the small socialistic clubs in the neighborhood. People looked aghast when he began to talk of the reforms which he thought necessary; and they trembled when he proclaimed his convictions, that "the sword and the torch ought to search the rotten foundations of society."

These opinions, certain utilitarian views of like eccentricity, and still stranger experiments which he openly carried on before the whole world, had led people more than once to doubt the soundness of his mind. The most charitable said, "He is an oddity." This eccentric man had naturally no great fondness for M. Seneschal, the mayor, a former lawyer, and a legitimist. He did not think much of the commonwealth attorney, a useless bookworm. But he detested M. Galpin. Still he bowed to the three men; and, without minding his patient, he said to them,—

"You see, gentlemen, Count Claudieuse is in a bad plight. He has been fired at with a gun loaded with small shot; and wounds made in that way are very puzzling. I trust no vital part has been injured; but I cannot answer for any thing. I have often in my practice seen very small injuries, wounds caused by a small-sized shot, which, nevertheless, proved fatal, and showed their true character only twelve or fifteen hours after the accident had happened."

He would have gone on in this way, if the magistrate had not suddenly interrupted him, saying,—

"Doctor, you know I am here because a crime has been committed. The criminal has to be found out, and to be punished: hence I request your assistance, from this moment, in the name of the Law."

III.

By this single phrase M. Galpin made himself master of the situation, and reduced the doctor to an inferior position, in which, it is true, he had the mayor and the commonwealth attorney to bear him company. There was nothing now to be thought of, but the crime that had been committed, and the judge who was to punish the author. But he tried in vain to assume all the rigidity of his official air and that contempt for human feelings which has made justice so hateful to thousands. His whole being was impregnated with intense satisfaction, up to his beard, cut and trimmed like the box-hedges of an old-fashioned garden.

"Well, doctor," he asked, "first of all, have you any objection to my questioning your patient?"

"It would certainly be better for him to be left alone," growled Dr. Seignebos. "I have made him suffer enough this last hour; and I shall directly begin again cutting out the small pieces of lead which have honeycombed his flesh. But if it must be"—

"It must be."

"Well, then, make haste; for the fever will set in presently."

M. Daubigeon could not conceal his annoyance. He called out,—

"Galpin, Galpin!"

The other man paid no attention. Having taken a note-book and a pencil from his pocket, he drew up close to the sick man's bed, and asked him in an undertone,—

"Are you strong enough, count, to answer my questions?"

"Oh, perfectly!"

"Then, pray tell me all you know of the sad events of to-night."

With the aid of his wife and Dr. Seignebos, the count raised himself on his pillows, and began thus,—

"Unfortunately, the little I know will be of no use in aiding justice to discover the guilty man. It may have been eleven o'clock, for I am not even quite sure of the hour, when I had gone to bed, and just blown out my candle: suddenly a bright light fell upon the window. I was amazed, and utterly confused; for I was in that state of sleepiness which is not yet sleep, but very much like it. I said to myself, 'What can this be?' but I did not get up: I only was roused by a great noise, like the crash of a falling wall; and then I jumped out of bed, and said to myself, 'The house is on fire!' What increased my anxiety was the fact, which I at once recollected, that there were in the courtyard, and all around the house, some sixteen thousand bundles of dry wood, which had been cut last year. Half dressed, I rushed downstairs. I was very much bewildered, I confess, and could hardly succeed in opening the outer door: still I did open it at last. But I had barely put my foot on the threshold, when I felt in my right side, a little above the hip, a fierce pain, and heard at the same time, quite close to me, a shot."

The magistrate interrupted him by a gesture.

"Your statement, count, is certainly remarkably clear. But there is one point we must try to establish. Were you really fired at the moment you showed yourself at the door?"

"Yes, sir."

"Then the murderer must have been quite near on the watch. He must have known that the fire would bring you out; and he was lying in wait for you."

"That was and still is my impression," declared the count.

M. Galpin turned to M. Daubigeon.

"Then," he said to him, "the murder is the principal fact with which we have to do; and the fire is only an aggravating circumstance,—the means which the criminal employed in order to succeed the better in perpetrating his crime."

Then, returning to the count, he said,—

"Pray go on."

"When I felt I was wounded," continued Count Claudieuse, "my first impulse was instinctively to rush forward to the place from which the gun seemed to have been fired at me. I had not proceeded three yards, when I felt the same pain once more in the shoulder and in the neck. This second wound was more serous than the first; for I lost my consciousness, my head began to swim and I fell."

"You had not seen the murderer?"

"I beg your pardon. At the moment when I fell, I thought I saw a man rush forth from behind a pile of fagots, cross the courtyard, and disappear in the fields."

"Would you recognize him?"

"No."

"But you saw how he was dressed: you can give me a description?"

"No, I cannot. I felt as if there was a veil before my eyes; and he passed me like a shadow."

The magistrate could hardly conceal his disappointment.

"Never mind," he said, "we'll find him out. But go on, sir."

The count shook his head.

"I have nothing more to say," he replied. "I had fainted; and when I recovered my consciousness, some hours later, I found myself here lying on this bed."

M. Galpin noted down the count's answers with scrupulous exactness: when he had done, he asked again,—

"We must return to the details of the attack, and examine them minutely. Now, however, it is important to know what happened after you fell. Who could tell us that?"

"My wife, sir."

"I thought so. The countess, no doubt, got up when you rose."

"My wife had not gone to bed."

The magistrate turned suddenly to the countess; and at a glance he perceived that her costume was not that of a lady who had been suddenly roused from slumber by the burning of her house.

"I see," he said to himself.

"Bertha," the count went on to state, "our youngest daughter, who is lying there on that bed, under the blanket, has the measles, and is suffering terribly. My wife was sitting up with her. Unfortunately the windows of her room look upon the garden, on the side opposite to that where the fire broke out."

"How, then, did the countess become aware of the accident?" asked the magistrate.

Without waiting for a more direct question, the countess came forward and said,—

"As my husband has just told you, I was sitting up with my little Bertha. I was rather tired; for I had sat up the night before also, and I had begun to nod, when a sudden noise aroused me. I was not quite sure whether I had really heard such a noise; but just then a second shot was heard. I left the room more astonished than frightened. Ah, sir! The fire had already made such headway, that the staircase was as light as in broad day. I went down in great haste. The outer door was open. I went out; and there, some five or six yards from me, I saw, by the light of the flames, the body of my husband lying on the ground. I threw myself upon him; but he did not even hear me; his heart had ceased to beat. I thought he was dead; I called for help; I was in despair."

M. Seneschal and M. Daubigeon trembled with excitement.

"Well, very well!" said M. Galpin, with an air of satisfaction,— "very well done!"

"You know," continued the countess, "how hard it is to rouse country-people. It seems to me I remained ever so long alone there, kneeling by the side of my husband. At last the brightness of the fire awakened some of the farm-hands, the workmen, and our servants. They rushed out, crying, 'Fire!' When they saw me, they ran up and helped me carry my husband to a place of safety; for the danger was increasing every minute. The fire was spreading with terrific violence, thanks to a furious wind. The barns were one vast mass of fire; the outbuildings were burning; the distillery was in a blaze; and the roof of the dwelling-house was flaming up in various places. And there was not one cool head among them all. I was so utterly bewildered, that I forgot all about my children; and their room was already in flames, when a brave, bold fellow rushed in, and snatched them from the very jaws of death. I did not come to myself till Dr. Seignebos arrived, and spoke to me words of hope. This fire will probably ruin us; but what matters that, so long as my husband and my children are safe?"

Dr. Seignebos had more than once given utterance to his contemptuous impatience: he did not appreciate these preliminary steps. The others, however, the mayor, the attorney, and even the servants, had hardly been able to suppress their excitement. He shrugged his shoulders, and growled between his teeth,—

"Mere formalities! How petty! How childish!"

After having taken off his spectacles, wiped them and replaced them twenty times, he had sat down at the rickety table in the corner of the room, and amused himself with arranging the fifteen or twenty shot he had extracted from the count's wounds, in long lines or small circles. But, when the countess uttered her last words, he rose, and, turning to M. Galpin, said in a curt tone,—

"Now, sir, I hope you will let me have my patient again."

The magistrate was not a little incensed: there was reason enough, surely; and, frowning fiercely, he said,—

"I appreciate, sir, the importance of your duties; but mine are, I think, by no means less solemn nor less urgent."

"Oh!"

"Consequently you will be pleased, sir, to grant me five minutes more."

"Ten, if it must be, sir. Only I warn you that every minute henceforth may endanger the life of my patient."

They had drawn near to each other, and were measuring each other with defiant looks, which betrayed the bitterest animosity. They would surely not quarrel at the bedside of a dying man? The countess seemed to fear such a thing; for she said reproachfully,—

"Gentlemen, I pray, gentlemen"—

Perhaps her intervention would have been of no avail, if M. Seneschal and M. Daubigeon had not stepped in, each addressing one of the two adversaries. M. Galpin was apparently the most obstinate of the two; for, in spite of all, he began once more to question the count, and said,—

"I have only one more question to ask you, sir: Where and how were you standing, where and how do you think the murderer was standing, at the moment when the crime was committed?"

"Sir," replied the count, evidently with a great effort, "I was standing, as I told you, on the threshold of my door, facing the courtyard. The murderer must have been standing some twenty yards off, on my right, behind a pile of wood."

When he had written down the answer of the wounded man, the magistrate turned once more to the physician, and said,—

"You heard what was said, sir. It is for you now to aid justice by telling us at what distance the murderer must have been when he fired."

"I don't guess riddles," replied the physician coarsely.

"Ah, have a care, sir!" said M. Galpin. "Justice, whom I here represent, has the right and the means to enforce respect. You are a physician, sir; and your science is able to answer my question with almost mathematical accuracy."

The physician laughed, and said,—

"Ah, indeed! Science has reached that point, has it? Which science? Medical jurisprudence, no doubt,—that part of our profession which is at the service of the courts, and obeys the judges' behests."

"Sir!"

But the doctor was not the man to allow himself to be defeated a second time. He went on coolly,—

"I know what you are going to say; there is no handbook of medical jurisprudence which does not peremptorily settle the question you ask me. I have studied these handbooks, these formidable weapons which you gentlemen of the bar know so well how to handle. I know the opinions of a Devergie and an Orfila, I know even what Casper and Tardieu, and a host of others teach on that subject. I am fully aware that these gentlemen claim to be able to tell you by the inch at what distance a shot has been fired. But I am not so skilful. I am only a poor country-practitioner, a simple healer of diseases. And before I give an opinion which may cost a poor devil his life, innocent though he be, I must have time to reflect, to consult data, and to compare other cases in my practice."

He was so evidently right in reality, if not in form, that even M. Galpin gave way.

"It is merely as a matter of information that I request your opinion, sir," he replied. "Your real and carefully-considered professional opinion will, of course, be given in a special statement."

"Ah, if that is the case!"

"Pray, inform me, then unofficially, what you think of the nature of the wounds of Count Claudieuse."

Dr. Seignebos settled his spectacles ceremoniously on his nose, and then replied,—

"My impression, so far as I am now able to judge, is that the count has stated the facts precisely as they were. I am quite ready to believe that the murderer was lying in ambush behind one of the piles of wood, and at the distance which he has mentioned. I am also able to affirm that the two shots were fired at different distances,—one much nearer than the other. The proof of it lies in the nature of the wounds, one of which, near the hip may be scientifically called"—

"But we know at what distance a ball is spent," broke in M. Seneschal, whom the doctor's dogmatic tone began to annoy.

"Ah, do we know that, indeed? You know it, M. Seneschal? Well, I declare I do not know it. To be sure, I bear in mind, what you seem to forget, that we have no longer, as in former days, only three or four kinds of guns. Did you think of the immense variety of fire-arms, French and English, American and German, which are nowadays found in everybody's hands? Do you not see, you who have been a lawyer and a magistrate, that the whole legal question will be based upon this grave and all-important point?"

Thereupon the physician resumed his instruments, resolved to give no other answer, and was about to go to work once more when fearful cries were heard without; and the lawyers, the mayor, and the countess herself, rushed at once to the door.

These cries were, unfortunately, not uttered without cause. The roof of the main building had just fallen in, burying under its ruins the poor drummer who had a few hours ago beaten the alarm, and one of the firemen, the most respected carpenter in Sauveterre, and a father of five children.

Capt. Parenteau seemed to be maddened by this disaster; and all vied with each other in efforts to rescue the poor fellows, who were uttering shrieks of horror that rose high above the crash of falling timbers. But all their endeavors were unavailing. One of the gendarmes and a farmer, who had nearly succeeded in reaching the sufferers, barely escaped being burnt themselves, and were only rescued after having been dangerously injured. Then only it seemed as if all became fully aware of the abominable crime committed by the incendiary. Then only the clouds of smoke and the columns of fire, which rose high into the air, were accompanied by fierce cries of vengeance rising heavenwards.

"Death to the incendiary! Death!"

At the moment M. Seneschal felt himself inspired with a sudden thought. He knew how cautious peasants are, and how difficult it is to make them tell what they know. He climbed, therefore, upon a heap of fallen beams, and said in a clear, loud voice,—

"Yes, my friends, you are right: death to the incendiary! Yes, the unfortunate victims of the basest of all crimes must be avenged. We must find out the incendiary; we must! You want it to be done, don't you? Well, it depends only on you. There must be some one among you who knows something about this matter. Let him come forward and tell us what he has seen or heard. Remember that the smallest trifle may be a clew to the crime. You would be as bad as the incendiary himself, if you concealed him. Just think it over, consider."

Loud voices were heard in the crowd; then suddenly a voice said,—

"There is one here who can tell."

"Who?"

"Cocoleu. He was there from the beginning. It was he who went and brought the children of the countess out of their room. What has become of him?—Cocoleu, Cocoleu!"

One must have lived in the country, among these simple-minded peasants, to understand the excitement and the fury of all these men and women as they crowded around the ruins of Valpinson. People in town do not mind brigands, in general: they have their gas, their strong doors, and the police. They are generally little afraid of fire. They have their fire-alarms; and at the first spark the neighbor cries, "Fire!" The engines come racing up; and water comes forth as if by magic. But it is very different in the country: here every man is constantly under a sense of his isolation. A simple latch protects his door; and no one watches over his safety at night. If a murderer should attack him, his cries could bring no help. If fire should break out, his house would be burnt down before the neighbors could reach it; and he is happy who can save his own life and that of his family. Hence all these good people, whom the mayor's words had deeply excited, were eager to find out the only man who knew anything about this calamity, Cocoleu.

He was well known among them, and for many years.

There was not one among them who had not given him a piece of bread, or a bowl of soup, when he was hungry; not one of them had ever refused him a night's rest on the straw in his barn, when it was raining or freezing, and the poor fellow wanted a shelter.

For Cocoleu was one of those unfortunate beings who labor under a grievous physical or moral deformity.

Some twenty years ago, a wealthy land-owner in Brechy had sent to the nearest town for half a dozen painters, whom he kept at his house nearly a whole summer, painting and decorating his newly-built house. One of these men had seduced a girl in the neighborhood, whom he had bewitched by his long white blouse, his handsome brown mustache, his good spirits, gay songs, and flattering speeches. But, when the work was done, the tempter had flown away with the others, without thinking any more of the poor girl than of the last cigar which he had smoked.

And yet she was expecting a child. When she could no longer conceal her condition, she was turned out of the house in which she had been employed; and her family, unable to support themselves, drove her away without mercy. Overcome with grief, shame, and remorse, poor Colette wandered from farm to farm, begging, insulted, laughed at, beaten even at times. Thus it came about, that in a dark wood, one dismal winter evening, she gave life to a male child. No one ever understood how mother and child managed to survive. But both lived; and for many a year they were seen in and around Sauveterre, covered with rags, and living upon the dear-bought generosity of the peasants.

Then the mother died, utterly forsaken by human help, as she had lived. They found her body, one morning, in a ditch by the wayside.

The child survived alone. He was then eight years old, quite strong and tall for his age. A farmer took pity on him, and took him home. The little wretch was not fit for anything: he could not even keep his master's cows. During his mother's lifetime, his silence, his wild looks, and his savage appearance, had been attributed to his wretched mode of life. But when people began to be interested in him, they found out that his intellect had never been aroused. He was an idiot, and, besides, subject to that terrible nervous affection which at times shakes the whole body and disfigures the face by the violence of uncontrollable convulsions. He was not a deaf-mute; but he could only stammer out with intense difficulty a few disjointed syllables. Sometimes the country people would say to him,—

"Tell us your name, and you shall have a cent."

Then it took him five minutes' hard work to utter, amid a thousand painful contortions, the name of his mother.

"Co-co-co-lette."

Hence came his name Cocoleu. It had been ascertained that he was utterly unable to do anything; and people ceased to interest themselves in his behalf. The consequence was, that he became a vagabond as of old.

It was about this time that Dr. Seignebos, on one of his visits, met him one day on the public road.

This excellent man had, among other extraordinary notions, the conviction that idiocy is nothing more than a defective state of the brains, which may be remedied by the use of certain well-known substances, such as phosphorus, for instance. He lost no time in seizing upon this admirable opportunity to test his theory. Cocoleu was sent for, and installed in his house. He subjected him to a treatment which he kept secret; and only a druggist at Sauveterre, who was also well known as entertaining very extraordinary notions, knew what had happened. At the end of eighteen months, Cocoleu had fallen off terribly: he talked perhaps, a little more fluently; but his intellect had not been perceptibly improved.

Dr. Seignebos was discouraged. He made up a parcel of things which he had given to his patient, put it into his hands, pushed him out of his door, and told him never to come back again.

The doctor had rendered Cocoleu a sad service. The poor idiot had lost the habit of privation: he had forgotten how to go from door to door, asking for alms; and he would have perished, if his good fortune had not led him to knock at the door of the house at Valpinson.

Count Claudieuse and his wife were touched by his wretchedness, and determined to take charge of him. They gave him a room and a bed at one of the farmhouses; but they could never induce him to stay there. He was by nature a vagabond; and the instinct was too strong for him. In winter, frost and snow kept him in for a little while; but as soon as the first leaves came out, he went wandering again through forest and field, remaining absent often for weeks altogether.

At last, however, something seemed to have been aroused in him, which looked like the instinct of a domesticated animal. His attachment to the countess resembled that of a dog, even in the capers and cries with which he greeted her whenever he saw her. Often, when she went out, he accompanied her, running and frolicking around her just like a dog. He was also very fond of little girls, and seemed to resent it when he was kept from them: for people were afraid his nervous attacks might affect the children.

With time he had also become capable of performing some simple service. He could be intrusted with certain messages: he could water the flowers, summon a servant, or even carry a letter to the post-office at Brechy. His progress in this respect was so marked, that some of the more cunning peasants began to suspect that Cocoleu was not so "innocent," after all, as he looked, and that he was cleverly playing the fool in order to enjoy life easily.

"We have him at last," cried several voices at once. "Here he is; here he is!"

The crowd made way promptly; and almost immediately a young man appeared, led and pushed forward by several persons. Cocoleu's clothes, all in disorder, showed clearly that he had offered a stout resistance. He was a youth of about eighteen years, very tall, quite beardless, excessively thin, and so loosely jointed, that he looked like a hunchback. A mass of reddish hair came down his low, retreating forehead. His small eyes, his enormous mouth bristling with sharp teeth, his broad flat nose, and his immense ears, gave to his face a strange idiotic expression, and to his whole appearance a most painful brutish air.

"What must we do with him?" asked the peasants of the mayor.

"We must take him before the magistrate, my friends," replied M. Seneschal,—"down there in that cottage, where you have carried the count."

"And we'll make him talk," threatened his captors. "You hear! Go on, quick!"

IV.

M. Galpin and the doctor had both considered it a point of honor who should show the most perfect indifference; and thus

- 28 -

they had betrayed by no sign their curiosity to know what was going on out doors. Dr. Seignebos was on the point of resuming the operation; and, as coolly as if he had been in his own rooms at home, he was washing the sponge which he had just used, and wiping his instruments. The magistrate, on the other hand, was standing in the centre of the room, his arms crossed, his eyes fixed upon the infinite, apparently. It may be he was thinking of his star which had at last brought him that famous criminal case for which he had ardently longed many a year.

Count Claudieuse, however, was very far from sharing their reserve. He was tossing about on his bed; and as soon as the mayor and his friend reappeared, looking quite upset, he exclaimed,—

"What does that uproar mean?"

And, when he had heard of the calamity, he added,—

"Great God! And I was complaining of my losses. Two men killed! That is a real misfortune. Poor men! to die because they were so brave,—Bolton hardly thirty years old; Guillebault, a father of a family, who leaves five children, and not a cent!"

The countess, coming in at that moment, heard his last words.

"As long as we have a mouthful of bread," she said in a voice full of deep emotion, "neither Bolton's mother, nor Guillebault's children, shall ever know what want is."

She could not say another word; for at that moment the peasants crowded into the room, pushing the prisoner before them.

"Where is the magistrate?" they asked. "Here is a witness!"

"What, Cocoleu!" exclaimed the count.

"Yes, he knows something: he said so himself. We want him to tell it to the magistrate. We want the incendiary to be caught."

Dr. Seignebos had frowned fiercely. He execrated Cocoleu, whose sight recalled to him that great failure which the good people of Sauveterre were not likely to forget soon.

"You do not really mean to examine him?" he asked, turning to M. Galpin.

"Why not?" answered the magistrate dryly.

"Because he is an imbecile, sir, an idiot. Because he cannot possibly understand your questions, or the importance of his answers."

"He may give us a valuable hint, nevertheless."

"He? A man who has no sense? You don't really think so. The law cannot attach any importance to the evidence of a fool."

M. Galpin betrayed his impatience by an increase of stiffness, as he replied,—

"I know my duty, sir."

"And I," replied the physician,—"I also know what I have to do. You have summoned me to assist you in this investigation. I obey; and I declare officially, that the mental condition of this unfortunate man makes his evidence utterly worthless. I appeal to the commonwealth attorney."

He had hoped for a word of encouragement from M. Daubigeon; but nothing came. Then he went on,—

"Take care, sir, or you may get yourself into trouble. What would you do if this poor fellow should make a formal charge against any one? Could you attach any weight to his word?"

The peasants were listening with open mouths. One of them said,—

"Oh! Cocoleu is not so innocent as he looks."

"He can say very well what he wants to say, the scamp!" added another.

"At all events, I am indebted to him for the life of my children," said the count gently. "He thought of them when I was unconscious, and when no one else remembered them. Come, Cocoleu, come nearer, my friend, don't be afraid: there is no one here to hurt you."

It was very well the count used such kind words; for Cocoleu was thoroughly terrified by the brutal treatment he had received, and was trembling in all his limbs.

- 30 -

"I am—not—a—afraid," he stammered out.

"Once more I protest," said the physician.

He had found out that he stood not alone in his opinion. Count Claudieuse came to his assistance, saying,—

"I really think it might be dangerous to question Cocoleu."

But the magistrate was master of the situation, and conscious of all the powers conferred upon him by the laws of France in such cases.

"I must beg, gentlemen," he said, in a tone which did not allow of any reply,—"I must beg to be permitted to act in my own way."

And sitting down, he asked Cocoleu,—

"Come, my boy, listen to me, and try to understand what I say. Do you know what has happened at Valpinson?"

"Fire," replied the idiot.

"Yes, my friend, fire, which burns down the house of your benefactor,—fire, which has killed two good men. But that is not all: they have tried to murder the count. Do you see him there in his bed, wounded, and covered with blood? Do you see the countess, how she suffers?"

Did Cocoleu follow him? His distorted features betrayed nothing of what might be going on within him.

"Nonsense!" growled the doctor, "what obstinacy! What folly!"

M. Galpin heard him, and said angrily,—

"Sir, do not force me to remind you that I have not far from here, men whose duty it is to see that my authority is respected here."

Then, turning again to the poor idiot, he went on,—

"All these misfortunes are the work of a vile incendiary. You hate him, don't you; you detest him, the rascal!"

"Yes," said Cocoleu.

"You want him to be punished, don't you?"

"Yes, yes!"

"Well, then you must help me to find him out, so that the gendarmes may catch him, and put him in jail. You know who it is; you have told these people and"—

He paused, and after a moment, as Cocoleu kept silent, he asked,—

"But, now I think of it, whom has this poor fellow talked to?"

Not one of the peasants could tell. They inquired; but no answer came. Perhaps Cocoleu had never said what he was reported to have said.

"The fact is," said one of the tenants at Valpinson, "that the poor devil, so to say, never sleeps, and that he is roaming about all night around the house and the farm buildings."

This was a new light for M. Galpin; suddenly changing the form of his interrogatory, he asked Cocoleu,—

"Where did you spend the night?"

"In—in—the—court—yard."

"Were you asleep when the fire broke out?"

"No."

"Did you see it commence?"

"Yes."

"How did it commence?"

The idiot looked fixedly at the Countess Claudieuse with the timid and abject expression of a dog who tries to read something in his master's eyes.

"Tell us, my friend," said the Countess gently,—"tell us."

A flash of intelligence shone in Cocoleu's eyes.

"They—they set it on fire," he stammered.

"On purpose?"

"Yes."

"Who?"

"A gentleman."

There was not a person present at this extraordinary scene who did not anxiously hold his breath as the word was uttered. The doctor alone kept cool, and exclaimed,—

"Such an examination is sheer folly!"

But the magistrate did not seem to hear his words; and, turning to Cocoleu, he asked him, in a deeply agitated tone of voice—

"Did you see the gentleman?"

"Yes."

"Do you know who he is?"

"Very—very—well."

"What is his name?"

"Oh, yes!"

"What is his name? Tell us."

Cocoleu's features betrayed the fearful anguish of his mind. He hesitated, and at last he answered, making a violent effort,— "Bois—Bois—Boiscoran!"

The name was received with murmurs of indignation and incredulous laughter. There was not a shadow of doubt or of suspicion. The peasants said,—

"M. de Boiscoran an incendiary! Who does he think will believe that story?"

"It is absurd!" said Count Claudieuse.

"Nonsense!" repeated the mayor and his friend.

Dr. Siegnebos had taken off his spectacles, and was wiping them with an air of intense satisfaction.

"What did I tell you?" he exclaimed. "But the gentleman did not condescend to attach any importance to my suggestions."

The magistrate was by far the most excited man in the crowd. He had turned excessively pale, and made, visibly, the greatest efforts to preserve his equanimity. The commonwealth attorney leaned over towards him, and whispered,—

"If I were in your place, I would stop here, and consider the answer as not given."

But M. Galpin was one of those men who are blinded by self-conceit, and who would rather be cut to pieces than admit that they have been mistaken. He answered,—

"I shall go on."

Then turning once more to Cocoleu, in the midst of so deep a silence that the buzzing of a fly would have been distinctly heard, he asked,—

"Do you know, my boy, what you say? Do you know that you are accusing a man of a horrible crime?"

Whether Cocoleu understood, or not, he was evidently deeply agitated. Big drops of perspiration rolled slowly down his temples; and nervous shocks agitated his limbs, and convulsed his features.

"I, I—am—telling the—truth!" he said at last.

"M. de. Boiscoran has set Valpinson on fire?"

"Yes."

"How did he do it?"

Cocoleu's restless eyes wandered incessantly from the count, who looked indignant, to the countess, who seemed to listen with painful surprise. The magistrate repeated,—

"Speak!"

After another moment's hesitation, the idiot began to explain what he had seen; and it took him many minutes to state, amid countless contortions, and painful efforts to speak, that he had seen M. de Boiscoran pull out some papers from his pocket, light them with a match, put them under a rick of straw near by, and push the burning mass towards two enormous piles of wood which were in close contact with a vat full of spirits.

"This is sheer nonsense!" cried the doctor, thus giving words to what they all seemed to feel.

But M. Galpin had mastered his excitement. He said solemnly,—

"At the first sign of applause or of displeasure, I shall send for the gendarmes, and have the room cleared."

Then, turning once more to Cocoleu, he said,—

"Since you saw M. de Boiscoran so distinctly, tell us how he was dressed."

"He had light trousers on," replied the idiot, stammering still most painfully, "a dark-brown shooting-jacket, and a big straw hat. His trousers were stuffed into his boots."

Two or three peasants looked at each other, as if they had at last hit upon a suspicious fact. The costume which Cocoleu had so accurately described was well known to them all.

"And when he had kindled the fire," said the magistrate again, "what did he do next?"

"He hid behind the woodpile."

"And then?"

"He loaded his gun, and, when master came out, he fired."

Count Claudieuse was so indignant that he forgot the pain which his wounds caused him, and raised himself on his bed.

"It is monstrous," he exclaimed, "to allow an idiot to charge an honorable man with such a crime! If he really saw M. de Boiscoran set the house on fire, and hide himself in order to murder me, why did he not come and warn me?"

Mr. Galpin repeated the question submissively, to the great amazement of the mayor and M. Daubigeon.

"Why did you not give warning?" he asked Cocoleu.

But the efforts which the unfortunate man had made during the last half-hour had exhausted his little strength. He broke out into stupid laughter; and almost instantly one of his fearful nervous attacks overcame him: he fell down yelling, and had to be carried away.

The magistrate had risen, pale and deeply excited, but evidently meditating on what was to be done next. The commonwealth attorney asked him in an undertone what he was going to do; and the lawyer replied,—

"Prosecute!"

"What?"

"Can I do otherwise in my position? God is my witness that I tried my best, by urging this poor idiot, to prove the absurdity of his accusation. But the result has disappointed me."

"And now?"

"Now I can no longer hesitate. There have been ten witnesses present at the examination. My honor is at stake. I must establish either the guilt or the innocence of the man whom Cocoleu accuses." Immediately, walking up to the count's bed, he asked,—

"Will you have the kindness, Count Claudieuse, to tell me what your relations are to M. de Boiscoran?"

Surprise and indignation caused the wounded man to blush deeply.

"Can it be possible, sir, that you believe the words of that idiot?"

"I believe nothing," answered the magistrate. "My duty is to unravel the truth; and I mean to do it."

"The doctor has told you what the state of Cocoleu's mind is?"

"Count, I beg you will answer my question."

Count Claudieuse looked angry; but he replied promptly,—

"My relations with M. de Boiscoran are neither good nor bad. We have none."

"It is reported, I have heard it myself, that you are on bad terms."

"On no terms at all. I never leave Valpinson, and M. de Boiscoran spends nine months of the year in Paris. He has never called at my house, and I have never been in his."

"You have been overheard speaking of him in unmeasured terms."

"That may be. We are neither of the same age, nor have we the same tastes or the same opinions. He is young: I am old. He likes Paris and the great world: I am fond of solitude and hunting. I am a Legitimist: he used to be an Orleanist, and now he is a Republican. I believe that the descendant of our old kings alone can save the country; and he is convinced that the happiness of France is possible only under a Republic. But two men may be enemies, and yet esteem each other. M. de Boiscoran is an honorable man; he has done his duty bravely in the war, he has fought well, and has been wounded."

M. Galpin noted down these answers with extreme care. When he had done so, he continued,—

"The question is not one of political opinions only. You have had personal difficulties with M. de Boiscoran."

"Of no importance."

"I beg pardon: you have been at law."

"Our estates adjoin each other. There is an unlucky brook between us, which is a source of constant trouble to the neighbors."

M. Galpin shook his head, and added,—

"These are not the only difficulties you have had with each other. Everybody in the country knows that you have had violent altercations."

Count Claudieuse seemed to be in great distress.

"It is true: we have used hard words. M. de Boiscoran had two wretched dogs that were continually escaping from his kennels, and came hunting in my fields. You cannot imagine how much game they destroyed."

"Exactly so. And one day you met M. de Boiscoran, and you warned him that you would shoot his dogs."

"I must confess I was furious. But I was wrong, a thousand times wrong: I did threaten"—

"That is it. You were both of you armed. You threatened one another: he actually aimed at you. Don't deny it. A number of persons have seen it; and I know it. He has told me so himself."

V.

There was not a person in the whole district who did not know of what a fearful disease poor Cocoleu was suffering; and everybody knew, also, that it was perfectly useless to try and help him. The two men who had taken him out had therefore laid him simply on a pile of wet straw, and then they had left him to himself, eager as they were to see and hear what was going on.

It must be said, in justice to the several hundred peasants who were crowding around the smoking ruins of Valpinson, that they treated the madman who had accused M. de Boiscoran of such a crime, neither with cruel jokes nor with fierce curses. Unfortunately, first impulses, which are apt to be good impulses, do not last long. One of those idle good-for-nothings, drunkards, envious scamps who are found in every community, in the country as well as in the city, cried out,—

"And why not?"

These few words opened at once a door to all kinds of bold guesses.

Everybody had heard something about the quarrel between Count Claudieuse and M. de Boiscoran. It was well known, moreover, that the provocation had always come from the count, and that the latter had invariably given way in the end. Why, therefore, might not M. de Boiscoran, impatient at last, have resorted to such means in order to avenge himself on a man whom they thought he must needs hate, and whom he probably feared at the same time?

"Perhaps he would not do it, because he is a nobleman, and because he is rich?" they added sneeringly.

The next step was, of course, to look out for circumstances which might support such a theory; and the opportunity was not lacking. Groups were formed; and soon two men and a woman declared aloud that they could astonish the world if they chose to talk. They were urged to tell what they knew; and, of course, they refused. But they had said too much already. Willing or not willing, they were carried up to the house, where, at that very moment, M. Galpin was examining Count Claudieuse. The excited crowd made such a disturbance, that M. Seneschal, trembling at the idea of a new accident, rushed out to the door.

"What is it now?" he asked.

"More witnesses," replied the peasants. "Here are some more witnesses."

The mayor turned round, and, after having exchanged glances with M. Daubigeon, he said to the magistrate,—

"They are bringing you some more witnesses, sir."

No doubt M. Galpin was little pleased at the interruption; but he knew the people well enough to bear in mind, that, unless he took them at the moment when they were willing to talk, he might never be able to get any thing out of them at any other time.

"We shall return some other time to our conversation," he said to Count Claudieuse.

Then, replying to M. Seneschal, he said,—

"Let the witnesses come in, but one by one."

The first who entered was the only son of a well-to-do farmer in the village of Brechy, called Ribot. He was a young fellow of about twenty-five, broad-shouldered, with a very small head, a low brow, and formidable crimson ears. For twenty miles all around, he was reputed to be an irresistible beau,—a reputation of which he was very proud. After having asked him his name, his first names, and his age, M. Galpin said,—

"What do you know?"

The young man straightened himself, and with a marvellously conceited air, which set all the peasants a-laughing, he replied,—

- 39 -

"I was out that night on some little private business of my own. I was on the other side of the chateau of Boiscoran. Somebody was waiting for me, and I was behind time: so I cut right across the marsh. I knew the rains of the last days would have filled all the ditches; but, when a man is out on such important business as mine was, he can always find his way"—

"Spare us those tedious details," said the magistrate coldly. The handsome fellow looked surprised, rather than offended, by the interruption, and then went on,—

"As your Honor desires. Well, it was about eight o'clock, or a little more, and it was growing dark, when I reached the Seille swamps. They were overflowing; and the water was two inches above the stones of the canal. I asked myself how I should get across without spoiling my clothes, when I saw M. de Boiscoran coming towards me from the other side."

"Are you quite sure it was he?"

"Why, I should think so! I talked to him. But stop, he was not afraid of getting wet. Without much ado, he rolled up his trousers, stuffed them into the tops of his tall boots, and went right through. Just then he saw me, and seemed to be surprised. I was as much so as he was. 'Why, is it you, sir?' I said. He replied 'Yes: I have to see somebody at Brechy.' That was very probably so; still I said again, 'But you have chosen a queer way.' He laughed. 'I did not know the swamps were overflowed,' he answered, 'and I thought I would shoot some snipes.' As he said this, he showed me his gun. At that moment I had nothing to say; but now, when I think it over, it looks queer to me."

M. Galpin had written down the statement as fast as it was given. Then he asked,—

"How was M. de Boiscoran dressed?"

"Stop. He had grayish trousers on, a shooting-jacket of brown velveteen, and a broad-brimmed panama hat."

The count and the countess looked distressed and almost overcome; nor did the mayor and his friend seem to be less troubled. One circumstance in Ribot's evidence seemed to have struck them with peculiar force,—the fact that he had seen M. de Boiscoran push his trousers inside his boots.

"You can go," said M. Galpin to the young man. "Let another witness come in."

The next one was an old man of bad reputation, who lived alone in an old hut two miles from Valpinson. He was called Father Gaudry. Unlike young Ribot, who had shown great assurance, the old man looked humble and cringing in his dirty, ill-smelling rags. After having given his name, he said,—

"It might have been eleven o'clock at night, and I was going through the forest of Rochepommier, along one of the little by-paths"—

"You were stealing wood!" said the magistrate sternly.

"Great God, what an idea!" cried the old man, raising his hands to heaven. "How can you say such a thing! I steal wood! No, my dear sir, I was very quietly going to sleep in the forest, so as to be up with daylight, and gather champignons and other mushrooms to sell at Sauveterre. Well, I was trotting along, when, all of a sudden, I hear footsteps behind me. Naturally, I was frightened."

"Because you were stealing!"

"Oh, no! my dear sir; only, at night, you understand. Well, I hid behind a tree; and almost at the same moment I saw M. de Boiscoran pass by. I recognized him perfectly in spite of the dark; for he seemed to be in a great rage, talked loud to himself, swore, gesticulated, and tore handfuls of leaves from the branches."

"Did he have a gun?"

"Yes, my dear sir; for that was the very thing that frightened me so. I thought he was a keeper."

The third and last witness was a good old woman, Mrs. Courtois, whose little farm lay on the other side of the forest of Rochepommier. When she was asked, she hesitated a moment, and then she said,—

"I do not know much; but I will tell you all I do know. As we expected to have a house full of workmen a few days hence, and as I was going to bake bread to-morrow, I was going with my ass to the mill on Sauveterre Mountain to fetch flour. The miller had not any ready; but he told me, if I could wait, he would let me have some: and so I staid to supper. About ten o'clock, they gave me a bag full of flour. The boys put it on my ass, and I went home. I was about half-way, and it was, perhaps, eleven o'clock, when, just at the edge of the forest of Rochepommier, my ass stumbled, and the bag fell off. I had a great deal of trouble, for I was not strong enough to lift it alone; and just then a man came out of the woods, quite near me. I called to him, and he came. It was M. de Boiscoran: I ask him to help me; and at once, without losing a moment, he puts his gun down, lifts the bag from the ground, and puts it on my ass. I thank him. He says, 'Welcome,' and—that is all."

The mayor had been all this time standing in the door of the chamber, performing the humble duty of a doorkeeper, and barring the entrance to the eager and curious crowd outside. When Mrs. Courtois retired, quite bewildered by her own words, and regretting what she had said, he called out,—

"Is there any one else who knows any thing?"

As nobody appeared, he closed the door, and said curtly,—

"Well, then, you can go home now, my friends. Let the law have free course."

The law, represented by the magistrate, was a prey at that moment to the most cruel perplexity. M. Galpin was utterly overcome by consternation. He sat at the little table, on which he had been writing, his head resting on his hands, thinking, apparently, how he could find a way out of this labyrinth.

All of a sudden he rose, and forgetting, for a moment, his customary rigidity, he let his mask of icy impassiveness drop off his face, and said,—

"Well?" as if, in his despair, he had hoped for some help or advice in his troubles,—"well?"

No answer came.

All the others were as much troubled as he was. They all tried to shake off the overwhelming impression made by this accumulation of evidence; but in vain. At last, after a moment's silence, the magistrate said with strange bitterness,—

"You see, gentlemen, I was right in examining Cocoleu. Oh! don't attempt to deny it: you share my doubts and my suspicions, I see it. Is there one among you who would dare assert that the terrible excitement of this poor man has not restored to him for a time the use of his reason? When he told you that he had witnessed the crime, and when he gave the name of the criminal, you looked incredulous. But then other witnesses came; and their united evidence, corresponding without a missing link, constitutes a terrible presumption."

He became animated again. Professional habits, stronger than every thing else, obtained once more the mastery.

"M. de Boiscoran was at Valpinson to-night: that is clearly established. Well, how did he get here? By concealing himself. Between his own house and Valpinson there are two public roads,—one by Brechy, and another around the swamps. Does M. de Boiscoran take either of the two? No. He cuts straight across the marshes, at the risk of sinking in, or of getting wet from head to foot. On his return he chooses, in spite of the darkness, the forest of Rochepommier, unmindful of the danger he runs to lose his way, and to wander about in it till daybreak. What was he doing this for? Evidently, in order not to be seen. And, in fact, whom does he meet?—a loose fellow, Ribot, who is himself in hiding on account of some love-intrigue; a wood-stealer, Gaudry, whose only anxiety is to avoid the gendarmes; an old woman, finally, Mrs. Courtois, who has been belated by an accident. All his precautions were well chosen; but Providence was watching."

"O Providence!" growled Dr. Seignebos,—"Providence!"

But M. Galpin did not even hear the interruption. Speaking faster and faster, he went on,—

"Would it at least be possible to plead in behalf of M. de Boiscoran a difference in time? No. At what time was he seen to come to this place? At nightfall. 'It was half-past eight,' says Ribot, 'when M. de Boiscoran crossed the canal at the Seille swamps.' He might, therefore, have easily reached Valpinson at half-past nine. At that hour the crime had not yet been committed. When was he

- 43 -

seen returning home? Gaudry and the woman Courtois have told you the hour,—after eleven o'clock. At that time Count Claudieuse had been shot, and Valpinson was on fire. Do we know any thing of M. de Boiscoran's temper at that time? Yes, we do. When he came this way he was quite cool. He is very much surprised at meeting Ribot; but he explains to him very fully how he happens to be at that place, and also why he has a gun.

"He says he is on his way to meet somebody at Brechy, and he thought he would shoot some birds. Is that admissible? Is it even likely? However, let us look at him on his way back. Gaudry says he was walking very fast: he seemed to be furious, and was pulling handfuls of leaves from the branches. What does Mrs. Courtois say? Nothing. When she calls him, he does not venture to run; that would have been a confession, but he is in a great hurry to help her. And then? His way for a quarter of an hour is the same as the woman's: does he keep her company? No. He leaves her hastily. He goes ahead, and hurries home; for he thinks Count Claudieuse is dead; he knows Valpinson is in flames; and he fears he will hear the bells ring, and see the fire raging."

It is not often that magistrates allow themselves such familiarity; for judges, and even lawyers, generally fancy they are too high above common mortals, on such occasions, to explain their views, to state their impressions, and to ask, as it were, for advice. Still, when the inquiry is only begun, there are, properly speaking, no fixed rules prescribed. As soon as a crime has been reported to a French magistrate, he is at liberty to do any thing he chooses in order to discover the guilty one. Absolutely master of the case, responsible only to his conscience, and endowed with extraordinary powers, he proceeds as he thinks best. But, in this affair at Valpinson, M. Galpin had been carried away by the rapidity of the events themselves. Since the first question addressed to Cocoleu, up to the present moment, he had not had time to consider. And his proceedings had been public; thus he felt naturally tempted to explain them.

"And you call this a legal inquiry?" asked Dr. Seignebos.

He had taken off his spectacles, and was wiping them furiously.

"An inquiry founded upon what?" he went on with such vehemence that no one dared interrupt him,—"founded upon the evidence of an unfortunate creature, whom I, a physician, testify to be not responsible for what he says. Reason does not go out and become lighted again, like the gas in a street-lamp. A man is an idiot, or he is not an idiot. He has always been one; and he always will be one. But you say the other statements are conclusive. Say, rather, that you think they are. Why? Because you are prejudiced by Cocoleu's accusation. But for it, you would never have troubled yourselves about what M. De Boiscoran did, or did not. He walked about the whole evening. He has a right to do so. He crossed the marsh. What hindered him? He went through the woods. Why should he not? He is met with by people. Is not that quite natural? But no: an idiot accuses him, and forthwith all he does looks suspicious. He talks. It is the insolence of a hardened criminal. He is silent. It is the remorse of a guilty man trembling with fear. Instead of naming M. de Boiscoran, Cocoleu might just as well have named me, Dr. Seignebos. At once, all my doings would have appeared suspicious; and I am quite sure a thousand evidences of my guilt would have been discovered. It would have been an easy matter. Are not my opinions more radical even than those of M. de Boiscoran? For there is the key to the whole matter. M. de Boiscoran is a Republican; M. de Boiscoran acknowledges no sovereignty but that of the people"—

"Doctor," broke in the commonwealth attorney,—"doctor, you are not thinking of what you say."

"I do think of it, I assure you"—

But he was once more interrupted, and this time by Count Claudieuse, who said,—

"For my part, I admit all the arguments brought up by the magistrate. But, above all probabilities, I put a fact,—the character of the accused. M. de Boiscoran is a man of honor and an excellent man. He is incapable of committing a mean and odious crime."

The others assented. M. Seneschal added,—

"And I, I will tell you another thing. What would have been the purpose of such a crime? Ah, if M. de Boiscoran had nothing to lose! But do you know among all your friends a happier man than he is?—young, handsome, in excellent health, immensely wealthy, esteemed and popular with everybody. Finally, there is another fact, which is a family secret, but which I may tell you, and which will remove at once all suspicions,—M. de Boiscoran is desperately in love with Miss Dionysia de Chandore. She returns his love; and the day before yesterday the wedding-day was fixed on the 20th of the next month."

In the meantime the hours had sped on. It was half-past three by the clock of the church in Brechy. Day was breaking; and the light of the lamps was turning pale. The morning mists began to disappear; and the sunlight fell upon the window-panes. But no one noticed this: all these men gathered around the bed of the wounded man were too deeply excited. M. Galpin had listened to the objection made by the others, without a word or a gesture. He had so far recovered his self-control, that it would have been difficult to see what impressions they made upon his mind. At last, shaking his head gravely, he said,—

"More than you, gentlemen, I feel a desire to believe M. de Boiscoran innocent. M. Daubigeon, who knows what I mean, will tell you so. In my heart I pleaded his cause long before you. But I am the representative of the law; and my duty is above my affections. Does it depend on me to set aside Cocoleu's accusation, however stupid, however absurd, it may be? Can I undo the three statements made by the witnesses, and confirming so strongly the suspicions aroused by the first charge?"

Count Claudieuse was distressed beyond expression. At last he said,—

"The worst thing about it is, that M. de Boiscoran thinks I am his enemy. I should not wonder if he went and imagined that these charges and vile suspicions have been suggested by my wife or by myself. If I could only get up! At least, let M. de Boiscoran know distinctly that I am ready to answer for him, as I would answer for myself. Cocoleu, the wretched idiot! Ah, Genevieve, my darling wife! Why did you induce him to talk? If you had not insisted, he would have kept silent forever."

The countess succumbed at last to the anxieties of this terrible night. At first she had been supported by that exaltation which is apt to accompany a great crisis; but latterly she had felt exhausted. She had sunk upon a stool, near the bed on which her two daughters were lying; and, her head hid in the pillow, she seemed to sleep. But she was not asleep. When her husband reproached her thus, she rose, pale, with swollen eyes and distorted features, and said in a piercing voice,—

"What? They have tried to kill my Trivulce; our children have been near unto death in the flames; and I should have allowed any means to be unused by which the guilty one may be found out? No! I have only done what it was my duty to do. Whatever may come of it, I regret nothing."

"But, Genevieve, M. de Boiscoran is not guilty: he cannot possibly be guilty. How could a man who has the happiness of being loved by Dionysia de Chandore, and who counts the days to his wedding,—how could he devise such a hideous crime?"

"Let him prove his innocence," replied the countess mercilessly.

The doctor smacked his lips in the most impertinent manner.

"There is a woman's logic for you," he murmured.

"Certainly," said M. Seneschal, "M. de Boiscoran's innocence will be promptly established. Nevertheless, the suspicion will remain. And our people are so constituted, that this suspicion will overshadow his whole life. Twenty years hence, they will meet him, and they will say, 'Oh, yes! the man who set Valpinson on fire!'"

It was not M. Galpin this time who replied, but the commonwealth attorney. He said sadly,—

"I cannot share your views; but that does not matter. After what has passed, our friend, M. Galpin cannot retrace his steps: his duty makes that impossible, and, even more so, what is due to the accused. What would all these people say, who have heard Cocoleu's deposition, and the evidence given by the witnesses, if the inquiry were stopped? They would certainly say M. de Boiscoran was guilty, but that he was not held responsible because he was rich and noble. Upon my honor I believe him to be innocent. But precisely because this is my conviction, I maintain that his innocence must be clearly established. No doubt he has the means of doing so. When he met Ribot, he told him he was on his way to see somebody at Brechy."

"But suppose he never went there?" objected M. Seneschal. "Suppose he did not see anybody there? Suppose it was only a pretext to satisfy Ribot's impertinent curiosity?"

"Well, then, he would only have to tell the truth in court. And look! Here's an important proof which almost by itself relieves M. de Boiscoran. Would he not have loaded his gun with a ball, if he should ever have really thought of murdering the count? But it was loaded with nothing but small-shot."

"And he would never have missed me at ten yards' distance," said the count.

Suddenly somebody was heard knocking furiously at the door.

"Come in!" cried M. Seneschal.

The door opened and three peasants appeared, looking bewildered, but evidently well pleased.

"We have just," said one of them, "found something curious."

"What?" asked M. Galpin.

"It looks very much like a case; but Pitard says it is the paper of a cartridge."

Count Claudieuse raised himself on his pillows, and said eagerly,—

"Let me see! I have during these last days fired several times quite near to the house to frighten the birds away that eat my fruit. I want to see if the paper is mine."

The peasant gave it to him.

It was a very thin lead form, such as contain the cartridges used in American breech-loading guns. What was singular was that it was blackened by burnt powder; but it had not been torn, nor had it blazed up in the discharge. It was so perfectly uninjured, that one could read the embossed letters of the name of the manufacturer, Clebb.

"That cartridge never belonged to me," said the count.

But as he uttered these words he turned deadly pale, so pale, that his wife came close to him, and looked at him with a glance full of terrible anguish.

"Well?"

He made no reply.

But at that moment such silence was so eloquent, that the countess felt sickened, and whispered to him,—

"Then Cocoleu was right, after all!"

Not one feature of this dramatic scene had escaped M. Galpin's eye. He had seen on every face signs of a kind of terror; still he made no remark. He took the metal case from the count's hands, knowing that it might become an important piece of evidence; and for nearly a minute he turned it round and round, looking at it from all sides, and examining it in the light with the utmost attention.

Then turning to the peasants, who were standing respectfully and uncovered close by the door, he asked them,—

"Where did you find this cartridge, my friends?"

"Close by the old tower, where they keep the tools, and where the ivy is growing all over the old castle."

M. Seneschal had in the meantime succeeded in recovering his self-control, and said now,—

"Surely the murderer cannot have fired from there. You cannot even see the door of the house from the old tower."

"That may be," replied the magistrate; "but the cartridge-case does not necessarily fall to the ground at the place where the gun is discharged. It falls as soon as the gun is cocked to reload."

This was so true, that even Dr. Seignebos had nothing to say.

"Now, my friends," said M. Galpin, "which of you has found the cartridge-case?"

"We were all together when we saw it, and picked it up."

"Well, then, all three of you must give me your names and your domicile, so that I can send for you when you are wanted."

This was done; and, when all formalities were attended to, they went off with numberless bows and doffings of hats. Just at that moment the furious gallop of a horse was heard approaching the house; the next moment the man who had been sent to Sauveterre for medicines came in. He was furious.

"That rascal of a druggist!" he said. "I thought he would never open his shop!"

Dr. Seignebos had eagerly seized the things that were sent him, then, bowing with mock respect to the magistrate, he said,—

"I know very well, sir, how pressing the necessity is to have the head of the culprit cut off; but I think it is almost as pressing to save the life of the murdered man. I have probably delayed the binding up of the count's wounds longer than I ought to have done; and I beg you will now leave me alone, so as to enable me to do my duty to him."

VI.

There was nothing more to be done for the magistrate, the commonwealth attorney, or the mayor. The doctor might assuredly have used more polite language; but people were accustomed to his brutal ways; for it is surprising with what readiness men are tolerated in France, under the pretext that they are as they are, and that they must be taken as they are. The three gentlemen, therefore, left the room, after having bid farewell to the countess, and after having promised to send the count news of all that might be discovered.

The fire was going out for want of fuel. A few hours had sufficed to destroy all that the hard work and incessant cares of many years had accomplished. This charming and much envied estate presented now nothing but a few half calcined walls, heaps of black and gray ashes, and still glowing timbers, from which columns of smoke were slowly rising upward. Thanks to Capt. Parenteau, all that they had been able to save had been carried to a distance, and safely stored away under the shelter of the ruins of the old castle. There, furniture and other articles were piled up pell-mell. There, carts and agricultural machines were standing about, empty casks, and sacks of oats and rye. There, also, the cattle were gathered, that had been drawn from their stalls with infinite labor, and at great risk of life,—horses, oxen, some sheep, and a dozen cows, who lowed piteously. Few of the people had left as yet. With greater zeal than ever the firemen, aided by the peasants, deluged the remains of the dwelling-house with water. They had nothing to fear from the fire; but they desired to keep the bodies of their unfortunate companions from being entirely consumed.

"What a terrible scourge fire is!" said M. Seneschal.

Neither M. Galpin nor the mayor made any answer. They also felt their hearts oppressed by the sad sight before them, in spite of all the intense excitement before; for a fire is nothing as long as the feverish excitement, and the hope of saving something, continue to keep us up, and as long as the red flames illumine the horizon; but the next day, when all is over, then we realize the extent of the misfortune.

The firemen recognized the mayor, and greeted him with cheers. He went rapidly towards them; and, for the first time since the alarm had been raised, the magistrate and the attorney were alone. They were standing close by each other, and for a moment kept silent, while each one tried to read in the other's eyes the secret of his thoughts. At last M. Daubigeon asked,—

"Well?"

M. Galpin trembled.

"This is a fearful calamity," he said.

"What is your opinion?"

"Ah! do I know it myself? I have lost my head: the whole thing looks to me like a nightmare."

"You cannot really believe that M. de Boiscoran is guilty?"

"I believe nothing. My reason tells me he is innocent. I feel he must be innocent; and yet I see terrible evidence rising against him."

The attorney was overwhelmed.

"Alas!" he said, "why did you, contrary to everybody's opinion, insist upon examining Cocoleu, a poor idiotic wretch?"

But the magistrate remonstrated—

"You do not mean to reproach me, sir, for having followed the impulses of my conscience?"

"I reproach you for nothing."

"A horrible crime has been committed; and my duty compelled me to do all that lies in the power of man to discover the culprit."

"Yes; and the man who is accused of the crime is your friend, and only yesterday you spoke of his friendship as your best chance of success in life."

"Sir?"

"Are you surprised to find me so well informed? Ah, you do not know that nothing escapes the idle curiosity of a village. I know that your dearest hope was to become a member of M. de Boiscoran's family, and that you counted upon him to back you in your efforts to obtain the hand of one of his cousins."

"I do not deny that."

"Unfortunately, you have been tempted by the prestige you might gain in a great and famous trial. You have laid aside all prudence; and your projects are forgotten. Whether M. de Boiscoran is innocent or guilty, his family will never forgive you your interference. If he is guilty, they will blame you for having handed him over to justice: if he is innocent, they will blame you even more for having suspected him."

M. Galpin hung his head as if to conceal his trouble. Then he asked,—

"And what would you do in my place?"

"I would withdraw from the case, although it is rather late."

"If I did so, I should risk my career."

"Even that would be better for you than to engage in an affair in which you cannot feel the calmness nor the impartiality which are the first and indispensable virtues of an upright magistrate."

The latter was becoming impatient. He exclaimed,—

"Sir, do you think I am a man to be turned aside from my duty by considerations of friendship or personal interest?"

"I said nothing of the kind."

"Did you not see just now how I carried on the inquiry? Did you see me start when Cocoleu first mentioned M. de Boiscoran's name? If he had denounced any one else, I should probably have let the matter rest there. But precisely because M. de Boiscoran is a friend of mine, and because I have great expectations from him, I have insisted and persisted, and I do so still."

The commonwealth attorney shrugged his shoulders.

"That is it exactly," he said. "Because M. de Boiscoran is a friend of yours, you are afraid of being accused of weakness; and you are going to be hard, pitiless, unjust even, against him. Because you had great expectations from him, you will insist upon finding him guilty. And you call yourself impartial?"

M. Galpin assumed all his usual rigidity, and said solemnly,—

"I am sure of myself!"

"Have a care!"

"My mind is made up, sir."

It was time for M. Seneschal to join them again: he returned, accompanied by Capt. Parenteau.

"Well, gentlemen," he asked, "what have you resolved?"

"We are going to Boiscoran," replied the magistrate.

"What! Immediately?"

"Yes: I wish to find M. de Boiscoran in bed. I am so anxious about it, that I shall do without my clerk."

Capt. Parenteau bowed, and said,—

"Your clerk is here, sir: he was but just inquiring for you." Thereupon he called out as loud as he could,—

"Mechinet, Mechinet!"

A small gray-haired man, jovial and cheerful, came running up, and at once proceeded to tell at full length how a neighbor had told him what had happened, and how the magistrate had left town, whereupon he, also, had started on foot, and come after him as fast as he could.

"Now will you go to Boiscoran?" asked the mayor.

"I do not know yet. Mechinet will have to look for some conveyance."

Quick like lightning, the clerk was starting off, when M. Seneschal held him back, saying,—

"Don't go. I place my horse and my carriage at your disposal. Any one of these peasants can drive you. Capt. Parenteau and I will get into some farmer's wagon, and thus get back to Sauveterre; for we ought to be back as soon as possible. I have just heard alarming news. There may be some disorder. The peasant-women who attend the market have brought in most exciting reports, and exaggerated the calamities of last night. They have started reports that ten or twelve men have been killed, and that the incendiary, M. de Boiscoran, has been arrested. The crowd has gone to poor Guillebault's widow; and there have been demonstrations before the houses of several of the principal inhabitants of Sauveterre."

In ordinary times, M. Seneschal would not have intrusted his famous horse, Caraby, for any thing in the world, to the hands of a stranger. He considered it the best horse in the province. But he was evidently terribly upset, and betrayed it in his manner, and by the very efforts he made to regain his official dignity and self-possession.

He made a sign, and his carriage was brought up, all ready. But, when he asked for somebody to drive, no one came forward. All these good people who had spent the night abroad were in great haste to return home, where their cattle required their presence. When young Ribot saw the others hesitate, he said,—

"Well, I'll drive the justice."

And, taking hold of the whip and the reins, he took his seat on the front-bench, while the magistrate, the commonwealth attorney, and the clerk filled the vehicle.

"Above all, take care of Caraby," begged M. Seneschal, who at the last moment felt almost overcome with anxiety for his favorite.

"Don't be afraid, sir," replied the young man, as he started the horse. "If I strike too hard, M. Mechinet will stop me."

This Mechinet, the magistrate's clerk, was almost a power in Sauveterre; and the greatest personages there paid their court to him. His official duties were of very humble nature, and ill paid; but he knew how to eke out his income by other occupations, of which the court took no notice; and these added largely both to his importance in the community and to his modest income.

As he was a skilful lithographer, he printed all the visiting-cards which the people of Sauveterre ordered at the principal printing-office of Sauveterre, where "The Independent" was published. An able accountant, he kept books and made up accounts for some of the principal merchants in town. Some of the country people who were fond of litigation came to him for legal advice; and he drew up all kinds of law papers. For many years now, he had been director of the firemen's band, and manager of the Orpheon. He was a correspondent of certain Paris societies, and thus obtained free admission to the theatre not only, but also to the sacred precincts behind the scenes. Finally he was always ready to give writing-lessons, French lessons to little girls, or music-lessons on the flute and the horn, to amateurs.

These varied talents had drawn upon him the hostility of all the other teachers and public servants of the community, especially that of the mayor's clerk, and the clerks of the bank and great institutions of Sauveterre. But all these enemies he had gradually conquered by the unmistakable superiority of his ability; so that they fell in with the universal habit, and, when any thing special happened, said to each other,—

"Let us go and consult Mechinet."

He himself concealed, under an appearance of imperturbable good nature, the ambition by which he was devoured: he wanted to become rich, and to rise in the world. In fact, Mechinet was a diplomat, working in secret, but as cunning as Talleyrand. He had succeeded already in making himself the one great personage of

Sauveterre. The town was full of him; nothing was done without him; and yet he had not an enemy in the place.

The fact is, people were afraid of him, and dreaded his terrible tongue. Not that he had ever injured anybody, he was too wise for that; but they knew the harm he might do, if he chose, as he was master of every important secret in Sauveterre, and the best informed man in town as regarded all their little intrigues, their private foibles, and their dark antecedents.

This gave him quite an exceptional position. As he was unmarried, he lived with his sisters, the Misses Mechinet, who were the best dressmakers in town, and, moreover, devout members of all kinds of religious societies. Through them he heard all that was going on in society, and was able to compare the current gossip with what he heard in court, or at the newspaper office. Thus he could say pleasantly,—

"How could any thing escape me, when I have the church and the press, the court and the theatre, to keep me informed?"

Such a man would have considered himself disgraced if he had not known every detail of M. de Boiscoran's private affairs. He did not hesitate, therefore, while the carriage was rolling along on an excellent road, in the fresh spring morning, to explain to his companions the "case," as he called it, of the accused nobleman.

M. de Boiscoran, called Jacques by his friends, was rarely on his estate, and then only staid a month or so there. He was living in Paris, where his family owned a comfortable house in University Street. His parents were still alive.

His father, the Marquis de Boiscoran, the owner of a large landed estate, a deputy under Louis Philippe, a representative in 1848, had withdrawn from public life when the Second Empire was established, and spent, since that time, all his money, and all his energies, in collecting rare old books, and especially costly porcelain, on which he had written a monograph.

His mother, a Chalusse by birth, had enjoyed the reputation of being one of the most beautiful and most gifted ladies at the court of the Citizen King. At a certain period in her life, unfortunately, slander had attacked her; and about 1845 or 1846, it was reported that she had had a remarkable affair with a young lawyer of distinction, who had since become one of the austerest and most renowned judges. As she grew old, the marchioness devoted herself more and more to politics, as other women become pious. While her husband boasted that he had not read a newspaper for ten years, she had made her *salon* a kind of parliamentary centre, which had its influence on political affairs.

Although Jacques de Boiscoran's parents were still alive, he possessed a considerable fortune of his own—five or six thousand dollars a year. This fortune, which consisted of the Chateau of Boiscoran, the farms, meadows, and forests belonging to it, had been left to him by one of his uncles, the oldest brother of his father, who had died a widower, and childless, in 1868. M. de Boiscoran was at this moment about twenty-six or twenty-seven years old, dark complexion, tall, strong, well made, not exactly a handsome man, but having, what was worth more, one of those frank, intelligent faces which prepossess one at first sight.

His character was less well known at Sauveterre than his person. Those who had had any business with him described him as an honorable, upright man: his companions spoke of him as cheerful and gay, fond of pleasure, and always in good humor. At the time of the Prussian invasion, he had been made a captain of one of the volunteer companies of the district. He had led his men bravely under fire, and conducted himself so well on the battlefield, that Gen. Chanzy had rewarded him, when wounded, with the cross of the legion of honor.

"And such a man should have committed such a crime at Valpinson," said M. Daubigeon to the magistrate. "No, it is impossible! And no doubt he will very easily scatter all our doubts to the four winds."

"And that will be done at once," said young Ribot; "for here we are."

In many of the provinces of France the name of *chateau* is given to almost any little country-house with a weathercock on its pointed roof. But Boiscoran was a real chateau. It had been built towards the end of the seventeenth century, in wretched taste, but massively, like a fortress. Its position is superb. It is surrounded on all sides by woods and forests; and at the foot of the sloping garden flows a little river, merrily splashing over its pebbly bed, and called the Magpie on account of its perpetual babbling.

VII.

It was seven o'clock when the carriage containing the justice drove into the courtyard at Boiscoran,—a vast court, planted with lime-trees, and surrounded by farm buildings. The chateau was wide awake. Before her house-door, the farmer's wife was cleaning the huge caldron in which she had prepared the morning soup; the maids were going and coming; and at the stable a groom was rubbing down with great energy a thorough-bred horse.

On the front-steps stood Master Anthony, M. de Boiscoran's own man, smoking his cigar in the bright sunlight, and overlooking the farm operations. He was a man of nearly fifty, still very active, who had been bequeathed to his new master by his uncle, together with his possessions. He was a widower now; and his daughter was in the marchioness' service.

As he had been born in the family, and never left it afterwards, he looked upon himself as one of them, and saw no difference between his own interests and those of his master. In fact, he was treated less like a servant than like a friend; and he fancied he knew every thing about M. de Boiscoran's affairs.

When he saw the magistrate and the commonwealth attorney come up to the door, he threw away his cigar, came down quickly, and, bowing deeply, said to them with his most engaging smile,—

"Ah, gentlemen! What a pleasant surprise! My master will be delighted."

With strangers, Anthony would not have allowed himself such familiarity, for he was very formal; but he had seen M. Daubigeon more than once at the chateau; and he knew the plans that had been discussed between M. Galpin and his master. Hence he was not a little amazed at the embarrassed stiffness of the two gentlemen, and at the tone of voice in which the magistrate asked him,—

"Has M. de Boiscoran gotten up yet?"

"Not yet," he replied; "and I have orders not to wake him. He came home late last night, and wanted to make up this morning."

Instinctively the magistrate and the attorney looked away, each fearing to meet the other's eyes.

"Ah! M. de Boiscoran came home late last night?" repeated M. Galpin.

"Towards midnight, rather after midnight than before."

"And when had he gone out?"

"He left here about eight."

"How was he dressed?"

"As usually. He had light gray trousers, a shooting-jacket of brown velveteen, and a large straw hat."

"Did he take his gun?"

"Yes, sir."

"Do you know where he went?"

But for the respect which he felt for his master's friends, Anthony would not have answered these questions, which he thought were extremely impertinent. But this last question seemed to him to go beyond all fair limits. He replied, therefore, in a tone of injured self-respect,—

"I am not in the habit of asking my master where he goes when he leaves the house, nor where he has been when he comes back."

M. Daubigeon understood perfectly well the honorable feelings which actuated the faithful servant. He said to him with an air of unmistakable kindness,—

"Do not imagine, my friend, that I ask you these questions from idle curiosity. Tell me what you know; for your frankness may be more useful to your master than you imagine."

Anthony looked with an air of perfect stupefaction, by turns at the magistrate and the commonwealth attorney, at Mechinet, and finally at Ribot, who had taken the lines, and tied Caraby to a tree.

"I assure you, gentlemen, I do not know where M. de Boiscoran has spent the evening."

"You have no suspicion?"

"No."

"Perhaps he went to Brechy to see a friend?"

"I do not know that he has any friends in Brechy."

"What did he do after he came home?"

The old servant showed evident signs of embarrassment.

"Let me think," he said. "My master went up to his bedroom, and remained there four or five minutes. Then he came down, ate a piece of a pie, and drank a glass of wine. Then he lit a cigar, and told me to go to bed, adding that he would take a little walk, and undress without my help."

"And then you went to bed?"

"Of course."

"So that you do not know what your master may have done?"

"I beg your pardon. I heard him open the garden door."

"He did not appear to you different from usual?"

"No: he was as he always is,—quite cheerful: he was singing."

"Can you show me the gun he took with him?"

"No. My master probably took it to his room."

M. Daubigeon was about to make a remark, when the magistrate stopped him by a gesture, and eagerly asked,—

"How long is it since your master and Count Claudieuse have ceased seeing each other?"

Anthony trembled, as if a dark presentiment had entered his mind. He replied,—

"A long time: at least I think so."

"You are aware that they are on bad terms?"

"Oh!"

"They have had great difficulties between them?"

"Something unpleasant has happened, I know; but it was not much. As they do not visit each other, they cannot well hate each other. Besides, I have heard master say a hundred times, that he looked upon Count Claudieuse as one of the best and most honorable men; that he respected him highly, and"—

For a minute or so M. Galpin kept silent, thinking whether he had forgotten any thing. Then he asked suddenly,—

"How far is it from here to Valpinson?"

"Three miles, sir," replied Anthony.

"If you were going there, what road would you take?"

"The high road which passes Brechy."

"You would not go across the marsh?"

"Certainly not."

"Why not?"

"Because the Seille is out of its banks, and the ditches are full of water."

"Is not the way much shorter through the forest?"

"Yes, the way is shorter; but it would take more time. The paths are very indistinct, and overgrown with briers."

The commonwealth attorney could hardly conceal his disappointment. Anthony's answers seemed to become worse and worse.

"Now," said the magistrate again, "if fire should break out at Valpinson, would you see it from here?"

"I think not, sir. There are hills and tall woods between."

"Can you hear the Brechy bells from here?"

"When the wind is north, yes, sir."

"And last night, how was it?"

"The wind was from the west, as it always is when we have a storm."

"So that you have heard nothing? You do not know what a terrible calamity"—

"A calamity? I do not understand you, sir."

This conversation had taken place in the court-yard: and at this moment there appeared two gendarmes on horseback, whom M. Galpin had sent for just before he left Valpinson.

When old Anthony saw them, he exclaimed,—

"Great God! what is the meaning of this? I must wake master."

The magistrate stopped him, saying harshly,—

"Not a step! Don't say a word!"

And pointing out Ribot to the gendarmes, he said,—

"Keep that lad under your eyes, and let him have no communication with anybody."

Then, turning again to Anthony, he said,—

"Now show us to M. de Boiscoran's bedroom."

VIII.

In spite of its grand feudal air, the chateau at Boiscoran was, after all, little more than a bachelor's modest home, and in a very bad state of preservation. Of the eighty or a hundred rooms which it contained, hardly more than eight or ten were furnished, and this only in the simplest possible manner,—a sitting-room, a dining-room, a few guest-chambers: this was all M. de Boiscoran required during his rare visits to the place. He himself used in the second story a small room, the door of which opened upon the great staircase.

When they reached this door, guided by old Anthony, the magistrate said to the servant,—

"Knock!"

The man obeyed: and immediately a youthful, hearty voice replied from within,—

"Who is there?"

"It is I," said the faithful servant. "I should like"—

"Go to the devil!" broke in the voice.

"But, sir"—

"Let me sleep, rascal. I have not been able to close an eye till now." The magistrate, becoming impatient, pushed the servant aside, and, seizing the door-knob tried to open it; it was locked inside. But he lost no time in saying,—

"It is I, M. de Boiscoran: open, if you please!"

"Ah, dear M. Galpin!" replied the voice cheerfully.

"I must speak to you."

"And I am at your service, illustrious jurist. Just give me time to veil my Apollonian form in a pair of trousers, and I appear."

Almost immediately, the door opened; and M. de Boiscoran presented himself, his hair dishevelled, his eyes heavy with sleep, but looking bright in his youth and full health, with smiling lips and open hands.

"Upon my word!" he said. "That was a happy inspiration you had, my dear Galpin. You come to join me at breakfast?"

And, bowing to M. Daubigeon, he added,—

"Not to say how much I thank you for bringing our excellent commonwealth attorney with you. This is a veritable judicial visit"—

But he paused, chilled as he was by M. Daubigeon's icy face, and amazed at M. Galpin's refusal to take his proffered hand.

"Why," he said, "what is the matter, my dear friend?"

The magistrate had never been stiffer in his life, when he replied,—

"We shall have to forget our relations, sir. It is not as a friend I come to-day, but as a magistrate."

M. de Boiscoran looked confounded; but not a shadow of trouble appeared on his frank and open face.

"I'll be hanged," he said, "if I understand"—

"Let us go in," said M. Galpin.

They went in; and, as they passed the door, Mechinet whispered into the attorney's ear,—

"Sir, that man is certainly innocent. A guilty man would never have received us thus."

"Silence, sir!" said the commonwealth attorney, however much he was probably of his clerk's opinion. "Silence!"

And grave and sad he went and stood in one of the window embrasures. M. Galpin remained standing in the centre of the room, trying to see every thing in it, and to fix it in his memory, down to the smallest details. The prevailing disorder showed clearly how hastily M. de Boiscoran had gone to bed the night before. His clothes, his boots, his shirt, his waistcoat, and his straw hat lay scattered about on the chairs and on the floor. He wore those light gray trousers, which had been succcessively seen and recognized by Cocoleu, by Ribot, by Gaudry, and by Mrs. Courtois.

"Now, sir," began M. de Boiscoran, with that slight angry tone of voice which shows that a man thinks a joke has been carried far enough, "will you please tell me what procures for me the honor of this early visit?"

Not a muscle in M. Galpin's face was moving. As if the question had been addressed to some one else, he said coldly,—

"Will you please show us your hands, sir?"

M. de Boiscoran's cheeks turned crimson; and his eyes assumed an expression of strange perplexity.

"If this is a joke," he said, "it has perhaps lasted long enough."

He was evidently getting angry. M. Daubigeon thought it better to interfere, and thus he said,—

"Unfortunately, sir, the question is a most serious one. Do what the magistrate desires."

More and more amazed, M. de Boiscoran looked rapidly around him. In the door stood Anthony, his faithful old servant, with anguish on his face. Near the fireplace, the clerk had improvised a table, and put his paper, his pens, and his horn inkstand in readiness. Then with a shrug of his shoulders, which showed that he failed to understand, M. de Boiscoran showed his hands.

They were perfectly clean and white: the long nails were carefully cleaned also.

"When did you last wash your hands?" asked M. Galpin, after having examined them minutely.

At this question, M. de Boiscoran's face brightened up; and, breaking out into a hearty laugh, he said,—

"Upon my word! I confess you nearly caught me. I was on the point of getting angry. I almost feared"—

"And there was good reason for fear," said M. Galpin; "for a terrible charge has been brought against you. And it may be, that on your answer to my question, ridiculous as it seems to you, your honor may depend, and perhaps your liberty."

This time there was no mistake possible. M. de Boiscoran felt that kind of terror which the law inspires even in the best of men, when they find themselves suddenly accused of a crime. He turned pale, and then he said in a troubled voice,—

"What! A charge has been brought against me, and you, M. Galpin, come to my house to examine me?"

"I am a magistrate, sir."

"But you were also my friend. If anyone should have dared in my presence to accuse you of a crime, of a mean act, of something infamous, I should have defended you, sir, with all my energy, without hesitation, and without a doubt. I should have defended you till absolute, undeniable evidence should have been brought forward of your culpability; and even then I should have pitied you, remembering that I had esteemed you so highly as to favor your alliance with my family. But you—I am accused, I do not know of what, falsely, wrongly; and at once you hasten hither, you believe the charge, and consent to become my judge. Well, let it be so! I washed my hands last night after coming home."

M. Galpin had not boasted too much in praising his self-possession and his perfect control over himself. He did not move when the terrible words fell upon his ear; and he asked again in the same calm tone,—

"What has become of the water you used for that purpose?"

"It is probably still there, in my dressing-room."

The magistrate at once went in. On the marble table stood a basin full of water. That water was black and dirty. At the bottom lay particles of charcoal. On the top, mixed with the soapsuds, were swimming some extremely slight but unmistakable fragments of charred paper. With infinite care the magistrate carried the basin to the table at which Mechinet had taken a seat; and, pointing at it, he asked M. de Boiscoran,—

"Is that the water in which you washed your hands last night after coming home?"

"Yes," replied the other with an air of careless indifference.

"You had been handling charcoal, or some inflammable material."

"Don't you see?"

Standing face to face, the commonwealth attorney and clerk exchanged rapid glances. They had had the same feeling at that moment. If M. de Boiscoran was innocent, he was certainly a marvellously cool and energetic man, or he was carrying out a long-premeditated plan of action; for every one of his answers seemed to tighten the net in which he was taken. The magistrate himself seemed to be struck by this; but it was only for a moment, and then, turning to the clerk, he said,—

"Write that down!"

He dictated to him the whole evidence, most minutely and accurately, correcting himself every now and then to substitute a better word, or to improve his style. When he had read it over he said,—

"Let us go on, sir. You were out last night?"

"Yes, sir."

"Having left the house at eight, you returned only around midnight."

"After midnight."

"You took your gun?"

"Yes, sir."

"Where is it?"

With an air of indifference, M. de Boiscoran pointed at it in the corner of the fireplace, and said,—

"There it is!"

M. Galpin took it up quickly. It was a superb weapon, double-barrelled, of unusually fine make, and very elegant. On the beautifully carved woodwork the manufacturer's name, Clebb, was engraven.

"When did you last fire this gun?" asked the magistrate.

"Some four or five days ago."

"What for?"

"To shoot some rabbits who infested my woods."

M. Galpin raised and lowered the cock with all possible care: he noticed that it was the Remington patent. Then he opened the chamber, and found that the gun was loaded. Each barrel had a cartridge in it. Then he put the gun back in its place, and, pulling from his pocket the leaden cartridge-case which Pitard had found, he showed it to M. de Boiscoran, and asked him,—

"Do you recognize this?"

"Perfectly!" replied the other. "It is a case of one of the cartridges which I have probably thrown away as useless."

"Do you think you are the only one in this country who has a gun by this maker?"

"I do not think it: I am quite sure of it."

"So that you must, as a matter of course, have been at a spot where such a cartridge-case as this has been found?"

"Not necessarily. I have often seen children pick up these things, and play with them."

The clerk, while he made his pen fly across his paper, could not resist the temptation of making all kinds of faces. He was too well acquainted with lawyers' tactics not to understand M. Galpin's policy perfectly well, and to see how cunningly it was devised to make every fact strengthen the suspicion against M. de Boiscoran.

"It is a close game," he said to himself.

The magistrate had taken a seat.

"If that is so," he began again, "I beg you will give me an account of how you spent the evening after eight o'clock: do not hurry, consider, take your time; for your answers are of the utmost importance."

M. de Boiscoran had so far remained quite cool; but his calmness betrayed one of those terrible storms within, which may break forth, no one knows when. This warning, and, even more so, the tone in which it was given, revolted him as a most hideous hypocrisy. And, breaking out all of a sudden, he cried,—

"After all, sir, what do you want of me? What am I accused of?"

M. Galpin did not stir. He replied,—

"You will hear it at the proper time. First answer my question, and believe me in your own interest. Answer frankly. What did you do last night?"

"How do I know? I walked about."

"That is no answer."

"Still it is so. I went out with no specific purpose: I walked at haphazard."

"Your gun on your shoulder?"

"I always take my gun: my servant can tell you so."

"Did you cross the Seille marshes?"

"No."

The magistrate shook his head gravely. He said,—

"You are not telling the truth."

"Sir!"

"Your boots there at the foot of the bed speak against you. Where does the mud come from with which they are covered?"

"The meadows around Boiscoran are very wet."

"Do not attempt to deny it. You have been seen there."

"But"—

"Young Ribot met you at the moment when you were crossing the canal."

M. de Boiscoran made no reply.

"Where were you going?" asked the magistrate.

For the first time a real embarrassment appeared in the features of the accused,—the embarrassment of a man who suddenly sees an abyss opening before him. He hesitated; and, seeing that it was useless to deny, he said,—

"I was going to Brechy."

"To whom?"

"To my wood-merchant, who has bought all this year's wood. I did not find him at home, and came back on the high road."

M. Galpin stopped him by a gesture.

"That is not so," he said severely.

"Oh!"

"You never went to Brechy."

"I beg your pardon."

"And the proof is, that, about eleven o'clock, you were hurriedly crossing the forest of Rochepommier."

"I?"

"Yes, you! And do not say No; for there are your trousers torn to pieces by the thorns and briers through which you must have made your way."

"There are briers elsewhere as well as in the forest."

"To be sure; but you were seen there."

"By whom?"

"By Gaudry the poacher. And he saw so much of you, that he could tell us in what a bad humor you were. You were very angry. You were talking loud, and pulling the leaves from the trees."

As he said so, the magistrate got up and took the shooting-jacket, which was lying on a chair not far from him. He searched the pockets, and pulled out of one a handful of leaves.

"Look here! you see, Gaudry has told the truth."

"There are leaves everywhere," said M. de Boiscoran half aloud.

"Yes; but a woman, Mrs. Courtois, saw you come out of the forest of Rochepommier. You helped her to put a sack of flour on her ass, which she could not lift alone. Do you deny it? No, you are right; for, look here! on the sleeve of your coat I see something white, which, no doubt, is flour from her bag."

M. de Boiscoran hung his head. The magistrate went on,—

"You confess, then, that last night, between ten and eleven you were at Valpinson?"

"No, sir, I do not."

"But this cartridge-case which I have just shown you was picked up at Valpinson, close by the ruins of the old castle."

"Well, sir, have I not told you before that I have seen a hundred times children pick up these cases to play with? Besides, if I had really been at Valpinson, why should I deny it?"

M. Galpin rose to his full height, and said in the most solemn manner,—

"I am going to tell you why! Last night, between ten and eleven, Valpinson was set on fire; and it has been burnt to the ground."

"Oh!"

"Last night Count Claudieuse was fired at twice."

"Great God!"

"And it is thought, in fact there are strong reasons to think, that you, Jacques de Boiscoran, are the incendiary and the assassin."

IX.

M. de Boiscoran looked around him like a man who has suddenly been seized with vertigo, pale, as if all his blood had rushed to his heart.

He saw nothing but mournful, dismayed faces.

Anthony, his old trusted servant, was leaning against the doorpost, as if he feared to fall. The clerk was mending his pen in the air, overcome with amazement. M. Daubigeon hung his head.

"This is horrible!" he murmured: "this is horrible!"

He fell heavily into a chair, pressing his hands on his heart, as if to keep down the sobs that threatened to rise. M. Galpin alone seemed to remain perfectly cool. The law, which he imagined he was representing in all its dignity, knows nothing of emotions. His thin lips even trembled a little, as if a slight smile was about to burst forth: it was the cold smile of the ambitious man, who thinks he has played his little part well.

Did not every thing tend to prove that Jacques de Boiscoran was the guilty man, and that, in the alternative between a friend, and an opportunity of gaining high distinction, he had chosen well? After the silence of a minute, which seemed to be a century, he went and stood, with arms crossed on his chest, before the accused, and asked him,—

"Do you confess?"

M. de Boiscoran sprang up as if moved by a spring, and said,—

"What? What do you want me to confess?"

"That you have committed the crime at Valpinson."

The young man pressed his hands convulsively on his brow, and cried out,—

"But I am mad! I should have committed such a fearful, cowardly crime? Is that possible? Is that likely? I might confess, and you would not believe me. No! I am sure you would not believe my own words."

He would have moved the marble on his mantelpiece sooner than M. Galpin. The latter replied in icy tones,—

"I am not part of the question here. Why will you refer to relations which must be forgotten? It is no longer the friend who speaks to you, not even the man, but simply the magistrate. You were seen"—

"Who is the wretch?"

"Cocoleu!"

M. de Boiscoran seemed to be overwhelmed. He stammered,—

"Cocoleu? That poor epileptic idiot whom the Countess Claudieuse has picked up?"

"The same."

"And upon the strength of the senseless words of a poor imbecile I am charged with incendiarism, with murder?"

Never had the magistrate made such efforts to assume an air of impassive dignity and icy solemnity, as when he replied,—

"For an hour, at least, poor Cocoleu has been in the full enjoyment of his faculties. The ways of Providence are inscrutable."

"But sir"—

"And what does Cocoleu depose? He says he saw you kindle the fire with your own hands, then conceal yourself behind a pile of wood, and fire twice at Count Claudieuse."

"And all that appears quite natural to you?"

"No! At first it shocked me as it shocked everybody. You seem to be far above all suspicion. But a moment afterwards they pick up the cartridge-case, which can only have belonged to you. Then, upon my arrival here, I surprise you in bed, and find the water in which you have washed your hands black with coal, and little pieces of charred paper swimming on top of it."

"Yes," said M. de Boiscoran in an undertone: "it is fate."

"And that is not all," continued the magistrate, raising his voice, "I examine you, and you admit having been out from eight o'clock till after midnight. I ask what you have been doing, and you refuse to tell me. I insist, and you tell a falsehood. In order to overwhelm you, I am forced to quote the evidence of young Ribot, of Gaudry, and Mrs. Courtois, who have seen you at the very places where you deny having been. That circumstance alone condemns you. Why should you not be willing to tell me what you have been doing during those four hours? You claim to be innocent. Help me, then, to establish your innocence. Speak, tell me what you were doing between eight and midnight."

M. de Boiscoran had no time to answer.

For some time already, half-suppressed cries, and the sound of a large crowd, had come up from the courtyard. A gendarme came in quite excited; and, turning to the magistrate and the commonwealth attorney, he said,—

"Gentlemen, there are several hundred peasants, men and women, in the yard, who clamor for M. de Boiscoran. They threaten to drag him down to the river. Some of the men are armed with pitchforks; but the women are the maddest. My comrade and I have done our best to keep them quiet."

And just then, as if to confirm what he said, the cries came nearer, growing louder and louder; and one could distinctly hear,—

"Drown Boiscoran! Let us drown the incendiary!"

The attorney rose, and told the gendarme,—

"Go down and tell these people that the authorities are this moment examining the accused; that they interrupt us; and that, if they keep on, they will have to do with me."

The gendarme obeyed his orders. M. de Boiscoran had turned deadly pale. He said to himself,—

"These unfortunate people believe my guilt!"

"Yes," said M. Galpin, who had overheard the words; "and you would comprehend their rage, for which there is good reason, if you knew all that has happened."

"What else?"

"Two Sauveterre firemen, one the father of five children, have perished in the flames. Two other men, a farmer from Brechy, and a gendarme who tried to rescue them, have been so seriously burned that their lives are in danger."

M. de Boiscoran said nothing.

"And it is you," continued the magistrate, "who is charged with all these calamities. You see how important it is for you to exculpate yourself."

"Ah! how can I?"

"If you are innocent, nothing is easier. Tell us how you employed yourself last night."

"I have told you all I can say."

The magistrate seemed to reflect for a full minute; then he said,—

"Take care, M. de Boiscoran: I shall have to have you arrested."

"Do so."

"I shall be obliged to order your arrest at once, and to send you to jail in Sauveterre."

"Very well."

"Then you confess?"

"I confess that I am the victim of an unheard-of combination of circumstances; I confess that you are right, and that certain fatalities can only be explained by the belief in Providence: but I swear by all that is holy in the world, I am innocent."

"Prove it."

"Ah! would I not do it if I could?"

"Be good enough, then, to dress, sir, and to follow the gendarmes."

Without a word, M. de Boiscoran went into his dressing-room, followed by his servant, who carried him his clothes. M. Galpin was so busy dictating to the clerk the latter part of the examination, that he seemed to forget his prisoner. Old Anthony availed himself of this opportunity.

"Sir," he whispered into his master's ear while helping him to put on his clothes.

"What?"

"Hush! Don't speak so loud! The other window is open. It is only about twenty feet to the ground: the ground is soft. Close by is one of the cellar openings; and in there, you know, there is the old hiding-place. It is only five miles to the coast, and I will have a good horse ready for you to-night, at the park-gate."

A bitter smile rose on M. de Boiscoran's lips, as he said,—

"And you too, my old friend: you think I am guilty?"

"I conjure you," said Anthony, "I answer for any thing. It is barely twenty feet. In your mother's name"—

But, instead of answering him, M. de Boiscoran turned round, and called M. Galpin. When he had come in, he said to him, "Look at that window, sir! I have money, fast horses; and the sea is only five miles off. A guilty man would have escaped. I stay here; for I am innocent."

In one point, at least, M. de Boiscoran had been right. Nothing would have been easier for him than to escape, to get into the garden, and to reach the hiding-place which his servant had suggested to him. But after that? He had, to be sure, with old Anthony's assistance, some chance of escaping altogether. But, after all, he might have been found out in his hiding-place, or he might have been overtaken in his ride to the coast. Even if he had succeeded, what would have become of him? His flight would necessarily have been looked upon as a confession of his guilt.

Under such circumstances, to resist the temptation to escape, and to make this resistance well known, was in fact not so much an evidence of innocence as a proof of great cleverness. M. Galpin, at all events, looked upon it in that light; for he judged others by himself. Carefully and cunningly calculating every step he took in life, he did not believe in sudden inspirations. He said, therefore, with an ironical smile, which was to show that he was not so easily taken in,—

"Very well, sir. This circumstance shall be mentioned, as well as the others, at the trial."

Very differently thought the commonwealth attorney and the clerk. If the magistrate had been too much engaged in his dictation to notice any thing, they had been perfectly able to notice the great excitement under which the accused had naturally labored. Perfectly amazed at first, and thinking, for a moment, that the whole was a joke, he had next become furiously angry; then fear and utter dejection had followed one another. But in precise proportion as the charges had accumulated, and the evidence had become overwhelming, he had, so far from becoming demoralized, seemed to recover his assurance.

"There is something curious about it," growled Mechinet. M. Daubigeon, on the other hand, said nothing; but when M. de Boiscoran came out of his dressing-room, fully dressed and ready, he said,—

"One more question, sir."

The poor man bowed. He was pale, but calm and self-possessed.

"I am ready to reply," he said.

"I'll be brief. You seemed to be surprised and indignant at any one's daring to accuse you. That was weakness. Justice is but the work of man, and must needs judge by appearances. If you reflect, you will see that the appearances are all against you."

"I see it but too clearly."

"If you were on a jury, you would not hesitate to pronounce a man guilty upon such evidence."

"No, sir, no!"

The commonwealth attorney bounded from his chair. He said,—

"You are not sincere!"

M. de Boiscoran sadly shook his head, and replied,—

"I speak to you without the slightest hope of convincing you, but in all sincerity. No, I should not condemn a man, as you say, if he asserted his innocence, and if I did not see any reason for his crime. For, after all, unless a man is mad, he does not commit a crime for nothing. Now I ask you, how could I, upon whom fortune has always smiled; I who am on the eve of marrying one whom I love passionately,—how could I have set Valpinson on fire, and tried to murder Count Claudieuse?"

M. Galpin had scarcely been able to disguise his impatience, when he saw the attorney take part in the affair. Seizing, therefore, the opportunity to interfere, he said,—

"Your reason, sir, was hatred. You hated the count and the countess mortally. Do not protest: it is of no use. Everybody knows it; and you yourself have told me so."

M. de Boiscoran looked as if he were growing still more pale, and then replied in a tone of crushing disdain,—

"Even if that were so, I do not see what right you have to abuse the confidence of a friend, after having declared, upon your arrival here, that all friendship between us had ceased. But that is not so. I never told you any such thing. As my feelings have never changed, I can repeat literally what I have said. I have told you that the count was a troublesome neighbor, a stickler for his rights, and almost absurdly attached to his preserves. I have also told you, that, if he declared my public opinions to be abominable, I looked upon his as ridiculous and dangerous. As for the countess, I have simply said, half in jest, that so perfect a person was not to my taste; and that I should be very unhappy if my wife were a Madonna, who hardly ever deigned to put her foot upon the ground."

"And that was the only reason why you once pointed your gun at Count Claudieuse? A little more blood rushing to your head would have made you a murderer on that day."

A terrible spasm betrayed M. de Boiscoran's fury; but he checked himself, and said,—

"My passion was less fiery than it may have looked. I have the most profound respect for the count's character. It is an additional grief to me that he should have accused me."

"But he has not accused you!" broke in M. Daubigeon. "On the contrary, he was the first and the most eager to defend you."

And, in spite of the signs which M. Galpin made, he continued,—

"Unfortunately that has nothing to do with the force of the evidence against you. If you persist in keeping silence, you must look for a criminal trial for the galleys. If you are innocent, why not explain the matter? What do you wait for? What do you hope?"

"Nothing."

Mechinet had, in the meantime, completed the official report.

"We must go," said M. Galpin

"Am I at liberty," asked M. de Boiscoran, "to write a few lines to my father and my mother? They are old: such an event may kill them."

"Impossible!" said the magistrate.

Then, turning to Anthony, he said,—

"I am going to put the seals on this room, and I shall leave it in the meanwhile in your keeping. You know your duty, and the penalties to which you would be subject, if, at the proper time, every thing is not found in the same condition in which it is left now. Now, how shall we get back to Sauveterre?"

After mature deliberation it was decided that M. de Boiscoran should go in one of his own carriages, accompanied by one of the gendarmes. M. Daubigeon, the magistrate, and the clerk would return in the mayor's carriage, driven by Ribot, who was furious at being kept under surveillance.

"Let us be off," said the magistrate, when the last formalities had been fulfilled.

M. de Boiscoran came down slowly. He knew the court was full of furious peasants; and he expected to be received with hootings. It was not so. The gendarme whom the attorney had sent down had done his duty so well, that not a cry was heard. But when he had taken his seat in the carriage, and the horse went off at a trot, fierce curses arose, and a shower of stones fell, one of which wounded a gendarme.

"Upon my word, you bring ill luck, prisoner," said the man, a friend of the other gendarme who had been so much injured at the fire.

M. de Boiscoran made no reply. He sank back into the corner, and seemed to fall into a kind of stupor, from which he did not rouse himself till the carriage drove into the yard of the prison at Sauveterre. On the threshold stood Master Blangin, the jailer, smiling with delight at the idea of receiving so distinguished a prisoner.

"I am going to give you my best room," he said, "but first I have to give a receipt to the gendarme, and to enter you in my book." Thereupon he took down his huge, greasy register, and wrote the name of Jacques de Boiscoran beneath that of Trumence Cheminot, a vagabond who had just been arrested for having broken into a garden.

It was all over. Jacques de Boiscoran was a prisoner, to be kept in close confinement.

SECOND PART

THE BOISCORAN TRIAL

I.

The Paris house of the Boiscoran family, No. 216 University Street, is a house of modest appearance. The yard in front is small; and the few square yards of damp soil in the rear hardly deserve the name of a garden. But appearances are deceptive. The inside is marvellously comfortable; careful and painstaking hands have made every provision for ease; and the rooms display that solid splendor for which our age has lost the taste. The vestibule contains a superb mosaic, brought home from Venice, in 1798, by one of the Boiscorans, who had degenerated, and followed the fortunes of Napoleon. The balusters of the great staircase are a masterpiece of iron work; and the wainscoting in the dining-room has no rival in Paris.

All this, however, is a mere nothing in comparison with the marquis's cabinet of curiosities. It fills the whole depth, and half the width, of the upper story; is lighted from above like a huge *atelier*; and would fill the heart of an artist with delight. Immense glass cases, which stand all around against the walls, hold the treasures of the marquis,—priceless collections of enamels, ivories, bronzes, unique manuscripts, matchless porcelains, and, above all, his *faiences*, his dear *faiences*, the pride and the torment of his old age.

The owner was well worthy of such a setting.

Though sixty-one years old at that time, the marquis was as straight as ever, and most aristocratically lean. He had a perfectly magnificent nose, which absorbed immense quantities of snuff; his mouth was large, but well furnished; and his brilliant eyes shone with that restless cunning which betrayed the amateur, who has continually to deal with sharp and eager dealers in curiosities and second-hand articles of *vertu*.

In the year 1845 he had reached the summit of his renown by a great speech on the question of public meetings; but at that hour his watch seemed to have stopped. All his ideas were those of an Orleanist. His appearance, his costume, his high cravat, his whiskers, and the way he brushed his hair, all betrayed the admirer and friend of the citizen king. But for all that, he did not trouble himself about politics; in fact, he troubled himself about nothing at all. With the only condition that his inoffensive passion should be respected, the marchioness was allowed to rule supreme in the house, administering her large fortune, ruling her only son, and deciding all questions without the right of appeal. It was perfectly useless to ask the marquis any thing: his answer was invariably,—

"Ask my wife."

The good man had, the evening before, purchased a little at haphazard, a large lot of *faiences*, representing scenes of the Revolution; and at about three o'clock, he was busy, magnifying-glass in hand, examining his dishes and plates, when the door was suddenly opened.

The marchioness came in, holding a blue paper in her hand. Six or seven years younger than her husband, she was the very companion for such an idle, indolent man. In her walk, in her manner, and in her voice, she showed at once the woman who stands at the wheel, and means to be obeyed. Her once celebrated beauty had left remarkable traces enough to justify her pretensions. She denied having any claims to being considered handsome, since it was impossible to deny or conceal the ravages of time, and hence by far her best policy was to accept old age with good grace. Still, if the marchioness did not grow younger, she pretended to be older than she really was. She had her gray hair puffed out with considerable affectation, so as to contrast all the more forcibly with her ruddy, blooming cheeks, which a girl might have envied and she often thought of powdering her hair.

She was so painfully excited, and almost undone, when she came into her husband's cabinet, that even he, who for many a year had made it a rule of his life to show no emotion, was seriously troubled. Laying aside the dish which he was examining, he said with an anxious voice,—

"What is the matter? What has happened?"

"A terrible misfortune."

"Is Jacques dead?" cried the old collector.

The marchioness shook her head.

"No! It is something worse, perhaps"—

The old man, who has risen at the sight of his wife, sank slowly back into his chair.

"Tell me," he stammered out,—"tell me. I have courage."

She handed him the blue paper which she had brought in, and said slowly,—

"Here. A telegram which I have just received from old Anthony, our son's valet."

With trembling hands the old marquis unfolded the paper, and read,—

"Terrible misfortune! Master Jacques accused of having set the chateau at Valpinson on fire, and murdered Count Claudieuse. Terrible evidence against him. When examined, hardly any defence. Just arrested and carried to jail. In despair. What must I do?"

The marchioness had feared lest the marquis should have been crushed by this despatch, which in its laconic terms betrayed Anthony's abject terror. But it was not so. He put it back on the table in the calmest manner, and said, shrugging his shoulders,—

"It is absurd!"

His wife did not understand it. She began again,—

"You have not read it carefully, my friend"—

"I understand," he broke in, "that our son is accused of a crime which he has not and can not have committed. You surely do not doubt his innocence? What a mother you would be! On my part, I assure you I am perfectly tranquil. Jacques an incendiary! Jacques a murderer! That is nonsense!"

"Ah! you did not read the telegram," exclaimed the marchioness.

"I beg your pardon."

"You did not see that there was evidence against him."

"If there had been none, he could not have been arrested. Of course, the thing is disagreeable: it is painful."

"But he did not defend himself."

"Upon my word! Do you think that if to-morrow somebody accused me of having robbed the till of some shopkeeper, I would take the trouble to defend myself?"

"But do you not see that Anthony evidently thinks our son is guilty?"

"Anthony is an old fool!" declared the marquis.

Then pulling out his snuffbox, and stuffing his nose full of snuff, he said,—

"Besides, let us consider. Did you not tell me that Jacques is in love with that little Dionysia Chandore?"

"Desperately. Like a real child."

"And she?"

"She adores Jacques."

"Well. And did you not also tell me that the wedding-day was fixed?"

"Yes, three days ago."

"Has Jacques written to you about the matter?"

"An excellent letter."

"In which he tells you he is coming up?"

"Yes: he wanted to purchase the wedding-presents himself." With a gesture of magnificent indifference the marquis tapped the top of his snuffbox, and said,—

"And you think a boy like our Jacques, a Boiscoran, in love, and beloved, who is about to be married, and has his head full of wedding-presents, could have committed such a horrible crime? Such things are not worth discussing, and, with your leave, I shall return to my occupation."

If doubt is contagious, confidence is still more so. Gradually the marchioness felt reassured by the perfect assurance of her husband.

The blood came back to her cheeks; and smiles reappeared on pale lips. She said in a stronger voice,—

"In fact, I may have been too easily frightened."

The marquis assented by a gesture.

"Yes, much too easily, my dear. And, between us, I would not say much about it. How could the officers help accusing our Jacques if his own mother suspects him?"

The marchioness had taken up the telegram, and was reading it over once more.

"And yet," she said, answering her own objections, "who in my place would not have been frightened? This name of Claudieuse especially"—

"Why? It is the name of an excellent and most honorable gentleman,—the best man in the world, in spite of his sea-dog manners."

"Jacques hates him, my dear."

"Jacques does not mind him any more than that."

"They have repeatedly quarrelled."

"Of course. Claudieuse is a furious legitimist; and as such he always talks with the utmost contempt of all of us who have been attached to the Orleans family."

"Jacques has been at law with him."

"And he has done right, only he ought to have carried the matter through. Claudieuse has claims on the Magpie, which divides our lands,—absurd claims. He wants at all seasons, and according as he may desire, to direct the waters of the little stream into his own channels, and thus drown the meadows at Boiscoran, which are lower than his own. Even my brother, who was an angel in patience and gentleness, had his troubles with this tyrant."

But the marchioness was not convinced yet.

"There was another trouble," she said.

"What?"

"Ah! I should like to know myself."

"Has Jacques hinted at any thing?"

"No. I only know this. Last year, at the Duchess of Champdoce's, I met by chance the Countess Claudieuse and her children. The young woman is perfectly charming; and, as we were going to give a ball the week after, it occurred to me to invite her at once. She refused, and did so in such an icy, formal manner, that I did not insist."

"She probably does not like dancing," growled the marquis.

"That same evening I mentioned the matter to Jacques. He seemed to be very angry, and told me, in a manner that was hardly compatible with respect, that I had been very wrong, and that he had his reasons for not desiring to come in contact with those people."

The marquis felt so secure, that he only listened with partial attention, looking all the time aside at his precious *faiences*.

"Well," he said at last, "Jacques detests the Claudieuses. What does that prove? God be thanked, we do not murder all the people we detest!"

His wife did not insist any longer. She only asked,—

"Well, what must we do?"

She was so little in the habit of consulting her husband, that he was quite surprised.

"The first thing is to get Jacques out of jail. We must see—we ought to ask for advice."

At this moment a light knock was heard at the door.

"Come in!" he said.

A servant came in, bringing a large envelope, marked "Telegraphic Despatch. Private."

"Upon my word!" cried the marquis. "I thought so. Now we shall be all right again."

The servant had left the room. He tore open the envelope; but at the first glance at the contents the smile vanished, he turned pale, and just said,—

"Great God!"

Quick as lightning, the marchioness seized the fatal paper. She read at a glance,—

"Come quick. Jacques in prison; close confinement; accused of horrible crime. The whole town says he is guilty, and that he has confessed. Infamous calumny! His judge is his former friend, Galpin, who was to marry his cousin Lavarande. Know nothing except that Jacques is innocent. Abominable intrigue! Grandpa Chandore and I will do what can be done. Your help indispensable. Come, come!

"DIONYSIA CHANDORE."

"Ah, my son is lost!" cried the marchioness with tears in her eyes. The marquis, however, had recovered already from the shock.

"And I—I say more than ever, with Dionysia, who is a brave girl, Jacques is innocent. But I see he is in danger. A criminal prosecution is always an ugly affair. A man in close confinement may be made to say any thing."

"We must do something," said the mother, nearly mad with grief.

"Yes, and without losing a minute. We have friends: let us see who among them can help us."

"I might write to M. Margeril."

The marquis, who had turned quite pale, became livid.

"What!" he cried. "You dare utter that name in my presence?"

"He is all powerful; and my son is in danger."

The marquis stopped her with a threatening gesture, and cried with an accent of bitter hatred,—

"I would a thousand times rather my son should die innocent on the scaffold than owe his safety to that man!"

His wife seemed to be on the point of fainting.

"Great God! And yet you know very well that I was only a little indiscreet."

"No more!" said the marquis harshly.

Then, recovering his self-control by a powerful effort, he went on,—

"Before we attempt any thing, we must know how the matter stands. You will leave for Sauveterre this evening."

"Alone?"

"No. I will find some able lawyer,—a reliable jurist, who is not a politician,—if such a one can be found nowadays. He will tell you what to do, and will write to me, so that I can do here whatever may be best. Dionysia is right. Jacques must be the victim of some abominable intrigue. Nevertheless, we shall save him; but we must keep cool, perfectly cool."

And as he said this he rang the bell so violently, that a number of servants came rushing in at once.

"Quick," he said; "send for my lawyer, Mr. Chapelain. Take a carriage."

The servant who took the order was so expeditious, that, in less than twenty minutes, M. Chapelain arrived.

"Ah! we want all your experience, my friend," said the marquis to him. "Look here. Read these telegrams."

Fortunately, the lawyer had such control over himself, that he did not betray what he felt; for he believed Jacques guilty, knowing as he did how reluctant courts generally are to order the arrest of a suspected person.

"I know the man for the marchioness," he said at last.

"Ah!"

"A young man whose modesty alone has kept him from distinguishing himself so far, although I know he is one of the best jurists at the bar, and an admirable speaker."

"What is his name?"

"Manuel Folgat. I shall send him to you at once."

Two hours later, M. Chapelain's *protégé* appeared at the house of the Boiscorans. He was a man of thirty-one or thirty-two, with large, wide-open eyes, whose whole appearance was breathing intelligence and energy.

The marquis was pleased with him, and after having told him all he knew about Jacques's position, endeavored to inform him as to the people down at Sauveterre,—who would be likely to be friends, and who enemies, recommending to him, above all, to trust M. Seneschal, an old friend of the family, and a most influential man in that community.

"Whatever is humanly possible shall be done, sir," said the lawyer.

That same evening, at fifteen minutes past eight, the Marchioness of Boiscoran and Manuel Folgat took their seats in the train for Orleans.

II.

The railway which connects Sauveterre with the Orleans line enjoys a certain celebrity on account of a series of utterly useless curves, which defy all common sense, and which would undoubtedly be the source of countless accidents, if the trains were not prohibited from going faster than eight or ten miles an hour.

The depot has been built—no doubt for the greater convenience of travellers—at a distance of two miles from town, on a place where formerly the first banker of Sauveterre had his beautiful gardens. The pretty road which leads to it is lined on both sides with inns and taverns, on market-days full of peasants, who try to rob each other, glass in hand, and lips overflowing with protestations of honesty. On ordinary days even, the road is quite lively; for the walk to the railway has become a favorite promenade. People go out to see the trains start or come in, to examine the new arrivals, or to exchange confidences as to the reasons why Mr. or Mrs. So-and-so have made up their mind to travel.

It was nine o'clock in the morning when the train which brought the marchioness and Manuel Folgat at last reached Sauveterre. The former was overcome by fatigue and anxiety, having spent the whole night in discussing the chances for her son's safety, and was all the more exhausted as the lawyer had taken care not to encourage her hopes.

For he also shared, in secret at least, M. Chapelain's doubts. He, also, had said to himself, that a man like M. de Boiscoran is not apt to be arrested, unless there are strong reasons, and almost overwhelming proofs of his guilt in the hands of the authorities.

The train was slackening speed.

"If only Dionysia and her father," sighed the marchioness, "have thought of sending a carriage to meet us."

"Why so?" asked Manuel Folgat.

"Because I do not want all the world to see my grief and my tears."

The young lawyer shook his head, and said,—

"You will certainly not do that, madame, if you are disposed to follow my advice."

She looked at him quite amazed; but he insisted.

"I mean you must not look as if you wished not to be seen: that would be a great, almost irreparable mistake. What would they think if they saw you in tears and great distress? They would say you were sure of your son's guilt; and the few who may still doubt will doubt no longer. You must control public opinion from the beginning; for it is absolute in these small communities, where everybody is under somebody else's immediate influence. Public opinion is all powerful; and say what you will, it controls even the jurymen in their deliberations."

"That is true," said the marchioness: "that is but too true."

"Therefore, madame, you must summon all your energy, conceal your maternal anxiety in your innermost heart, dry your tears, and show nothing but the most perfect confidence. Let everybody say, as he sees you, 'No mother could look so who thinks her son guilty.'"

The marchioness straightened herself, and said,—

"You are right, sir; and I thank you. I must try to impress public opinion as you say; and, so far from wishing to find the station deserted, I shall be delighted to see it full of people. I will show you what a woman can do who thinks of her son's life."

The Marchioness of Boiscoran was a woman of rare power.

Drawing her comb from her dressing-case, she repaired the disorder of her coiffure; with a few skilful strokes she smoothed her dress; her features, by a supreme effort of will, resumed their usual serenity; she forced her lips to smile without betraying the effort it cost her; and then she said in a clear, firm voice,—

"Look at me, sir. Can I show myself now?"

The train stopped at the station. Manuel Folgat jumped out lightly; and, offering the marchioness his hand to assist her, he said,—

"You will be pleased with yourself, madam. Your courage will not be useless. All Sauveterre seems to be here."

This was more than half true. Ever since the night before, a report had been current,—no one knew how it had started,—that the "murderer's mother," as they charitably called her, would arrive by the nine o'clock train; and everybody had determined to happen to be at the station at that hour. In a place where gossip lives for three days upon the last new dress from Paris, such an opportunity for a little excitement was not to be neglected. No one thought for a moment of what the poor old lady would probably feel upon being compelled thus to face a whole town; for at Sauveterre curiosity has at least the merit, that it is not hypocritical. Everybody is openly indiscreet, and by no means ashamed of it. They place themselves right in front of you, and look at you, and try to find out the secret of your joy or your grief.

It must be borne in mind, however, that public opinion was running strongly against M. de Boiscoran. If there had been nothing against him but the fire at Valpinson, and the attempts upon Count Claudieuse, that would have been a small matter. But the fire had had terrible consequences. Two men had perished in it; and two others had been so severely wounded as to put their lives in jeopardy. Only the evening before, a sad procession had passed through the streets of Sauveterre. In a cart covered with a cloth, and followed by two priests, the almost carbonized remains of Bolton the drummer, and of poor Guillebault, had been brought home. The whole city had seen the widow go to the mayor's office, holding in her arms her youngest child, while the four others clung to her dress.

All these misfortunes were traced back to Jacques, who was loaded with curses; and the people now thought of receiving his mother, the marchioness, with fierce hootings.

"There she is, there she is!" they said in the crowd, when she appeared in the station, leaning upon M. Folgat's arm.

But they did not say another word, so great was their surprise at her appearance. Immediately two parties were formed. "She puts a bold face on it," said some; while others declared, "She is quite sure of her son's innocence."

At all events, she had presence of mind enough to see what an impression she produced, and how well she had done to follow M. Folgat's advice. It gave her additional strength. As she distinguished in the crowd some people whom she knew, she went up to them, and, smiling, said,—

"Well, you know what has happened to us. It is unheard of! Here is the liberty of a man like my son at the mercy of the first foolish notion that enters the head of a magistrate. I heard the news yesterday by telegram, and came down at once with this gentleman, a friend of ours, and one of the first lawyers of Paris."

M. Folgat looked embarrassed: he would have liked more considerate words. Still he could not help supporting the marchioness in what she had said.

"These gentlemen of the court," he said in measured tones, "will perhaps be sorry for what they have done."

Fortunately a young man, whose whole livery consisted in a gold-laced cap, came up to them at this moment.

"M. de Chandore's carriage is here," he said.

"Very well," replied the marchioness.

And bowing to the good people of Sauveterre, who were quite dumfounded by her assurance, she said,—

"Pardon me if I leave you so soon; but M. de Chandore expects us. I shall, however, be happy to call upon you soon, on my son's arm."

The house of the Chandore family stands on the other side of the New-Market Place, at the very top of the street, which is hardly more than a line of steps, which the mayor persistently calls upon the municipal council to grade, and which the latter as persistently refuse to improve. The building is quite new, massive but ugly, and has at the side a pretentious little tower with a peaked roof, which Dr. Seignebos calls a perpetual menace of the feudal system.

It is true the Chandores once upon a time were great feudal lords, and for a long time exhibited a profound contempt for all who could not boast of noble ancestors and a deep hatred of revolutionary ideas. But if they had ever been formidable, they had long since ceased to be so. Of the whole great family,—one of the most numerous and most powerful of the province,—only one member survived, the Baron de Chandore, and a girl, his granddaughter, betrothed to Jacques de Boiscoran. Dionysia was an orphan. She was barely three years old, when within five months, she lost her father, who fell in a duel, and her mother, who had not the strength to survive the man whom she had loved. This was certainly for the child a terrible misfortune; but she was not left uncared for nor unloved. Her grandfather bestowed all his affections upon her; and the two sisters of her mother, the Misses Lavarande, then already no longer young, determined never to marry, so as to devote themselves exclusively to their niece. From that day the two good ladies had wished to live in the baron's house; but from the beginning he had utterly refused to listen to their propositions, asserting that he was perfectly able himself to watch over the child, and wanted to have her all to himself. All he would grant was, that the ladies might spend the day with Dionysia whenever they chose.

Hence arose a certain rivalry between the aunts and the grandfather, which led both parties to most amazing exaggerations. Each one did what could be done to engage the affections of the little girl; each one was willing to pay any price for the most trifling caress. At five years Dionysia had every toy that had ever been invented. At ten she was dressed like the first lady of the land, and had jewelry in abundance.

The grandfather, in the meantime, had been metamorphosed from head to foot. Rough, rigid, and severe, he had suddenly become a "love of a father." The fierce look had vanished from his eyes, the scorn from his lips; and both had given way to soft glances and smooth words. He was seen daily trotting through the streets, and going from shop to shop on errands for his grandchild. He invited her little friends, arranged picnics for her, helped her drive her hoops, and if needs be, led in a cotillion.

If Dionysia looked displeased, he trembled. If she coughed, he turned pale. Once she was sick: she had the measles. He staid up for twelve nights in succession, and sent to Paris for doctors, who laughed in his face.

And yet the two old ladies found means to exceed his folly.

If Dionysia learned any thing at all, it was only because she herself insisted upon it: otherwise the writing-master and the music-master would have been sent away at the slightest sign of weariness.

Sauveterre saw it, and shrugged its shoulders.

"What a wretched education!" the ladies said. "Such weakness is absolutely unheard of. They tender the child a sorry service."

There was no doubt that such almost incredible spoiling, such blind devotion, and perpetual worship, came very near making of Dionysia the most disagreeable little person that ever lived. But fortunately she had one of those happy dispositions which cannot be spoiled; and besides, she was perhaps saved from the danger by its very excess. As she grew older she would say with a laugh,—

"Grandpapa Chandore, my aunts Lavarande, and I, we do just what we choose."

That was only a joke. Never did a young girl repay such sweet affection with rarer and nobler qualities.

She was thus leading a happy life, free from all care, and was just seventeen years old, when the great event of her life took place. M. de Chandore one morning met Jacques de Boiscoran, whose uncle had been a friend of his, and invited him to dinner. Jacques accepted the invitation, and came. Dionysia saw him, and loved him.

Now, for the first time in her life, she had a secret unknown to Grandpapa Chandore and to her aunts; and for two years the birds and the flowers were the only confidants of this love of hers, which grew up in her heart, sweet like a dream, idealized by absence, and fed by memory.

For Jacques's eyes remained blind for two years.

But the day on which they were opened he felt that his fate was sealed. Nor did he hesitate a moment; and in less than a month after that, the Marquis de Boiscoran came down to Sauveterre, and in all form asked Dionysia's hand for his son.

Ah! that was a heavy blow for Grandpapa Chandore.

He had, of course, often thought of the future marriage of his grandchild; he had even at times spoken of it, and told her that he was getting old, and should feel very much relieved when he should have found her a good husband. But he talked of it as a distant thing, very much as we speak of dying. M. de Boiscoran brought his true feelings out. He shuddered at the idea of giving up Dionysia, of seeing her prefer another man to himself, and of loving her children best of all. He was quite inclined to throw the ambassador out of the window.

Still he checked his feelings, and replied that he could give no reply till he had consulted his granddaughter.

Poor grandpapa! At the very first words he uttered, she exclaimed,—

"Oh, I am so happy! But I expected it."

M. de Chandore bent his head to conceal a tear which burned in his eyes. Then he said very low,—

"Then the thing is settled."

At once, rather comforted by the joy that was sparkling in his grandchild's eyes, he began reproaching himself for his selfishness, and for being unhappy, when his Dionysia seemed to be so happy. Jacques had, of course, been allowed to visit the house as a lover; and the very day before the fire at Valpinson, after having long and carefully counted the days absolutely required for all the purchases of the trousseau, and all the formalities of the event, the wedding-day had been finally fixed.

Thus Dionysia was struck down in the very height of her happiness, when she heard, at the same time, of the terrible charges brought against M. de Boiscoran, and of his arrest.

At first, thunderstruck, she had lain nearly ten minutes unconscious in the arms of her aunts, who, like the grandfather, were themselves utterly overcome with terror. But, as soon as she came to, she exclaimed,—

"Am I mad to give way thus? Is it not evident that he is innocent?"

Then she had sent her telegram to the marquis, knowing well, that, before taking any measures, it was all important to come to an understanding with Jacques's family. Then she had begged to be left alone; and she had spent the night in counting the minutes that must pass till the hour came when the train from Paris would bring her help.

At eight o'clock she had come down to give orders herself that a carriage should be sent to the station for the marchioness, adding that they must drive back as fast as they could. Then she had gone into the sitting-room to join her grandfather and her aunts. They talked to her; but her thoughts were elsewhere.

At last a carriage was heard coming up rapidly, and stopping before the house. She got up, rushed into the hall, and cried,—

"Here is Jacques's mother!"

III.

We cannot do violence to our natural feelings without paying for it. The marchioness had nearly fainted when she could at last take refuge in the carriage: she was utterly overcome by the great effort she had made to present to the curious people of Sauveterre a smiling face and calm features.

"What a horrible comedy!" she murmured, as she sank back on the cushions.

"Admit, at least, madam," said the lawyer, "that it was necessary. You have won over, perhaps, a hundred persons to your son's side."

She made no reply. Her tears stifled her. What would she not have given for a few moments' solitude, to give way to all the grief of her heart, to all the anxiety of a mother! The time till she reached the house seemed to her an eternity; and, although the horse was driven at a furious rate, she felt as if they were making no progress. At last the carriage stopped.

The little servant had jumped down, and opened the door, saying,—

"Here we are."

The marchioness got out with M. Folgat's assistance; and her foot was hardly on the ground, when the house-door opened, and Dionysia threw herself into her arms, too deeply moved to speak. At last she broke forth,—

"Oh, my mother, my mother! what a terrible misfortune!"

In the passage M. de Chandore was coming forward. He had not been able to follow his granddaughter's rapid steps.

"Let us go in," he said to the two ladies: "don't stand there!"

For at all the windows curious eyes were peeping through the blinds.

He drew them into the sitting-room. Poor M. Folgat was sorely embarrassed what to do with himself. No one seemed to be aware of his existence. He followed them, however. He entered the room, and standing by the door, sharing the general excitement, he was watching by turns, Dionysia, M. de Chandore, and the two spinsters.

Dionysia was then twenty years old. It could not be said that she was uncommonly beautiful; but no one could ever forget her again who had once seen her. Small in form, she was grace personified; and all her movements betrayed a rare and exquisite perfection. Her black hair fell in marvellous masses over her head, and contrasted strangely with her blue eyes and her fair complexion. Her skin was of dazzling whiteness. Every thing in her features spoke of excessive timidity. And yet, from certain movements of her lips and her eyebrows, one might have suspected no lack of energy.

Grandpapa Chandore looked unusually tall by her side. His massive frame was imposing. He did not show his seventy-two years, but was as straight as ever, and seemed to be able to defy all the storms of life. What struck strangers most, perhaps, was his dark-red complexion, which gave him the appearance of an Indian chieftain, while his white beard and hair brought the crimson color still more prominently out. In spite of his herculean frame and his strange complexion, his face bore the expression of almost child-like goodness. But the first glance at his eyes proved that the gentle smile on his lips was not to be taken alone. There were flashes in his gray eyes which made people aware that a man who should dare, for instance, to offend Dionysia, would have to pay for it pretty dearly.

As to the two aunts, they were as tall and thin as a couple of willow-rods, pale, discreet, ultra-aristocratic in their reserve and their coldness; but they bore in their faces an expression of happy peace and sentimental tenderness, such as is often seen in old maids whose temper has not been soured by celibacy. They dressed absolutely alike, as they had done now for forty years, preferring neutral colors and modest fashions, such as suited their simple taste.

They were crying bitterly at that moment; and M. Folgat felt instinctively that there was no sacrifice of which they were not capable for their beloved niece's sake.

"Poor Dionysia!" they whispered.

The girl heard them, however; and, drawing herself up, she said,—

"But we are behaving shamefully. What would Jacques say, if he could see us from his prison! Why should we be so sad? Is he not innocent?"

Her eyes shone with unusual brilliancy: her voice had a ring which moved Manuel Folgat deeply.

"I can at least, in justice to myself," she went on saying, "assure you that I have never doubted him for a moment. And how should I ever have dared to doubt? The very night on which the fire broke out, Jacques wrote me a letter of four pages, which he sent me by one of his tenants, and which reached me at nine o'clock. I showed it to grandpapa. He read it, and then he said I was a thousand times right, because a man who had been meditating such a crime could never have written that letter."

"I said so, and I still think so," added M. de Chandore; "and every sensible man will think so too; but"—

His granddaughter did not let him finish.

"It is evident therefore, that Jacques is the victim of an abominable intrigue; and we must unravel it. We have cried enough: now let us act!"

Then, turning to the marchioness, she said,—

"And my dear mother, I sent for you, because we want you to help us in this great work."

"And here I am," replied the old lady, "not less certain of my son's innocence than you are."

Evidently M. de Chandore had been hoping for something more; for he interrupted her, asking,—

"And the marquis?"

"My husband remained in Paris."

The old gentleman's face assumed a curious expression.

"Ah, that is just like him," he said. "Nothing can move him. His only son is wickedly accused of a crime, arrested, thrown into prison. They write to him; they hope he will come at once. By no means. Let his son get out of trouble as he can. He has his *faïences* to attend to. Oh, if I had a son!"

"My husband," pleaded the marchioness, "thinks he can be more useful to Jacques in Paris than here. There will be much to be done there."

"Have we not the railway?"

"Moreover," she went on, "he intrusted me to this gentleman." She pointed out M. Folgat.

"M. Manuel Folgat, who has promised us the assistance of his experience, his talents, and his devotion."

When thus formally introduced, M. Folgat bowed, and said,—

"I am all hope. But I think with Miss Chandore, that we must go to work without losing a second. Before I can decide, however, upon what is to be done, I must know all the facts."

"Unfortunately we know nothing," replied M. de Chandore,— "nothing, except that Jacques is kept in close confinement."

"Well, then, we must try to find out. You know, no doubt, all the law officers of Sauveterre?"

"Very few. I know the commonwealth attorney."

"And the magistrate before whom the matter has been brought."

The older of the two Misses Lavarande rose, and exclaimed,—

"That man, M. Galpin, is a monster of hypocrisy and ingratitude. He called himself Jacques's friend; and Jacques liked him well enough to induce us, my sister and myself, to give our consent to a marriage between him and one of our cousins, a Lavarande. Poor child. When she learned the sad truth, she cried, 'Great God! God be blessed that I escaped the disgrace of becoming the wife of such a man!'"

"Yes," added the other old lady, "if all Sauveterre thinks Jacques guilty, let them also say, 'His own friend has become his judge.'"

M. Folgat shook his head, and said,—

"I must have more minute information. The marquis mentioned to me a M. Seneschal, mayor of Sauveterre."

M. de Chandore looked at once for his hat, and said,—

"To be sure! He is a friend of ours; and, if any one is well informed, he is. Let us go to him. Come."

M. Seneschal was indeed a friend of the Chandores, the Lavarandes, and also of the Boiscorans. Although he was a lawyer he had become attached to the people whose confidential adviser he had been for more than twenty years. Even after having retired from business, M. Seneschal had still retained the full confidence of his former clients. They never decided on any grave question, without consulting him first. His successor did the business for them; but M. Seneschal directed what was to be done.

Nor was the assistance all on one side. The example of great people like M. de Chandore and Jacques's uncle had brought many a peasant on business into M. Seneschal's office; and when he was, at a later period of his life, attacked by the fever of political ambition, and offered to "sacrifice himself for his country" by becoming mayor of Sauveterre, and a member of the general council, their support had been of great service to him.

Hence he was well-nigh overcome when he returned, on that fatal morning, to Sauveterre. He looked so pale and undone, that his wife was seriously troubled.

"Great God, Augustus! What has happened?" she asked.

"Something terrible has happened," he replied in so tragic a manner, that his wife began to tremble.

To be sure, Mrs. Seneschal trembled very easily. She was a woman of forty-five or fifty years, very dark, short, and fat, trying hard to breathe in the corsets which were specially made for her by the Misses Mechinet, the clerk's sisters. When she was young, she had been rather pretty: now she still kept the red cheeks of her younger days, a forest of jet black hair, and excellent teeth. But she was not happy. Her life had been spent in wishing for children, and she had none.

She consoled herself, it is true, by constantly referring to all the most delicate details on the subject, mentioning not to her intimate friends only, but to any one who would listen, her constant disappointments, the physicians she had consulted, the pilgrimages she had undertaken, and the quantities of fish she had eaten, although she abominated fish. All had been in vain, and as her hopes fled with her years, she had become resigned, and indulged now in a kind of romantic sentimentality, which she carefully kept alive by reading novels and poems without end. She had a tear ready for every unfortunate being, and some words of comfort for every grief. Her charity was well known. Never had a poor woman with children appealed to her in vain. In spite of all that, she was not easily taken in. She managed her household with her hand as well as with her eye; and no one surpassed her in the extent of her washings, or the excellence of her dinners.

She was quite ready, therefore, to sigh and to sob when her husband told her what had happened during the night. When he had ended, she said,—

"That poor Dionysia is capable of dying of it. In your place, I would go at once to M. de Chandore, and inform him in the most cautious manner of what has happened."

"I shall take good care not to do so," replied M. Seneschal; "and I tell you expressly not to go there yourself."

For he was by no means a philosopher; and, if he had been his own master, he would have taken the first train, and gone off a hundred miles, so as not to see the grief of the Misses Lavarande and Grandpapa Chandore. He was exceedingly fond of Dionysia: he had been hard at work for years to settle and to add to her fortune, as if she had been his own daughter, and now to witness her grief! He shuddered at the idea. Besides, he really did not know what to believe, and influenced by M. Galpin's assurance, misled by public opinion, he had come to ask himself if Jacques might not, after all, have committed the crimes with which he was charged.

Fortunately his duties were on that day so numerous and so troublesome, that he had no time to think. He had to provide for the recovery and the transportation of the remains of the two unfortunate victims of the fire; he had to receive the mother of one, and the widow and children of the other, and to listen to their complaints, and try to console them by promising the former a small pension, and the latter some help in the education of their children. Then he had to give directions to have the wounded men brought home; and, after that, he had gone out in search of a house for Count Claudieuse and his wife, which had given him much trouble. Finally, a large part of the afternoon had been taken up by an angry discussion with Dr. Seignebos. The doctor, in the name of outraged society, as he called it, and in the name of justice and humanity, demanded the immediate arrest of Cocoleu, that wretch whose unconscious statement formed the basis of the accusation. He demanded with a furious oath that the epileptic idiot should be sent to the hospital, and kept there so as to be professionally examined by experts. The mayor had for some time refused to grant the request, which seemed to him unreasonable; but he doctor had talked so loud and insisted so strongly, that at last he had sent two gendarmes to Brechy with orders to bring back Cocoleu.

They had returned several hours later with empty hands. The idiot had disappeared; and no one in the whole district had been able to give any information as to this whereabouts.

"And you think that is natural?" exclaimed Dr. Seignebos, whose eyes were glaring at the mayor from under his spectacles. "To me that looks like an absolute proof that a plot has been hatched to ruin M. de Boiscoran."

"But can't you be quiet?" M. Seneschal said angrily. "Do you think Cocoleu is lost? He will turn up again."

The doctor had left him without insisting any longer; but before going home, he had dropped in at his club, and there, in the presence of twenty people he had declared that he had positive proof of a plot formed against M. de Boiscoran, whom the Monarchists had never forgiven for having left them; and that the Jesuits were certainly mixed up with the business.

This interference was more injurious than useful to Jacques; and the consequences were soon seen. That same evening, when M. Galpin crossed the New-Market Place, he was wantonly insulted. Very naturally he went, almost in a fury, to call upon the mayor, to hold him responsible for this insult offered to Justice in his person, and asking for energetic punishment. M. Seneschal promised to take the proper measures, and went to the commonwealth attorney to act in concert with him. There he learned what had happened at Boiscoran, and the terrible result of the examination.

So he had come home, quite sorrowful, distressed at Jacques's situation, and very much disturbed by the political aspect which the matter was beginning to wear. He had spent a bad night, and in the morning had displayed such fearful temper, that his wife had hardly dared to say a word to him. But even that was not all. At two o'clock precisely, the funeral of Bolton and Guillebault was to take place; and he had promised Capt. Parenteau that he would be present in his official costume, and accompanied by the whole municipal council. He had already given orders to have his uniform gotten ready, when the servant announced visitors,—M. de Chandore and friend.

"That was all that was wanting!" he exclaimed

But, thinking it over, he added,—

"Well, it had to come sooner or later. Show them in!"

M. Seneschal was too good to be so troubled in advance, and to prepare himself for a heart-rending scene. He was amazed at the easy, almost cheerful manner with which M. de Chandore presented to him his companion.

"M. Manuel Folgat, my dear Seneschal, a famous lawyer from Paris, who has been kind enough to come down with the Marchioness de Boiscoran."

"I am a stranger here, M. Seneschal," said Folgat: "I do not know the manner of thinking, the customs, the interests, the prejudices, of this country; in fact, I am totally ignorant, and I know I would commit many a grievous blunder, unless I could secure the assistance of an able and experienced counsellor. M. de Boiscoran and M. de Chandore have both encouraged me to hope that I might find such a man in you."

"Certainly, sir, and with all my heart," replied M. Seneschal, bowing politely, and evidently flattered by this deference on the part of a great Paris lawyer.

He had offered his guests seats. He had sat down himself, and resting his elbow on the arm of his big office-chair, he rubbed his clean-shaven chin with his hand.

"This is a very serious matter, gentlemen," he said at last.

"A criminal charge is always serious," replied M. Folgat.

"Upon my word," cried M. de Chandore, "you are not in doubt about Jacques's innocence?"

M. Seneschal did not say, No. He was silent, thinking of the wise remarks made by his wife the evening before.

"How can we know," he began at last, "what may be going on in young brains of twenty-five when they are set on fire by the remembrance of certain insults! Wrath is a dangerous counsellor."

Grandpapa Chandore refused to hear any more.

"What! do you talk to me of wrath?" he broke in; "and what do you see of wrath in this Valpinson affair? I see nothing in it, for my part, but the very meanest crime, long prepared and coolly carried out."

The mayor very seriously shook his head, and said,—

"You do not know all that has happened."

"Sir," added M. Folgat, "it is precisely for the purpose of hearing what has happened that we come to you."

"Very well," said M. Seneschal.

Thereupon he went to work to describe the events which he had witnessed at Valpinson, and those, which, as he had learned from the commonwealth attorney, had taken place at Boiscoran; and this he did with all the lucidity of an experienced old lawyer who is accustomed to unravel the mysteries of complicated suits. He wound up by saying,—

"Finally, do you know what Daubigeon said to me, whose evidence you will certainly know how to appreciate? He said in so many words, 'Galpin could not but order the arrest of M. de Boiscoran. Is he guilty? I do not know what to think of it. The accusation is overwhelming. He swears by all the gods that he is innocent; but he will not tell how he spent the night.'"

M. de Chandore, in spite of his vigor, was near fainting, although his face remained as crimson as ever. Nothing on earth could make him turn pale.

"Great God!" he murmured, "what will Dionysia say?"

Then, turning to M. Folgat, he said aloud,—

"And yet Jacques had something in his mind for that evening."

"Do you think so?"

"I am sure of it. But for that, he would certainly have come to the house, as he has done every evening for a month. Besides, he said so himself in the letter which he sent Dionysia by one of his tenants, and which she mentioned to you. He wrote, 'I curse from the bottom of my heart the business which prevents me from spending the evening with you; but I cannot possibly defer it any longer. To-morrow!'"

"You see," said M. Seneschal.

"The letter is of such a nature," continued the old gentleman, "that I repeat, No man who premeditated such a hideous crime could possibly have written it. Nevertheless, I confess to you, that, when I heard the fatal news, this very allusion to some pressing business impressed me painfully."

But the young lawyer seemed to be far from being convinced.

"It is evident," he said, "that M. de Boiscoran will on no account let it be known where he went."

"He told a falsehood, sir," insisted M. Seneschal. "He commenced by denying that he had gone the way on which the witnesses met him."

"Very naturally, since he desires to keep the place unknown to which he went."

"He did not say any more when he was told that he was under arrest."

"Because he hopes he will get out of this trouble without betraying his secret."

"If that were so, it would be very strange."

"Stranger things than that have happened."

"To allow himself to be accused of incendiarism and murder when he is innocent!"

"To be innocent, and to allow one's self to be condemned, is still stranger; and yet there are instances"—

The young lawyer spoke in that short, imperious tone which is, so to say, the privilege of his profession, and with such an accent of assurance, that M. de Chandore felt his hopes revive. M. Seneschal was sorely troubled.

"And what do you think, sir?" he asked.

"That M. de Boiscoran must be innocent," replied the young advocate. And, without leaving time for objections, he continued,—

"That is the opinion of a man who is not influenced by any consideration. I come here without any preconceived notions. I do not know Count Claudieuse any more than M. de Boiscoran. A crime has been committed: I am told the circumstances; and I at once come to the conclusion that the reasons which led to the arrest of the accused would lead me to set him at liberty."

"Oh!"

"Let me explain. If M. de Boiscoran is guilty, he has shown, in the way in which he received M. Galpin at the house, a perfectly unheard-of self-control, and a matchless genius for comedy. Therefore, if he is guilty, he is immensely clever"—

"But."

"Allow me to finish. If he is guilty, he has in the examination shown a marvellous want of self-control, and, to be brief, a nameless stupidity: therefore, if he is guilty, he is immensely stupid"—

"But."

"Allow me to finish. Can one and the same person be at once so unusually clever and so unusually stupid? Judge yourself. But again: if M. de Boiscoran is guilty, he ought to be sent to the insane asylum, and not to prison; for any one else but a madman would have poured out the dirty water in which he had washed his blackened hands, and would have buried anywhere that famous breech-loader, of which the prosecution makes such good use."

"Jacques is safe!" exclaimed M. de Chandore.

M. Seneschal was not so easily won over.

"That is specious pleading," he said. "Unfortunately, we want something more than a logic conclusion to meet a jury with an abundance of witnesses on the other side."

"We will find more on our side."

"What do you propose to do?"

"I do not know. I have just told you my first impression. Now I must study the case, and examine the witnesses, beginning with old Anthony."

M. de Chandore had risen. He said,—

"We can reach Boiscoran in an hour. Shall I send for my carriage?"

"As quickly as possible," replied the young lawyer.

M. de Chandore's servant was back in a quarter of an hour, and announced that the carriage was at the door. M. de Chandore and M. Folgat took their seats; and, while they were getting in, the mayor warned the young Paris lawyer,—

"Above all, be prudent and circumspect. The public mind is already but too much inflamed. Politics are mixed up with the case. I am afraid of some disturbance at the burial of the firemen; and they bring me word that Dr. Seignebos wants to make a speech at the graveyard. Good-by and good luck!"

The driver whipped the horse, and, as the carriage was going down through the suburbs, M. de Chandore said,—

"I cannot understand why Anthony did not come to me immediately after his master had been arrested. What can have happened to him?"

IV.

M. Seneschal's horse was perhaps one of the very best in the whole province; but M. de Chandore's was still better. In less than fifty minutes they had driven the whole distance to Boiscoran; and during this time M. de Chandore and M. Folgat had not exchanged fifty words.

When they reached Boiscoran, the courtyard was silent and deserted. Doors and windows were hermetically closed. On the steps of the porch sat a stout young peasant, who, at the sight of the newcomers, rose, and carried his hand to his cap.

"Where is Anthony?" asked M. de Chandore.

"Up stairs, sir."

The old gentleman tried to open the door: it resisted.

"O sir! Anthony has barricaded the door from the inside."

"A curious idea," said M. de Chandore, knocking with the butt-end of his whip.

He was knocking fiercer and fiercer, when at last Anthony's voice was heard from within,—

"Who is there?"

"It is I, Baron Chandore."

The bars were removed instantly, and the old valet showed himself in the door. He looked pale and undone. The disordered condition of his beard, his hair, and his dress, showed that he had not been to bed. And this disorder was full of meaning in a man who ordinarily prided himself upon appearing always in the dress of an English gentleman.

M. de Chandore was so struck by this, that he asked, first of all,—

"What is the matter with you, my good Anthony?"

Instead of replying, Anthony drew the baron and his companion inside; and, when he had fastened the door again, he crossed his arms, and said,—

"The matter is—well, I am afraid."

The old gentleman and the lawyer looked at each other. They evidently both thought the poor man had lost his mind. Anthony saw it, and said quickly,—

"No, I am not mad, although, certainly, there are things passing here which could make one doubtful of one's own senses. If I am afraid, it is for good reasons."

"You do not doubt your master?" asked M. Folgat.

The servant cast such fierce, threatening glances at the lawyer, that M. de Chandore hastened to interfere.

"My dear Anthony," he said, "this gentleman is a friend of mine, a lawyer, who has come down from Paris with the marchioness to defend Jacques. You need not mistrust him, nay, more than that, you must tell him all you know, even if"—

The trusty old servant's face brightened up, and he exclaimed,—

"Ah! If the gentleman is a lawyer. Welcome, sir. Now I can say all that weighs on my heart. No, most assuredly I do not think Master Jacques guilty. It is impossible he should be so: it is absurd to think of it. But what I believe, what I am sure of, is this,—there is a plot to charge him with all the horrors of Valpinson."

"A plot?" broke in M. Folgat, "whose? how? and what for?"

"Ah! that is more than I know. But I am not mistaken; and you would think so too, if you had been present at the examination, as I was. It was fearful, gentlemen, it was unbearable, so that even I was stupefied for a moment, and thought my master was guilty, and advised him to flee. The like has never been heard of before, I am sure. Every thing went against him. Every answer he made sounded like a confession. A crime had been committed at Valpinson; he had been seen going there and coming back by side paths. A fire had been kindled; his hands bore traces of charcoal. Shots had been fired; they found one of his cartridge-cases close to the spot where Count Claudieuse had been wounded. There it was I saw the plot. How could all these circumstances have agreed so precisely if they had not been pre-arranged, and calculated beforehand? Our poor M. Daubigeon had tears in his eyes; and even that meddlesome fellow, Mechinet, the clerk, was quite overcome. M. Galpin was the only one who looked pleased; but then he was the magistrate, and he put the questions. He, my master's friend!—a man who was constantly coming here, who ate our bread, slept in our beds, and shot our game. Then it was, 'My dear Jacques,' and 'My dear Boiscoran' always, and no end of compliments and caresses; so that I often thought one of these days I should find him blackening my master's boots. Ah! he took his revenge yesterday; and you ought to have seen with what an air he said to master, 'We are friends no longer.' The rascal! No, we are friends no longer; and, if God was just, you ought to have all the shot in your body that has wounded Count Claudieuse."

M. de Chandore was growing more and more impatient. As soon, therefore, as Anthony's breath gave out a moment, he said,—

"Why did you not come and tell me all that immediately?"

The old servant ventured to shrug his shoulders slightly, and replied,—

"How could I? When the examination was over, that man, Galpin, put the seals everywhere,—strips of linen, fastened on with sealing-wax, as they do with dead people. He put one on every opening, and on some of them two. He put three on the outer door. Then he told me that he appointed me keeper of the house, that I would be paid for it, but that I would be sent to the galleys if any one touched the seals with the tip of the finger. When he had handed master over to the gendarmes, that man, Galpin, went away, leaving me here alone, dumfounded, like a man who has been knocked in the head. Nevertheless, I should have come to you, sir, but I had an idea, and that gave me the shivers."

Grandpapa Chandore stamped his foot, and said,—

"Come to the point, to the point!"

"It was this: you must know, gentlemen, that, in the examination, that breech-loading gun played a prominent part. That man, Galpin looked at it carefully, and asked master when he had last fired it off. Master said, 'About five days ago. You hear, I say, five days.' Thereupon, that man, Galpin, puts the gun down, without looking at the barrels."

"Well?" asked M. Folgat.

"Well, sir, I—Anthony—I had the evening before—I say the evening before—cleaned the gun, washed it, and"—

"Upon my word," cried M. de Chandore, "why did you not say so at once? If the barrels are clean, that is an absolute proof that Jacques is innocent."

The old servant shook his head, and said,—

"To be sure, sir. But are they clean?"

"Oh!"

"Master may have been mistaken as to the time when he last fired the gun, and then the barrels would be soiled; and, instead of helping him, my evidence might ruin him definitely. Before I say any thing, I ought to be sure."

"Yes," said Folgat, approvingly, "and you have done well to keep silence, my good man, and I cannot urge you too earnestly not to say a word of it to any one. That fact may become a decisive argument for the *defence*."

"Oh! I can keep my tongue, sir. Only you may imagine how impatient it has made me to see these accursed seals which prevent me from going to look at the gun. Oh, if I had dared to break one of them!"

"Poor fellow!"

"I thought of doing it; but I checked myself. Then it occurred to me that other people might think of the same thing. The rascals who have formed this abominable plot against Master Jacques are capable of any thing, don't you think so? Why might not they come some night, and break the seals? I put the steward on guard in the garden, beneath the windows. I put his son as a sentinel into the courtyard; and I have myself stood watch before the seals with arms in my hands all the time. Let the rascals come on; they will find somebody to receive them."

In spite of all that is said, lawyers are better than their reputation. Lawyers, accused of being sceptics above all men, are, on the contrary, credulous and simple-minded. Their enthusiasm is sincere; and, when we think they play a part, they are in earnest. In the majority of cases, they fancy their own side the just one, even though they should be beaten. Hour by hour, ever since his arrival at Sauveterre, M. Folgat's faith in Jacques's innocence had steadily increased. Old Anthony's tale was not made to shake his growing conviction. He did not admit the existence of a plot, however; but he was not disinclined to believe in the cunning calculations of some rascal, who, availing himself of circumstances known to him alone, tried to let all suspicion fall upon M. de Boiscoran, instead of himself.

But there were many more questions to be asked; and Anthony was in such a state of feverish excitement, that it was difficult to induce him to answer. For it is not so easy to examine a man, however inclined he may be to answer. It requires no small self-possession, much care, and an imperturbable method, without which the most important facts are apt to be overlooked. M. Folgat began, therefore, after a moment's pause, once more, saying,—

"My good Anthony, I cannot praise your conduct in this matter too highly. However, we have not done with it yet. But as I have eaten nothing since I left Paris last night, and as I hear the bell strike twelve o'clock"—

M. de Chandore seemed to be heartily ashamed, and broke in,—

"Ah, forgetful old man that I am! Why did I not think of it? But you will pardon me, I am sure. I am so completely upset. Anthony, what can you let us have?"

"The housekeeper has eggs, potted fowl, ham"—

"Whatever can be made ready first will be the best," said the young lawyer.

"In a quarter of an hour the table shall be set," replied the servant.

He hurried away, while M. de Chandore invited M. Folgat into the sitting-room. The poor grandfather summoned all his energy to keep up appearances.

"This fact about the gun will save him, won't it?" he asked.

"Perhaps so," replied the famous advocate.

And they were silent,—the grandfather thinking of the grief of his grandchild, and cursing the day on which he had opened his house to Jacques, and with him to such heart-rending anguish; the lawyer arranging in his mind the facts he had learned, and preparing the questions he was going to ask. They were both so fully absorbed by their thoughts, that they started when Anthony reappeared, and said,—

"Gentlemen, breakfast is ready!"

The table had been set in the dining-room; and, when the two gentlemen had taken their seats, old Anthony placed himself, his napkin over his arm, behind them; but M. de Chandore called him, saying,—

"Put another plate, Anthony, and breakfast with us."

"Oh, sir," protested the old servant,—"sir"—

"Sit down," repeated the baron: "if you eat after us, you will make us lose time, and an old servant like you is a member of the family."

Anthony obeyed, quite overcome, but blushing with delight at the honor that was done him; for the Baron de Chandore did not usually distinguish himself to familiarity. When the ham and eggs of the housekeeper had been disposed of, M. Folgat said,—

"Now let us go back to business. Keep cool, my dear Anthony, and remember, that, unless we get the court to say that there is no case, your answers may become the basis of our defence. What were M. de Boiscoran's habits when he was here?"

"When he was here, sir, he had, so to say, no habits. We came here very rarely, and only for a short time."

"Never mind: what was he doing here?"

"He used to rise late; he walked about a good deal; he sometimes went out hunting; he sketched; he read, for master is a great reader, and is as fond of his books as the marquis, his father, is of his porcelains."

"Who came here to see him?"

"M. Galpin most frequently, Dr. Seignebos, the priest from Brechy, M. Seneschal, M. Daubigeon."

"How did he spend his evenings?"

"At M. de Chandore's, who can tell you all about it."

"He had no other relatives in this country?"

"No."

"You do not know that he had any lady friend?"

Anthony looked as if he would have blushed.

"Oh, sir!" he said, "you do not know, I presume, that master is engaged to Miss Dionysia?"

The Baron de Chandore was not a baby, as he liked to call it. Deeply interested as he was, he got up, and said,—

"I want to take a little fresh air."

And he went out, understanding very well that his being Dionysia's grandfather might keep Anthony from telling the truth.

"That is a sensible man," thought M. Folgat.

Then he added aloud,—

"Now we are alone, my dear Anthony, you can speak frankly. Did M. de Boiscoran keep a mistress?"

"No, sir."

"Did he ever have one?"

"Never. They will tell you, perhaps, that once upon a time he was rather pleased with a great, big red-haired woman, the daughter of a miller in the neighborhood, and that the gypsy of a woman came more frequently to the chateau than was needful,—now on one pretext, and now on another. But that was mere childishness. Besides, that was five years ago, and the woman has been married these three years to a basket-maker at Marennes."

"You are quite sure of what you say?"

"As sure as I am of myself. And you would be as sure of it yourself, if you knew the country as I know it, and the abominable tongues the people have. There is no concealing any thing from them. I defy a man to talk three times to a woman without their finding it out, and making a story of it. I say nothing of Paris"—

M. Folgat listened attentively. He asked,—

"Ah! was there any thing of the kind in Paris?"

Anthony hesitated; at last he said,—

"You see, master's secrets are not my secrets, and, after the oath I have sworn,"—

"It may be, however, that his safety depends upon your frankness in telling me all," said the lawyer. "You may be sure he will not blame you for having spoken."

For several seconds the old servant remained undecided; then he said,—

"Master, they say, has had a great love-affair."

"When?"

"I do not know when. That was before I entered his service. All I know is, that, for the purpose of meeting the person, master had bought at Passy, at the end of Vine Street, a beautiful house, in the centre of a large garden, which he had furnished magnificently."

"Ah!"

"That is a secret, which, of course, neither master's father nor his mother knows to this day; and I only know it, because one day master fell down the steps, and dislocated his foot, so that he had to send for me to nurse him. He may have bought the house under his own name; but he was not known by it there. He passed for an Englishmen, a Mr. Burnett; and he had an English maid-servant."

"And the person?"

"Ah, sir! I not only do not know who she is, but I cannot even guess it, she took such extraordinary precautions! Now that I mean to tell you every thing, I will confess to you that I had the curiosity to question the English maid. She told me that she was no farther than I was, that she knew, to be sure, a lady was coming there from time to time; but that she had never seen even the end of her nose. Master always arranged it so well, that the girl was invariably out on some errand or other when the lady came and when she went away. While she was in the house, master waited upon her himself. And when they wanted to walk in the garden, they sent the servant away, on some fool's errand, to Versailles or to Fontainebleau; and she was mad, I tell you."

M. Folgat began to twist his mustache, as he was in the habit of doing when he was specially interested. For a moment, he thought he saw the woman—that inevitable woman who is always at the bottom of every great event in man's life; and just then she vanished from his sight; for he tortured his mind in vain to discover a possible if not probable connection between the mysterious visitor in Vine Street and the events that had happened at Valpinson. He could not see a trace. Rather discouraged, he asked once more,—

"After all, my dear Anthony, this great love-affair of your master's has come to an end?"

"It seems so, sir, since Master Jacques was going to marry Miss Dionysia."

That reason was perhaps not quite as conclusive as the good old servant imagined; but the young advocate made no remark.

"And when do you think it came to an end?"

"During the war, master and the lady must have been parted; for master did not stay in Paris. He commanded a volunteer company; and he was even wounded in the head, which procured him the cross."

"Does he still own the house in Vine Street?"

"I believe so."

"Why?"

"Because, some time ago, when master and I went to Paris for a week, he said to me one day, 'The War and the commune have cost me dear. My cottage has had more than twenty shells, and it has been in turn occupied by *Francs-tireurs*, Communists and Regulars. The walls are broken; and there is not a piece of furniture uninjured. My architect tells me, that all in all, the repairs will cost me some ten thousand dollars.'"

"What? Repairs? Then he thought of going back there?"

"At that time, sir, master's marriage had not been settled. Yet"—

"Still that would go to prove that he had at that time met the mysterious lady once more, and that the war had not broken off their relations."

"That may be."

"And has he never mentioned the lady again?"

"Never."

At this moment M. de Chandore's cough was heard in the hall,—that cough which men affect when they wish to announce their coming. Immediately afterwards he reappeared; and M. Folgat said to him, to show that his presence was no longer inconvenient,—

"Upon my word, sir, I was just on the point of going in search of you, for fear that you felt really unwell."

"Thank you," replied the old gentleman, "the fresh air has done me good."

He sat down; and the young advocate turned again to Anthony, saying,—

"Well, let us go on. How was he the day before the fire?"

"Just as usual."

"What did he do before he went out?"

"He dined as usual with a good appetite; then he went up stairs and remained there for an hour. When he came down, he had a letter in his hand, which he gave to Michael, our tenant's son, and told him to carry it to Sauveterre, to Miss Chandore."

"Yes. In that letter, M. de Boiscoran told Miss Dionysia that he was retained here by a matter of great importance."

"Ah!"

"Have you any idea what that could have been?"

"Not at all, sir, I assure you."

"Still let us see. M. de Boiscoran must have had powerful reasons to deprive himself of the pleasure of spending the evening with Miss Dionysia?"

"Yes, indeed."

"He must also have had his reasons for taking to the marshes, on his way out, instead of going by the turnpike, and for coming back through the woods."

Old Anthony was literally tearing his hair, as he exclaimed,—

"Ah, sir! These are the very words M. Galpin said."

"Unfortunately every man in his senses will say so."

"I know, sir: I know it but too well. And Master Jacques himself knew it so well that at first he tried to find some pretext; but he has never told a falsehood. And he who is such a clever man could not find a pretext that had any sense in it. He said he had gone to Brechy to see his wood-merchant"—

"And why should he not?"

Anthony shook his head, and said,—

"Because the wood-merchant at Brechy is a thief, and everybody knows that master has kicked him out of the house some three years ago. We sell all our wood at Sauveterre."

M. Folgat had taken out a note-book, and wrote down some of Anthony's statements, preparing thus the outline of his defence. This being done, he commenced again,—

"Now we come to Cocoleu."

"Ah the wretch!" cried Anthony.

"You know him?"

"How could I help knowing him, when I lived all my life here at Boiscoran in the service of master's uncle?"

"Then what kind of a man is he?"

"An idiot, sir or, as they here call it, an innocent, who has Saint Vitus dance into the bargain, and epilepsy moreover."

"Then it is perfectly notorious that he is imbecile?"

"Yes, sir, although I have heard people insist that he is not quite so stupid as he looks, and that, as they say here, he plays the ass in order to get his oats"—

M. de Chandore interrupted him, and said,—

- 118 -

"On this subject Dr. Seignebos can give you all the information you may want: he kept Cocoleu for nearly two years at his own house."

"I mean to see the doctor," replied M. Folgat. "But first of all we must find this unfortunate idiot."

"You heard what M. Seneschal said: he has put the gendarmes on his track."

Anthony made a face, and said,—

"If the gendarmes should take Cocoleu, Cocoleu must have given himself up voluntarily."

"Why so?"

"Because, gentlemen, there is no one who knows all the by-ways and out-of-the-way corners of the country so well as that idiot; for he has been hiding all his life like a savage in all the holes and hiding-places that are about here; and, as he can live perfectly well on roots and berries, he may stay away three months without being seen by any one."

"Is it possible?" exclaimed M. Folgat angrily.

"I know only one man," continued Anthony, "who could find out Cocoleu, and that is our tenant's son Michael,—the young man you saw down stairs."

"Send for him," said M. de Chandore.

Michael appeared promptly, and, when he had heard what he was expected to do, he replied,—

"The thing can be done, certainly; but it is not very easy. Cocoleu has not the sense of a man; but he has all the instincts of a brute. However, I'll try."

There was nothing to keep either M. de Chandore or M. Folgat any longer at Boiscoran; hence, after having warned Anthony to watch the seals well, and get a glimpse, if possible, of Jacques's gun, when the officers should come for the different articles, they left the chateau. It was five o'clock when they drove into town again. Dionysia was waiting for them in the sitting-room. She rose as they entered, looking quite pale, with dry, brilliant eyes.

"What? You are alone here!" said M. de Chandore. "Why have they left you alone?"

"Don't be angry, grandpapa. I have just prevailed on the marchioness, who was exhausted with fatigue to lie down for an hour or so before dinner."

"And your aunts?"

"They have gone out, grandpapa. They are probably, by this time at M. Galpin's."

M. Folgat started, and said,—

"Oh!"

"But that is foolish in them!" exclaimed the old gentleman.

The young girl closed his lips by a single word. She said,—

"I asked them to go."

V.

Yes, the step taken by the Misses Lavarande was foolish. At the point which things had reached now, their going to see M. Galpin was perhaps equivalent to furnishing him the means to crush Jacques. But whose fault was it, but M. de Chandore's and M. Folgat's? Had they not committed an unpardonable blunder in leaving Sauveterre without any other precaution than to send word through M. Seneschal's servant, that they would be back for dinner, and that they need not be troubled about them?

Not be troubled? And that to the Marchioness de Boiscoran and Dionysia, to Jacques's mother and Jacques's betrothed.

Certainly, at first, the two wretched women preserved their self-control in a manner, trying to set each other an example of courage and confidence. But, as hour after hour passed by, their anxiety became intolerable; and gradually, as they confided their apprehensions to each other, their grief broke out openly. They thought of Jacques being innocent, and yet treated like one of the worst criminals, alone in the depth of his prison, given up to the most horrible inspirations of despair. What could have been his feelings during the twenty-four hours which had brought him no news from his friends? Must he not fancy himself despised and abandoned.

"That is an intolerable thought!" exclaimed Dionysia at lat. "We must get to him at any price."

"How?" asked the marchioness.

"I do not know; but there must be some way. There are things which I would not have ventured upon as long as I was alone; but, with you by my side, I can risk any thing. Let us go to the prison."

The old lady promptly put a shawl around her shoulders, and said,—

"I am ready; let us go."

They had both heard repeatedly that Jacques was kept in close confinement; but neither of them realized fully what that meant. They had no idea of this atrocious measure, which is, nevertheless, rendered necessary by the peculiar forms of French law-proceedings,—a measure which, so to say, immures a man alive, and leaves him in his cell alone with the crime with which he is charged, and utterly at the mercy of another man, whose duty it is to extort the truth from him. The two ladies only saw the want of liberty, a cell with its dismal outfittings, the bars at the window, the bolts at the door, the jailer shaking his bunch of keys at his belt, and the tramp of the solitary sentinel in the long passages.

"They cannot refuse me permission," said the old lady, "to see my son."

"They cannot," repeated Dionysia. "And, besides, I know the jailer, Blangin: his wife was formerly in our service."

When the young girl, therefore, raised the heavy knocker at the prison-door, she was full of cheerful confidence. Blangin himself came to the door; and, at the sight of the two poor ladies, his broad face displayed the utmost astonishment.

"We come to see M. de Boiscoran," said Dionysia boldly.

"Have you a permit, ladies?" asked the keeper.

"From whom?"

"From M. Galpin."

"We have no permit."

"Then I am very sorry to have to tell you, ladies, that you cannot possibly see M. de Boiscoran. He is kept in close confinement, and I have the strictest orders."

Dionysia looked threatening, and said sharply,—

"Your orders cannot apply to this lady, who is the Marchioness de Boiscoran."

"My orders apply to everybody, madam."

"You would not, I am sure, keep a poor, distressed mother from seeing her son!"

"Ah! but—madam—it does not rest with me. I? Who am I? Nothing more than one of the bolts, drawn or pushed at will."

For the first time, it entered the poor girl's head that her effort might fail: still she tried once more, with tears in her eyes,—

"But I, my dear M. Blangin, think of me! You would not refuse me? Don't you know who I am? Have you never heard your wife speak of me?"

The jailer was certainly touched. He replied,—

"I know how much my wife and myself are indebted to your kindness, madam. But—I have my orders, and you surely would not want me to lose my place, madam?"

"If you lose your place, M. Blangin, I, Dionysia de Chandore, promise you another place twice as good."

"Madame!"

"You do not doubt my word, M. Blangin, do you?"

"God forbid, madam! But it is not my place only. If I did what you want me to do, I should be severely punished."

The marchioness judged from the jailer's tone that Dionysia was not likely to prevail over him, and so she said,—

"Don't insist, my child. Let us go back."

"What? Without finding out what is going on behind these pitiless walls; without knowing even whether Jacques is dead or alive?"

There was evidently a great struggle going on in the jailer's heart. All of a sudden he cast a rapid glance around, and then said, speaking very hurriedly,—

"I ought not to tell you—but never mind—I cannot let you go away without telling you that M. de Boiscoran is quite well."

"Ah!"

"Yesterday, when they brought him here, he was, so to say, overcome. He threw himself upon his bed, and he remained there without stirring for over two hours. I think he must have been crying."

A sob, which Dionysia could not suppress, made Blangin start.

"Oh, reassure yourself, madame!" he added quickly. "That state of things did not last long. Soon M. de Boiscoran got up, and said, 'Why, I am a fool to despair!'"

"Did you hear him say so?" asked the old lady.

"Not I. It was Trumence who heard it."

"Trumence?"

"Yes, one of our jail-birds. Oh! he is only a vagabond, not bad at all; and he has been ordered to stand guard at the door of M. de Boiscoran's cell, and not for a moment to lose sight of it. It was M. Galpin who had that idea, because the prisoners sometimes in their first despair,—a misfortune happens so easily,—they become weary of life—Trumence would be there to prevent it."

The old lady trembled with horror. This precautionary measure, more than any thing else, gave her the full measure of her son's situation.

"However," M. Blangin went on, "there is nothing to fear. M. de Boiscoran became quite calm again, and even cheerful, if I may say so. When he got up this morning, after having slept all night like a dormouse, he sent for me, and asked me for paper, ink, and pen. All the prisoners ask for that the second day. I had orders to let him have it, and so I gave it to him. When I carried him his breakfast, he handed me a letter for Miss Chandore."

"What?" cried Dionysia, "you have a letter for me, and you don't give it to me?"

"I do not have it now, madam. I had to hand it, as is my duty, to M. Galpin, when he came accompanied by his clerk, Mechinet, to examine M. de Boiscoran."

"And what did he say?"

"He opened the letter, read it, put it into his pocket, and said, 'Well.'"

Tears of anger this time sprang from Dionysia's eyes; and she cried,—

"What a shame? This man reads a letter written by Jacques to me! That is infamous!"

And, without thinking of thanking Blangin, she drew off the old lady, and all the way home did not say a word.

"Ah, poor child, you did not succeed," exclaimed the two old aunts, when they saw their niece come back.

But, when they had heard every thing, they said,—

"Well, we'll go and see him, this little magistrate, who but the day before yesterday was paying us abject court to obtain the hand of our cousin. And we'll tell him the truth; and, if we cannot make him give us back Jacques, we will at least trouble him in his triumph, and take down his pride."

How could poor Dionysia help adopting the notions of the old ladies, when their project offered such immediate satisfaction to her indignation, and at the same time served her secret hopes?

"Oh, yes! You are right, dear aunts," she said. "Quick, don't lose any time; go at once!"

Unable to resist her entreaties, they started instantly, without listening to the timid objections made by the marchioness. But the good ladies were sadly mistaken as to the state of mind of M. Galpin. The ex-lover of one of their cousins was not bedded on roses by any means. At the beginning of this extraordinary affair he had taken hold of it with eagerness, looking upon it as an admirable opportunity, long looked for, and likely to open wide the doors to his burning ambition. Then having once begun, and the investigation being under way, he had been carried away by the current, without having time to reflect. He had even felt a kind of unhealthy satisfaction at seeing the evidence increasing, until he felt justified and compelled to order his former friend to be sent to prison. At that time he was fairly dazzled by the most magnificent expectations. This preliminary inquiry, which in a few hours already had led to the discovery of a culprit the most unlikely of all men in the province, could not fail to establish his superior ability and matchless skill.

But, a few hours later, M. Galpin looked no longer with the same eye upon these events. Reflection had come; and he had begun to doubt his ability, and to ask himself, if he had not, after all, acted rashly. If Jacques was guilty, so much the better. He was sure, in that case, immediately after the verdict, to obtain brilliant promotion. Yes, but if Jacques should be innocent? When that thought occurred to M. Galpin for the first time, it made him shiver to the marrow of his bones. Jacques innocent!—that was his own condemnation, his career ended, his hopes destroyed, his prospects ruined forever. Jacques innocent!—that was certain disgrace. He would be sent away from Sauveterre, where he could not remain after such a scandal. He would be banished to some out-of-the-way village, and without hope of promotion.

In vain he tried to reason that he had only done his duty. People would answer, if they condescended at all to answer, that there are flagrant blunders, scandalous mistakes, which a magistrate must not commit; and that for the honor of justice, and in the interest of the law, it is better, under certain circumstances, to let a guilty man escape, than to punish an innocent one.

With such anxiety on his mind, the most cruel that can tear the heart of an ambitious man, M. Galpin found his pillow stuffed with thorns. He had been up since six o'clock. At eleven, he had sent for his clerk, Mechinet; and they had gone together to the jail to recommence the examination. It was then that the jailer had handed him the prisoner's letter for Dionysia. It was a short note, such as a sensible man would write who knows full well that a prisoner cannot count upon the secrecy of his correspondence. It was not even sealed, a fact which M. Blangin had not noticed.

"Dionysia, my darling," wrote the prisoner, "the thought of the terrible grief I cause you is my most cruel, and almost my only sorrow. Need I stoop to assure you that I am innocent? I am sure it is not needed. I am the victim of a fatal combination of circumstances, which could not but mislead justice. But be reassured, be hopeful. When the time comes, I shall be able to set matters right.

"JACQUES."

"Well," M. Galpin had really said after reading this letter. Nevertheless it had stung him to the quick.

"What assurance!" he had said to himself.

Still he had regained courage while ascending the steps of the prison. Jacques had evidently not thought it likely that his note would reach its destination directly, and hence it might be fairly presumed that he had written for the eyes of justice as well as for his lady-love. The fact that the letter was not sealed even, gave some weight to this presumption.

"After all we shall see," said M. Galpin, while Blangin was unlocking the door.

But he found Jacques as calm as if he had been in his chateau at Boiscoran, haughty and even scornful. It was impossible to get any thing out of him. When he was pressed, he became obstinately silent, or said that he needed time to consider. The magistrate had returned home more troubled than ever. The position assumed by Jacques puzzled him. Ah, if he could have retraced his steps!

But it was too late. He had burnt his vessels, and condemned himself to go on to the end. For his own safety, for his future life, it was henceforth necessary that Jacques de Boiscoran should be found guilty; that he should be tried in open court, and there be sentenced. It must be. It was a question of life or death for him.

He was in this state of mind when the two Misses Lavarande called at his house, and asked to see him. He shook himself; and in an instant his over-excited mind presented to him all possible contingencies. What could the two old ladies want of him?

"Show them in," he said at last.

They came in, and haughtily declined the chairs that were offered.

"I hardly expected to have the honor of a visit from you, ladies," he commenced.

The older of the two, Miss Adelaide, cut him short, saying,—

"I suppose not, after what has passed."

And thereupon, speaking with all the eloquence of a pious woman who is trying to wither an impious man, she poured upon him a stream of reproaches for what she called his infamous treachery. What? How could he appear against Jacques, who was his friend, and who had actually aided him in obtaining the promise of a great match. By that one hope he had become, so to say, a member of the family. Did he not know that among kinsmen it was a sacred duty to set aside all personal feelings for the purpose of protecting that sacred patrimony called family honor?

M. Galpin felt like a man upon whom a handful of stones falls from the fifth story of a house. Still he preserved his self-control, and even asked himself what advantage he might obtain from this extraordinary scene. Might it open a door for reconciliation?

As soon, therefore, as Miss Adelaide stopped, he began justifying himself, painting in hypocritical colors the grief it had given him, swearing that he was able to control the events, and that Jacques was as dear to him now as ever.

"If he is so dear to you," broke in Miss Adelaide, "why don't you set him free?"

"Ah! how can I?"

"At least give his family and his friends leave to see him."

"The law will not let me. If he is innocent, he has only to prove it. If he is guilty, he must confess. In the first case, he will be set free; in the other case, he can see whom he wishes."

"If he is so dear to you, how could you dare read the letter he had written to Dionysia?"

"It is one of the most painful duties of my profession to do so."

"Ah! And does that profession also prevent you from giving us that letter after having read it?"

"Yes. But I may tell you what is in it."

He took it out of a drawer, and the younger of the two sisters, Miss Elizabeth, copied it in pencil. Then they withdrew, almost without saying good-by.

M. Galpin was furious. He exclaimed,—

"Ah, old witches! I see clearly you do not believe in Jacques's innocence. Why else should his family be so very anxious to see him? No doubt they want to enable him to escape by suicide the punishment of his crime. But, by the great God, that shall not be, if I can help it!"

M. Folgat was, as we have seen, excessively annoyed at this step taken by the Misses Lavarande; but he did not let it be seen. It was very necessary that he at least should retain perfect presence of mind and calmness in this cruelly tried family. M. de Chandore, on the other hand, could not conceal his dissatisfaction so well; and, in spite of his deference to his grandchild's wishes, he said,—

"I am sure, my dear child, I don't wish to blame you. But you know your aunts, and you know, also, how uncompromising they are. They are quite capable of exasperating M. Galpin."

"What does it matter?" asked the young girl haughtily. "Circumspection is all very well for guilty people; but Jacques is innocent."

"Miss Chandore is right," said M. Folgat, who seemed to succumb to Dionysia like the rest of the family. "Whatever the ladies may have done, they cannot make matters worse. M. Galpin will be none the less our bitter enemy."

Grandpapa Chandore started. He said,—

"But"—

"Oh! I do not blame him," broke in the young lawyer; "but I blame the laws which make him act as he does. How can a magistrate remain perfectly impartial in certain very important cases, like this one, when his whole future career depends upon his success? A man may be a most upright magistrate, incapable of unfairness, and conscientious in fulfilling all his duties, and yet he is but a man. He has his interest at stake. He does not like the court to find that that there is no case. The great rewards are not always given to the lawyer who has taken most pains to find out the truth."

"But M. Galpin was a friend of ours, sir."

"Yes; and that is what makes me fear. What will be his fate on the day when M. Jacques's innocence is established?"

They were just coming home, quite proud of their achievement, and waving in triumph the copy of Jacques's letter. Dionysia seized upon it; and, while she read it aside, Miss Adelaide described the interview, stating how haughty and disdainful she had been, and how humble and repentant M. Galpin had seemed to be.

"He was completely undone," said the two old ladies with one voice: "he was crushed, annihilated."

"Yes, you have done a nice thing," growled the old baron; "and you have much reason to boast, forsooth."

"My aunts have done well," declared Dionysia. "Just see what Jacques has written! It is clear and precise. What can we fear when he says, 'Be reassured: when the time comes, I shall be able to set matters right'?"

M. Folgat took the letter, read it, and shook his head. Then he said,—

"There was no need of this letter to confirm my opinion. At the bottom of this affair there is a secret which none of us have found out yet. But M. de Boiscoran acts very rashly in playing in this way with a criminal prosecution. Why did he not explain at once? What was easy yesterday may be less easy to-morrow, and perhaps impossible in a week."

"Jacques, sir, is a superior man," cried Dionysia, "and whatever he says is perfectly sure to be the right thing."

His mother's entrance prevented the young lawyer from making any reply. Two hours' rest had restored to the old lady a part of her energy, and her usual presence of mind; and she now asked that a telegram should be sent to her husband.

"It is the least we can do," said M. de Chandore in an undertone, "although it will be useless, I dare say. Boiscoran does not care that much for his son. Pshaw! Ah! if it was a rare *faience*, or a plate that is wanting in his collection, then would it be a very different story."

Still the despatch was drawn up and sent, at the very moment when a servant came in, and announced that dinner was ready. The meal was less sad than they had anticipated. Everybody, to be sure, felt a heaviness at heart as he thought that at the same hour a jailer probably brought Jacques his meal to his cell; nor could Dionysia keep from dropping a tear when she saw M. Folgat sitting in her lover's place. But no one, except the young advocate, thought that Jacques was in real danger.

M. Seneschal, however, who came in just as coffee was handed round, evidently shared M. Folgat's apprehensions. The good mayor came to hear the news, and to tell his friends how he had spent the day. The funeral of the firemen had passed off quietly, although amid deep emotion. No disturbance had taken place, as was feared; and Dr. Seignebos had not spoken at the graveyard. Both a disturbance and a row would have been badly received, said M. Seneschal; for he was sorry to say, the immense majority of the people of Sauveterre did not doubt M. de Boiscoran's guilt. In several groups he had heard people say, "And still you will see they will not condemn him. A poor devil who should commit such a horrible crime would be hanged sure enough; but the son of the Marquis de Boiscoran—you will see, he'll come out of it as white as snow."

The rolling of a carriage, which stopped at the door, fortunately interrupted him at this point.

"Who can that be?" asked Dionysia, half frightened.

They heard in the passage the noise of steps and voices, something like a scuffle; and almost instantly the tenant's son Michael pushed open the door of the sitting-room, crying out,—

"I have gotten him! Here he is!"

And with these words he pushed in Cocoleu, all struggling, and looking around him, like a wild beast caught in a trap.

"Upon my word, my good fellow," said M. Seneschal, "you have done better than the gendarmes!"

The manner in which Michael winked with his eye showed that he had not a very exalted opinion of the cleverness of the gendarmes.

"I promised the baron," he said, "I would get hold of Cocoleu somehow or other. I knew that at certain times he went and buried himself, like the wild beast that he is, in a hole which he has scratched under a rock in the densest part of the forest of Rochepommier. I had discovered this den of his one day by accident; for a man might pass by a hundred times, and never dream of where it was. But, as soon as the baron told me that the innocent had disappeared, I said to myself, 'I am sure he is in his hole: let us go and see.' So I gathered up my legs; I ran down to the rocks: and there was Cocoleu. But it was not so easy to pull him out of his den. He would not come; and, while defending himself, he bit me in the hand, like the mad dog that he is."

And Michael held up his left hand, wrapped up in a bloody piece of linen.

"It was pretty hard work to get the madman here. I was compelled to tie him hand and foot, and to carry him bodily to my father's house. There we put him into the little carriage, and here he is. Just look at the pretty fellow!"

He was hideous at that moment, with his livid face spotted all over with red marks, his hanging lips covered with white foam, and his brutish glances.

"Why would you not come?" asked M. Seneschal.

The idiot looked as if he did not hear.

"Why did you bite Michael?" continued the mayor.

Cocoleu made no reply.

"Do you know that M. de Boiscoran is in prison because of what you have said?"

Still no reply.

"Ah!" said Michael, "it is of no use to question him. You might beat him till to-morrow, and he would rather give up the ghost than say a word."

"I am—I am hungry," stammered Cocoleu.

M. Folgat looked indignant.

"And to think," he said, "that, upon the testimony of such a thing, a capital charge has been made!"

Grandpapa Chandore seemed to be seriously embarrassed. He said,—

"But now, what in the world are we to do with the idiot?"

"I am going to take him," said M. Seneschal, "to the hospital. I will go with him myself, and let Dr. Seignebos know, and the commonwealth attorney."

Dr. Seignebos was an eccentric man, beyond doubt; and the absurd stories which his enemies attributed to him were not all unfounded. But he had, at all events, the rare quality of professing for his art, as he called it, a respect very nearly akin to enthusiasm. According to his views, the faculty were infallible, as much so as the pope, whom he denied. He would, to be sure, in confidence, admit that some of his colleagues were amazing donkeys; but he would never have allowed any one else to say so in his presence. From the moment that a man possessed the famous diploma which gives him the right over life and death, that man became in his eyes an august personage for the world at large. It was a crime, he thought, not to submit blindly to the decision of a physician. Hence his obstinacy in opposing M. Galpin, hence the bitterness of his contradictions, and the rudeness with which he had requested the "gentlemen of the law" to leave the room in which *his* patient was lying.

"For these devils," he said, "would kill one man in order to get the means of cutting off another man's head."

And thereupon, resuming his probes and his sponge, he had gone to work once more, with the aid of the countess, digging out grain by grain the lead which had honeycombed the flesh of the count. At nine o'clock the work was done.

"Not that I fancy I have gotten them all out," he said modestly, "but, if there is any thing left, it is out of reach, and I shall have to wait for certain symptoms which will tell me where they are."

As he had foreseen, the count had grown rather worse. His first excitement had given way to perfect prostration; and he seemed to be insensible to what was going on around him. Fever began to show itself; and, considering the count's constitution, it was easily to be foreseen that delirium would set in before the day was out.

"Nevertheless, I think there is hardly any danger," said the doctor to the countess, after having pointed out to her all the probable symptoms, so as to keep her from being alarmed. Then he recommended to her to let no one approach her husband's bed, and M. Galpin least of all.

This recommendation was not useless; for almost at the same moment a peasant came in to say that there was a man from Sauveterre at the door who wished to see the count.

"Show him in," said the doctor; "I'll speak to him."

It was a man called Tetard, a former constable, who had given up his place, and become a dealer in stones. But besides being a former officer of justice and a merchant, as his cards told the world, he was also the agent of a fire insurance company. It was in this capacity that he presumed, as he told the countess, to present himself in person. He had been informed that the farm buildings at Valpinson, which were insured in his company, had been destroyed by fire; that they had been purposely set on fire by M. de Boiscoran; and that he wished to confer with Count Claudieuse on the subject. Far from him, he added, to decline the responsibility of his company: he only wished to establish the facts which would enable him to fall back upon M. de Boiscoran, who was a man of fortune, and would certainly be condemned to make compensation for the injury done. For this purpose, certain formalities had to be attended to; and he had come to arrange with Count Claudieuse the necessary measures.

"And I," said Dr. Seignebos,—"I request you to take to your heels." He added with a thundering voice,—

"I think you are very bold to dare to speak in that way of M. de Boiscoran."

M. Tetard disappeared without saying another word; and the doctor, very much excited by this scene, turned to the youngest daughter of the countess, the one with whom she was sitting up when the fire broke out, and who was now decidedly better: after that nothing could keep him at Valpinson. He carefully pocketed the pieces of lead which he had taken from the count's wounds, and then, drawing the countess out to the door, he said,—

"Before I go away, madam, I should like to know what you think of these events."

The poor lady, who looked as pale as death itself, could hardly hold up any longer. There seemed to be nothing alive in her but her eyes, which were lighted up with unusual brilliancy.

"Ah! I do not know, sir," she replied in a feeble voice. "How can I collect my thoughts after such terrible shocks?"

"Still you questioned Cocoleu."

"Who would not have done so, when the truth was at stake?"

"And you were not surprised at the name he mentioned?"

"You must have seen, sir."

"I saw; and that is exactly why I ask you, and why I want to know what you really think of the state of mind of the poor creature."

"Don't you know that he is idiotic?"

"I know; and that is why I was so surprised to see you insist upon making him talk. Do you really think, that, in spite of his habitual imbecility, he may have glimpses of sense?"

"He had, a few moments before, saved my children from death."

"That proves his devotion for you."

"He is very much attached to me indeed, just like a poor animal that I might have picked up and cared for."

"Perhaps so. And still he showed more than mere animal instinct."

"That may well be so. I have more than once noticed flashes of intelligence in Cocoleu."

The doctor had taken off his spectacles, and was wiping them furiously.

"It is a great pity that one of these flashes of intelligence did not enlighten him when he saw M. de Boiscoran make a fire and get ready to murder Count Claudieuse."

The countess leaned against the door-posts, as if about to faint.

"But it is exactly to his excitement at the sight of the flames, and at hearing the shots fired, that I ascribe Cocoleu's return to reason."

"May be," said the doctor, "may be."

Then putting on his spectacles again, he added,—

"That is a question to be decided by the professional men who will have to examine the poor imbecile creature."

"What! Is he going to be examined?"

"Yes, and very thoroughly, madam, I tell you. And now I have the honor of wishing you good-bye. However, I shall come back to-night, unless you should succeed during the day in finding lodgings in Sauveterre,—an arrangement which would be very desirable for myself, in the first place, and not less so for your husband and your daughter. They are not comfortable in this cottage."

Thereupon he lifted his hat, returned to town, and immediately asked M. Seneschal in the most imperious manner to have Cocoleu arrested. Unfortunately the gendarmes had been unsuccessful; and Dr. Seignebos, who saw how unfortunate all this was for Jacques, began to get terribly impatient, when on Saturday night, towards ten o'clock, M. Seneschal came in, and said,—

"Cocoleu is found."

The doctor jumped up, and in a moment his hat on his head, and stick in hand, asked,—

"Where is he?"

"At the hospital. I have seen him myself put into a separate room."

"I am going there."

"What, at this hour?"

"Am I not one of the hospital physicians? And is it not open to me by night and by day?"

"The sisters will be in bed."

The doctor shrugged his shoulders furiously; then he said,—

"To be sure, it would be a sacrilege to break the slumbers of these good sisters, these dear sisters, as you say. Ah, my dear mayor! When shall we have laymen for our hospitals? And when will you put good stout nurses in the place of these holy damsels?"

M. Seneschal had too often discussed that subject with the doctor, to open it anew. He kept silent, and that was wise; for Dr. Seignebos sat down, saying,—

"Well, I must wait till to-morrow."

VI.

"The hospital in Sauveterre," says the guide book, "is, in spite of its limited size, one of the best institutions of the kind in the department. The chapel and the new additions were built at the expense of the Countess de Maupaison, the widow of one of the ministers of Louis Philippe."

But what the guide book does not say is, that the hospital was endowed with three free beds for pregnant women, by Mrs. Seneschal, or that the two wings on both sides of the great entrance-gate have also been built by her liberality. One of these wings, the one on the right, is used by the janitor, a fine-looking old man, who formerly was beadle at the cathedral, and who loves to think of the happy days when he added to the splendor of the church by his magnificent presence, his red uniform, his gold bandelaire, his halbert, and his gold-headed cane.

This janitor was, on Sunday morning, a little before eight o'clock, smoking his pipe in the yard, when he saw Dr. Seignebos coming in. The doctor was walking faster than usual, his hat over his face, and his hands thrust deep into his pockets, evident signs of a storm. Instead of coming, as he did every day before making the rounds, into the office of the sister-druggist, he went straight up to the room of the lady superior. There, after the usual salutations, he said,—

"They have no doubt brought you, my sister, last night, a patient, an idiot, called Cocoleu?"

"Yes, doctor."

"Where has he been put?"

"The mayor saw him himself put into the little room opposite the linen room."

"And how did he behave?"

"Perfectly well: the sister who kept the watch did not hear him stir."

"Thanks, my sister!" said Dr. Seignebos.

He was already in the door, when the lady superior recalled him.

"Are you going to see the poor man, doctor?" she asked.

"Yes, my sister; why?"

"Because you cannot see him."

"I cannot?"

"No. The commonwealth attorney has sent us orders not to let any one, except the sister who nurses him, come near Cocoleu,— no one, doctor, not even the physician, a case of urgency, of course, excepted."

Dr. Seignebos smiled ironically. Then he said, laughing scornfully,—

"Ah, these are your orders, are they? Well, I tell you that I do not mind them in the least. Who can prevent me from seeing my patient? Tell me that! Let the commonwealth attorney give his orders in his court-house as much as he chooses: that is all right. But in my hospital! My sister, I am going to Cocoleu's room."

"Doctor, you cannot go there. There is a gendarme at the door."

"A gendarme?"

"Yes, he came this morning with the strictest orders."

For a moment the doctor was overcome. Then he suddenly broke out with unusual violence, and a voice that made the windows shake,—

"This is unheard of! This is an abominable abuse of power! I'll have my rights, and justice shall be done me, if I have to go to Thiers!"

Then he rushed out without ceremony, crossed the yard, and disappeared like an arrow, in the direction of the court-house. At that very moment M. Daubigeon was getting up, feeling badly because he had had a bad, sleepless night, thanks to this unfortunate affair of M. de Boiscoran, which troubled him sorely; for he was almost of M. Galpin's opinion. In vain he recalled Jacques's noble character, his well-known uprightness, his keen sense of honor, the evidence was so strong, so overwhelming! He wanted to doubt; but experience told him that a man's past is no guarantee for his future. And, besides, like many great criminal lawyers, he thought, what he would never have ventured to say openly, that some great criminals act while they are under the influence of a kind of vertigo, and that this explains the stupidity of certain crimes committed by men of superior intelligence.

Since his return from Boiscoran, he had kept close in his house; and he had just made up his mind not to leave the house that day, when some one rang his bell furiously. A moment later Dr. Seignebos fell into the room like a bombshell.

"I know what brings you, doctor," said M. Daubigeon. "You come about that order I have given concerning Cocoleu."

"Yes, indeed, sir! That order is an insult."

"I have been asked to give it as a matter of necessity, by M. Galpin."

"And why did you not refuse? You alone are responsible for it in my eyes. You are commonwealth attorney, consequently the head of the bar, and superior to M. Galpin."

M. Daubigeon shook his head and said,—

"There you are mistaken, doctor. The magistrate in such a case is independent of myself and of the court. He is not even bound to obey the attorney-general, who can make suggestions to him, but cannot give him orders. M. Galpin, in his capacity as examining magistrate, has his independent jurisdiction, and is armed with almost unlimited power. No one in the world can say so well as an examining magistrate what the poet calls,—

"'Such is my will, such are my orders, and my will is sufficient.'

"'Hoc volo, hoc jubeo, sit pro ratione voluntas.'"

For once Dr. Seignebos seemed to be convinced by M. Daubigeon's words. He said,—

"Then, M. Galpin has even the right to deprive a sick man of his physician's assistance."

"If he assumes the responsibility, yes. But he does not mean to go so far. He was, on the contrary, about to ask you, although it is Sunday, to come and be present at a second examination of Cocoleu. I am surprised that you have not received his note, and that you did not meet him at the hospital."

"Well, I am going at once."

And he went back hurriedly, and was glad he had done so; for at the door of the hospital he came face to face against M. Galpin, who was just coming in, accompanied by his faithful clerk, Mechinet.

"You came just in time, doctor," began the magistrate, with his usual solemnity.

But, short and rapid as the doctor's walk had been, it had given him time to reflect, and to grow cool. Instead of breaking out into recriminations, he replied in a tone of mock politeness,—

"Yes, I know. It is that poor devil to whom you have given a gendarme for a nurse. Let us go up: I am at your service."

The room in which Cocoleu had been put was large, whitewashed, and empty, except that a bed, a table and two chairs, stood about. The bed was no doubt a good one; but the idiot had taken off the mattress and the blankets, and lain down in his clothes on the straw bed. Thus the magistrate and the physician found him as they entered. He rose at their appearance; but, when he saw the gendarme, he uttered a cry, and tried to hide under the bed. M. Galpin ordered the gendarme to pull him out again. Then he walked up to him, and said,—

"Don't be afraid, Cocoleu. We want to do you no harm; only you must answer our questions. Do you recollect what happened the other night at Valpinson?"

Cocoleu laughed,—the laugh of an idiot,—but he made no reply. And then, for a whole hour, begging, threatening, and promising by turns, the magistrate tried in vain to obtain one word from him. Not even the name of the Countess Claudieuse had the slightest effect. At last, utterly out of patience, he said,—

"Let us go. The wretch is worse than a brute."

"Was he any better," asked the doctor, "when he denounced M. de Boiscoran?"

But the magistrate pretended not to hear; and, when they were about to leave the room, he said to the doctor,—

"You know that I expect your report, doctor?"

"In forty-eight hours I shall have the honor to hand it to you," replied the latter.

But as he went off, he said half aloud,—

"And that report is going to give you some trouble, my good man."

The report was ready then, and his reason for not giving it in, was that he thought, the longer he could delay it, the more chance he would probably have to defeat the plan of the prosecution.

"As I mean to keep it two days longer," he thought on his way home, "why should I not show it to this Paris lawyer who has come down with the marchioness? Nothing can prevent me, as far as I see, since that poor Galpin, in his utter confusion, has forgotten to put me under oath."

But he paused. According to the laws of medical jurisprudence, had he the right, or not, to communicate a paper belonging to the case to the counsel of the accused? This question troubled him; for, although he boasted that he did not believe in God, he believed firmly in professional duty, and would have allowed himself to be cut in pieces rather than break its laws.

"But I have clearly the right to do so," he growled. "I can only be bound by my oath. The authorities are clear on that subject. I have in my favor the decisions of the Court of Appeals of 27 November, and 27 December, 1828; those of the 13th June, 1835; of the 3d May, 1844; of the 26th June, 1866."

The result of this mediation was, that, as soon as he had breakfasted, he put his report in his pocket, and went by side streets to M. de Chandore's house. The marchioness and the two aunts were still at church, where they had thought it best to show themselves; and there was no one in the sitting-room but Dionysia, the old baron, and M. Folgat. The old gentleman was very much surprised to see the doctor. The latter was his family physician, it is true; but, except in cases of sickness, the two never saw each other, their political opinions were so very different.

"If you see me here," said the physician, still in the door, "it is simply because, upon my honor and my conscience, I believe M. Boiscoran is innocent."

Dionysia would have liked to embrace the doctor for these words of his; and with the greatest eagerness she pushed a large easy-chair towards him, and said in her sweetest voice,—

"Pray sit down, my dear doctor."

"Thanks," he answered bruskly. "I am very much obliged to you." Then turning to M. Folgat, he said, according to his odd notion,—

"I am convinced that M. Boiscoran is the victim of his republican opinions which he has so boldly professed; for, baron, your future son-in-law is a republican."

Grandpapa Chandore did not move. If they had come and told him Jacques had been a member of the Commune, he would not have been any more moved. Dionysia loved Jacques. That was enough for him.

"Well," the doctor went on, "I am a Radical, I, M."—

"Folgat," supplied the young lawyer.

"Yes, M. Folgat, I am a Radical; and it is my duty to defend a man whose political opinions so closely resemble mine. I come, therefore, to show you my medical report, if you can make any use of it in your defence of M. Boiscoran, or suggest to me any ideas."

"Ah!" exclaimed the young man. "That is a very valuable service."

"But let us understand each other," said the physician earnestly. "If I speak of listening to your suggestions, I take it for granted that they are based upon facts. If I had a son, and he was to die on the scaffold I would not use the slightest falsehood to save him."

He had, meanwhile, drawn the report from a pocket in his long coat, and now put in on the table with these words,—

"I shall call for it again to-morrow morning. In the meantime you can think it over. I should like, however, to point out to you the main point, the culminating point, if I may say so."

At all events he was "saying so" with much hesitation, and looking fixedly at Dionysia as if to make her understand that he would like her to leave the room. Seeing that she did not take the hint, he added,—

"A medical and legal discussion would hardly interest the young lady."

"Why, sir, why, should I not be deeply, passionately, interested in any thing that regards the man who is to be my husband?"

"Because ladies are generally very sensational," said the doctor uncivilly, "very sensitive."

"Don't think so, doctor. For Jacques's sake, I promise you I will show you quite masculine energy."

The doctor knew Dionysia well enough to see that she did not mean to go: so he growled,—

"As you like it."

Then, turning again to M. Folgat, he said,—

"You know there were two shots fired at Count Claudieuse. One, which hit him in the side, nearly missed him; the other, which struck his shoulder and his neck, hit well."

"I know," said the advocate.

"The difference in the effect shows that the two shots were fired from different distances, the second much nearer than the first."

"I know, I know!"

"Excuse me. If I refer to these details, it is because they are important. When I was sent for in the middle of the night to come and see Count Claudieuse, I at once set to work extracting the particles of lead that had lodged in his flesh. While I was thus busy, M. Galpin arrived. I expected he would ask me to show him the shot: but no, he did not think of it; he was too full of his own ideas. He thought only of the culprit, of *his* culprit. I did not recall to him the A B C of his profession: that was none of my business. The physician has to obey the directions of justice, but not to anticipate them."

"Well, then?"

"Then M. Galpin went off to Boiscoran, and I completed my work. I have extracted fifty-seven shot from the count's wound in the side, and a hundred and nine from the wound on the shoulder and the neck; and, when I had done that, do you know what I found out?"

He paused, waiting to see the effect of his words; and, when everybody's attention seemed to him fully roused, he went on,—

"I found out that the shot in the two wounds was not alike."

M. de Chandore and M. Folgat exclaimed at one time,—

"Oh!"

"The shot that was first fired," continued Dr. Seignebos, "and which has touched the side, is the very smallest sized 'dust.' That in the shoulder, on the other hand, is quite large sized, such as I think is used in shooting hares. However, I have some samples."

And with these words, he opened a piece of white paper, in which were ten or twelve pieces of lead, stained with coagulated blood, and showing at once a considerable difference in size. M. Folgat looked puzzled.

"Could there have been two murderers?" he asked half aloud.

"I rather think," said M. de Chandore, "that the murderer had, like many sportsmen, one barrel ready for birds, and another for hares or rabbits."

"At all events, this fact puts all premeditation out of question. A man does not load his gun with small-shot in order to commit murder."

Dr. Seignebos thought he had said enough about it, and was rising to take leave, when M. de Chandore asked him how Count Claudieuse was doing.

"He is not doing well," replied the doctor. "The removal, in spite of all possible precautions, has worn him out completely; for he is here in Sauveterre since yesterday, in a house which M. Seneschal has rented for him provisionally. He has been delirious all night through; and, when I came to see him this morning, I do not think he knew me."

"And the countess?" asked Dionysia.

"The countess, madam, is quite as sick as her husband, and, if she had listened to me, she would have gone to bed, too. But she is a woman of uncommon energy, who derives from her affection for her husband an almost incomprehensible power of resistance. As to Cocoleu," he added, standing already near the door, "an examination of his mental condition might produce results which no one seems to expect now. But we will talk of that hereafter. And now, I must bid you all good-by."

"Well?" asked Dionysia and M. de Chandore, as soon as they had heard the street door close behind Dr. Seignebos.

But M. Folgat's enthusiasm had cooled off very rapidly.

"Before giving an opinion," he said cautiously, "I must study the report of this estimable doctor."

Unfortunately, the report contained nothing that the doctor had not mentioned. In vain did the young advocate try all the afternoon to find something in it that might be useful for the defence. There were arguments in it, to be sure, which might be very valuable when the trial should come on, but nothing that could be used to make the prosecution give up the case.

The whole house was, therefore, cruelly disappointed and dejected, when, about five o'clock, old Anthony came in from Boiscoran. He looked very sad, and said,—

"I have been relieved of my duties. At two o'clock M. Galpin came to take off the seals. He was accompanied by his clerk Mechinet, and brought Master Jacques with him, who was guarded by two gendarmes in citizen's clothes. When the room was opened, that unlucky man Galpin asked Master Jacques if those were the clothes which he wore the night of the fire, his boots, his gun, and the water in which he washed his hands. When he had acknowledged every thing, the water was carefully poured into a bottle, which they sealed, and handed to one of the gendarmes. Then they put master's clothes in a large trunk, his gun, several parcels of cartridge, and some other articles, which the magistrate said were needed for the trial. That trunk was sealed like the bottle, and put on the carriage; then that man Galpin went off, and told me that I was free."

"And Jacques," Dionysia asked eagerly,—"how did he look?"

"Master, madam, laughed contemptuously."

"Did you speak to him?" asked M. Folgat.

"Oh, no, sir! M. Galpin would not allow me."

"And did you have time to look at the gun?"

"I could but just glance at the lock."

"And what did you see?"

The brow of the old servant grew still darker, as he replied sadly,—

"I saw that I had done well to keep silent. The lock is black. Master must have used his gun since I cleaned it."

Grandpapa Chandore and M. Folgat exchanged looks of distress. One more hope was lost.

"Now," said the young lawyer, "tell me how M. de Boiscoran usually charged his gun."

"He used cartridges, sir, of course. They sent him, I think, two thousand with the gun,—some for balls, some with large shot, and others with shot of every size. At this season, when hunting is prohibited, master could shoot nothing but rabbits, or those little birds, you know, which come to our marshes: so he always loaded one barrel with tolerably large shot, and the other with small-shot."

But he stopped suddenly, shocked at the impression which his statement seemed to produce. Dionysia cried,—

"That is terrible! Every thing is against us!"

M. Folgat did not give her time to say any more. He asked,—

"My dear Anthony, did M. Galpin take all of your master's cartridges away with him?"

"Oh, no! certainly not."

"Well, you must instantly go back to Boiscoran, and bring me three or four cartridges of every number of shot."

"All right," said the old man. "I'll be back in a short time."

He started immediately; and, thanks to his great promptness, he reappeared at seven o'clock, at the moment when the family got up from dinner, and put a large package of cartridges on the table.

M. de Chandore and M. Folgat had quickly opened some of them; and, after a few failures, they found two numbers of shot which seemed to correspond exactly to the samples left them by the doctor.

"There is an incomprehensible fatality in all this," said the old gentleman in an undertone.

The young lawyer, also, looked discouraged.

"It is madness," he said, "to try to establish M. de Boiscoran's innocence without having first communicated with him."

"And if you could do so to-morrow?" asked Dionysia.

"Then, madam, he might give us the key to this mystery, which we are in vain trying to solve; or, at least, he might tell us the way to find it all out. But that is not to be thought of. M. de Boiscoran is held in close confinement, and you may rest assured M. Galpin will see to it that no communication is held with his prisoner."

"Who knows?" said the young girl.

And immediately she drew M. de Chandore aside into one of the little card-rooms adjoining the parlor, and asked him,—

"Grandpapa, am I rich?"

Never in her life had she thought of that, and she was to a certain extent utterly ignorant of the value of money.

"Yes, you are rich, my child," replied the old gentleman.

"How much do I have?"

"You have in your own right, as coming to you from your poor father and from your mother, twenty-five thousand francs a year, or a capital of about five hundred and fifty thousand francs."

"And is that a good deal?"

"It is so much, that you are one of the richest heiresses of the district; but you have, besides, considerable expectations."

Dionysia was so preoccupied, that she did not even protest. She went on asking,—

"What do they call here to be well off?"

"That depends, my child. If you will tell me"—

She interrupted him, putting down her foot impatiently, saying,—

"Nothing. Please answer me!"

"Well, in our little town, an income of eight hundred or a thousand francs makes anybody very well off."

"Let us say a thousand."

"Well, a thousand would make a man very comfortable."

"And what capital would produce such an income?"

"At five per cent, it would take twenty thousand francs."

"That is to say, about the income of a year."

"Exactly."

"Never mind. I presume that is quite a large sum, and it would be rather difficult for you, grandpapa, to get it together by to-morrow morning?"

"Not at all. I have that much in railway coupon-bonds; and they are just as good as current money."

"Ah! Do you mean to say, that, if I gave anybody twenty thousand francs in such bonds, it would be just the same to him as if I gave him twenty thousand francs in bank-notes?"

"Just so."

Dionysia smiled. She thought she saw light. Then she went on,—

"If that is so, I must beg you, grandpapa, to give me twenty thousand francs in coupon-bonds."

The old gentleman started.

"You are joking," he said. "What do you want with so much money? You are surely joking."

"Not at all. I have never in my life been more serious," replied the young girl in a tone of voice which could not be mistaken. "I beseech you, grandpapa, if you love me, give me these twenty thousand francs this evening, right now. You hesitate? O God! You may kill me if you refuse."

No, M. de Chandore was hesitating no longer.

"Since you will have it so," he said, "I am going up stairs to get it."

She clapped her hands with joy.

"That's it," she said. "Make haste and dress; for I have to go out, and you must go with me."

Then going up to her aunts and the marchioness, she said to them,—

"I hope you will excuse me, if I leave you; but I must go out."

"At this hour?" cried Aunt Elizabeth. "Where are you going?"

"To my dressmakers, the Misses Mechinet. I want a dress."

"Great God!" cried Aunt Adelaide, "the child is losing her mind!"

"I assure you I am not, aunt."

"Then let me go with you."

"Thank you, no. I shall go alone; that is to say, alone with dear grandpapa."

And as M. de Chandore came back, his pockets full of bonds, his hat on his head, and his cane in his hand, she carried him off, saying,—

"Come, quick, dear grandpapa, we are in a great hurry."

VII.

Although M. de Chandore was literally worshipping his grandchild on his knees, and had transferred all his hopes and his affections to her who alone survived of his large family, he had still had his thoughts when he went up stairs to take from his money-box so large a sum of money. As soon, therefore, as they were outside of the house, he said,—

"Now that we are alone, my dear child, will you tell me what you mean to do with all this money?"

"That is my secret," she replied.

"And you have not confidence enough in your old grandfather to tell him what it is, darling?"

He stopped a moment; but she drew him on, saying,—

"You shall know it all, and in less than an hour. But, oh! You must not be angry, grandpapa. I have a plan, which is no doubt very foolish. If I told you, I am afraid you would stop me; and if you succeeded, and then something happened to Jacques, I should not survive the misery. And think of it, what you would feel, if you were to think afterwards, 'If I had only let her have her way!'"

"Dionysia, you are cruel!"

"On the other hand, if you did not induce me to give up my project, you would certainly take away all my courage; and I need it all, I tell you, grandpapa, for what I am going to risk."

"You see, my dear child, and you must pardon me for repeating it once more, twenty thousand francs are a big sum of money; and there are many excellent and clever people who work hard, and deny themselves every thing, a whole life long, without laying up that much."

"Ah, so much the better!" cried the young girl. "So much the better. I do hope there will be enough so as to meet with no refusal!"

Grandpapa Chandore began to comprehend.

"After all," he said, "you have not told me where we are going."

"To my dressmakers."

"To the Misses Mechinet?"

"Yes."

M. de Chandore was sure now.

"We shall not find them at home," he said. "This is Sunday; and they are no doubt at church."

"We shall find them, grandpapa; for they always take tea at half-past seven, for their brother's, the clerk's sake. But we must make haste."

The old gentleman did make haste; but it is a long way from the New-Market Place to Hill Street; for the sisters Mechinet lived on the Square, and, if you please, in a house of their own,—a house which was to be the delight of their days, and which had become the trouble of their nights.

They bought the house the year before the war, upon their brother's advice, and going halves with him, paying a sum of forty-seven thousand francs, every thing included. It was a capital bargain; for they rented out the basement and the first story to the first grocer in Sauveterre. The sisters did not think they were imprudent in paying down ten thousand francs in cash, and in binding themselves to pay the rest in three yearly instalments. The first year all went well; but then came the war and numerous disasters. The income of the sisters and of the brother was much reduced, and they had nothing to live upon but his pay as clerk; so that they had to use the utmost economy, and even contract some debts, in order to pay the second instalment. When peace came, their income increased again, and no one doubted in Sauveterre but that they would manage to get out of their difficulties, as the brother was one of the hardest working men, and the sisters were patronized by "the most distinguished" ladies of the whole country.

"Grandpapa, they are at home," said Dionysia, when they reached the Square.

"Do you think so?"

"I am sure. I see light in their windows."

M. de Chandore stopped.

"What am I to do next?" he asked.

"You are going to give me the bonds, grandpapa, and to wait for me here, walking up and down, whilst I am going to the Misses Mechinet. I would ask you to come up too; but they would be frightened at seeing you. Moreover, if my enterprise does not succeed, it would not matter much as long as it concerned only a little girl."

The old gentleman's last doubts began to vanish.

"You won't succeed, my poor girl," he said.

"O God!" she replied, checking her tears with difficulty, "why will you discourage me?"

He said nothing. Suppressing a sigh, he pulled the papers out of his pockets, and helped Dionysia to stuff them, as well as she could, into her pocket and a little bag she had in her hand. When she had done, she said,—

"Well, good-bye, grandpapa. I won't be long."

And lightly, like a bird, she crossed the street, and ran up to her dressmakers. The old ladies and their brother were just finishing their supper, which consisted of a small piece of pork and a light salad, with an abundance of vinegar. At the unexpected entrance of Miss Chandore they all started up.

"You, miss," cried the elder of the two,—"you!"

Dionysia understood perfectly well what that simple "you" meant. It meant, with the help of the tone of voice, "What? your betrothed is charged with an abominable crime; there is overwhelming evidence against him; he is in jail, in close confinement; everybody knows he will be tried at the assizes, and he will be condemned—and you are here?"

But Dionysia kept on smiling, as she had entered.

"Yes," she replied, "it is I. I must have two dresses for next week; and I come to ask you to show me some samples."

The Misses Mechinet, always acting upon their brother's advice, had made an arrangement with a large house in Bordeaux, by which they received samples of all their goods, and were allowed a discount on whatever they sold.

"I will do so with pleasure," said the older sister. "Just allow me to light a lamp. It is almost dark."

While she was wiping the chimney, and trimming the wick, she asked her brother,—

"Are you not going to the Orpheon?"

"Not to-night," he replied.

"Are you not expected to be there?"

"No: I sent them word I would not come. I have to lithograph two plates for the printer, and some very urgent copying to do for the court."

While he was thus replying, he had folded up his napkin, and lighted a candle.

"Good-night!" he said to his sisters. "I won't see you again to-night," and, bowing deeply to Miss Chandore, he went out, his candle in his hand.

"Where is your brother going?" Dionysia asked eagerly.

"To his room, madam. His room is just opposite on the other side of the staircase."

Dionysia was as red as fire. Was she thus to let her opportunity slip,—an opportunity such as she had never dared hope for? Gathering up all her courage, she said,—

"But, now I think of it, I want to say a few words to your brother, my dear ladies. Wait for me a moment. I shall be back in a moment." And she rushed out, leaving the dressmakers stupefied, gazing after her with open mouths, and asking themselves if the grand calamity had bereft the poor lady of reason.

The clerk was still on the landing, fumbling in his pocket for the key of his room.

"I want to speak to you instantly," said Dionysia.

Mechinet was so utterly amazed, that he could not utter a word. He made a movement as if he wanted to go back to his sisters; but the young girl said,—

"No, in your room. We must not be overheard. Open sir, please. Open, somebody might come."

The fact is, he was so completely overcome, that it took him half a minute to find the keyhole, and put the key in. At last, when the door was opened, he moved aside to let Dionysia pass: but she said, "No, go in!"

He obeyed. She followed him, and, as soon as she was in the room, she shut the door again, pushing even a bolt which she had noticed. Mechinet the clerk was famous in Sauveterre for his coolness. Dionysia was timidity personified, and blushed for the smallest trifle, remaining speechless for some time. At this moment, however, it was certainly not the young girl who was embarrassed.

"Sit down, M. Mechinet," she said, "and listen to me."

He put his candlestick on a table, and sat down.

"You know me, don't you?" asked Dionysia.

"Certainly I do, madam."

"You have surely heard that I am to be married to M. de Boiscoran?"

The clerk started up, as if he had been moved by a spring, beat his forehead furiously with his hand, and said,—

"Ah, what a fool I was! Now I see."

"Yes, you are right," replied the girl. "I come to talk to you about M. de Boiscoran, my betrothed, my husband."

She paused; and for a minute Mechinet and the young girl remained there face to face, silent and immovable, looking at each other, he asking himself what she could want of him, and she trying to guess how far she might venture.

"You can no doubt imagine, M. Mechinet, what I have suffered, since M. de Boiscoran has been sent to prison, charged with the meanest of all crimes!"

"Oh, surely, I do!" replied Mechinet.

And, carried away by his emotion, he added,—

"But I can assure you, madam, that I, who have been present at all the examinations, and who have no small experience in criminal matters,—that I believe M. de Boiscoran innocent. I know M. Galpin does not think so, nor M. Daubigeon, nor any of the gentlemen of the bar, nor the town; but, nevertheless, that is my conviction. You see, I was there when they fell upon M. de Boiscoran, asleep in his bed. Well, the very tone of his voice, as he cried out, 'Oh, my dear Galpin!' told me that the man is not guilty."

"Oh, sir," stammered Dionysia, "thanks, thanks!"

"There is nothing to thank me for, madam; for time has only confirmed my conviction. As if a guilty man ever bore himself as M. de Boiscoran does! You ought to have seen him just now, when we had gone to remove the seals, calm, dignified, answering coldly all the questions that were asked. I could not help telling M. Galpin what I thought. He said I was a fool. Well, I maintain, on the contrary, that he is. Ah! I beg your pardon, I mean that he is mistaken. The more I see of M. de Boiscoran, the more he gives me the impression that he has only a word to say to clear up the whole matter."

Dionysia listened to him with such absorbing interest, that she well-nigh forgot why she had come.

"Then," she asked, "you think M. de Boiscoran is not much overcome?"

"I should lie if I said he did not look sad, madam," was the reply. "But he is not overcome. After the first astonishment, his presence of mind returned; and M. Galpin has in vain tried these three days by all his ingenuity and his cleverness"—

Here he stopped suddenly, like a drunken man who recovers his consciousness for a moment, and becomes aware that he has said too much in his cups. He exclaimed,—

"Great God! what am I talking about? For Heaven's sake, madam, do not let anybody hear what I was led by my respectful sympathy to tell you just now."

Dionysia felt that the decisive moment had come. She said,—

"If you knew me better, sir, you would know that you can rely upon my discretion. You need not regret having given me by your confidence some little comfort in my great sorrow. You need not; for"—

Her voice nearly failed her, and it was only with a great effort she could add,—

"For I come to ask you to do even more than that for me, oh! yes, much more."

Mechinet had turned painfully pale. He broke in vehemently,—

"Not another word, madam: your hope already is an insult to me. You ought surely to know that by my profession, as well as by my oath, I am bound to be as silent as the very cell in which the prisoners are kept. If I, the clerk, were to betray the secret of a criminal prosecution"—

Dionysia trembled like an aspen-leaf; but her mind remained clear and decided. She said,—

"You would rather let an innocent man perish."

"Madam!"

"You would let an innocent man be condemned, when by a single word you could remove the mistake of which he is the victim? You would say to yourself, 'It is unlucky; but I have sworn not to speak'? And you would see him with quiet conscience mount the scaffold? No, I cannot believe that! No, that cannot be true!"

"I told you, madam, I believe in M. de Boiscoran's innocence."

"And you refuse to aid me in establishing his innocence? O God! what ideas men form of their duty! How can I move you? How can I convince you? Must I remind you of the torture this man suffers, whom they charge with being an assassin? Must I tell you what horrible anguish we suffer, we, his friends, his relatives?—how his mother weeps, how I weep, I, his betrothed! We know he is innocent; and yet we cannot establish his innocence for want of a friend who would aid us, who would pity us!"

In all his life the clerk had not heard such burning words. He was moved to the bottom of his heart. At last he asked, trembling,—

"What do you want me to do, madam?"

"Oh! very little, sir, very little,—just to send M. de Boiscoran ten lines, and to bring us his reply."

The boldness of the request seemed to stun the clerk. He said,—

"Never!"

"You will not have pity?"

"I should forfeit my honor."

"And, if you let an innocent one be condemned, what would that be?"

Mechinet was evidently suffering anguish. Amazed, overcome, he did not know what to say, what to do. At last he thought of one reason for refusing, and stammered out,—

"And if I were found out? I should lose my place, ruin my sisters, destroy my career for life."

With trembling hands, Dionysia drew from her pocket the bonds which her grandfather had given her, and threw them in a heap on the table. She began,—

"There are twenty thousand francs."

The clerk drew back frightened. He cried,—

"Money! You offer me money!"

"Oh, don't be offended!" began the young girl again, with a voice that would have moved a stone. "How could I want to offend you, when I ask of you more than my life? There are services which can never be paid. But, if the enemies of M. de Boiscoran should find out that you have aided us, their rage might turn against you."

Instinctively the clerk unloosed his cravat. The struggle within him, no doubt, was terrible. He was stifled.

"Twenty thousand francs!" he said in a hoarse voice.

"Is it not enough?" asked the young girl. "Yes, you are right: it is very little. But I have as much again for you, twice as much."

With haggard eyes, Mechinet had approached the table, and was convulsively handling the pile of papers, while he repeated,—

"Twenty thousand francs! A thousand a year!"

"No, double that much, and moreover, our gratitude, our devoted friendship, all the influence of the two families of Boiscoran and Chandore; in a word, fortune, position, respect."

But by this time, thanks to a supreme effort of will, the clerk had recovered his self-control.

"No more, madam, say no more!"

And with a determined, though still trembling voice, he went on,—

"Take your money back again, madam. If I were to do what you want me to do, if I were to betray my duty for money, I should be the meanest of men. If, on the other hand, I am actuated only by a sincere conviction and an interest in the truth, I may be looked upon as a fool; but I shall always be worthy of the esteem of honorable men. Take back that fortune, madam, which has made an honest man waver for a moment in his conscience. I will do what you ask, but for nothing."

If grandpapa was getting tired of walking up and down in the Square, the sisters of Mechinet found time pass still more slowly in their workroom. They asked each other,—

"What can Miss Dionysia have to say to brother?"

At the end of ten minutes, their curiosity, stimulated by the most absurd suppositions, had become such martyrdom to them, that they made up their minds to knock at the clerk's door.

"Ah, leave me alone!" he cried out, angry at being thus interrupted. But then he considered a moment, opened hastily, and said quite gently,—

"Go back to your room, my dear sisters, and, if you wish to spare me a very serious embarrassment, never tell anybody in this world that Miss Chandore has had a conversation with me."

Trained to obey, the two sisters went back, but not so promptly that they should have not seen the bonds which Dionysia had thrown upon the table, and which were quite familiar in their appearance to them, as they had once owned some of them themselves. Their burning desire to know was thus combined with vague terror; and, when they got back to their room, the younger asked,—

"Did you see?"

"Yes, those bonds," replied the other.

"There must have been five or six hundred."

"Even more, perhaps."

"That is to say, a very big sum of money."

"An enormous one."

"What can that mean, Holy Virgin! And what have we to expect?"

"And brother asking us to keep his secret!"

"He looked as pale as his shirt, and terribly distressed."

"Miss Dionysia was crying like a Magdalen."

It was so. Dionysia, as long as she had been uncertain of the result, had felt in her heart that Jacques's safety depended on her courage and her presence of mind. But now, assured of success, she could no longer control her excitement; and, overcome by the effort, she had sunk down on a chair and burst out into tears.

The clerk shut the door, and looked at her for some time; then, having overcome his own emotions, he said to her,—

"Madame."

But, as she heard his voice, she jumped up, and taking his hands into hers, she broke out,—

"O sir! How can I thank you! How can I ever make you aware of the depth of my gratitude!"

"Don't speak of that," he said almost rudely, trying to conceal his deep feeling.

"I will say nothing more," she replied very gently; "but I must tell you that none of us will ever forget the debt of gratitude which we owe you from this day. You say the great service which you are about to render us is not free from danger. Whatever may happen, you must remember, that, from this moment, you have in us devoted friends."

The interruption caused by his sisters had had the good effect of restoring to Mechinet a good portion of his habitual self-possession. He said,—

"I hope no harm will come of it; and yet I cannot conceal from you, madam, that the service which I am going to try to render you presents more difficulties than I thought."

"Great God!" murmured Dionysia.

"M. Galpin," the clerk went on saying, "is, perhaps, not exactly a superior man; but he understands his profession; he is cunning, and exceedingly suspicious. Only yesterday he told me that he knew the Boiscoran family would try every thing in the world to save M. de Boiscoran from justice. Hence he is all the time on the watch, and takes all kinds of precautions. If he dared to it, he would have his bed put across his cell in the prison."

"That man hates me, M. Mechinet!"

"Oh, no, madam! But he is ambitious: he thinks his success in his profession depends upon his success in this case; and he is afraid the accused might escape or be carried off."

Mechinet was evidently in great perplexity, and scratched his ear. Then he added,—

"How am I to go about to let M. de Boiscoran have your note? If he knew beforehand, it would be easy. But he is unprepared. And then he is just as suspicious as M. Galpin. He is always afraid lest they prepare him a trap; and he is on the lookout. If I make him a sign, I fear he will not understand me; and, if I make him a sign, will not M. Galpin see it? That man is lynx-eyed."

"Are you never alone with M. de Boiscoran?"

"Never for an instant, madam. I only go in with the magistrate, and I come out with him. You will say, perhaps, that in leaving, as I am behind, I might drop the note cleverly. But, when we leave, the jailer is there, and he has good eyes. I should have to dread, besides, M. de Boiscoran's own suspicions. If he saw a letter coming to him in that way, from me, he is quite capable of handing it at once to M. Galpin."

He paused, and after a moment's meditation he went on,—

"The safest way would probably be to win the confidence of M. Blangin, the keeper of the jail, or of some prisoner, whose duty it is to wait on M. de Boiscoran, and to watch him."

"Trumence!" exclaimed Dionysia.

The clerk's face expressed the most startled surprise. He said,—

"What! You know his name?"

"Yes, I do; for Blangin mentioned him to me; and the name struck me the day when M. de Boiscoran's mother and I went to the jail, not knowing what was meant by 'close confinement.'"

The clerk was disappointed.

"Ah!" he said, "now I understand M. Galpin's great trouble. He has, no doubt, heard of your visit, and imagined that you wanted to rob him of his prisoner."

He murmured some words, which Dionysia could not hear; and then, coming to some decision, apparently, he said,—

"Well, never mind! I'll see what can be done. Write your letter, madam: here are pens and ink."

The young girl made no reply, but sat down at Mechinet's table; but, at the moment when she was putting pen to paper she asked,—

"Has M. de Boiscoran any books in his prison?"

"Yes, madam. At his request M. Galpin himself went and selected, in M. Daubigeon's library, some books of travels and some of Cooper's novels for him."

Dionysia uttered a cry of delight.

"O Jacques!" she said, "how glad I am you counted upon me!" and, without noticing how utterly Mechinet seemed to be surprised, she wrote,—

"We are sure of your innocence, Jacques, and still we are in despair. Your mother is here, with a Paris lawyer, a M. Folgat, who is devoted to your interests. What must we do? Give us your instructions. You can reply without fear, as you have *our* book.

"DIONYSIA."

"Read this," she said to the clerk, when she had finished. But he did not avail himself of the permission. He folded the paper, and slipped it into an envelope, which he sealed.

"Oh, you are very kind!" said the young girl, touched by his delicacy.

- 161 -

"Not at all, madam. I only try to do a dishonest thing in the most honest way. To-morrow, madam, you shall have your answer."

"I will call for it."

Mechinet trembled.

"Take care not to do so," he said. "The good people of Sauveterre are too cunning not to know that just now you are not thinking much of dress; and your calls here would look suspicious. Leave it to me to see to it that you get M. de Boiscoran's answer."

While Dionysia was writing, the clerk had made a parcel of the bonds which she had brought. He handed it to her, and said,—

"Take it, madam. If I want money for Blangin, or for Trumence, I will ask you for it. And now you must go: you need not go in to my sisters. I will explain your visit to them."

VIII.

"What can have happened to Dionysia, that she does not come back?" murmured Grandpapa Chandore, as he walked up and down the Square, and looked, for the twentieth time, at his watch. For some time the fear of displeasing his grandchild, and of receiving a scolding, kept him at the place where she had told him to wait for her; but at last it was too much for him, and he said,—

"Upon my word, this is too much! I'll risk it."

And, crossing the road which separates the Square from the houses, he entered the long, narrow passage in the house of the sisters Mechinet. He was just putting his foot on the first step of the stairs, when he saw a light above. He distinguished the voice of his granddaughter, and then her light step.

"At last!" he thought.

And swiftly, like a schoolboy who hears his teacher coming, and fears to be caught in the act, he slipped back into the Square. Dionysia was there almost at the same moment, and fell on his neck, saying,—

"Dear grandpapa, I bring you back your bonds," and then she rained a shower of kisses upon the old gentleman's furrowed cheeks.

If any thing could astonish M. de Chandore, it was the idea that there should exist in this world a man with a heart hard, cruel, and barbarous enough, to resist his Dionysia's prayers and tears, especially if they were backed by twenty thousand francs. Nevertheless, he said mournfully,—

"Ah! I told you, my dear child, you would not succeed."

"And you were mistaken, dear grandpapa, and you are still mistaken; for I have succeeded!"

"But—you bring back the money?"

"Because I have found an honest man, dearest grandpapa,—a most honorable man. Poor fellow, how I must have tempted his honesty! For he is very much embarrassed, I know it from good authority, ever since he and his sisters bought that house. It was more than comfort, it was a real fortune, I offered him. Ah! you ought to have seen how his eyes brightened up, and how his hands trembled, when he took up the bonds! Well, he refused to take them, after all; and the only reward he asks for the very good service which he is going to render us"—

M. de Chandore expressed his assent by a gesture, and then said,—

"You are right, darling: that clerk is a good man, and he has won our eternal gratitude."

"I ought to add," continued Dionysia, "that I was ever so brave. I should never have thought that I could be so bold. I wish you had been hid in some corner, grandpapa, to see me and hear me. You would not have recognized your grandchild. I cried a little, it is true, when I had carried my point."

"Oh, dear, dear child!" murmured the old gentleman, deeply moved.

"You see, grandpapa, I thought of nothing but of Jacques's danger, and of the glory of proving myself worthy of him, who is so brave himself. I hope he will be satisfied with me."

"He would be hard to please, indeed, if he were not!" exclaimed M. de Chandore.

The grandfather and his child were standing all the while under the trees in the great Square while they were thus talking to each other; and already a number of people had taken the opportunity of passing close by them, with ears wide open, and all eagerness, to find out what was going on: it is a way people have in small towns. Dionysia remembered the clerk's kindly warnings; and, as soon as she became aware of it, she said to her grandfather,—

"Come, grandpapa. People are listening. I will tell you the rest as we are going home."

And so, on their way, she told him all the little details of her interview; and the old gentleman declared, in all earnest, that he did not know which to admire most,—her presence of mind, or Mechinet's disinterestedness.

"All the more reason," said the young girl, "why we should not add to the dangers which the good man is going to run for us. I promised him to tell nobody, and I mean to keep my promise. If you believe me, dear grandpapa, we had better not speak of it to anybody, not even to my aunts."

"You might just as well declare at once, little scamp, that you want to save Jacques quite alone, without anybody's help."

"Ah, if I could do that! Unfortunately, we must take M. Folgat into our confidence; for we cannot do without his advice."

Thus it was done. The poor aunts, and even the marchioness, had to be content with Dionysia's not very plausible explanation of her visit. And a few hours afterwards M. de Chandore, the young girl, and M. Folgat held a council in the baron's study. The young lawyer was even more surprised by Dionysia's idea, and her bold proceedings, then her grandfather; he would never have imagined that she was capable of such a step, she looked so timid and innocent, like a mere child. He was about to compliment her; but she interrupted him eagerly, saying,—

"There is nothing to boast of. I ran no risk."

"A very substantial risk, madam, I assure you."

"Pshaw!" exclaimed M. de Chandore.

"To bribe an official," continued M. Folgat, "is a very grave offence. The Criminal Code has a certain paragraph, No. 179, which does not trifle, and punishes the man who bribes, as well as the man who is bribed."

"Well, so much the better!" cried Dionysia. "If poor M. Mechinet has to go to prison, I'll go with him!"

And, without noticing the dissatisfaction expressed in her grandfather's features, she added, turning to M. Folgat,—

"After all, sir, you see that your wishes have been fulfilled. We shall be able to communicate with M. de Boiscoran: he will give us his instructions."

"Perhaps so, madam."

"How? Perhaps? You said yourself"—

"I told you, madam, it would be useless, perhaps even imprudent, to take any steps before we know the truth. But will we know it? Do you think that M. de Boiscoran, who has good reasons for being suspicious of every thing, will at once tell us all in a letter which must needs pass through several hands before it can reach us?"

"He will tell us all, sir, without reserve, without fear, and without danger."

"Oh!"

"I have taken my precautions. You will see."

"Then we have only to wait."

Alas, yes! They had to wait, and that was what distressed Dionysia. She hardly slept that night. The next day was one unbroken torment. At each ringing of the bell, she trembled, and ran to see.

At last, towards five o'clock, when nothing had come, she said,—

"It is not to be to-day, provided, O God! that poor Mechinet has not been caught."

And, perhaps in order to escape for a time the anguish of her fears, she agreed to accompany Jacques's mother, who wanted to pay some visits.

Ah, if she had but known! She had not left the house ten minutes, when one of those street-boys, who abound at all hours of the day on the great Square, appeared, bringing a letter to her address. They took it to M. de Chandore, who, while waiting for dinner, was walking in the garden with M. Folgat.

"A letter for Dionysia!" exclaimed the old gentleman, as soon as the servant had disappeared. "Here is the answer we have been waiting for!"

He boldly tore it open. Alas! It was useless. The note within the envelope ran thus,—

"31:9, 17, 19, 23, 25, 28, 32, 101, 102, 129, 137, 504, 515—37:2, 3, 4, 5, 7, 8, 10, 11, 13, 14, 24, 27, 52, 54, 118, 119, 120, 200, 201— 41:7, 9, 17, 21, 22, 44, 45, 46"—

And so on, for two pages.

"Look at this, and try to make it out," said M. de Chandore, handing the letter to M. Folgat.

The young man actually tried it; but, after five minutes' useless efforts, he said,—

"I understand now why Miss Chandore promised us that we should know the truth. M. de Boiscoran and she have formerly corresponded with each other in cipher."

Grandpapa Chandore raised his hands to heaven.

"Just think of these little girls! Here we are utterly helpless without her, as she alone can translate those hieroglyphics for you."

If Dionysia had hoped, by accompanying the marchioness on her visits, to escape from the sad presentiments that oppressed her, she was cruelly disappointed. They went to M. Seneschal's house first; but the mayor's wife was by no means calculated to give courage to others in an hour of peril. She could do nothing but embrace alternately Jacques's mother and Dionysia, and, amid a thousand sobs, tell them over and over again, that she looked upon one as the most unfortunate of mothers, and upon the other as the most unfortunate of betrothed maidens.

"Does the woman think Jacques is guilty?" thought Dionysia, and felt almost angry.

And that was not all. As they returned home, and passed the house which had been provisionally taken for Count Claudieuse and his family, they heard a little boy calling out,—

"O mamma, come quick! Here are the murderer's mother and his sweetheart."

Thus the poor girl came home more downcast than before. Immediately, however, her maid, who had evidently been on the lookout for her return, told her that her grandfather and the lawyer from Paris were waiting for her in the baron's study. She hastened there without stopping to take off her bonnet; and, as soon as she came in, M. de Chandore handed her Jacques's letter, saying,—

"Here is your answer."

She could not repress a little cry of delight, and rapidly touched the letter with her lips, repeating,—

"Now we are safe, we are safe!"

M. de Chandore smiled at the happiness of his granddaughter.

"But, Miss Hypocrite," he said, "it seems you had great secrets to communicate to M. de Boiscoran, since you resorted to cipher, like arch conspirators. M. Folgat and I tried to read it; but it was all Greek to us."

Now only the young lady remembered M. Folgat's presence, and, blushing deeply, she said,—

"Latterly Jacques and I had been discussing the various methods to which people resort who wish to carry on a secret correspondence: this led him to teach me one of the ways. Two correspondents choose any book they like, and each takes a copy of the same edition. The writer looks in his volume for the words he wants, and numbers them; his correspondent finds them by the aid of these numbers. Thus, in Jacques's letters, the numbers followed by a colon refer to the pages, and the others to the order in which the words come."

"Ah, ah!" said Grandpapa Chandore, "I might have looked a long time."

"It is a very simple method," replied Dionysia, "very well known, and still quite safe. How could an outsider guess what book the correspondents have chosen? Then there are other means to mislead indiscreet people. It may be agreed upon, for instance, that the numbers shall never have their apparent value, or that they shall vary according to the day of the month or the week. Thus, to-day is Monday, the second day of the week. Well, I have to deduct one from each number of a page, and add one to each number of a word."

"And you will be able to make it all out?" asked M. de Chandore.

"Certainly, dear grandpapa. Ever since Jacques explained it to me, I have tried to learn it as a matter of course. We have chose a book which I am very fond of, Cooper's 'Spy;' and we amused ourselves by writing endless letters. Oh! it is very amusing, and it takes time, because one does not always find the words that are needed, and then they have to be spelled letter by letter."

"And M. de Boiscoran has a copy of Cooper's novels in his prison?" asked M. Folgat.

"Yes, sir. M. Mechinet told me so. As soon as Jacques found he was to be kept in close confinement, he asked for some of Cooper's novels, and M. Galpin, who is so cunning, so smart, and so suspicious, went himself and got them for him. Jacques was counting upon me."

"Then, dear child, go and read your letter, and solve the riddle," said M. de Chandore.

When she had left, he said to his companion,—

"How she loves him! How she loves this man Jacques! Sir, if any thing should happen to him, she would die."

M. Folgat made no reply; and nearly an hour passed, before Dionysia, shut up in her room, had succeeded in finding all the words of which Jacques's letter was composed. But when she had finished, and came back to her grandfather's study, her youthful face expressed the most profound despair.

"This is horrible!" she said.

The same idea crossed, like a sharp arrow, the minds of M. de Chandore and M. Folgat. Had Jacques confessed?

"Look, read yourself!" said Dionysia, handing them the translation.

Jacques wrote,—

"Thanks for your letter, my darling. A presentiment had warned me, and I had asked for a copy of Cooper.

"I understand but too well how grieved you must be at seeing me kept in prison without my making an effort to establish my innocence. I kept silence, because I hoped the proof of my innocence would come from outside. I see that it would be madness to hope so any longer, and that I must speak. I shall speak. But what I have to say is so very serious, that I shall keep silence until I shall have had an opportunity of consulting with some one in whom I can feel perfect confidence. Prudence alone is not enough now: skill also is required. Until now I felt secure, relying on my innocence. But the last examination has opened my eyes, and I now see the danger to which I am exposed.

"I shall suffer terribly until the day when I can see a lawyer. Thank my mother for having brought one. I hope he will pardon me, if I address myself first to another man. I want a man who knows the country and its customs.

"That is why I have chosen M. Magloire; and I beg you will tell him to hold himself ready for the day on which, the examination being completed, I shall be relieved from close confinement.

"Until then, nothing can be done, nothing, unless you can obtain that the case be taken out of M. G——'s hands, and be given to some one else. That man acts infamously. He wants me to be guilty. He would himself commit a crime in order to charge me with it, and there is no kind of trap he does not lay for me. I have the greatest difficulty in controlling myself every time I see this man enter my cell, who was my friend, and now is my accuser.

"Ah, my dear ones! I pay a heavy price for a fault of which I have been, until now, almost unconscious.

"And you, my only friend, will you ever be able to forgive me the terrible anxiety I cause you?

"I should like to say much more; but the prisoner who has handed me your note says I must be quick, and it takes so much time to pick out the words!

"J."

When the letter had been read, M. Folgat and M. de Chandore sadly turned their heads aside, fearing lest Dionysia should read in their eyes the secret of their thoughts. But she felt only too well what it meant.

"You cannot doubt Jacques, grandpapa!" she cried.

"No," murmured the old gentleman feebly, "no."

"And you, M. Folgat—are you so much hurt by Jacques's desire to consult another lawyer?"

"I should have been the first, madam, to advise him to consult a native."

Dionysia had to summon all her energy to check her tears.

"Yes," she said, "this letter is terrible; but how can it be otherwise? Don't you see that Jacques is in despair, that his mind wanders after all these fearful shocks?"

Somebody knocked gently at the door.

"It is I," said the marchioness.

Grandpapa Chandore, M. Folgat, and Dionysia looked at each other for a moment; and then the advocate said,—

"The situation is too serious: we must consult the marchioness." He rose to open the door. Since the three friends had been holding the council in the baron's study, a servant had come five times in succession to knock at the door, and tell them that the soup was on the table.

"Very well," they had replied each time.

At last, as they did not come down yet, Jacques's mother had come to the conclusion that something extraordinary had occurred.

"Now, what could this be, that they should keep it from her?" she thought. If it were something good, they would not have concealed it from her. She had come up stairs, therefore, with the firm resolution to force them to let her come in. When M. Folgat opened the door, she said instantly,—

"I mean to know all!"

Dionysia replied to her,—

"Whatever you may hear, my dear mother, pray remember, that if you allow a single word to be torn from you, by joy or by sorrow, you cause the ruin of an honest man, who has put us all under such obligations as can never be fully discharged. I have been fortunate enough to establish a correspondence between Jacques and us."

"O Dionysia!"

"I have written to him, and I have received his answer. Here it is."

The marchioness was almost beside herself, and eagerly snatched at the letter. But, as she read on, it was fearful to see how the blood receded from her face, how her eyes grew dim, her lips turned pale, and at last her breath failed to come. The letter slipped from her trembling hands; she sank into a chair, and said, stammering,—

"It is no use to struggle any longer: we are lost!"

There was something grand in Dionysia's gesture and the admirable accent of her voice, as she said,—

"Why don't you say at once, my mother, that Jacques is an incendiary and an assassin?"

Raising her head with an air of dauntless energy, with trembling lips, and fierce glances full of wrath and disdain, she added,—

"And do I really remain the only one to defend him,—him, who, in his days of prosperity, had so many friends? Well, so be it!"

Naturally, M. Folgat had been less deeply moved than either the marchioness or M. de Chandore; and hence he was also the first to recover his calmness.

"We shall be two, madam, at all events," he said; "for I should never forgive myself, if I allowed myself to be influenced by that letter. It would be inexcusable, since I know by experience what your heart has told you instinctively. Imprisonment has horrors which affect the strongest and stoutest of minds. The days in prison are interminable, and the nights have nameless terrors. The innocent man in his lonely cell feels as if he were becoming guilty, as the man of soundest intellect would begin to doubt himself in a madhouse"—

Dionysia did not let him conclude. She cried,—

"That is exactly what I felt, sir; but I could not express it as clearly as you do."

Ashamed at their lack of courage, M. de Chandore and the marchioness made an effort to recover from the doubts which, for a moment, had well-nigh overcome them.

"But what is to be done?" asked the old lady.

"Your son tells us, madam, we have only to wait for the end of the preliminary examination."

"I beg your pardon," said M. de Chandore, "we have to try to get the case handed over to another magistrate."

M. Folgat shook his head.

"Unfortunately, that is not to be dreamt of. A magistrate acting in his official capacity cannot be rejected like a simple juryman."

"However"—

"Article 542 of the Criminal Code is positive on the subject."

"Ah! What does it say?" asked Dionysia.

"It says, in substance, madam, that a demand for a change of magistrate, on the score of well-founded suspicion, can only be entertained by a court of appeals, because the magistrate, within his legitimate sphere, is a court in himself. I do not know if I express myself clearly?"

"Oh, very clearly!" said M. de Chandore. "Only, since Jacques wishes it"—

"To be sure; but M. de Boiscoran does not know"—

"I beg your pardon. He knows that the magistrate is his mortal enemy."

"Be it so. But how would that help us? Do you think that a demand for a change of venue would prevent M. Galpin from carrying on the proceedings? Not at all. He would go on until the decision comes from the Court of Appeals. He could, it is true, issue no final order; but that is the very thing M. de Boiscoran ought to desire, since such an order would make an end to his close confinement, and enable him to see an advocate."

"That is atrocious!" murmured M. de Chandore.

"It is atrocious, indeed; but such are the laws of France."

In the meantime Dionysia had been meditating; and now she said to the young advocate,—

"I have understood you perfectly, and to-morrow your objections shall be known to M. de Boiscoran."

"Above all," said the lawyer, "explain to him clearly that any such steps as he proposes to take will turn to his disadvantage. M. Galpin is our enemy; but we can make no specific charge against him. They would always reply, 'If M. de Boiscoran is innocent, why does he not speak?'"

This is what Grandpapa Chandore would not admit.

"Still," he said, "if we could bring influential men to help us?"

"Can you?"

"Certainly. Boiscoran has old friends, who, no doubt, are all-powerful still under the present government. He was, in former years, very intimate with M. de Margeril."

M. Folgat's expression was very encouraging.

"Ah!" he said, "if M. de Margeril could give us a lift! But he is not easily approached."

"We might send Boiscoran to see him, at least. Since he remained in Paris for the purpose of assisting us there, now he will have an opportunity. I will write to him to-night."

Since the name of Margeril had been mentioned, the marchioness had become, if possible, paler than ever. At the old gentleman's last words she rose, and said anxiously,—

"Do not write, sir: it would be useless. I do not wish it."

Her embarrassment was so evident, that the others were quite surprised.

"Have Boiscoran and M. de Margeril had any difficulty?" asked M. de Chandore.

"Yes."

"But," cried Dionysia, "it is a matter of life and death for Jacques."

Alas! The poor woman could not speak of the suspicions which had darkened the whole life of the Marquis de Boiscoran, nor of the cruel penalty which the wife was now called upon to pay for a slight imprudence.

"If it is absolutely necessary," she said with a half-stifled voice, "if that is our very last hope, then I will go and see M. de Margeril myself."

M. Folgat was the only one who suspected what painful antecedents there might be in the life of the marchioness, and how she was harassed by their memory now. He interposed, therefore, saying,—

"At all events, my advice is to await the end of the preliminary investigation. I may be mistaken, however, and, before any answer is sent to M. Jacques, I desire that the lawyer to whom he alludes should be consulted."

"That is certainly the wisest plan," said M. de Chandore. And, ringing for a servant, he sent him at once to M. Magloire, to ask him to call after dinner. Jacques de Boiscoran had chosen wisely. M. Magloire was looked upon in Sauveterre as the most eloquent and most skilful lawyer, not only of the district, but of the whole province. And what is rarer still, and far more glorious, he had, besides, the reputation of being unsurpassed in integrity and a high sense of honor. It was well known that he would never have consented to plead a doubtful cause; and they told of him a number of heroic stories, in which he had thrown clients out of the window, who had been so ill-advised to come to him, money in hand, to ask him to undertake an unclean case. He was naturally not a rich man, and preserved, at fifty-four or five, all the habits of a frugal and thrifty young man.

After having married quite young, M. Magloire had lost his wife after a few months, and had never recovered from the loss. Although thirty years old, the wound had never healed; and regularly, on certain days, he was seen wending his way to the cemetery, to place flowers on a modest grave there. Any other man would have been laughed at for such a thing at Sauveterre; but with him they dared not do so, for they all respected him highly. Young and old knew and reverenced the tall man with the calm, serene face, the clear, bright eyes, and the eloquent lips, which, in their well-cut, delicate lines, by turns glowed with scorn, with tenderness, or with disdain.

Like Dr. Seignebos, M. Magloire also was a Republican; and, at the last Imperial elections, the Bonapartists had had the greatest trouble, aided though they were by the whole influence of the government, and shrinking from no unfair means, to keep him out of the Chamber. Nor would they have been successful after all, but for the influence of Count Claudieuse, who had prevailed upon a number of electors to abstain from voting.

This was the man, who, towards nine o'clock, presented himself, upon the invitation of M. de Chandore, at his house, where he was anxiously expected by all the inmates. His greeting was affectionate, but at the same time so sad, that it touched Dionysia's heart most painfully. She thought she saw that M. Magloire was not far from believing Jacques guilty.

And she was not mistaken; for M. Magloire let them see it clearly, in the most delicate manner, to be sure, but still so as to leave no doubt. He had spent the day in court, and there had heard the opinions of the members of the court, which was by no means favorable to the accused. Under such circumstances, it would have evidently been a grave blunder to yield to Jacques's wishes, and to apply for a change of venue from M. Galpin to some other magistrate.

"The investigation will last a year," cried Dionysia, "since M. Galpin is determined to obtain from Jacques the confession of a crime which he has not committed."

M. Magloire shook his head, and replied,—

"I believe, on the contrary, madam, that the investigation will be very soon concluded."

"But if Jacques keeps silent?"

"Neither the silence of an accused, nor any other caprice or obstinacy of his, can interfere with the regular process. Called upon to produce his justification, if he refuses to do so, the law proceeds without him."

"Still, sir, if an accused person has reasons"—

"There are no reasons which can force a man to let himself be accused unjustly. But even that case has been foreseen. The accused is at liberty not to answer a question which may inculpate him. *Nemo tenetur prodere se ipsum.* But you must admit that such a refusal to answer justifies a judge in believing that the charges are true which the accused does not refute."

The great calmness of the distinguished lawyer of Sauveterre terrified his listeners more and more, except M. Folgat. When they heard him use all those technical terms, they felt chilled through and through like the friends of a wounded man who hear the grating noise of the surgeon's knife.

"My son's situation appears to you very serious, sir?" asked the marchioness in a feeble voice.

"I said it was dangerous, madam."

"You think, as M. Folgat does, that every day adds to the danger to which he is exposed?"

"I am but too sure of that. And if M. de Boiscoran is really innocent"—

"Ah, M. Magloire!" broke in Dionysia, "how can you, who are a friend of Jacques's, say so?"

M. Magloire looked at the young girl with an air of deep and sincere pity, and then said,—

"It is precisely because I am his friend, madam, that I am bound to tell you the truth. Yes, I know and I appreciate all the noble qualities which distinguish M. de Boiscoran. I have loved him, and I love him still. But this is a matter which we have to look at with the mind, and not with the heart. Jacques is a man; and he will be judged by men. There is clear, public, and absolute evidence of his guilt on hand. What evidence has he to offer of his innocence? Moral evidence only."

"O God!" murmured Dionysia.

"I think, therefore, with my honorable brother"—

And M. Magloire bowed to M. Folgat.

"I think, that, if M. de Boiscoran is innocent, he has adopted an unfortunate system. Ah! if luckily there should be an *alibi*. He ought to make haste, great haste, to establish it. He ought not to allow matters to go on till he is sent up into court. Once there, an accused is three-fourths condemned already."

For once it looked as if the crimson in M. de Chandore's cheeks was growing pale.

"And yet," he exclaimed, "Jacques will not change his system: any one who knows his mulish obstinacy might be quite sure of that."

"And unfortunately he has made up his mind," said Dionysia, "as M. Magloire, who knows him so well, will see from this letter of his."

Until now nothing had been said to let the Sauveterre lawyer suspect that communications had been opened with the prisoner. Now that the letter had been alluded to, it became necessary to take him into confidence. At first he was astonished, then he looked displeased; and, when he had been told every thing, he said,—

"This is great imprudence! This is too daring!"

Then looking at M. Folgat, he added,—

"Our profession has certain rules which cannot be broken without causing trouble. To bribe a clerk, to profit by his weakness and his sympathy"—

The Paris lawyer had blushed imperceptibly. He said,—

"I should never have advised such imprudence; but, when it was once committed, I did not feel bound to insist upon its being abandoned: and even if I should be blamed for it, or more, I mean to profit by it."

M. Magloire did not reply; but, after having read Jacques's letter, he said,—

"I am at M. de Boiscoran's disposal; and I shall go to him as soon as he is no longer in close confinement. I think, as Miss Dionysia does, that he will insist upon saying nothing. However, as we have the means of reaching him by letter,—well, here I am myself ready to profit by the imprudence that has been committed!—beseech him, in the name of his own interest, in the name of all that is dear to him, to speak, to explain, to prove his innocence."

Thereupon M. Magloire bowed, and withdrew suddenly, leaving his audience in consternation, so very evident was it, that he left so suddenly in order to conceal the painful impression which Jacques's letter had produced upon him.

"Certainly," said M. de Chandore, "we will write to him; but we might just as well whistle. He will wait for the end of the investigation."

"Who knows?" murmured Dionysia.

And, after a moment's reflection, she added,—

"We can try, however."

And, without vouchsafing any further explanation, she left the room, and hastened to her chamber to write the following letter:—

"I must speak to you. There is a little gate in our garden which opens upon Charity Lane, I will wait for you there. However late it may be when you get these lines, come!

"DIONYSIA."

- 178 -

Then having put the note into an envelope, she called the old nurse, who had brought her up, and, with all the recommendations which extreme prudence could suggest, she said to her,—

"You must see to it that M. Mechinet the clerk gets this note to-night. Go! make haste!"

IX.

During the last twenty-four hours, Mechinet had changed so much, that his sisters recognized him no longer. Immediately after Dionysia's departure, they had come to him, hoping to hear at last what was meant by that mysterious interview; but at the first word he had cried out with a tone of voice which frightened his sisters to death,—

"That is none of your business! That is nobody's business!" and he had remained alone, quite overcome by his adventure, and dreaming of the means to make good his promise without ruining himself. That was no easy matter.

When the decisive moment arrived, he discovered that he would never be able to get the note into M. de Boiscoran's hands, without being caught by that lynx-eyed M. Galpin: as the letter was burning in his pocket, he saw himself compelled, after long hesitation, to appeal for help to the man who waited on Jacques,—to Trumence, in fine. The latter was, after all, a good enough fellow; his only besetting sin being unconquerable laziness, and his only crime in the eyes of the law perpetual vagrancy. He was attached to Mechinet, who upon former occasions, when he was in jail, had given him some tobacco, or a little money to buy a glass of wine. He made therefore no objection, when the clerk asked him to give a letter to M. de Boiscoran, and to bring back an answer. He acquitted himself, moreover, faithfully and honestly of his commission. But, because every thing had gone well once, it did not follow that Mechinet felt quite at peace. Besides being tormented by the thought that he had betrayed his duty, he felt wretched in being at the mercy of an accomplice. How easily might he not be betrayed! A slight indiscretion, an awkward blunder, an unlucky accident, might do it. What would become of him then?

He would lose his place and all his other employments, one by one. He would lose confidence and consideration. Farewell to all ambitious dreams, all hopes of wealth, all dreams of an advantageous marriage. And still, by an odd contradiction, Mechinet did not repent what he had done, and felt quite ready to do it over again. He was in this state of mind when the old nurse brought him Dionysia's letter.

"What, again?" he exclaimed.

And when he had read the few lines, he replied,—

"Tell your mistress I will be there!" But in his heart he thought some untoward event must have happened.

The little garden-gate was half-open: he had only to push it to enter. There was no moon; but the night was clear, and at a short distance from him, under the trees, he recognized Dionysia, and went towards her.

"Pardon me, sir," she said, "for having dared to send for you."

Mechinet's anxiety vanished instantly. He thought no longer of his strange position. His vanity was flattered by the confidence which this young lady put in him, whom he knew very well as the noblest, the most beautiful, and the richest heiress in the whole country.

"You were quite right to send for me, madam," he replied, "if I can be of any service to you."

In a few words she had told him all; and, when she asked his advice, he replied,—

"I am entirely of M. Folgat's opinion, and think that grief and isolation begin to have their effect upon M. de Boiscoran's mind."

"Oh, that thought is maddening!" murmured the poor girl.

"I think, as M. Magloire does, that M. de Boiscoran, by his silence, only makes his situation much worse. I have a proof of that. M. Galpin, who, at first, was all doubt and anxiety, is now quite reassured. The attorney-general has written him a letter, in which he compliments his energy."

"And then."

"Then we must induce M. de Boiscoran to speak. I know very well that he is firmly resolved not to speak; but if you were to write to him, since you can write to him"—

"A letter would be useless."

"But"—

"Useless, I tell you. But I know a means."

"You must use it promptly, madam: don't lose a moment. There is no time."

The night was clear, but not clear enough for the clerk to see how very pale Dionysia was.

"Well, then, I must see M. de Boiscoran: I must speak to him."

She expected the clerk to start, to cry out, to protest. Far from it: he said in the quietest tone,—

"To be sure; but how?"

"Blangin the keeper, and his wife, keep their places only because they give them a support. Why might I not offer them, in return for an interview with M. de Boiscoran, the means to go and live in the country?"

"Why not?" said the clerk.

And in a lower voice, replying to the voice of his conscience, he went on,—

"The jail in Sauveterre is not at all like the police-stations and prisons of larger towns. The prisoners are few in number; they are hardly guarded. When the doors are shut, Blangin is master within."

"I will go and see him to-morrow," declared Dionysia.

There are certain slopes on which you must glide down. Having once yielded to Dionysia's suggestions, Mechinet had, unconsciously, bound himself to her forever.

"No: do not go there, madam," he said. "You could not make Blangin believe that he runs no danger; nor could you sufficiently arouse his cupidity. I will speak to him myself."

"O sir!" exclaimed Dionysia, "how can I ever?"—

"How much may I offer him?" asked the clerk.

"Whatever you think proper—any thing."

"Then, madam, I will bring you an answer to-morrow, here, and at the same hour."

And he went away, leaving Dionysia so buoyed up by hope, that all the evening, and the next day, the two aunts and the marchioness, neither of whom was in the secret, asked each other incessantly,—

"What is the matter with the child?"

She was thinking, that, if the answer was favorable, ere twenty-four hours had gone by, she would see Jacques; and she kept saying to herself,—

"If only Mechinet is punctual!"

He was so. At ten o'clock precisely, he pushed open the little gate, just as the night before, and said at once,—

"It is all right!"

Dionysia was so terribly excited, that she had to lean against a tree.

"Blangin agrees," the clerk went on. "I promised him sixteen thousand francs. Perhaps that is rather much?"

"It is very little."

"He insists upon having them in gold."

"He shall have it."

"Finally, he makes certain conditions with regard to the interview, which will appear rather hard to you."

The young girl had quite recovered by this time.

"What are they?"

"Blangin is taking all possible precautions against detection, although he is quite prepared for the worst. He has arranged it this way: To-morrow evening, at six o'clock, you will pass by the jail. The door will stand open, and Blangin's wife, whom you know very well, as she has formerly been in your service, will be standing in the door. If she does not speak to you, you keep on: something has happened. If she does speak to you, go up to her, you, quite alone, and she will show you into a small room which adjoins her own. There you will stay till Blangin, perhaps at a late hour, thinks he can safely take you to M. de Boiscoran's cell. When the interview is over, you come back into the little room, where a bed will be ready for you, and you spend the night there; for this is the hardest part of it: you cannot leave the prison till next day."

This was certainly terrible; still, after a moment's reflection, Dionysia said,—

"Never mind! I accept. Tell Blangin, M. Mechinet, that it is all right."

That Dionysia should accept all the conditions of Blangin the jailer was perfectly natural; but to obtain M. de Chandore's consent was a much more difficult task. The poor girl understood this so well, that, for the first time in her life, she felt embarrassed in her grandfather's presence. She hesitated, she prepared her little speech, and she selected carefully her words. But in spite of all her skill, in spite of all the art with which she managed to present her strange request, M. de Chandore had no sooner understood her project than he exclaimed,—

"Never, never, never!"

Perhaps in his whole life the old gentleman had never expressed himself in so positive a manner. His brow had never looked so dark. Usually, when his granddaughter had a petition, his lips might say, "No;" but his eyes always said, "Yes."

"Impossible!" he repeated, and in a tone of voice which seemed to admit of no reply.

Surely, in all these painful events, he had not spared himself, and he had so far done for Dionysia all that she could possibly expect of him. Her will had been his will. As she had prompted, he had said, "Yes," or "No." What more could he have said or done?

Without telling him what she was going to do with it, Dionysia had asked him for twenty thousand francs, and he had given them to her, however big the sum might be everywhere, however immense in a small town like Sauveterre. He was quite ready to give her as much again, or twice as much, without asking any more questions.

But for Dionysia to leave her home one evening at six o'clock, and not to return to it till the next morning—

"That I cannot permit," he repeated.

But for Dionysia to spend a night in the Sauveterre jail, in order to have an interview with her betrothed, who was accused of incendiarism and murder; to remain there all night, alone, absolutely at the mercy of the jailer, a hard, coarse, covetous man—

"That I will never permit," exclaimed the old gentleman once more.

Dionysia remained calm, and let the storm pass. When her grandfather became silent, she said,—

"But if I must?"

M. de Chandore shrugged his shoulders. She repeated in a louder tone,—

"If I must, in order to decide Jacques to abandon this system that will ruin him, to induce him to speak before the investigation is completed?"

"That is not your business, my child," said the old gentleman.

"Oh!"

"That is the business of his mother, the Marchioness of Boiscoran. Whatever Blangin agrees to venture for your sake, he will do as well for her sake. Let the marchioness go and spend the night at the jail. I agree to that. Let her see her son. That is her duty."

"But surely she will never shake Jacques's resolution."

"And you think you have more influence over him than his mother?"

"It is not the same thing, dear papa."

"Never mind!"

This "never mind" of Grandpapa Chandore was as positive as his "impossible;" but he had begun to discuss the question, and to discuss means to listen to arguments on the other side.

"Do not insist, my dear child," he said again. "My mind is made up; and I assure you"—

"Don't say so, papa," said the young girl.

And her attitude was so determined, and her voice so firm, that the old gentleman was quite overwhelmed for a moment.

"But, if I am not willing," he said.

"You will consent, dear papa, you will certainly not force your little granddaughter, who loves you so dearly, to the painful necessity of disobeying you for the first time in her life."

"Because, for the first time in her life I am not doing what my granddaughter wants me to do?"

"Dear papa, let me tell you."

"Rather listen to me, poor child, and let me show you to what dangers, to what misfortunes, you expose yourself. To go and spend a night at this prison would be risking, understand me well, your honor,—that tender, delicate honor which is tarnished by a breath, which involves the happiness and the peace of your whole life."

"But Jacques's honor and life are at stake."

"Poor imprudent girl! How do you know but he would be the very first to blame you cruelly for such a step?"

"He?"

"Men are made so: the most perfect devotion irritates them at times."

"Be it so. I would rather endure Jacques's unjust reproaches than the idea of not having done my duty."

M. de Chandore began to despair.

"And if I were to beg you, Dionysia, instead of commanding. If your old grandfather were to beseech you on his knees to abandon your fatal project."

"You would cause me fearful pain, dear papa: but it would be all in vain; for I must resist your prayers, as I must resist your orders."

"Inexorable!" cried the old gentleman. "She is immovable!" And suddenly changing his tone, he cried,—

"But, after all, I am master here."

"Dear papa, pray!"

"And since nothing can move you, I will speak to Mechinet, I will let Blangin know my will."

Dionysia, turning as pale as death, but with burning eyes, drew back a step, and said,—

"If you do that, grandpapa, if you destroy my last hope"—

"Well?"

"I swear to you by the sacred memory of my mother, I will be in a convent to-morrow, and you will never see me again in your life, not even if I should die, which would certainly soon"—

M. de Chandore, raising his hands to heaven, and with an accent of genuine despair, exclaimed,—

"Ah, my God! Are these our children? And is this what is in store for us old people? We have spent a lifetime in watching over them; we have submissively gratified all their fancies; they have been our greatest anxiety, and our sweetest hope; we have given them our life day by day, and we would not hesitate to give them our life's blood drop by drop; they are every thing to us, and we imagine they love us—poor fools that we are! One fine day, a man goes by, a careless, thoughtless man, with a bright eye and a ready tongue, and it is all over. Our child is no longer our own; our child no longer knows us. Go, old man, and die in your corner."

Overwhelmed by his grief, the old man staggered and sank into a chair, as an old oak, cut by the woodman's axe, trembles and falls.

"Ah, this is fearful!" murmured Dionysia. "What you say, grandpapa, is too fearful. How can you doubt me?"

She had knelt down. She was weeping; and her hot tears fell upon the old gentleman's hands. He started up as he felt them on his icy-cold hand; and, making one more effort, he said,—

"Poor, poor child! And suppose Jacques is guilty, and, when he sees you, confesses his crime, what then?"

Dionysia shook her head.

"That is impossible," she said; "and still, even if it were so, I ought to be punished as much as he is; for I know, if he had asked me, I should have acted in concert with him."

"She is mad!" exclaimed M. de Chandore, falling back into his chair. "She is mad!"

But he was overcome; and the next day, at five in the afternoon, his heart torn by unspeakable grief, he went down the steep street with his daughter on his arm. Dionysia had chosen her simplest and plainest dress; and the little bag she carried on her arm contained not sixteen but twenty thousand francs. As a matter of course, it had been necessary to take the marchioness into their confidence; but neither she, nor the Misses Lavarande, nor M. Folgat, had raised an objection. Down to the prison, grandfather and grandchild had not exchanged a word; but, when they reached it, Dionysia said,—

"I see Mrs. Blangin at the door: let us be careful."

They came nearer. Mrs. Blangin saluted them.

"Come, it is time," said the young girl. "Till to-morrow, dear papa! Go home quickly, and be not troubled about me."

Then joining the keeper's wife, she disappeared inside the prison.

X.

The prison of Sauveterre is in the castle at the upper end of town, in a poor and almost deserted suburb. This castle, once upon a time of great importance, had been dismantled at the time of the siege of Rochelle; and all that remains are a few badly-repaired ruins, ramparts with fosses that have been filled up, a gate surmounted by a small belfry, a chapel converted into a magazine, and finally two huge towers connected by an immense building, the lower rooms in which are vaulted.

Nothing can be more mournful than these ruins, enclosed within an ivy-covered wall; and nothing would indicate the use that is made of them, except the sentinel which stands day and night at the gate. Ancient elm-trees overshadow the vast courts; and on the old walls, as well as in every crevice, there grow and bloom enough flowers to rejoice a hundred prisoners. But this romantic prison is without prisoners.

"It is a cage without birds," says the jailer often in his most melancholy voice.

He takes advantage of this to raise his vegetables all along the slopes; and the exposure is so excellent, that he is always the first in Sauveterre who had young peas. He has also taken advantage of this—with leave granted by the authorities—to fit up very comfortable lodgings for himself in one of the towers. He has two rooms below, and a chamber up stairs, which you reach by a narrow staircase in the thickness of the wall. It was to this chamber that the keeper's wife took Dionysia with all the promptness of fear. The poor girl was out of breath. Her heart was beating violently; and, as soon as she was in the room, she sank into a chair.

"Great God!" cried the woman. "You are not sick, my dear young lady? Wait, I'll run for some vinegar."

"Never mind," replied Dionysia in a feeble voice. "Stay here, my dear Colette: don't go away!"

For Colette was her name, though she was as dark as gingerbread, nearly forty-five years old, and boasted of a decided mustache on her upper lip.

"Poor young lady!" she said. "You feel badly at being here."

"Yes," replied Dionysia. "But where is your husband?"

"Down stairs, on the lookout, madam. He will come up directly." Very soon afterwards, a heavy step was heard on the stairs; and Blangin came in, looking pale and anxious, like a man who feels that he is running a great risk.

"Neither seen nor known," he cried. "No one is aware of your presence here. I was only afraid of that dog of a sentinel; and, just as you came by, I had managed to get him round the corner, offering him a drop of something to drink. I begin to hope I shall not lose my place."

Dionysia accepted these words as a summons to speak out.

"Ah!" she said, "don't mind your place: don't you know I have promised you a better one?"

And, with a gayety which was very far from being real, she opened her little bag, and put upon the table the rolls which it contained.

"Ah, that is gold!" said Blangin with eager eyes.

"Yes. Each one of these rolls contains a thousand francs; and here are sixteen."

An irresistible temptation seized the jailer.

"May I see?" he asked.

"Certainly!" replied the young girl. "Look for yourself and count."

She was mistaken. Blangin did not think of counting, not he. What he wanted was only to gratify his eye by the sight of the gold, to hear its sound, to handle it.

With feverish eagerness he tore open the wrappings, and let the pieces fall in cascades upon the table; and, as the heap increased, his lips turned white, and perspiration broke out on his temples.

"And all that is for me?" he said with a stupid laugh.

"Yes, it is yours," replied Dionysia.

"I did not know how sixteen thousand francs would look. How beautiful gold is! Just look, wife."

But Colette turned her head away. She was quite as covetous as her husband, and perhaps even more excited; but she was a woman, and she knew how to dissemble.

"Ah, my dear young lady!" she said, "never would my old man and myself have asked you for money, if we had only ourselves to think of. But we have children."

"Your duty is to think of your children," replied Dionysia.

"I know sixteen thousand francs is a big sum. Perhaps you will be sorry to give us so much money."

"I am not sorry at all: I would even add to it willingly." And she showed them one of the other four rolls in her bag.

"Then, to be sure, what do I care for my place!" cried Blangin. And, intoxicated by the sight and the touch of the gold, he added,—

"You are at home here, madam; and the jail and the jailer are at your disposal. What do you desire? Just speak. I have nine prisoners, not counting M. de Boiscoran and Trumence. Do you want me to set them all free?"

"Blangin!" said his wife reprovingly.

"What? Am I not free to let the prisoners go?"

"Before you play the master, wait, at least, till you have rendered our young lady the service which she expects from you."

"Certainly."

"Then go and conceal this money," said the prudent woman; "or it might betray us."

And, drawing from her cupboard a woollen stocking, she handed it to her husband, who slipped the sixteen thousand francs into it, retaining about a dozen gold-pieces, which he kept in his pocket so as always to have in his hands some tangible evidence of his new fortune. When this was done, and the stocking, full to overflowing, had been put back in the cupboard under a pile of linen, she ordered her husband,—

"Now, you go down. Somebody might be coming; and, if you were not there to open when they knock, that might look suspicious."

Like a well-trained husband, Blangin obeyed without saying a word; and then his wife bethought herself how to entertain

Dionysia. She hoped, she said, her dear young lady would do her the honor to take something. That would strengthen her, and, besides, help her to pass the time; for it was only seven o'clock, and Blangin could not take her to M. de Boiscoran's cell before ten, without great danger.

"But I have dined," Dionysia objected. "I do not want any thing."

The woman insisted only the more. She remembered (God be thanked!) her dear young lady's taste; and she had made her an admirable broth, and some beautiful dessert. And, while thus talking, she set the table, having made up her mind that Dionysia must eat at all hazards; at least, so says the tradition of the place.

The eager zeal of the woman had, at least, this advantage,—that it prevented Dionysia from giving way to her painful thoughts.

Night had come. It was nine o'clock; then it struck ten. At last, the watch came round to relieve the sentinels. A quarter of an hour after that, Blangin reappeared, holding a lantern and an enormous bunch of keys in his hands.

"I have seen Trumence to bed," he said. "You can come now, madam."

Dionysia was all ready.

"Let us go," she said simply.

Then she followed the jailer along interminable passages, through a vast vaulted hall, in which their steps resounded as in a church, then through a long gallery. At last, pointing at a massive door, through the cracks of which the light was piercing, he said,—

"Here we are."

But Dionysia seized his arm, and said in an almost inaudible voice,—

"Wait a moment."

She was almost overcome by so many successive emotions. She felt her legs give way under her, and her eyes become dim. In her heart she preserved all her usual energy; but the flesh escaped from her will and failed her at the last moment.

"Are you sick?" asked the jailer. "What is the matter?"

She prayed to God for courage and strength: when her prayer was finished, she said,—

"Now, let us go in."

And, making a great noise with the keys and the bolts, Blangin opened the door to Jacques de Boiscoran's cell.

Jacques counted no longer the days, but the hours. He had been imprisoned on Friday morning, June 23, and this was Wednesday night, June 28, He had been a hundred and thirty-two hours, according to the graphic description of a great writer, "living, but struck from the roll of the living, and buried alive."

Each one of these hundred and thirty-two hours had weighed upon him like a month. Seeing him pale and haggard, with his hair and beard in disorder, and his eyes shining brightly with fever, like half-extinguished coals, one would hardly have recognized in him the happy lord of Boiscoran, free from care and trouble, upon whom fortune had ever smiled,—that haughty sceptical young man, who from the height of the past defied the future.

The fact is, that society, obliged to defend itself against criminals, has invented no more fearful suffering than what is called "close confinement." There is nothing that will sooner demoralize a man, crush his will, and utterly conquer the most powerful energy. There is no struggle more distressing than the struggle between an innocent man accused of some crime, and the magistrate,—a helpless being in the hands of a man armed with unlimited power.

If great sorrow was not sacred, to a certain degree, Dionysia might have heard all about Jacques. Nothing would have been easier. She would have been told by Blangin, who was watching M. de Boiscoran like a spy, and by his wife, who prepared his meals, through what anguish he had passed since his imprisonment.

Stunned at first, he had soon recovered; and on Friday and Saturday he had been quiet and confident, talkative, and almost cheerful. But Sunday had been a fatal day. Two gendarmes had carried him to Boiscoran to take off the seals; and on his way out he had been overwhelmed with insults and curses by the people who had recognized him. He had come back terribly distressed.

On Tuesday, he had received Dionysia's letter, and answered it. This had excited him fearfully, and, during a part of the night, Trumence had seen him walk up and down in his cell with all the gestures and incoherent imprecations of a madman.

He had hoped for a letter on Wednesday. When none came, he had sunk into a kind of stupor, during which M. Galpin had been unable to draw a word from him. He had taken nothing all day long but a little broth and a cup of coffee. When the magistrate left him, he had sat down, leaning his head on his elbows, facing the window; and there he had remained, never moving, and so deeply absorbed in his reveries, that he had taken no notice when they brought him light. He was still in this state, when, a little after ten o'clock, he heard the grating of the bolts of his cell. He had become so well acquainted with the prison that he knew all its regulations. He knew at what hours his meals were brought, at what time Trumence came to clean up his room, and when he might expect the magistrate. After night, he knew he was his own master till next morning. So late a visit therefore, must needs bring him some unexpected news, his liberty, perhaps,—that visitor for whom all prisoners look so anxiously.

He started up. As soon as he distinguished in the darkness the jailer's rugged face, he asked eagerly,—

"Who wants me?"

Blangin bowed. He was a polite jailer. Then he replied,—

"Sir, I bring you a visitor."

And, moving aside, he made way for Dionysia, or, rather, he pushed her into the room; for she seemed to have lost all power to move.

"A visitor?" repeated M. de Boiscoran.

But the jailer had raised his lantern, and the poor man could recognize his betrothed.

"You," he cried, "you here!"

And he drew back, afraid of being deceived by a dream, or one of those fearful hallucinations which announce the coming of insanity, and take hold of the brains of sick people in times of over-excitement.

"Dionysia!" he barely whispered, "Dionysia!"

If not her own life (for she cared nothing for that), but Jacques's life, had at that moment depended on a single word, Dionysia could not have uttered it. Her throat was parched, and her lips refused to move. The jailer took it upon himself to answer,—

"Yes," he said, "Miss Chandore."

"At this hour, in my prison!"

"She had something important to communicate to you. She came to me"—

"O Dionysia!" stammered Jacques, "what a precious friend"—

"And I agreed," said Blangin in a paternal tone of voice, "to bring her in secretly. It is a great sin I commit; and if it ever should become known—But one may be ever so much a jailer, one has a heart, after all. I tell you so merely because the young lady might not think of it. If the secret is not kept carefully, I should lose my place, and I am a poor man, with wife and children."

"You are the best of men!" exclaimed M. de Boiscoran, far from suspecting the price that had been paid for Blangin's sympathy, "and, on the day on which I regain my liberty, I will prove to you that we whom you have obliged are not ungrateful."

"Quite at your service," replied the jailer modestly.

Gradually, however, Dionysia had recovered her self-possession. She said gently to Blangin,—

"Leave us now, my good friend."

As soon as he had disappeared, and without allowing M. de Boiscoran to say a word, she said, speaking very low,—

"Jacques, grandpapa has told me, that by coming thus to you at night, alone, and in secret, I run the risk of losing your affection, and of diminishing your respect."

"Ah, you did not think so!"

"Grandpapa has more experience than I have, Jacques. Still I did not hesitate. Here I am; and I should have run much greater risks; for your honor is at stake, and your honor is my honor, as your life is my life. Your future is at stake, *our* future, our happiness, all our hopes here below."

Inexpressible joy had illumined the prisoner's face.

"O God!" he cried, "one such moment pays for years of torture."

But Dionysia had sworn to herself, as she came, that nothing should turn her aside from her purpose. So she went on,—

"By the sacred memory of my mother, I assure you, Jacques, that I have never for a moment doubted your innocence."

The unhappy man looked distressed.

"You," he said; "but the others? But M. de Chandore?"

"Do you think I would be here, if he thought you were guilty? My aunts and your mother are as sure of it as I am."

"And my father? You said nothing about him in your letter."

"Your father remained in Paris in case some influence in high quarters should have to be appealed to."

Jacque shook his head, and said,—

"I am in prison at Sauveterre, accused of a fearful crime, and my father remains in Paris! It must be true that he never really loved me. And yet I have always been a good son to him down to this terrible catastrophe. He has never had to complain of me. No, my father does not love me."

Dionysia could not allow him to go off in this way.

"Listen to me, Jacques," she said: "let me tell you why I ran the risk of taking this serious step, that may cost me so dear. I come to you in the name of all your friends, in the name of M. Folgat, the great advocate whom your mother has brought down from Paris and in the name of M. Magloire, in whom you put so much confidence. They all agree you have adopted an abominable system. By refusing obstinately to speak, you rush voluntarily into the gravest danger. Listen well to what I tell you. If you wait till the examination is over, you are lost. If you are once handed over to the court, it is too late for you to speak. You will only, innocent as you are, make one more on the list of judicial murders."

Jacques de Boiscoran had listened to Dionysia in silence, his head bowed to the ground, as if to conceal its pallor from her. As soon as she stopped, all out of breath, he murmured,—

"Alas! Every thing you tell me I have told myself more than once."

"And you did not speak?"

"I did not."

"Ah, Jacques, you are not aware of the danger you run! You do not know"—

"I know," he said, interrupting her in a harsh, hoarse voice,—"I know that the scaffold, or the galleys, are at the end."

Dionysia was petrified with horror.

Poor girl! She had imagined that she would only have to show herself to triumph over Jacques's obstinacy, and that, as soon as she had heard what he had to say, she would feel reassured. And instead of that—

"What a misfortune!" she cried. "You have taken up these fearful notions, and you will not abandon them!"

"I must keep silent."

"You cannot. You have not considered!—"

"Not considered," he repeated.

And in a lower tone he added,—

"And what do you think I have been doing these hundred and thirty mortal hours since I have been alone in this prison,—alone to confront a terrible accusation, and a still more terrible emergency?"

"That is the difficulty, Jacques: you are the victim of your own imagination. And who could help it in your place? M. Folgat said so only yesterday. There is no man living, who, after four days' close confinement, can keep his mind cool. Grief and solitude are bad counsellors. Jacques, come to yourself; listen to your dearest friends who speak to you through me. Jacques, your Dionysia beseeches you. Speak!"

"I cannot."

"Why not?"

She waited for some seconds; and, as he did not reply, she said, not without a slight accent of bitterness in her voice,—

"Is it not the first duty of an innocent man to establish his innocence?"

The prisoner, with a movement of despair, clasped his hands over his brow. Then bending over Dionysia, so that she felt his breath in her hair, he said,—

"And when he cannot, when he cannot, establish his innocence?"

She drew back, pale unto death, tottering so that she had to lean against the wall, and cast upon Jacques de Boiscoran glances in which the whole horror of her soul was clearly expressed.

"What do you say?" she stammered. "O God!"

He laughed, the wretched man! with that laugh which is the last utterance of despair. And then he replied,—

"I say that there are circumstances which upset our reason; unheard-of circumstances, which could make one doubt of one's self. I say that every thing accuses me, that every thing overwhelms me, that every thing turns against me. I say, that if I were in M. Galpin's place, and if he were in mine, I should act just as he does."

"That is insanity!" cried Dionysia.

But Jacques de Boiscoran did not hear her. All the bitterness of the last days rose within him: he turned red, and became excited. At last, with gasping vice, he broke forth,—

"Establish my innocence! Ah! that is easily said. But how? No, I am not guilty: but a crime has been committed; and for this crime justice will have a culprit. If it is not I who fired at Count Claudieuse, and set Valpinson on fire, who is it? 'Where were you,' they ask me, 'at the time of the murder?' Where was I? Can I tell it? To clear myself is to accuse others. And if I should be mistaken? Or if, not being mistaken, I should be unable to prove the truthfulness of my accusation? The murderer and the incendiary, of course, took all possible precautions to escape detection, and to let the punishment fall upon me. I was warned beforehand. Ah, if we could always foresee, could know beforehand! How can I defend myself? On the first day I said, 'Such a charge cannot reach me: it is a cloud that a breath will scatter.' Madman that I was! The cloud has become an avalanche, and I may be crushed. I am neither a child nor a coward; and I have always met phantoms face to face. I have measured the danger, and I know it is fearful."

Dionysia shuddered. She cried,—

"What will become of us?"

This time M. de Boiscoran heard her, and was ashamed of his weakness. But, before he could master his feelings, the young girl went on, saying,—

"But never mind. These are idle thoughts. Truth soars invincible, unchangeable, high above all the ablest calculations and the most skilful combinations. Jacques, you must tell the truth, the whole truth, without subterfuge or concealment."

"I can do so no longer," murmured he.

"Is it such a terrible secret?"

"It is improbable."

Dionysia looked at him almost with fear. She did not recognize his old face, nor his eye, nor the tone of his voice. She drew nearer to him, and taking his hand between her own small white hands, she said,—

"But you can tell it to me, your friend, your"—

He trembled, and, drawing back, he said,—

"To you less than anybody else."

And, feeling how mortifying such an answer must be, he added,—

"Your mind is too pure for such wretched intrigues. I do not want your wedding-dress to be stained by a speck of that mud into which they have thrown me."

Was she deceived? No; but she had the courage to seem to be deceived. She went on quietly,—

"Very well, then. But the truth will have to be told sooner or later."

"Yes, to M. Magloire."

"Well, then, Jacques, write down at once what you mean to tell him. Here are pen and ink: I will carry it to him faithfully."

"There are things, Dionysia, which cannot be written."

She felt she was beaten; she understood that nothing would ever bend that iron will, and yet she said once more,—

"But if I were to beseech you, Jacques, by our past and our future, by that great and eternal love which you have sworn?"

"Do you really wish to make my prison hours a thousand times harder than they are? Do you want to deprive me of my last remnant of strength and of courage? Have you really no confidence in me any longer? Could you not believe me a few days more?"

He paused. Somebody knocked at the door; and almost at the same time Blangin the jailer called out through the wicket,—

"Time is passing. I want to be down stairs when they relieve guard. I am running a great risk. I am a father of a family."

"Go home now, Dionysia," said Jacques eagerly, "go home. I cannot think of your being seen here."

Dionysia had paid dear enough to know that she was quite safe; still she did not object. She offered her brow to Jacques, who touched it with his lips; and half dead, holding on to the walls, she went back to the jailer's little room. They had made up a bed for her, and she threw herself on it, dressed as she was, and remained there, immovable, as if she had been dead, overcome by a kind of stupor which deprived her even of the faculty of suffering.

It was bright daylight, it was eight o'clock, when she felt somebody pulling her sleeve. The jailer's wife said to her,—

"My dear young lady, this would be a good time for you to slip away. Perhaps they will wonder to see you alone in the street; but they will think you are coming home from seven o'clock mass."

Without saying a word, Dionysia jumped down, and in a moment she had arranged her hair and her dress. Then Blangin came, rather troubled at not seeing her leave the house; and she said to him, giving him one of the thousand-franc rolls that were still in her bag,—

"This is for you: I want you to remember me, if I should need you again."

And, dropping her veil over her face, she went away.

XI.

Baron Chandore had had one terrible night in his life, every minute of which he had counted by the ebbing pulse of his only son.

The evening before, the physicians had said,—

"If he lives this night, he may be saved."

At daybreak he had expired.

Well, the old gentleman had hardly suffered more during that fatal night than he did this night, during which Dionysia was away from the house. He knew very well that Blangin and his wife were honest people, in spite of their avarice and their covetousness; he knew that Jacques de Boiscoran was an honourable man.

But still, during the whole night, his old servant heard him walk up and down his room; and at seven o'clock in the morning he was at the door, looking anxiously up and down the street. Towards half-past seven, M. Folgat came up; but he hardly wished him good-morning, and he certainly did not hear a word of what the lawyer told him to reassure him. At last, however, the old man cried,—

"Ah, there she is!"

He was not mistaken. Dionysia was coming round the corner. She came up to the house in feverish haste, as if she had known that her strength was at an end, and would barely suffice to carry her to the door.

Grandpapa Chandore met her with a kind of fierce joy, pressed her in his arms, and said over and over again,—

"O Dionysia! Oh, my darling child, how I have suffered! How long you have been! But it is all over now. Come, come, come!"

And he almost carried her into the parlor, and put her down tenderly into a large easy-chair. He knelt down by her, smiling with happiness; but, when he had taken her hands in his, he said,—

"Your hands are burning. You have a fever!"

He looked at her: she had raised her veil.

"You are pale as death!" he went on. "Your eyes are red and swollen!"

"I have cried, dear papa," she replied gently.

"Cried! Why?"

"Alas, I have failed!"

As if moved by a sudden shock, M. de Chandore started up, and cried,—

"By God's holy name the like has not been heard since the world was made! What! you went, you Dionysia de Chandore, to him in his prison; you begged him"—

"And he remained inflexible. Yes, dear papa. He will say nothing till after the preliminary investigation is over."

"We were mistaken in the man: he has no courage and no feeling."

Dionysia had risen painfully, and said feebly,—

"Ah, dear papa! Do not blame him, do not accuse him! he is so unhappy!"

"But what reasons does he give?"

"He says the facts are so very improbable that he should certainly not be believed; and that he should ruin himself if he were to speak as long as he is kept in close confinement, and has no advocate. He says his position is the result of a wicked conspiracy. He says he thinks he knows the guilty one, and that he will denounce the person, since he is forced to do so in self-defence."

M. Folgat, who had until now remained a silent witness of the scene, came up, and asked,—

"Are you quite sure, madam, that that was what M. de Boiscoran said?"

"Oh, quite sure, sir! And, if I lived a thousand years, I should never forget the look of his eyes, or the tone of his voice."

M. de Chandore did not allow her to be interrupted again.

"But surely, my dear child, Jacques told you—you—something more precise?"

"No."

"You did not ask him even what those improbable facts were?"

"Oh, yes!"

"Well?"

"He said that I was the very last person who could be told."

"That man ought to be burnt over a slow fire," said M. de Chandore to himself. Then he added in a louder voice,—

"And you do not think all this very strange, very extraordinary?"

"It seems to me horrible!"

"I understand. But what do you think of Jacques?"

"I think, dear papa, that he cannot act otherwise, or he would not do it. Jacques is too intelligent and too courageous to deceive himself easily. As he alone knows every thing, he alone can judge. I, of course, am bound to respect his will more than anybody else."

But the old gentleman did not think himself bound to respect it; and, exasperated as he was by this resignation of his grandchild, he was on the point of telling her his mind fully, when she got up with some effort, and said, in an almost inaudible voice,—

"I am broken to pieces! Excuse me, grandpapa, if I go to my room." She left the parlor. M. de Chandore accompanied her to the door, remained there till he had seen her get up stairs, where her maid was waiting for her, and then came back to M. Folgat.

"They are going to kill me, sir!" he cried, with an explosion of wrath and despair which was almost frightful in a man of his age. "She had in her eyes the same look that her mother had when she told me, after her husband's death, 'I shall not survive him.' And she did not survive my poor son. And then I, old man, was left alone with that child; and who knows but she may have in her the germ of the same disease which killed her mother? Alone! And for these twenty years I have held my breath to listen if she is still breathing as naturally and regularly"—

"You are needlessly alarmed," began the advocate.

But Grandpapa Chandore shook his head, and said,—

"No, no. I fear my child has been hurt in her heart's heart. Did you not see how white she looked, and how faint her voice was? Great God! wilt thou leave me all alone here upon earth? O God! for which of my sins dost thou punish me in my children? For mercy's sake, call me home before she also leaves me, who is the joy of my life. And I can do nothing to turn aside this fatality— stupid inane old man that I am! And this Jacques de Boiscoran—if he were guilty, after all? Ah the wretch! I would hang him with my own hands!"

Deeply moved, M. Folgat had watched the old gentleman's grief. Now he said,—

"Do not blame M. de Boiscoran, sir, now that every thing is against him! Of all of us, he suffers, after all, most; for he is innocent."

"Do you still think so?"

"More than ever. Little as he has said, he has told Miss Dionysia enough to confirm me in my conjecture, and to prove to me that I have guessed right."

"When?"

"The day we went to Boiscoran."

The baron tried to remember.

"I do not recollect," he said.

"Don't you remember," said the lawyer, "that you left us, so as to permit Anthony to answer my questions more freely?"

"To be sure!" cried M. de Chandore, "to be sure! And then you thought"—

"I thought I had guessed right, yes, sir; but I am not going to do any thing now. M. de Boiscoran tells us that the facts are improbable. I should, therefore, in all probability, soon be astray; but, since we are now bound to be passive till the investigation is completed, I shall employ the time in examining the country people, who will, probably, tell me more than Anthony did. You have, no doubt, among your friends, some who must be well informed,—M. Seneschal, Dr. Seignebos."

The latter did not keep M. Folgat waiting long; for his name had hardly been mentioned, when he himself repeated it in the passage, telling a servant,—

"Say it is I, Dr. Seignebos, Dr. Seignebos."

He fell like a bombshell into the room. It was four days now since he had last presented himself there; for he had not come himself for his report and the shot he had left in M. Folgat's hands. He had sent for them, excusing himself on the score of his many engagements. The fact was, however, that he had spent nearly the whole of these four days at the hospital, in company with one of his brother-practitioners, who had been sent for by the court to proceed, "jointly with Dr. Seignebos," to an examination of Cocoleu's mental condition.

"And this is what brings me here," he cried, still in the door; "for this opinion, if it is not put into proper order, will deprive M. de Boiscoran of his best and surest chance of escape."

After what Dionysia had told them, neither M. de Chandore nor M. Folgat attached much importance to the state of Cocoleu's mind: still this word "escape" attracted their attention. There is nothing unimportant in a criminal trial.

"Is there any thing new?" asked the advocate.

The doctor first went to close the doors carefully, and then, putting his cane and broad-brimmed hat upon the table, he said,—

"No, there is nothing new. They still insist, as before, upon ruining M. de Boiscoran; and, in order to do that, they shrink from nothing."

"They! Who are they?" asked M. de Chandore.

The doctor shrugged his shoulders contemptuously.

"Are you really in doubt, sir?" he replied. "And yet the facts speak clearly enough. In this department, there is a certain number of physicians who are not very keenly alive to the honor of their profession, and who are, to tell the truth, consummate apes."

Grave as the situation was, M. Folgat could hardly suppress a smile, the doctor's manner was so very extraordinary.

"But there is one of these apes," he went on, "who, in length of ears and thickness of skin, surpasses all the others. Well, he is the very one whom the court has chosen and associated with me."

Upon this subject it was desirable to put a check upon the doctor. M. de Chandore therefore interrupted him, saying,—

"In fine"—

"In fine, my learned brother is fully persuaded that his mission as a physician employed by a court of justice is to say 'Amen' to all the stories of the prosecution. 'Cocoleu is an idiot,' says M. Galpin peremptorily. 'He is an idiot, or ought to be one,' reechoes my learned brother. 'He spoke on the occasion of the crime by an inspiration from on high,' the magistrate goes on to say. 'Evidently,' adds the brother, 'there was an inspiration from on high.' For this is the conclusion at which my learned brother arrives in his report: 'Cocoleu is an idiot who had been providentially inspired by a flash of reason.' He does not say it in these words; but it amounts to the same thing."

He had taken off his spectacles, and was wiping them industriously.

"But what do you think, doctor?" asked M. Folgat.

Dr. Seignebos solemnly put on again his spectacles, and replied coldly,—

"My opinion, which I have fully developed in my report, is, that Cocoleu is not idiotic at all."

M. Chandore started: the proposition seemed to him monstrous. He knew Cocoleu very well; he had seen him wander through the streets of Sauveterre during the eighteen months which the poor creature had spent under the doctor's treatment.

"What! Cocoleu not idiotic?" he repeated.

"No!" Dr. Seignebos declared peremptorily; "and you have only to look at him to be convinced. Has he a large flat face, disproportionate mouth, a yellow, tanned complexion, thick lips, defective teeth, and squinting eyes? Does his deformed head sway from side to side, being too heavy to be supported by his neck? Is his body deformed, and his spine crooked? Do you find that his stomach is big and pendent, that his hands drop upon his thighs, that his legs are awkward, and the joints unusually large? These are the symptoms of idiocy, gentleman, and you do not find them in Cocoleu. I, for my part, see in him a scamp, who has an iron constitution, who uses his hands very cleverly, climbs trees like a monkey, and leaps ditches ten feet wide. To be sure, I do not pretend that his intellect is normal; but I maintain that he is one of those imbeciles who have certain faculties very fully developed, while others, more essential, are missing."

While M. Folgat listened with the most intense interest, M. de Chandore became impatient, and said,—

"The difference between an idiot and an imbecile"—

"There is a world between them," cried the doctor.

And at once he went on with overwhelming volubility,—

"The imbecile preserves some fragments of intelligence. He can speak, make known his wants, and express his feelings. He associates ideas, compares impressions, remembers things, and acquires experience. He is capable of cunning and dissimulation. He hates and likes and fears. If he is not always sociable, he is susceptible of being influenced by others. You can easily obtain perfect control over him. His inconsistency is remarkable; and still he shows, at times, invincible obstinacy. Finally, imbeciles are, on account of this semi-lucidity, often very dangerous. You find among them almost all those monomaniacs whom society is compelled to shut up in asylums, because they cannot master their instincts."

"Very well said," repeated M. Folgat, who found here some elements of a plea,—"very well said."

The doctor bowed.

"Such a creature is Cocoleu. Does it follow that I hold him responsible for his actions? By no means! But it follows that I look upon him as a false witness brought forth to ruin an honest man."

It was evident that such views did not please M. de Chandore.

"Formerly," he said, "you did not think so."

"No, I even said the contrary," replied Dr. Seignebos, not without dignity. "I had not studied Cocoleu sufficiently, and I was taken in by him: I confess it openly. But this avowal of mine is an evidence of the cunning and the astute obstinacy of these wretched creatures, and of their capacity to carry out a design. After a year's experience, I sent Cocoleu away, declaring, and certainly believing, that he was incurable. The fact is, he did not want to be cured. The country-people, who observe carefully and shrewdly, were not taken in; they will tell you, almost to a man, that Cocoleu is bad, but not an idiot. That is the truth. He has found out, that, by exaggerating his imbecility, he could live without work; and he has done it. When he was taken in by Count Claudieuse, he was clever enough to show just so much intelligence as was necessary to make him endurable, without being compelled to do any work."

"In a word," said M. de Chandore incredulously, "Cocoleu is a great actor."

"Great enough to have deceived me," replied the doctor: "yes, sir."

Then turning to M. Folgat, he went on,—

"All this I had told my learned brother, before taking him to the hospital. There we found Cocoleu more obstinate than ever in his silence, which even M. Galpin had not induced him to break. All our efforts to obtain a word from him were fruitless, although it was very evident to me that he understood very well. I proposed to resort to quite legitimate means, which are employed to discover feigned defects and diseases; but my learned brother refused and was encouraged in his resistance by M. Galpin: I do not know upon what ground. Then I asked that the Countess Claudieuse should be sent for, as she has a talent of making him talk. M. Galpin would not permit it—and there we are."

It happens almost daily, that two physicians employed as experts differ in their opinions. The courts would have a great deal to do, if they had to force them to agree. They appoint simply a third expert, whose opinion is decisive. This was necessarily to be done in Cocoleu's case.

"And as necessarily," continued Dr. Seignebos, "the court, having appointed a first ass, will associate with me a second ass. They will agree with each other, and I shall be accused and convicted of ignorance and presumption."

He came, therefore, as he now said, to ask M. de Chandore to render him a little service. He wanted the two families, Chandore and Boiscoran, to employ all their influence to obtain that a commission of physicians from outside—if possible, from Paris— should be appointed to examine Cocoleu, and to report on his mental condition.

"I undertake," he said, "to prove to really enlightened men, that this poor creature is partly pretending to be imbecile, and that his obstinate speechlessness is only adopted in order to avoid answers which would compromise him."

At first, however, neither M. de Chandore nor M. Folgat gave any answer. They were considering the question.

"Mind," said the doctor again, shocked at their silence, "mind, I pray, that if my view is adopted, as I have every reason to hope, a new turn will be given to the whole case."

Why yes! The ground of the accusation might be taken from under the prosecution; and that was what kept M. Folgat thinking.

"And that is exactly," he commenced at last, "what makes me ask myself whether the discovery of Cocoleu's rascality would not be rather injurious than beneficial to M. de Boiscoran."

The doctor was furious. He cried,—

"I should like to know"—

"Nothing can be more simple," replied the advocate. "Cocoleu's idiocy is, perhaps the most serious difficulty in the way of the prosecution, and the most powerful argument for the defence. What can M. Galpin say, if M. de Boiscoran charges him with basing a capital charge upon the incoherent words of a creature void of intelligence, and, consequently, irresponsible."

"Ah! permit me," said Dr. Seignebos.

But M. de Chandore heard every syllable.

"Permit yourself, doctor," he said. "This argument of Cocoleu's imbecility is one which you have pleaded from the beginning, and which appeared to you, you said, so conclusive, that there was no need of looking for any other."

Before the doctor could find an answer, M. Folgat went on,—

"Let it be, on the contrary, established that Cocoleu really knows what he says, and all is changed. The prosecution is justified, by an opinion of the faculty, in saying to M. de Boiscoran, 'You need not deny any longer. You have been seen; here is a witness.'"

These arguments must have struck Dr. Seignebos very forcibly; for he remained silent for at least ten long seconds, wiping his gold spectacles with a pensive air. Had he really done harm to Jacques de Boiscoran, while he meant to help him? But he was not the man to be long in doubt. He replied in a dry tone,—

"I will not discuss that, gentlemen. I will ask you, only one question: 'Yes or no, do you believe in M. de Boiscoran's innocence?'"

"We believe in it fully," replied the two men.

"Then, gentlemen, it seems to me we are running no risk in trying to unmask an impostor."

That was not the young lawyer's opinion.

"To prove that Cocoleu knows what he says," he replied, "would be fatal, unless we can prove at the same time that he has told a falsehood, and that his evidence has been prompted by others. Can we prove that? Have we any means to prove that his obstinacy in not replying to any questions arises from his fear that his answers might convict him of perjury?"

The doctor would hear nothing more. He said rather uncourteously,—

"Lawyer's quibbles! I know only one thing; and that is truth."

"It will not always do to tell it," murmured the lawyer.

"Yes, sir, always," replied the physician,—"always, and at all hazards, and whatever may happen. I am M. de Boiscoran's friend; but I am still more the friend of truth. If Cocoleu is a wretched impostor, as I am firmly convinced, our duty is to unmask him."

Dr. Seignebos did not say—and he probably did not confess it to himself—that it was a personal matter between Cocoleu and himself. He thought Cocoleu had taken him in, and been the cause of a host of small witticisms, under which he had suffered cruelly, though he had allowed no one to see it. To unmask Cocoleu would have given him his revenge, and return upon his enemies the ridicule with which they had overwhelmed him.

"I have made up my mind," he said, "and, whatever you may resolve, I mean to go to work at once, and try to obtain the appointment of a commission."

"It might be prudent," M. Folgat said, "to consider before doing any thing, to consult with M. Magloire."

"I do not want to consult with Magloire when duty calls."

"You will grant us twenty-four hours, I hope."

Dr. Seignebos frowned till he looked formidable.

"Not an hour," he replied; "and I go from here to M. Daubigeon, the commonwealth attorney."

Thereupon, taking his hat and cane, he bowed and left, as dissatisfied as possible, without stopping even to answer M. de

Chandore, who asked him how Count Claudieuse was, who was, according to reports in town, getting worse and worse.

"Hang the old original!" cried M. de Chandore before the doctor had left the passage.

Then turning to M. Folgat, he added,—

"I must, however, confess that you received the great news which he brought rather coldly."

"The very fact of the news being so very grave," replied the advocate, "made me wish for time to consider. If Cocoleu pretends to be imbecile, or, at least, exaggerates his incapacity, then we have a confirmation of what M. de Boiscoran last night told Miss Dionysia. It would be the proof of an odious trap of a long-premeditated vengeance. Here is the turning-point of the affair evidently."

M. de Chandore was bitterly undeceived.

"What!" he said, "you think so, and you refuse to support Dr. Seignebos, who is certainly an honest man?"

The young lawyer shook his head.

"I wanted to have twenty-four hours' delay, because we must absolutely consult M. de Boiscoran. Could I tell the doctor so? Had I a right to take him into Miss Dionysia's secret?"

"You are right," murmured M. de Chandore, "you are right."

But, in order to write to M. de Boiscoran, Dionysia's assistance was necessary; and she did not reappear till the afternoon, looking very pale, but evidently armed with new courage.

M. Folgat dictated to her certain questions to ask the prisoner.

She hastened to write them in cipher; and about four o'clock the letter was sent to Mechinet, the clerk.

The next evening the answer came.

"Dr. Seignebos is no doubt right, my dear friends," wrote Jacques. "I have but too good reasons to be sure that Cocoleu's imbecility is partly assumed, and that his evidence has been prompted by others. Still I must beg you will take no steps that would lead to another medical investigation. The slightest imprudence may ruin me. For Heaven's sake wait till the end of the preliminary investigation, which is now near at hand, from what M. Galpin tells me."

The letter was read in the family circle; and the poor mother uttered a cry of despair as she heard those words of resignation.

"Are we going to obey him," she said, "when we all know that he is ruining himself by his obstinacy?"

Dionysia rose, and said,—

"Jacques alone can judge his situation, and he alone, therefore, has the right to command. Our duty is to obey. I appeal to M. Folgat."

The young advocate nodded his head.

"Every thing has been done that could be done," he said. "Now we can only wait."

XII.

The famous night of the fire at Valpinson had been a godsend to the good people of Sauveterre. They had henceforth an inexhaustible topic of discussion, ever new and ever rich in unexpected conjectures,—the Boiscoran case. When people met in the streets, they simply asked,—

"What are they doing now?"

Whenever, therefore, M. Galpin went from the court-house to the prison, or came striding up National Street with his stiff, slow step, twenty good housewives peeped from behind their curtains to read in his face some of the secrets of the trial. They saw, however, nothing there but traces of intense anxiety, and a pallor which became daily more marked. They said to each other,—

"You will see poor M. Galpin will catch the jaundice from it."

The expression was commonplace; but it conveyed exactly the feelings of the ambitious lawyer. This Boiscoran case had become like a festering wound to him, which irritated him incessantly and intolerably.

"I have lost my sleep by it," he told the commonwealth attorney. Excellent M. Daubigeon, who had great trouble in moderating his zeal, did not pity him particularly. He would say in reply,—

"Whose fault is it? But you want to rise in the world; and increasing fortune is always followed by increasing care.

"Ah!" said the magistrate. "I have only done my duty, and, if I had to begin again, I would do just the same."

Still every day he saw more clearly that he was in a false position. Public opinion, strongly arrayed against M. de Boiscoran, was not, on that account, very favorable to him. Everybody believed Jacques guilty, and wanted him to be punished with all the rigor of the law; but, on the other hand, everybody was astonished that M. Galpin should choose to act as magistrate in such a case. There was a touch of treachery in this proceeding against a former friend, in looking everywhere for evidence against him, in driving him into court, that is to say, towards the galleys or the scaffold; and this revolted people's consciences.

The very way in which people returned his greeting, or avoided him altogether, made the magistrate aware of the feelings they entertained for him. This only increased his wrath against Jacques, and, with it his trouble. He had been congratulated, it is true, by the attorney-general; but there is no certainty in a trial, as long as the accused refuses to confess. The charges against Jacques, to be sure, were so overwhelming, that his being sent before the court was out of question. But by the side of the court there is still the jury.

"And in fine, my dear," said the commonwealth attorney, "you have not a single eye-witness. And from time immemorial an eye-witness has been looked upon as worth a hundred hearsays."

"I have Cocoleu," said M. Galpin, who was rather impatient of all these objections.

"Have the doctors decided that he is not an idiot?"

"No: Dr. Seignebos alone maintains that doctrine."

"Well, at least Cocoleu is willing to repeat his evidence?"

"No."

"Why, then you have virtually no witness!"

Yes, M. Galpin understood it but too well, and hence his anxiety. The more he studied *his* accused, the more he found him in an enigmatic and threatening position, which was ominous of evil.

"Can he have an *alibi?*" he thought. "Or does he hold in reserve one of those unforeseen revelations, which at the last moment destroy the whole edifice of the prosecution, and cover the prosecuting attorney with ridicule?"

Whenever these thoughts occurred to him, they made big drops of perspiration run down his temples; and then he treated his poor clerk Mechinet like a slave. And that was not all. Although he lived more retired than ever, since this case had begun, many a report reached him from the Chandore family.

To be sure, he was a thousand miles from imagining that they had actually opened communications with the prisoner, and, what is more, that this intercourse was carried on by Mechinet, his own clerk. He would have laughed if one had come and told him that Dionysia had spent a night in prison, and paid Jacques a visit. But he heard continually of the hopes and the plans of the friends and relations of his prisoner; and he remembered, not without secret fear and trembling, that they were rich and powerful, supported by relations in high places, beloved and esteemed by everybody. He knew that Dionysia was surrounded by devoted and intelligent men, by M. de Chandore, M. Seneschal, Dr. Seignebos, M. Magloire, and, finally, that advocate whom the Marchioness de Boiscoran had brought down with her from Paris, M. Folgat.

"And Heaven knows what they would not try," he thought, "to rescue the guilty man from the hands of justice!"

It may well be said, therefore, that never was prosecution carried on with as much passionate zeal or as much minute assiduity. Every one of the points upon which the prosecution relied became, for M. Galpin, a subject of special study. In less than a fortnight he examined sixty-seven witnesses in his office. He summoned the fourth part of the population of Brechy. He would have summoned the whole country, if he had dared.

But all his efforts were fruitless. After weeks of furious investigations, the inquiry was still at the same point, the mystery was still impenetrable. The prisoner had not refuted any of the charges made against him; but the magistrate had, also, not obtained a single additional piece of evidence after those he had secured on the first day.

There must be an end of this, however.

One warm afternoon in July, the good ladies in National Street thought they noticed that M. Galpin looked even more anxious than usual. They were right. After a long conference with the commonwealth attorney and the presiding judge, the magistrate had made up his mind. When he reached the prison, he went to Jacques's cell and there, concealing his embarrassment under the greatest stiffness, he said,—

"My painful duty draws to an end, sir: the inquiry with which I have been charged will be closed. To-morrow the papers, with a list of the objects to be used as evidence, will be sent to the attorney-general, to be submitted to the court."

Jacques de Boiscoran did not move.

"Well," he said simply.

"Have you nothing to add, sir?" asked M. Galpin.

"Nothing, except that I am innocent."

M. Galpin found it difficult to repress his impatience. He said,—

"Well, then, prove it. Refute the charges which have been brought against you, which overwhelm you, which induce me, the court, and everybody else, to consider you guilty. Speak, and explain your conduct."

Jacques kept obstinately silent.

"Your resolution is fixed," said the magistrate once more, "you refuse to say any thing?"

"I am innocent."

M. Galpin saw clearly that it was useless to insist any longer.

"From this moment," he said, "you are no longer in close confinement. You can receive the visits of your family in the prison parlor. The advocate whom you will choose will be admitted to your cell to consult with you."

"At last!" exclaimed Jacques with explosive delight; and then he added,—

"Am I at liberty to write to M. de Chandore?"

"Yes," replied M. Galpin, "and, if you choose to write at once, my clerk will be happy to carry your letter this evening to its destination."

Jacques de Boiscoran availed himself on the spot of this permission; and he had done very soon, for the note which he wrote, and handed to M. Mechinet, contained only the few words,—

"I shall expect M. Magloire to-morrow morning at nine.

"J."

Ever since the day on which they had come to the conclusion that a false step might have the most fatal consequences, Jacques de Boiscoran's friends had abstained from doing anything. Besides, what would have been the use of any efforts? Dr. Seignebos's request, though unsupported, had been at least partially granted; and the court had summoned a physician from Paris, a great authority on insanity, to determine Cocoleu's mental condition. It was on a Saturday that Dr. Seignebos came triumphantly to announce the good news. It was the following Tuesday that he had to report his discomfiture. In a furious passion he said,—

"There are asses in Paris as well as elsewhere! Or, rather, in these days of trembling egotism and eager servility, an independent man is as difficult to find in Paris as in the provinces. I was looking for a *savant* who would be inaccessible to petty considerations; and they send me a trifling fellow, who does not dare to be disagreeable to the gentlemen of the bar. Ah, it was a cruel disappointment!"

And all the time worrying his spectacles, he went on,—

"I had been informed of the arrival of my learned brother; and I went to receive him myself at the railway station. The train comes in; and at once I make out my man in the crowd: a fine head, well set in grizzly hair, a noble eye, eloquent lips. 'There he is!' I say to myself. 'Hm!' He looked rather dandyish, to be sure, a lot of decorations in his buttonhole, whiskers trimmed as carefully as the box in my garden, and, instead of honest spectacles, a pair of eye-glasses. But no man is perfect. I go up to him, I give him my name, we shake hands, I ask him to breakfast, he accepts; and here we are at table, he doing justice to my Bordeaux, and I explaining to him the case systematically. When we have done, he wishes to see Cocoleu. We go to the hospital; and there, after merely glancing at the creature, he says, 'That man is simply the most complete idiot I have ever seen in my life!' I was a little taken aback, and tried to explain the matter to him; but he refuses to listen to me. I beseech him to see Cocoleu once more: he laughs at me. I feel hurt, and ask him how he explains the evidence which this idiot gave on the night of the fire. He laughs again, and replies that he does not explain it. I begin to discuss the question; and he marches off to court. And do you know where he dined that day? At the hotel with my other learned brother of the commission; and there they drew up a report which makes of Cocoleu the most perfect imbecile that was ever dreamed of."

He was walking up and down in the room with long strides, and, unwilling to listen, he went on,—

"But Master Galpin need not think of crowing over us yet. The end is not yet; they will not get rid of Dr. Seignebos so easily. I have said that Cocoleu was a wretched cheat, a miserable impostor, a false witness, and I shall prove it. Boiscoran can count upon me."

He broke off here, and, placing himself before M. Folgat, he added,—

"And I say M. de Boiscoran may count upon me, because I have my reasons. I have formed very singular suspicions, sir,—very singular."

M. Folgat, Dionysia, and the marchioness urged him to explain; but he declared that the moment had not come yet, that he was not perfectly sure yet.

And he left again, vowing that he was overworked, that he had forsaken his patients for forty-eight hours, and that the Countess Claudieuse was waiting for him, as her husband was getting worse and worse.

"What can the old man suspect?" Grandpapa Chandore asked again, an hour after the doctor had left.

M. Folgat might have replied that these probable suspicions were no doubt his own suspicions, only better founded, and more fully developed. But why should he say so, since all inquiry was prohibited, and a single imprudent word might ruin every thing? Why, also, should he excite new hopes, when they must needs wait patiently till it should seem good to M. Galpin to make an end to this melancholy suspense?

They heard very little nowadays of Jacques de Boiscoran. The examinations took place only at long intervals; and it was sometimes four or five days before Mechinet brought another letter.

"This is intolerable agony," repeated the marchioness over and over again.

The end was, however, approaching.

Dionysia was alone one afternoon in the sitting-room, when she thought she heard the clerk's voice in the hall. She went out at once and found him there.

"Ah!" she cried, "the investigation is ended!" For she knew very well that nothing less would have emboldened Mechinet to show himself openly at their house.

"Yes, indeed, madam!" replied the good man; "and upon M. Galpin's own order I bring you this letter from M. de Boiscoran."

She took it, read it at a single glance, and forgetting every thing, half delirious with joy, she ran to her grandfather and M. Folgat, calling upon a servant at the same time to run and fetch M. Magloire.

In less than an hour, the eminent advocate of Sauveterre arrived; and when Jacques's letter had been handed to him, he said with some embarrassment,—

"I have promised M. de Boiscoran my assistance, and he shall certainly have it. I shall be at the prison to-morrow morning as soon as the doors open, and I will tell you the result of our interview."

He would say nothing more. It was very evident that he did not believe in the innocence of his client, and, as soon as he had left, M. de Chandore exclaimed,—

"Jacques is mad to intrust his defence to a man who doubts him."

"M. Magloire is an honorable man, papa," said Dionysia; "and, if he thought he could compromise Jacques, he would resign."

Yes, indeed, M. Magloire was an honorable man, and quite accessible to tender sentiments; for he felt very reluctant to go and see the prisoner, charged as he was with an odious crime, and, as he thought, justly charged,—a man who had been his friend, and whom, in spite of all, he could not help loving still.

He could not sleep for it that night; and noticed his anxious air as he crossed the street next morning on his way to the jail. Blangin the keeper was on the lookout for him, and cried,—

"Ah, come quick, sir! The accused is devoured with impatience."

Slowly, and his heart beating furiously, the famous advocate went up the narrow stairs. He crossed the long passage; Blangin opened a door; he was in Jacques de Boiscoran's cell.

"At last you are coming," exclaimed the unhappy young man, throwing himself on the lawyer's neck. "At last I see an honest face, and hold a trusty hand. Ah! I have suffered cruelly, so cruelly, that I am surprised my mind has not given way. But now you are here, you are by my side, I am safe."

The lawyer could not speak. He was terrified by the havoc which grief had made of the noble and intelligent face of his friend. He was shocked at the distortion of his features, the unnatural brilliancy of his eyes, and the convulsive laugh on his lips.

"Poor man!" he murmured at last.

Jacques misunderstood him: he stepped back, as white as the walls of his cell.

"You do not think me guilty?" he exclaimed.

An inexpressibly sad expression convulsed his features.

"To be sure," he went on with his terrible convulsive laughter, "the charges must be overwhelming indeed, if they have convinced my best friends. Alas! why did I refuse to speak that first day? My honor!—what a phantom! And still, victimized as I am by an infamous conspiracy, I should still refuse to speak, if my life alone were at stake. But my honor is at stake. Dionysia's honor, the honor of the Boiscorans. I shall speak. You, M. Magloire, shall know the truth, you shall see my innocence in a word."

And, seizing M. Magloire's hand, he pressed it almost painfully, as he added in a hoarse voice,—

"One word will explain the whole thing to you: I was the lover of the Countess Claudieuse!"

XIII.

If he had been less distressed, Jacques de Boiscoran would have seen how wisely he had acted in choosing for his defender the great advocate of Sauveterre. A stranger, M. Folgat, for instance, would have heard him silently, and would have seen in the revelation nothing but the fact without giving it a personal value. In M. Magloire, on the contrary, he saw what the whole country would feel. And M. Magloire, when he heard him declare that the Countess Claudieuse had been his mistress, looked indignant, and exclaimed,—

"That is impossible."

At least Jacques was not surprised. He had been the first to say that they would refuse to believe him when he should speak; and this conviction had largely influenced him in keeping silence so long.

"It is impossible, I know," he said; "and still it is so."

"Give me proofs!" said M. Magloire.

"I have no proofs."

The melancholy and sympathizing expression of the great lawyer changed instantly. He sternly glanced at the prisoner, and his eye spoke of amazement and indignation.

"There are things," he said, "which it is rash to affirm when one is not able to support them with proof. Consider"—

"My situation forces me to tell all."

"Why, then, did you wait so long?"

"I hoped I should be spared such a fearful extremity."

"By whom?"

"By the countess."

M. Magloire's face became darker and darker.

"I am not often accused of partiality," he said. "Count Claudieuse is, perhaps, the only enemy I have in this country; but he is a bitter, fierce enemy. To keep me out of the chamber, and to prevent my obtaining many votes, he stooped to acts unworthy of a gentleman. I do not like him. But in justice I must say that I look upon the countess as the loftiest, the purest, and noblest type of the woman, the wife, and the mother."

A bitter smile played on Jacques's lips.

"And still I have been her lover," he said.

"When? How? The countess lived at Valpinson: you lived in Paris."

"Yes; but every year the countess came and spent the month of September in Paris; and I came occasionally to Boiscoran."

"It is very singular that such an intrigue should never have been suspected even."

"We managed to take our precautions."

"And no one ever suspected any thing?"

"No one."

But Jacques was at last becoming impatient at the attitude assumed by M. Magloire. He forgot that he had foreseen all the suspicions to which he found now he was exposed.

"Why do you ask all these questions?" he said. "You do not believe me. Well, be it so! Let me at least try to convince you. Will you listen to me?"

M. Magloire drew up a chair, and sitting down, not as usually, but across the chair, and resting his arms on the back, he said,—

"I listen."

Jacques de Boiscoran, who had been almost livid, became crimson with anger. His eyes flashed wrath. That he, he should be treated thus! Never had all the haughtiness of M. Galpin offended him half as much as this cool, disdainful condescension on the part of M. Magloire. It occurred to him to order him out of his room. But what then? He was condemned to drain the bitter cup to the very dregs: for he must save himself; he must get out of this abyss.

"You are cruel, Magloire," he said in a voice of ill-suppressed indignation, "and you make me feel all the horrors of my situation to the full. Ah, do not apologize! It does not matter. Let me speak."

He walked up and down a few times in his cell, passing his hand repeatedly over his brow, as if to recall his memory. Then he began, in a calmer tone of voice,—

"It was in the first days of the month of August, in 1866, and at Boiscoran, where I was on a visit to my uncle, that I saw the Countess Claudieuse for the first time. Count Claudieuse and my uncle were, at that time, on very bad terms with each other, thanks to that unlucky little stream which crosses our estates; and a common friend, M. de Besson, had undertaken to reconcile them at a dinner to which he had invited both. My uncle had taken me with him. The countess had come with her husband. I was just twenty years old; she was twenty-six. When I saw her, I was overcome. It seemed to me that I had never in all my life met a woman so perfectly beautiful and graceful; that I had never seen so charming a face, such beautiful eyes, and such a sweet smile.

"She did not seem to notice me. I did not speak to her; and still I felt within me a kind of presentiment that this woman would play a great, a fatal part in my life.

"This impression was so strong, that, as we left the house, I could not keep from mentioning it to my uncle. He only laughed, and said that I was a fool, and that, if my existence should ever be troubled by a woman, it would certainly not be by the Countess Claudieuse.

"He was apparently right. It was hard to imagine that any thing should ever again bring me in contact with the countess. M. de Besson's attempt at reconciliation had utterly failed; the countess lived at Valpinson; and I went back to Paris.

"Still I was unable to shake off the impression; and the memory of the dinner at M. de Besson's house was still in my mind, when a month later, at a party at my mother's brother's, M. de Chalusse, I thought I recognized the Countess Claudieuse. It was she. I bowed, and, seeing that she recognized me, I went up to her, trembling, and she allowed me to sit down by her.

"She told me then that she had come up to Paris for a month, as she did every year, and that she was staying at her father's, the Marquis de Tassar. She had come to this party much against her inclination, as she disliked going out. She did not dance; and thus I talked to her till the moment when she left.

"I was madly in love when we parted; and still I made no effort to see her again. It was mere chance again which brought us together.

"One day I had business at Melun, and, reaching the station rather late, I had but just time to jump into the nearest car. In the compartment was the countess. She told me—and that is all I ever recollected of the conversation—that she was on her way to Fontainebleau to see a friend, with whom she spent every Tuesday and Saturday. Usually she took the nine o'clock train.

"This was on a Tuesday; and during the next three days a great struggle went on in my heart. I was desperately in love with the countess, and still I was afraid of her. But my evil star conquered; and the next Saturday, at nine o'clock, I was at the station again.

"The countess has since confessed to me that she expected me. When she saw me, she made a sign; and, when they opened the doors, I managed to find a place by her side."

M. Magloire had for some minutes given signs of great impatience; now he broke forth,—

"This is too improbable!"

At first Jacques de Boiscoran made no reply. It was no easy task for a man, tried as he had been of late, to stir up thus the ashes of the past; and it made him shudder. He was amazed at seeing on his lips this secret which he had so long buried in his innermost heart. Besides, he had loved, loved in good earnest; and his love had been returned. And there are certain sensations which come to us only once in life, and which can never again be effaced. He was moved to tears. But as the eminent advocate of Sauveterre repeated his words, and even added,—

"No, it is not credible!"

"I do not ask you to believe me," he said gently: "I only ask you to hear me."

And, overcoming with all his energy the kind of torpor which was mastering him, he continued,—

"This trip to Fontainebleau decided our fate. Other trips followed. The countess spent her days with her friend, and I passed the long hours in roaming through the woods. But in the evening we met again at the station. We took a *coupe*, which I had engaged beforehand, and I accompanied her in a carriage to her father's house.

"Finally, one evening, she left her friend's house at the usual hour; but she did not return to her father's house till the day after."

"Jacques!" broke in M. Magloire, shocked, as if he had heard a curse,—"Jacques!"

M. de Boiscoran remained unmoved.

"Oh!" he said, "I know you must think it strange. You fancy that there is no excuse for the man who betrays the confidence of a woman who has once given herself to him. Wait, before you judge me."

And he went on, in a firmer tone of voice,—

"At that time I thought I was the happiest man on earth; and my heart was full of the most absurd vanity at the thought that she was mine, this beautiful woman, whose purity was high above all calumny. I had tied around my neck one of those fatal ropes which death alone can sever, and, fool that I was, I considered myself happy.

"Perhaps she really loved me at that time. At least she did not hesitate, and, overcome by the only real great passion of her life, she told me all that was in her innermost heart. At that time she did not think yet of protecting herself against me, and of making me her slave. She told me the secret of her marriage, which had at one time created such a sensation in the whole country.

"When her father, the Marquis de Brissac, had given up his place, he had soon begun to feel his inactivity weigh upon him, and at the same time he had become impatient at the narrowness of his means. He had ventured upon hazardous speculations. He had lost every thing he had; and even his honor was at stake. In his despair he was thinking of suicide, when chance brought to his house a former comrade, Count Claudieuse. In a moment of confidence, the marquis confessed every thing; and the other had promised to rescue him, and save him from disgrace. That was noble and grand. It must have cost an immense sum. And the friends of our youth who are capable of rendering us such services are rare in our day. Unfortunately, Count Claudieuse could not all the time be the hero he had been at first. He saw Genevieve de Tassar. He was struck with her beauty; and overcome by a sudden passion—forgetting that she was twenty, while he was nearly fifty—he made his friend aware that he was still willing to render him all the services in his power, but that he desired to obtain Genevieve's hand in return.

"That very evening the ruined nobleman entered his daughter's room, and, with tears in his eyes, explained to her his terrible situation. She did not hesitate a moment.

"'Above all,' she said to her father, 'let us save our honor, which even your death would not restore. Count Claudieuse is cruel to forget that he is thirty years older than I am. From this moment I hate and despise him. Tell him I am willing to be his wife.'

"And when her father, overcome with grief, told her that the count would never accept her hand in this form, she replied,—

"'Oh, do not trouble yourself about that! I shall do the thing handsomely, and your friend shall have no right to complain. But I know what I am worth; and you must remember hereafter, that, whatever service he may render you, you owe him nothing.'

"Less than a fortnight after this scene, Genevieve had allowed the count to perceive that he was not indifferent to her and a month later she became his wife.

"The count, on his side, had acted with the utmost delicacy and tact; so that no one suspected the cruel position of the Marquis de Tassar. He had placed two hundred thousand francs in his hands to settle his most pressing debts. In his marriage-contract he had acknowledged having received with his wife a dower of the same amount; and finally, he had bound himself to pay to his father-in-law and his wife an annual income of ten thousand francs. This had absorbed more than half of all he possessed."

M. Magloire no longer thought of protesting. Sitting stiffly on his chair, his eyes wide open, like a man who asks himself whether he is asleep or awake, he murmured,—

"That is incomprehensible! That is unheard of!"

Jacques was becoming gradually excited. He went on,—

"This is, at least, what the countess told me in her first hours of enthusiasm. But she told it to me calmly, coldly, like a thing that was perfectly natural. 'Certainly,' she said, 'Count Claudieuse has never had to regret the bargain he made. If he has been generous, I have been faithful. My father owes his life to him; but I have given him years of happiness to which he was not entitled. If he has received no love, he has had all the appearance of it, and an appearance far more pleasant than the reality.'

"When I could not conceal my astonishment, she added, laughing heartily,—

"'Only I brought to the bargain a mental reservation. I reserved to myself the right to claim my share of earthly happiness whenever it should come within my reach. That share is yours, Jacques; and do not fancy that I am troubled by remorse. As long as my husband thinks he is happy, I am within the terms of the contract.'

"That was the way she spoke at that time, Magloire; and a man of more experience would have been frightened. But I was a child; I loved her with all my heart. I admired her genius; I was overcome by her sophisms.

"A letter from Count Claudieuse aroused us from our dreams.

"The countess had committed the only and the last imprudence of her whole life: she had remained three weeks longer in Paris than was agreed upon; and her impatient husband threatened to come for her.

"'I must go back to Valpinson,' she said; 'for there is nothing I would not do to keep up the reputation I have managed to make for myself. My life, your life, my daughter's life—I would give them all, without hesitation, to protect my reputation.'

"This happened—ah! the dates have remained fixed in my mind as if engraven on bronze—on the 12th October.

"'I cannot remain longer than a month,' she said to me, 'without seeing you. A month from to-day, that is to say, on 12th November, at three o'clock precisely, you must be in the forest of Rochepommier, at the Red Men's Cross-roads. I will be there.'

"And she left Paris. I was in such a state of depression, that I scarcely felt the pain of parting. The thought of being loved by such a woman filled me with extreme pride, and, no doubt, saved me from many an excess. Ambition was rising within me whenever I thought of her. I wanted to work, to distinguish myself, to become eminent in some way.

"'I want her to be proud of me,' I said to myself, ashamed at being nothing at my age but the son of a rich father.'"

Ten times, at least, M. Magloire had risen from his chair, and moved his lips, as if about to make some objection. But he had pledged himself, in his own mind, not to interrupt Jacques, and he did his best to keep his pledge.

"In the meantime," Jacques went on, "the day fixed by the countess was drawing near. I went down to Boiscoran; and on the appointed day, at the precise hour, I was in the forest at the Red Men's Cross-roads. I was somewhat behind time, and I was extremely sorry for it: but I did not know the forest very well, and the place chosen by the countess for the rendezvous is in the very thickest part of the old wood. The weather was unusually severe for the season. The night before, a heavy snow had fallen: the paths were all white; and a sharp wind blew the flakes from the heavily-loaded branches. From afar off, I distinguished the countess, as she was walking, up and down in a kind of feverish excitement, confining herself to a narrow space, where the ground was dry, and where she was sheltered from the wind by enormous masses of stone. She wore a dress of dark-red silk, very long, a cloak trimmed with fur, and a velvet hat to match her dress. In three minutes I was by her side. But she did not draw her hand from her muff to offer it to me; and, without giving me time to apologize for the delay, she said in a dry tone,—

"'When did you reach Boiscoran?'

"'Last night.'

"'How childish you are!' she exclaimed, stamping her foot. 'Last night! And on what pretext?'

"'I need no pretext to visit my uncle.'

"'And was he not surprised to see you drop from the clouds at this time of the year?'

"'Why, yes, a little,' I answered foolishly, incapable as I was of concealing the truth.

"Her dissatisfaction increased visibly.

"'And how did you get here?' she commenced again. 'Did you know this cross-road?'

"'No, I inquired about it.'

"'From whom?'

"'From one of my uncle's servants; but his information was so imperfect, that I lost my way.'

"She looked at me with such a bitter, ironical smile, that I stopped.

"'And all that, you think, is very simple,' she broke in. 'Do you really imagine people will think it very natural that you should thus fall like a bombshell upon Boiscoran, and immediately set out for the Red Men's Cross-roads in the forest? Who knows but you have been followed? Who knows but behind one of these trees there may be eyes even now watching us?'

"And as she looked around with all the signs of genuine fear, I answered,—

"'And what do you fear? Am I not here?'

"I think I can even now see the look in her eyes as she said,—

"'I fear nothing in the world—do you hear me? nothing in the world, except being suspected; for I cannot be compromised. I like to do as I do; I like to have a lover. But I do not want it to be known; because, if it became known, there would be mischief. Between my reputation and my life I have no choice. If I were to be surprised here by any one, I would rather it should be my husband than a stranger. I have no love for the count, and I shall never forgive him for having married me; but he has saved my father's honor, and I owe it to him to keep his honor unimpaired. He is my husband, besides, and the father of my child: I bear his name, and I want it to be respected. I should die with grief and shame and rage, if I had to give my arm to a man at whom people might look and smile. Wives are absurdly stupid when they do not feel that all the scorn with which their unfortunate husbands are received in the great world falls back upon them. No. I do not love the count, Jacques, and I love you. But remember, that, between him and you, I should not hesitate a moment, and that I should sacrifice your life and your honor, with a smile on my lips, even though my heart should break, if I could, by doing so, spare him the shadow of a suspicion.'

"I was about to reply; but she said,—

"'No more! Every minute we stay here increases the danger. What pretext will you plead for your sudden appearance at Boiscoran?'

"'I do not know,' I replied.

"'You must borrow some money from your uncle, a considerable sum, to pay your debts. He will be angry, perhaps; but that will explain your sudden fancy for travelling in the month of November. Good-by, good-by!'

"All amazed, I cried,—

"'What! You will not let me see you again, at least from afar?'

"'During this visit that would be the height of imprudence. But, stop! Stay at Boiscoran till Sunday. Your uncle never stays away from high mass: go with him to church. But be careful, control yourself. A single imprudence, one blunder, and I should despise you. Now we must part. You will find in Paris a letter from me.'"

Jacques paused here, looking to read in M. Magloire's face what impression his recital had produced so far. But the famous lawyer remained impassive. He sighed, and continued,—

"I have entered into all these details, Magloire, because I want you to know what kind of a woman the countess is, so that you may understand her conduct. You see that she did not treat me like a traitor: she had given me fair warning, and shown me the abyss into which I was going to fall. Alas! so far from being terrified, these dark sides of her character only attracted me the more. I admired her imperious air, her courage, and her prudence, even her total lack of principle, which contrasted so strangely with her fear of public opinion. I said to myself with foolish pride,—

"'She certainly is a superior woman!'

"She must have been pleased with my obedience at church; for I managed to check even a slight trembling which seized me when I saw her and bowed to her as she passed so close to me that my hand touched her dress. I obeyed her in other ways also. I asked my uncle for six thousand francs, and he gave them to me, laughing; for he was the most generous man on earth: but he said at the same time,—

"'I thought you had not come to Boiscoran merely for the purpose of exploring the forest of Rochepommier.'

"This trifling circumstance increased my admiration for the Countess Claudieuse. How well she had foreseen my uncle's astonishment, when I had not even dreamed of it!

"'She has a genius for prudence,' I thought.

"Yes, indeed she had a genius for it, and a genius for calculation also, as I soon found out. When I reached Paris, I found a letter from her waiting for me; but it was nothing more than a repetition of all she had told me at our meeting. This letter was followed by several others, which she begged me to keep for her sake, and which all had a number in the upper corner.

"The first time I saw her again, I asked her,—

"'What are these numbers?'

"'My dear Jacques,' she replied, 'a woman ought always to know how many letters she has written to her lover. Up to now, you must have had nine.'

"This occurred in May, 1867, at Rochefort, where she had gone to be present at the launching of a frigate, and where I had followed her, at her suggestion, with a view to spending a few hours in each other's company. Like a fool, I laughed at the idea of this epistolary responsibility, and then I thought no more of it. I was at that time too busy otherwise. She had recalled to me the fact that time was passing, in spite of the sadness of our separation, and that the month of September, the month of her freedom, was drawing near. Should we be compelled again, like the year before, to resort to these perilous trips to Fontainebleau? Why not get a house in a remote quarter of town?

"Every wish of hers was an order for me. My uncle's liberality knew no end. I bought a house."

At last in the midst of all of Jacques's perplexities, there appeared a circumstance which might furnish tangible evidence.

M. Magloire started, and asked eagerly,—

"Ah, you bought a house?"

"Yes, a nice house with a large garden, in Vine Street, Passy."

"And you own it still?"

"Yes."

"Of course you have the title-papers?"

- 231 -

Jacques looked in despair.

"Here, again, fate is against me. There is quite a tale connected with that house."

The features of the Sauveterre lawyer grew dark again, much quicker than they had brightened up just now.

"Ah!" he said,—"a tale, ah!"

"I was scarcely of age," resumed Jacques, "when I wanted to purchase this house. I dreaded difficulties. I was afraid my father might hear of it; in fine, I wanted to be as prudent as the countess was. I asked, therefore, one of my English friends, Sir Francis Burnett, to purchase it in his name. He agreed; and he handed me, with the necessary bills of sale, also a paper in which he acknowledged my right as proprietor."

"But then"—

"Oh! wait a moment. I did not take these papers to my rooms in my father's house. I put them into a drawer of a bureau in my house at Passy. When the war broke out, I forgot them. I had left Paris before the siege began, you know, being in command of a company of volunteers from this department. During the two sieges, my house was successively occupied by the National Guards, the soldiers of the Commune, and the regular troops. When I got back there, I found the four walls pierced with holes by the shells; but all the furniture had disappeared, and with it the papers."

"And Sir Francis Burnett?"

"He left France at the beginning of the invasion; and I do not know what has become of him. Two friends of his in England, to whom I wrote, replied,—the one that he was probably in Australia; the other that he was dead."

"And you have taken no other steps to secure your rights to a piece of property which legally belongs to you?"

"No, not till now."

"You mean to say virtually that there is in Paris a house which has no owner, is forgotten by everybody, and unknown even to the tax-gatherer?"

"I beg your pardon! The taxes have always been regularly paid; and the whole neighborhood knows that I am the owner. But the individuality is not the same. I have unceremoniously assumed the identity of my friend. In the eyes of the neighbors, the small dealers near by, the workmen and contractors whom I have employed, for the servants and the gardener, I am Sir Francis Burnett. Ask them about Jacques de Boiscoran, and they will tell you, 'Don't know.' Ask them about Sir Francis Burnett, and they will answer, 'Oh, very well!' and they will give you my portrait."

M. Magloire shook his head as if he were not fully convinced.

"Then," he asked again, "you declare that the Countess Claudieuse has been at this house?"

"More than fifty times in three years."

"If that is so, she must be known there."

"No."

"But"—

"Paris is not like Sauveterre, my dear friend; and people are not solely occupied with their neighbors' doings. Vine Street is quite a deserted street; and the countess took the greatest precautions in coming and going."

"Well, granted, as far as the outside world is concerned. But within? You must have had somebody to stay in the house and keep it in order when you were away, and to wait upon you when you were there?"

"I had an English maid-servant."

"Well, this girl must know the countess?"

"She has never caught a glimpse of her even."

"Oh!"

"When the countess was coming down, or when she was going away, or when we wanted to walk in the garden, I sent the girl on some errand. I have sent her as far as Orleans to get rid of her for twenty-four hours. The rest of the time we staid up stairs, and waited upon ourselves."

Evidently M. Magloire was suffering. He said,—

"You must be under a mistake. Servants are curious, and to hide from them is only to make them mad with curiosity. That girl has watched you. That girl has found means to see the countess when she came there. She must be examined. Is she still in your service?"

"No, she left me when the war broke out."

"Why?"

"She wanted to return to England."

"Then we cannot hope to find her again?"

"I believe not."

"We must give it up, then. But your man-servant? Old Anthony was in your confidence. Did you never tell him any thing about it?"

"Never. Only once I sent for him to come to Vine Street when I had sprained my foot in coming down stairs."

"So that it is impossible for you to prove that the Countess Claudieuse ever came to your house in Passy? You have no evidence of it, and no eye-witness?"

"I used to have evidence. She had brought a number of small articles for her private use; but they have disappeared during the war."

"Ah, yes!" said M. Magloire, "always the war! It has to answer for every thing."

Never had any of M. Galpin's examinations been half as painful to Jacques de Boiscoran as this series of quick questions, which betrayed such distressing incredulity.

"Did I not tell you, Magloire," he resumed, "that the countess had a genius for prudence? You can easily conceal yourself when you can spend money without counting it. Would you blame me for not having any proofs to furnish? Is it not the duty of every man of honor to do all he can to keep even a shadow of suspicion from her who has confided herself to his hands? I have done my duty, and whatever may come of it, I shall not regret it. Could I foresee such unheard-of emergencies? Could I foresee that a day might come when I, Jacques de Boiscoran, should have to denounce the Countess Claudieuse, and should be compelled to look for evidence and witnesses against her?"

The eminent advocate of Sauveterre looked aside; and, instead of replying, he said in a somewhat changed voice,—

"Go on, Jacques, go on!"

Jacques de Boiscoran tried to overcome the discouragement which well-nigh mastered him, and said,—

"It was on the 2d September, 1867, that the Countess Claudieuse for the first time entered this house in Passy, which I had purchased and furnished for her; and during the five weeks which she spent in Paris, she came almost every day, and spent several hours there.

"At her father's house she enjoyed absolute and almost uncontrolled independence. She left her daughter—for she had at that time but one child—with her mother, the Marchioness de Tassar; and she was free to go and to come as she liked.

"When she wanted still greater freedom, she went to see her friend in Fontainebleau; and every time she did this she secured twenty-four or forty-eight hours over and above the time for the journey. I, for my part, was as perfectly free from all control. Ostensibly, I had gone to Ireland; in reality, I lived in Vine Street.

"These five weeks passed like a dream; and yet I must confess, the parting was not as painful as might have been supposed. Not that the bright prism was broken; but I always felt humiliated by the necessity of being concealed. I began to be tired of these incessant precautions; and I was quite ready to give up being Sir Francis Burnett, and to resume my identity.

"We had, besides, promised each other never to remain a month without seeing each other, at least for a few hours; and she had invented a number of expedients by which we could meet without danger.

"A family misfortune came just then to our assistance. My father's eldest brother, that kind uncle who had furnished me the means to purchase my house in Passy, died, and left me his entire fortune. As owner of Boiscoran, I could, henceforth, live as much as I chose in the province; and at all events come there whenever I liked, without anybody's inquiring for my reasons."

XIV.

Jacques de Boiscoran was evidently anxious to have done with his recital, to come to that night of the fire at Valpinson, and to learn at last from the eminent advocate of Sauveterre what he had to fear or to hope. After a moment's silence, for his breath was giving out, and after a few steps across his cell, he went on in a bitter tone of voice,—

"But why trouble you with all these details, Magloire? Would you believe me any more than you do now, if I were to enumerate to you all my meetings with the Countess Claudieuse, or if I were to repeat all her most trifling words?

"We had gradually learnt to calculate all our movements, and made our preparations so accurately, that we met constantly, and feared no danger. We said to each other at parting, or she wrote to me, 'On such a day, at such an hour, at such a place;' and however distant the day, or the hour, or the place, we were sure to meet. I had soon learned to know the country as well as the cleverest of poachers; and nothing was so useful to us as this familiarity with all the unknown hiding-places. The countess, on her side, never let three months pass by without discovering some urgent motive which carried her to Rochelle, to Angouleme, or to Paris; and I was there to meet her. Nothing kept her from these excursions; even when indisposed, she braved the fatigues of the journey. It is true, my life was well-nigh spent in travelling; and at any moment, when least expected, I disappeared for whole weeks. This will explain to you that restlessness at which my father sneered, and for which you, yourself, Magloire, used to blame me."

"That is true," replied the latter. "I remember."

Jacques de Boiscoran did not seem to notice the encouragement.

"I should not tell the truth if I were to say that this kind of life was unpleasant to me. Mystery and danger always add to the charms of love. The difficulties only increased my passion. I saw something sublime in this success with which two superior beings devoted all their intelligence and cleverness to the carrying-on of a secret intrigue. The more fully I became aware of the veneration with which the countess was looked up to by the whole country, the more I learned to appreciate her ability in dissembling and her profound perversity; and I was all the more proud of her. I felt the pride setting my cheeks aglow when I saw her at Brechy; for I came there every Sunday for her sake alone, to see her pass calm and serene in the imposing security of her lofty reputation. I laughed at the simplicity of all these honest, good people, who bowed so low to her, thinking they saluted a saint; and I congratulated myself with idiotic delight at being the only one who knew the true Countess Claudieuse,—she who took her revenge so bravely in our house in Passy!

"But such delights never last long.

"It had not taken me long to find out that I had given myself a master, and the most imperious and exacting master that ever lived. I had almost ceased to belong to myself. I had become her property; and I lived and breathed and thought and acted for her alone. She did not mind my tastes and my dislikes. She wished a thing, and that was enough. She wrote to me, 'Come!' and I had to be instantly on the spot: she said to me, 'Go!' an I had to leave at once. At first I accepted these evidences of her despotism with joy; but gradually I became tired of this perpetual abdication of my own will. I disliked to have no control over myself, to be unable to dispose of twenty-four hours in advance. I began to feel the pressure of the halter around my neck. I thought of flight. One of my friends was to set out on a voyage around the world, which was to last eighteen months or two years, and I had an idea of accompanying him. There was nothing to retain me. I was, by fortune and position, perfectly independent. Why should I not carry out my plan?

"Ah, why? The prism was not broken yet. I cursed the tyranny of the countess; but I still trembled when I heard her name mentioned. I thought of escaping from her; but a single glance moved me to the bottom of my heart. I was bound to her by the thousand tender threads of habit and of complicity,—those threads which seem to be more delicate than gossamer, but which are harder to break than a ship's cable.

"Still, this idea which had occurred to me brought it about that I uttered for the first time the word 'separation' in her presence, asking her what she would do if I should leave her. She looked at me with a strange air and asked me, after a moment's hesitation,—

"'Are you serious? Is it a warning?'

"I dared not carry matters any farther, and, making an effort to smile, I said,—

"'It is only a joke.'

"'Then,' she said, 'let us not say any thing more about it. If you should ever come to that, you would soon see what I would do.'

"I did not insist; but that look remained long in my memory, and made me feel that I was far more closely bound than I had thought. From that day it became my fixed idea to break with her."

"Well, you ought to have made an end of it," said Magloire.

Jacques de Boiscoran shook his head.

"That is easily said," he replied. "I tried it; but I could not do it. Ten times I went to her, determined to say, 'Let us part;' and ten times, at the last moment, my courage failed me. She irritated me. I almost began to hate her; but I could not forget how much I had loved her, and how much she had risked for my sake. Then—why should I not confess it?—I was afraid of her.

"This inflexible character, which I had so much admired, terrified me; and I shuddered, seized with vague and sombre apprehensions, when I thought what she was capable of doing. I was thus in the utmost perplexity, when my mother spoke to me of a match which she had long hoped for. This might be the pretext which I had so far failed to find. At all events, I asked for time to consider; and, the first time I saw the countess again, I gathered all my courage, and said to her,—

"'Do you know what has happened? My mother wants me to marry.'

"She turned as pale as death; and looking me fixedly in the eyes, as if wanting to read my innermost thoughts, she asked,—

"'And you, what do you want?'

"'I,' I replied with a forced laugh,—'I want nothing just now. But the thing will have to be done sooner or later. A man must have a home, affections which the world acknowledges'—

"'And I,' she broke in; 'what am I to you?'

"'You,' I exclaimed, 'you, Genevieve! I love you with all the strength of my heart. But we are separated by a gulf: you are married.'

"She was still looking at me fixedly.

"'In other words,' she said, 'you have loved me as a pastime. I have been the amusement of your youth, the poetry of twenty years, that love-romance which every man wants to have. But you are becoming serious; you want sober affections, and you leave me. Well, be it so. But what is to become of me when you are married?'

"I was suffering terribly.

"'You have your husband,' I stammered, 'your children'—

"She stopped me.

"'Yes,' she said. 'I shall go back go live at Valpinson, in that country full of associations, where every place recalls a rendezvous. I shall live with my husband, whom I have betrayed; with daughters, one of whom—That cannot be, Jacques.'

"I had a fit of courage.

"'Still,' I said, 'I may have to marry. What would you do?'

"'Oh! very little,' she replied. 'I should hand all your letters to Count Claudieuse.'"

During the thirty years which he had spent at the bar, M. Magloire had heard many a strange confession; but never in his life had all his ideas been overthrown as in this case.

"That is utterly confounding," he murmured.

But Jacques went on,—

"Was this threat of the countess meant in earnest? I did not doubt it; but affecting great composure, I said,—

"'You would not do that.'

"'By all that I hold dear and sacred in this world,' she replied, 'I would do it.'

"Many months have passed by since that scene, Magloire, many events have happened; and still I feel as if it had taken place yesterday. I see the countess still, whiter than a ghost. I still hear her trembling voice; and I can repeat to you her words almost literally,—

"'Ah! you are surprised at my determination, Jacques. I understand that. Wives who have betrayed their husbands have not accustomed their lovers to be held responsible by them. When they are betrayed, they dare not cry out; when they are abandoned, they submit; when they are sacrificed, they hide their tears, for to cry would be to avow their wrong. Who would pity them, besides? Have they not received their well-known punishment? Hence it is that all men agree, and there are some of them cynical enough to confess it, that a married woman is a convenient lady-love, because she can never be jealous, and she may be abandoned at any time. Ah! we women are great cowards. If we had more courage, you men would look twice before you would dare speak of love to a married woman. But what no one dares I will dare. It shall not be said that in our common fault there are two parts, and that you shall have had all the benefit of it, and that I must bear all the punishment. What? You might be free to-morrow to console yourself with a new love; and I—I should have to sink under my shame and remorse. No, no! Such bonds as those that bind us, riveted by long years of complicity, are not broken so easily.

"'You belong to me; you are mine; and I shall defend you against all and every one, with such arms as I possess. I told you that I valued my reputation more than my life; but I never told you that I valued life. On the eve of your wedding-day, my husband shall know all. I shall not survive the loss of my honor; but at least I shall have my revenge. If you escape the hatred of Count Claudieuse, your name will be bound up with such a tragic affair that your life will be ruined forever.'

"That was the way she spoke, Magloire, and with a passion of which I can give you no idea. It was absurd, it was insane, I admit. But is not all passion absurd and insane? Besides, it was by no means a sudden inspiration of her pride, which made her threaten me with such vengeance. The precision of her phrases, the accuracy of her words, all made me feel that she had long meditated such a blow, and carefully calculated the effect of every word.

"I was thunderstruck.

"And as I kept silence for some time, she asked me coldly,—

"'Well?'

"I had to gain time, first of all.

"'Well,' I said, 'I cannot understand your passion. This marriage which I mentioned has never existed as yet, except in my mother's imagination.'

"'True?' she asked.

"'I assure you.'

"She examined me with suspicious eyes. At last she said,—

"'Well, I believe you. But now you are warned: let us think no more of such horrors.'

"She might think no more of them, but I could not.

"I left her with fury in my heart.

"She had evidently settled it all. I had for lifetime this halter around my neck, which held me tighter day by day and, at the slightest effort to free myself, I must be prepared for a terrible scandal; for one of those overwhelming adventures which destroy a man's whole life. Could I ever hope to make her listen to reason? No, I was quite sure I could not.

"I knew but too well that I should lose my time, if I were to recall to her that I was not quite as guilty as she would make me out; if I were to show her that her vengeance would fall less upon myself than upon her husband and her children; and that, although she might blame the count for the conditions of their marriage, her daughters, at least, were innocent.

"I looked in vain for an opening out of this horrible difficulty. Upon my honor, Magloire, there were moments when I thought I would pretend getting married, for the purpose of inducing the countess to act, and of bringing upon myself these threats which were hanging over me. I fear no danger; but I cannot bear to know it to exist, and to wait for it with folded hands: I must go forth and meet it.

"The thought that the countess should use her husband for the purpose of keeping me bound shocked me. It seemed to me ridiculous and ignoble that she should make her husband the guardian of her love. Did she think I was afraid of her?

"In the meantime, my mother had asked me what was the result of my reflections on the subject of marriage; and I blushed with shame as I told her that I was not disposed to marry as yet, as I felt too young to accept the responsibility of a family. It was so; but, under other circumstances, I should hardly have put in that plea. I was thus hesitating, and thinking how and when I should be able to make an end of it, when the war broke out. I felt naturally bound to offer my services. I hastened to Boiscoran. They had just organized the volunteers of the district; and they made me their captain. With them I joined the army of the Loire. In my state of mind, war had nothing fearful for me: every excitement was welcome that made me forget the past. There was, consequently, no merit in my courage. Nevertheless, as the weeks passed, and then the months, without my hearing a word about the Countess Claudieuse, I began secretly to hope that she had forgotten me; and that, time and absence doing their work, she was giving me up.

"When peace was made, I returned to Boiscoran; and the countess gave no more signs of life now than before. I began to feel reassured, and to recover possession of myself, when one day M. de Chandore invited me to dinner. I went. I saw Miss Dionysia.

"I had known her already for some time; and the recollection of her had, perhaps, had its influence upon my desire to quit the countess. Still I had always had self-control enough to avoid her lest I should draw some fatal vengeance upon her. When I was brought in contact with her by her grandfather, I had no longer the heart to avoid her; and, on the day on which I thought I read in her eyes that she loved me I made up my mind, and I resolved to risk every thing.

"But how shall I tell you what I suffered, Magloire, and with what anxiety I asked every evening when I returned to Boiscoran,—

"'No letter yet?'

"None came; and still it was impossible that the Countess Claudieuse should not have heard of my marriage. My father had called on M. de Chandore, and asked him for the hand of his grand-daughter for me. I had been publicly acknowledged as her betrothed; and nothing was now to be done but to fix the wedding-day.

"This silence frightened me."

Exhausted and out of breath, Jacque de Boiscoran paused here, pressing both of his hands on his chest, as if to check the irregular beating of his heart.

He was approaching the catastrophe.

And yet he looked in vain to the advocate for a word or a sign of encouragement. M. Magloire remained impenetrable: his face remained as impassive as an iron mask.

At last, with a great effort, Jacques resumed,—

"Yes, this calm frightened me more than a storm would have done. To win Dionysia's love was too great happiness. I expected a catastrophe, something terrible. I expected it with such absolute certainty, that I had actually made up my mind to confess every thing to M. de Chandore. You know him, Magloire. The old gentleman is the purest and brightest type of honor itself. I could intrust my secrets to him with as perfect safety as I formerly intrusted Genevieve's name to the night winds.

"Alas! why did I hesitate? why did I delay?

"One word might have saved me; and I should not be here, charged with an atrocious crime, innocent, and yet condemned to see how you doubt the truth of my words.

"But fate was against me.

"After having for a week postponed my confession every day to the next, one evening, after Dionysia and I had been talking of presentiments, I said to myself, 'To-morrow it shall be done.'

"The next morning, I went to Boiscoran much earlier than usual, and on foot, because I wanted to give some orders to a dozen workmen whom I employed in my vineyards. I took a short cut through the fields. Alas! not a single detail has escaped from my memory. When I had given my orders, I returned to the high road, and there met the priest from Brechy, who is a friend of mine.

"'You must,' he said, 'keep me company for a little distance. As you are on your way to Sauveterre, it will not delay you much to take the cross-road which passes by Valpinson and the forest of Rochepommier.'

"On what trifles our fate depends!

"I accompanied the priest, and only left him at the point where the high-road and the cross-road intersect. As soon as I was alone, I hastened on; and I was almost through the wood, when, all of a sudden, some twenty yards before me, I saw the Countess Claudieuse coming towards me. In spite of my emotion, I kept on my way, determined to bow to her, but to pass her without speaking. I did so, and had gone on a little distance, when I heard her call me,—

"'Jacques!'

"I stopped; or, rather, I was nailed to the spot by that voice which for a long time had held such entire control over my heart. She came up to me, looking even more excited than I was. Her lips trembled, and her eyes wandered to and fro.

"'Well,' she said, 'it is no longer a fancy: this time you marry Miss Chandore.'

"The time for half-measures had passed.

"'Yes,' I replied.

"'Then it is really true,' she said again. 'It is all over now. I suppose it would be in vain to remind you of those vows of eternal love which you used to repeat over and over again. Look down there under that old oak. They are the same trees, this is the same landscape, and I am still the same woman; but your heart has changed.'

"I made no reply.

"'You love her very much, do you?' she asked me.

"I kept obstinately silent.

"'I understand,' she said, 'I understand you but too well. And Dionysia? She loves you so much she cannot keep it to herself. She stops her friends to tell them all about her marriage, and to assure them of her happiness. Oh, yes, indeed, very happy! That love which was my disgrace is her honor. I was forced to conceal it like a crime: she can display it as a virtue. Social forms are, after all, very absurd and unjust; but a fool is he who tries to defy them.'

"Tears, the very first tears I had ever seen her shed, glittered in her long silky eyelashes.

"'And to be nothing more to you,—nothing at all! Ah, I was too cautious! Do you recollect the morning after your uncle's death, when you, now a rich man, proposed that we should flee? I refused; I clung to my reputation. I wanted to be respected. I thought it possible to divide life into two parts,—one to be devoted to pleasure; the other, to the hypocrisy of duty. Poor fool that I was! And still I discovered long ago that you were weary of me. I knew you so well! Your heart was like an open book to me, in which I read your most secret thoughts. Then I might have retained you. I ought to have been humble, obliging, submissive. Instead of that, I tried to command.

"'And you,' she said after a short pause,—'are you happy?'

"'I cannot be completely happy as long as I know that you are unhappy. But there is no sorrow which time does not heal. You will forget'—

"'Never!' she cried.

"And, lowering her voice, she added,—

"'Can I forget you? Alas! my crime is fearful; but the punishment is still more so.'

"People were coming down the road.

"'Compose yourself,' I said.

"She made an effort to control her emotion. The people passed us, saluting politely. And after a moment she said again,—

"'Well, and when is the wedding?'

"I trembled. She herself insisted upon an explanation.

"'No day has as yet been fixed,' I replied. 'Had I not to see you first? You uttered once grave threats.'

"'And you were afraid?'

"'No: I was sure I knew you too well to fear that you would punish me for having loved you, as if that had been a crime. So many things have happened since the day when you made those threats!'

"'Yes,' she replied, 'many things indeed! My poor father is incorrigible. Once more he has committed himself fearfully; and once more my husband has been compelled to sacrifice a large sum to save him. Ah, Count Claudieuse has a noble heart; and it is a great pity I should be the only one towards whom he has failed to show generosity. Every kindness which he shows me is a new grievance for me; but, having accepted them all, I have forfeited the right to strike him, as I had intended to do. You may marry Dionysia, Jacques; you have nothing to fear from me.'

"Ah! I had not hoped for so much, Magloire. Overcome with joy, I seized her hand, and raising it to my lips, I said,—

"'You are the kindest of friends.'

"But promptly, as if my lips had burnt her hand, she drew it back, and said, turning very pale,—

"'No, don't do that!'

"Then, overcoming her emotion to a certain degree, she added,—

"'But we must meet once more. You have my letters, I dare say.'

"'I have them all.'

"'Well, you must bring them to me. But where? And how? I can hardly absent myself at this time. My youngest daughter—our daughter, Jacques—is very ill. Still, an end must be made. Let us see, on Thursday—are you free then? Yes. Very well, then come on Thursday evening, towards nine o'clock, to Valpinson. You will find me at the edge of the wood, near the towers of the old castle, which my husband has repaired.'

"'Is that quite prudent?' I asked.

"'Have I ever left any thing to chance?' she replied, 'and would I be apt, at this time, to be imprudent? Rely on me. Come, we must part, Jacques. Thursday, and be punctual!'

"Was I really free? Was the chain really broken? And had I become once more my own master?

"I thought so, and in my almost delirious joy I forgave the countess all the anxieties of the last year. What do I say? I began to accuse myself of injustice and cruelty. I admired her for sacrificing herself to my happiness. I felt, in the fulness of my gratitude, like kneeling down, and kissing the hem of her dress.

"It had become useless now to confide my secret to M. de Chandore. I might have gone back to Boiscoran. But I was more than half-way; I kept on; and, when I reached Sauveterre, my face bore such evident trances of my relief, that Dionysia said to me,—

"'Something very pleasant must have happened to you, Jacques.'

"Oh, yes, very pleasant! For the first time, I breathed freely as I sat by her side. I could love her now, without fearing that my love might be fatal to her.

"This security did not last long. As I considered the matter, I thought it very singular that the countess should have chosen such a place for our meeting.

"'Can it be a trap?' I asked, as the day drew nearer.

"All day long on Thursday I had the most painful presentiments. If I had known how to let the countess know, I should certainly not have gone. But I had no means to send her word; and I knew her well enough to be sure that breaking my word would expose me to her full vengeance. I dined at the usual hour; and, when I had finished, I went up to my room, where I wrote to Dionysia not to expect me that evening, as I should be detained by a matter of the utmost importance.

"I handed the note to Michael, the son of one of my tenants, and told him to carry it to town without losing a minute. Then I tied up all of the countess's letters in a parcel, put it in my pocket, took my gun, and went out. It might have been eight o'clock; but it was still broad daylight."

Whether M. Magloire accepted every thing that the prisoner said as truth, or not, he was evidently deeply interested. He had drawn up his chair, and at every statement he uttered half-loud exclamations.

"Under any other circumstances," said Jacques, "I should have taken one of the two public roads in going to Valpinson. But troubled, as I was, by vague suspicions, I thought only of concealing myself and cut across the marshes. They were partly overflowed; but I counted upon my intimate familiarity with the ground, and my agility. I thought, moreover, that here I should certainly not be seen, and should meet no one. In this I was mistaken. When I reached the Seille Canal, and was just about to cross it, I found myself face to face with young Ribot, the son of a farmer at Brechy. He looked so very much surprised at seeing me in such a place, that I thought to give him some explanation; and, rendered stupid by my troubles, I told him I had business at Brechy, and was crossing the marshes to shoot some birds.

"'If that is so,' he replied, laughing, 'we are not after the same kind of game.'

"He went his way; but this accident annoyed me seriously. I continued on my way, swearing, I fear, at young Ribot, and found that the path became more and more dangerous. It was long past nine when I reached Valpinson at last. But the night was clear, and I became more cautious than ever.

"The place which the countess had chosen for our meeting was about two hundred yards from the house and the farm buildings, sheltered by other buildings, and quite close to the wood. I approached it through this wood.

"Hid among the trees, I was examining the ground, when I noticed the countess standing near one of the old towers: she wore a simple costume of light muslin, which could be seen at a distance. Finding every thing quiet, I went up to her; and, as soon as she saw me, she said,—

"'I have been waiting for you nearly an hour.'

"I explained to her the difficulties I had met with on my way there; and then I asked her,—

"'But where is your husband?'

"'He is laid up with rheumatism,' she replied.

"'Will he not wonder at your absence?'

"'No: he knows I am sitting up with my youngest daughter. I left the house through the little door of the laundry.'

"And, without giving me time to reply, she asked,—

"'Where are my letters?'

"'Here they are,' I said, handing them to her.

"She took them with feverish haste, saying in an undertone,—

"'There ought to be twenty-four.'

"And, without thinking of the insult, she went to work counting them.

"'They are all here,' she said when she had finished.

"Then, drawing a little package from her bosom, she added,—

"'And here are yours.'

"But she did not give them to me.

"'We'll burn them,' she said.

"I started with surprise.

"'You cannot think of it,' I cried, 'here, and at this hour. The fire would certainly be seen.'

"'What? Are you afraid? However, we can go into the wood. Come, give me some matches.'

"I felt in my pockets; but I had none.

"'I have no matches,' I said.

"'Oh, come!—you who smoke all day long,—you who, even in my presence, could never give up your cigars.'

"'I left my match-box, yesterday, at M. de Chandore's.'

"She stamped her foot vehemently.

"'Since that is so, I'll go in and get some.'

"This would have delayed us, and thus would have been an additional imprudence. I saw that I must do what she wanted, and so I said,—

"'That is not necessary. Wait!'

"All sportsmen know that there is a way to replace matches. I employed the usual means. I took a cartridge out of my gun, emptied it and its shot, and put in, instead a piece of paper. Then, resting my gun on the ground, so as to prevent a loud explosion, I made the powder flash up.

"We had fire, and put the letters to the flame.

"A few minutes later, and nothing was left of them but a few blackened fragments, which I crumbled in my hands, and scattered to the winds. Immovable, like a statue, the Countess Claudieuse had watched my operations.

"'And that is all,' she said, 'that remains of five years of our life, of our love, and of your vows,—ashes.'

"I replied by a commonplace remark. I was in a hurry to be gone.

"She felt this, and cried with great vehemence,—

"'Ah! I inspire you with horror.'

"'We have just committed a marvellous imprudence,' I said.

"'Ah! what does it matter?'

"Then, in a hoarse voice, she added,—

"'Happiness awaits you, and a new life full of intoxicating hopes: it is quite natural that you should tremble. I, whose life is ended, and who have nothing to look for,—I, in whom you have killed every hope,—I am not afraid.'

"I saw her anger rising within her, and said very quietly,—

"'I hope you do not repent of your generosity, Genevieve.'

"'Perhaps I do,' she replied, in an accent which made me tremble. 'How you must laugh at me! What a wretched thing a woman is who is abandoned, who resigns, and sheds tears!'

"Then she went on fiercely,—

"'Confess that you have never loved me really!'

"'Ah, you know very well the contrary!'

"'Still you abandon me for another,—for that Dionysia!'

"'You are married: you cannot be mine.'

"'Then if I were free—if I had been a widow'—

"'You would be my wife you know very well.'

"She raised her arms to heaven, like a drowning person; and, in a voice which I thought they could hear at the house, she cried,—

"'His wife! If I were a widow, I would be his wife! O God! Luckily, that thought, that terrible thought, never occurred to me before.'"

All of a sudden, at these words, the eminent advocate of Sauveterre rose from his chair, and, placing himself before Jacques de Boiscoran, he asked, looking at him with one of those glances which seem to pierce our innermost heart,—

"And then?"

Jacques had to summon all the energy that was left him to be able to continue with a semblance of calmness, at least,—

"Then I tried every thing in the world to quiet the countess, to move her, and bring her back to the generous feelings of former days. I was so completely upset that I hardly knew what I was saying. I hated her bitterly, and still I could not help pitying her. I am a man; and there is no man living who would not feel deeply moved at seeing himself the object of such bitter regrets and such terrible despair. Besides, my happiness and Dionysia's honor were at stake. How do I know what I said? I am not a hero of romance. No doubt I was mean. I humbled myself, I besought her, I told falsehoods, I vowed to her that it was my family, mainly, who made me marry. I hoped I should be able, by great kindness and caressing words, to soften the bitterness of the parting. She listened to me, remaining as impassive as a block of ice; and, when I paused, she said with a sinister laugh,—

"'And you tell me all that! Your Dionysia! Ah! if I were a woman like other women, I would say nothing to-day, and, before the year was over, you would again be at my feet.'

"She must have been thinking of our meeting at the cross-roads. Or was this the last outburst of passion at the moment when the last ties were broken off? I was going to speak again; but she interrupted me bruskly, saying,—

"'Oh, that is enough! Spare me, at least, the insult of your pity! I'll see. I promise nothing. Good-by!'

"And she escaped toward the house, while I remained rooted to the spot, almost stupefied, and asking myself if she was not, perhaps at that moment, telling Count Claudieuse every thing. It was at that moment that I drew from my gun, almost mechanically, the burnt cartridge and put in a fresh one. Then, as nothing stirred, I went off with rapid strides."

"What time was it?" asked M. Magloire.

"I could not tell you precisely. My state of mind was such, that I had lost all idea of time. I went back through the forest of Rochepommier."

"And you saw nothing?"

"No."

"Heard nothing?"

"Nothing."

"Still, from your statement, you could not have been far from Valpinson when the fire broke out."

"That is true, and, in the open country, I should certainly have seen the fire; but I was in a dense wood: the trees cut off all view."

"And these same trees prevented the sound of the two shots fired at Count Claudieuse from reaching your ear?"

"They might have helped to prevent it; but there was no need for that. I was walking against the wind, which was very high; and it is an established fact, that, under such circumstances, the sound of a gun is not heard beyond fifty yards."

M. Magloire once more could hardly restrain his impatience; and, utterly unconscious that he was even harsher than the magistrate, he said,—

"And you think your statement explains every thing?"

"I believe that my statement, which is founded upon the most exact truth, explains the charges brought against me by M. Galpin. It explains how I tried to keep my visit to Valpinson secret; how I was met in going and in coming back, and at hours which correspond with the time of the fire. It explains, finally, how I came at first to deny. It explains how one of my cartridge-cases was found near the ruins, and why I had to wash my hands when I reached home."

Nothing seemed to be able to shake the lawyer's conviction. He asked,—

"And the day after, when they came to arrest you, what was your first impression?"

"I thought at once of Valpinson."

"And when you were told that a crime had been committed?"

"I said to myself, 'The countess wants to be a widow.'"

All of M. Magloire's blood seemed to rise in his face. He cried,—

"Unhappy man! How can you dare accuse the Countess Claudieuse of such a crime?"

Indignation gave Jacques strength to reply,—

"Whom else should I accuse? A crime has been committed, and under such circumstances that it cannot have been committed by any one except by her or by myself. I am innocent: consequently she is guilty."

"Why did you not say so at once?"

Jacques shrugged his shoulders, and replied in a tone of bitter irony,—

"How many times, and in how many ways, do you want me to give you my reasons? I kept silent the first day, because I did not then know the circumstances of the crime, and because I was reluctant to accuse a woman who had given me her love, and who had become criminal from passion; because, in fine, I did not think at that time that I was in danger. After that I kept silent because I hoped justice would be able to discover the truth, or the countess would be unable to bear the idea that I, the innocent one, should be accused. Still later, when I saw my danger, I was afraid."

The advocates' feelings seemed to be revolted. He broke in,—

"You do not tell the truth, Jacques; and I will tell you why you kept silent. It is very difficult to make up a story which is to account for every thing. But you are a clever man: you thought it over, and you made out a story. There is nothing lacking in it, except probability. You might tell me that the Countess Claudieuse has unfairly enjoyed the reputation of a saint, and that she has given you her love; perhaps I might be willing to believe it. But when you say she has set her own house on fire, and taken up a gun to shoot her husband, that I can never, never admit."

"Still it is the truth."

"No; for the evidence of Count Claudieuse is precise. He has seen his murderer; it was a man who fired at him."

"And who tells you that Count Claudieuse does not know all, and wants to save his wife, and ruin me? There would be a vengeance for him."

The objection took the advocate by surprise; but he rejected it at once, and said,—

"Ah! be silent, or prove."

"All the letters are burned."

"When one has been a woman's lover for five years, there are always proofs."

"But you see there are none."

"Do not insist," repeated M. Magloire.

And, in a voice full of pity and emotion, he added,—

"Unhappy man! Do you not feel, that, in order to escape from one crime, you are committing another which is a thousand times worse?"

Jacques stood wringing his hand, and said—

"It is enough to drive me mad."

"And even if I, your friend," continued M. Magloire, "should believe you, how would that help you? Would any one else believe it? Look here I will tell you exactly what I think. Even if I were perfectly sure of all the facts you mention, I should never plead them in my defence, unless I had proofs. To plead them, understand me well, would be to ruin yourself inevitably."

"Still they must be pleaded; for they are the truth."

"Then," said M. Magloire, "you must look for another advocate."

And he went toward the door. He was on the point of leaving, when Jacques cried out, almost in agony,—

"Great God, he forsakes me!"

"No," replied the advocate; "but I cannot discuss matters with you in the state of excitement in which you now are. You will think it over, and I will come again to-morrow."

He left; and Jacques de Boiscoran fell, utterly undone, on one of the prison chairs.

"It is all over," he stammered: "I am lost."

XV.

During all this time, they were suffering intense anxiety at M. de Chandore's house. Ever since eight o'clock in the morning the two aunts, the old gentleman, the marchioness, and M. Folgat had been assembled in the dining-room, and were there waiting for the result of the interview. Dionysia had only come down later; and her grandfather could not help noticing that she had dressed more carefully than usual.

"Are we not going to see Jacques again?" she replied with a smile full of confidence and joy.

She had actually persuaded herself that one word from Jacques would suffice to convince the celebrated lawyer, and that he would reappear triumphant on M. Magloire's arm. The others did not share these expectations. The two aunts, looking as yellow as their old laces, sat immovable in a corner. The marchioness was trying to hide her tears; and M. Folgat endeavored to look absorbed in a volume of engravings. M. de Chandore, who possessed less self-control, walked up and down in the room, repeating every ten minutes,—

"It is wonderful how long time seems when you are waiting!"

At ten o'clock no news had come.

"Could M. Magloire have forgotten his promise?" said Dionysia, becoming anxious.

"No, he has not forgotten it," replied a newcomer, M. Seneschal. It was really the excellent mayor, who had met M. Magloire about an hour before, and who now came to hear the news, for his own sake, as he said, but especially for his wife's sake, who was actually ill with anxiety.

Eleven o'clock, and no news. The marchioness got up, and said,—

"I cannot stand this uncertainty a minute longer. I am going to the prison."

"And I will go with you, dear mother," declared Dionysia.

But such a proceeding was hardly suitable. M. de Chandore opposed it, and was supported by M. Folgat, as well as by M. Seneschal.

"We might at least send somebody," suggested the two aunts timidly.

"That is a good idea," replied M. de Chandore.

He rang the bell; and old Anthony came in. He had established himself the evening before in Sauveterre, having heard that the preliminary investigation was finished.

- 256 -

As soon as he had been told what they wanted him to do, he said,—

"I shall be back in half an hour."

He nearly ran down the steep street, hastened along National Street, and then climbed up more slowly Castle Street. When M. Blangin, the keeper, saw him appear, he turned very pale; for M. Blangin had not slept since Dionysia had given him the seventeen thousand francs. He, once upon a time the special friend of all gendarmes, now trembled when one of them entered the jail. Not that he felt any remorse about having betrayed his duty; oh, no! but he feared discovery.

More than ten times he had changed the hiding-place of his precious stocking; but, wherever he put it, he always fancied that the eyes of his visitors were riveted upon that very spot. He recovered, however, from his fright when Anthony told him his errand, and replied in the most civil manner,—

"M. Magloire came here at nine o'clock precisely. I took him immediately to M. de Boiscoran's cell; and ever since they have been talking, talking."

"Are you quite sure?"

"Of course I am. Must I not know every thing that happens in my jail? I went and listened. You can hear nothing from the passage: they have shut the wicket, and the door is massive."

"That is strange," murmured the old servant.

"Yes, and a bad sign," declared the keeper with a knowing air. "I have noticed that the prisoners who take so long to state their case to their advocate always catch the maximum of punishment."

Anthony, of course, did not report to his masters the jailer's mournful anticipations; but what he told them about the length of the interview did not tend to relieve their anxiety.

Gradually the color had faded from Dionysia's cheeks; and the clear ring of her voice was half drowned in tears, when she said, that it would have been better, perhaps, if she had put on mourning, and that seeing the whole family assembled thus reminded her of a funeral.

The sudden arrival of Dr. Seignebos cut short her remarks. He was in a great passion, as usual; and as soon as he entered, he cried,—

"What a stupid town Sauveterre is! Nothing but gossip and idle reports! The people are all of them old women. I feel like running away, and hiding myself. On my way here, twenty curious people have stopped me to ask me what M. de Boiscoran is going to do now. For the town is full of rumors. They know that Magloire is at the jail now; and everybody wants to be the first to hear Jacques's story."

He had put his immense broad brimmed hat on the table, and, looking around the room at all the sad faces he asked,—

"And you have no news yet?"

"Nothing," replied M. Seneschal and M. Folgat at the same breath.

"And we are frightened by this delay," added Dionysia.

"And why?" asked the physician.

Then taking down his spectacles, and wiping them diligently, he said,—

"Did you think, my dear young lady, that Jacques de Boiscoran's affair could be settled in five minutes? If they let you believe that, they did wrong. I, who despise all concealment, I will tell you the truth. At the bottom of all these occurrences at Valpinson, there lies, I am perfectly sure, some dark intrigue. Most assuredly we shall put Jacques out of his trouble; but I fear it will be hard work."

"M. Magloire!" announced old Anthony.

The eminent advocate of Sauveterre entered. He looked so undone, and bore so evidently the traces of his excitement, that all had the same terrible thought which Dionysia expressed.

"Jacques is lost!"

M. Magloire did not say no.

"I believe he is in danger."

"Jacques," murmured the old marchioness,—"my son!"

"I said in danger," repeated the advocate; "but I ought to have said, he is in a strange, almost incredible, unnatural position."

"Let us hear," said the marchioness.

The lawyer was evidently very much embarrassed; and he looked with unmistakable distress, first at Dionysia, and then at the two old aunts. But nobody noticed this, and so he said,—

"I must ask to be left alone with these gentlemen."

In the most docile manner the Misses Lavarande rose, and took their niece and Jacques's mother with them: the latter was evidently near fainting. As soon as the door was shut, Grandpapa Chandore, half mad with grief, exclaimed,—

"Thanks, M. Magloire, thanks for having given me time to prepare my poor child for the terrible blow. I see but too well what you are going to say. Jacques is guilty."

"Stop," said the advocate: "I have said nothing of the kind. M. de Boiscoran still protests energetically that he is innocent; but he states in his defence a fact which is so entirely improbable, so utterly inadmissible"—

"But what does he say?" asked M. Seneschal.

"He says that the Countess Claudieuse has been his mistress."

Dr. Seignebos started, and, readjusting his spectacles, he cried triumphantly,—

"I said so! I have guessed it!"

M. Folgat had, on this occasion, very naturally, no deliberative voice. He came from Paris, with Paris ideas; and, whatever he might have been told, the name of the Countess Claudieuse revealed to him nothing. But, from the effect which it produced upon the others, he could judge what Jacques's accusation meant. Far from being of the doctor's opinion M. de Chandore and M. Seneschal both seemed to be as much shocked as M. Magloire.

"That is incredible," said one.

"That is impossible," added the other.

M. Magloire shook his head, and said,—

"That is exactly what I told Jacques."

But the doctor was not the man to be surprised at what public opinion said, much less to fear it. He exclaimed,—

"Don't you hear what I say? Don't you understand me? The proof that the thing is neither so incredible nor so impossible is, that I had suspected it. And there were signs of it, I should think. Why on earth should a man like Jacques, young, rich, well made, in love with a charming girl, and beloved by her, why should he amuse himself with setting houses on fire, and killing people? You tell me he did not like Count Claudieuse. Upon my word! If everybody who does not like Dr. Seignebos were to come and fire at him forthwith, do you know my body would look like a sieve! Among you all, M. Folgat is the only one who has not been struck with blindness."

The young lawyer tried modestly to protest.

"Sir"—

But the other cut him short, and went on,—

"Yes, sir, you saw it all; and the proof of it is, that you at once went to work in search of the real motive, the heart,—in fine, the woman at the bottom of the riddle. The proof of it is, that you went and asked everybody,—Anthony, M. de Chandore, M. Seneschal, and myself,—if M. de Boiscoran had not now, or had not had, some love-affair in the country. They all said No, being far from suspecting the truth. I alone, without giving you a positive answer, told you that I thought as you did, and told you so in M. de Chandore's presence."

"That is so!" replied the old gentleman and M. Folgat.

Dr. Seignebos was triumphant. Gesticulating, and continually handling his spectacles, he added,—

"You see I have learnt to mistrust appearances; and hence I had my misgivings from the beginning. I watched the Countess Claudieuse the night of the fire; and I saw that she looked embarrassed, troubled, suspicious. I wondered at her readiness to yield to M. Galpin's whim, and to allow Cocoleu to be examined; for I knew that she was the only one who could ever make that so-called idiot talk. You see I have good eyes, gentlemen, in spite of my spectacles. Well, I swear by all I hold most sacred, on my Republican faith, I am ready to affirm upon oath, that, when Cocoleu uttered Jacques de Boiscoran's name, the countess exhibited no sign of surprise."

Never before, in their life, had the mayor of Sauveterre and Dr. Seignebos been able to agree on any subject. This question was not likely to produce such an effect all of a sudden: hence M. Seneschal said,—

"I was present at Cocoleu's examination, and I noticed, on the contrary, the amazement of the countess."

The doctor raised his shoulders, and said,—

"Certainly she said, 'Ah!' But that is no proof. I, also, could very easily say, 'Ah!' if anybody should come and tell me that the mayor of Sauveterre was in the wrong; and still I should not be surprised."

"Doctor!" said M. de Chandore, anxious to conciliate,— "doctor!"

But Dr. Seignebos had already turned to M. Magloire, whom he was anxious to convert, and went on,—

"Yes, the face of the Countess Claudieuse, expressed amazement; but her eyes spoke of bitter, fierce hatred, of joy, and of vengeance. And that is not all. Will you please tell me, Mr. Mayor, when Count Claudieuse was roused by the fire, was the countess by him? No, she was nursing her youngest daughter, who had the measles. Hm! What do you think of measles which make sitting up at night necessary? And when the two shots were fired, where was the countess then? Still with her daughter, and on the other side of the house from where the fire was."

The mayor of Sauveterre was no less obstinate than the doctor. He at once objected,—

"I beg you will notice, doctor, that Count Claudieuse himself deposed how, when he ran to the fire, he found the door shut from within, just as he had left it a few hours before."

Dr. Seignebos returned a most ironical bow, and then asked,—

"Is there really only one door in the chateau at Valpinson?"

"To my knowledge," said M. de Chandore, "there are at least three."

"And I must say," added M. Magloire, "that according to M. de Boiscoran's statement, the countess, on that evening, had gone out by the laundry-door when she came to meet him."

"What did I say?" exclaimed the doctor.

And, wiping his glasses in a perfect rage, he added,—

"And the children! Does Mr. Mayor think it natural that the Countess Claudieuse, this incomparable mother in his estimation, should forget her children in the height of the fire?"

"What! The poor woman is called out by the discharge of fire-arms; she sees her house on fire; she stumbles over the lifeless body of her husband: and you blame her for not having preserved all her presence of mind."

"That is one view of it; but it is not the one I take. I rather think that the countess, having been delayed out of doors, was prevented by the fire from getting in again. I think, also, that Cocoleu came very opportunely; and that it was very lucky Providence should inspire his mind with that sublime idea of saving the children at the risk of his life."

This time M. Seneschal made no reply.

"Supported by all these facts," continued the doctor, "my suspicions became so strong that I determined to ascertain the truth, if I could. The next day I questioned the countess, and, I must confess, rather treacherously. Her replies and her looks were not such as to modify my views. When I asked her, looking straight into her eyes, what she thought of Cocoleu's mental condition, she nearly fainted; and she could hardly make me hear her when she said that she occasionally caught glimpses of intelligence in him. When I asked her if Cocoleu was fond of her, she said, in a most embarrassed manner, that his devotion was that of an animal which is grateful for the care taken of him. What do you think of that, gentlemen? To me it appeared that Cocoleu was at the bottom of the whole affair; that he knew the truth; and that I should be able to save Jacques, if I could prove Cocoleu's imbecility to be assumed, and his speechlessness to be an imposture. And I would have proved it, if they had associated with me any one else but this ass and this jackanapes from Paris."

He paused for a few seconds; but, without giving anybody time to reply, he went on,—

"Now, let us go back to our point of departure, and draw our conclusions. Why do you think it so improbable and impossible that the countess Claudieuse should have betrayed her duties? Because she has a world-wide reputation for purity and prudence. Well. But was not Jacques de Boiscoran's reputation as a man of honor also above all doubt? According to your views, it is absurd to suspect the countess of having had a lover. According to my notions, it is absurd that Jacques should, overnight, have become a scoundrel."

"Oh! that is not the same thing," said M. Seneschal.

"Certainly not!" replied the doctor; "and there you are right, for once. If M. de Boiscoran had committed this crime, it would be one of those absurd crimes which are revolting to us; but, if committed by the countess, it is only the catastrophe prepared by Count Claudieuse on the day when he married a woman thirty years younger than he was."

The great wrath of Dr. Seignebos was not always as formidable as it looked. Even when he appeared to be almost beside himself, he never said more than he intended to say, possessed as he was of that admirable southern quality, which enabled him to pour forth fire and flames, and to remain as cold as ice within, But in this case he showed what he thought fully. He had said quite enough, too, and had presented the whole affair under such a new aspect, that his friends became very thoughtful.

"You would have converted me, doctor," said M. Folgat, "if I had not been of your opinion before."

"I am sure," added M. de Chandore, after hearing the doctor, "the thing no longer looks impossible."

"Nothing is impossible," said M. Seneschal, like a philosopher.

The eminent advocate of Sauveterre alone remained unmoved.

"Well," said he, "I had rather admit one hour of utter insanity even than five years of such monstrous hypocrisy. Jacques may have committed the crime, and be nothing but a madman; but, if the countess is guilty, one might despair of mankind, and renounce all faith in this world. I have seen her, gentlemen, with her husband and her children. No one can feign such looks of tenderness and affection."

"He will never give her up!" growled Dr. Seignebos,—

And touching his friend on the shoulder,—for M. Magloire had been his friend for many years, and they were quite intimate,—he said,—

"Ah! There I recognize my friend, the strange lawyer, who judges others by himself, and refuses to believe any thing bad. Oh, do not protest! For we love and honor you for that very faith, and are proud to see you among us Republicans. But I must confess you are not the man to bring light into such a dark intrigue. At twenty-eight you married a girl whom you loved dearly: you lost her, and ever since you have remained faithful to her memory, and lived so far from all passions that you no longer believe in their existence. Happy man! Your heart is still at twenty; and with your grey hair you still believe in the smiles and looks of woman."

There was much truth in this; but there are certain truths which we are not overfond of hearing.

"My simplicity has nothing to do with the matter," said M. Magloire. "I affirm and maintain that a man who has been for five years the lover of a woman must have some proof of it."

"Well, there you are mistaken, master," said the physician, arranging his spectacles with an air of self-conceit, which, under other circumstances, would have been irresistibly ludicrous.

"When women determine to be prudent and suspicious," remarked M. de Chandore, "they never are so by halves."

"It is evident, besides," added M. Folgat, "that the Countess Claudieuse would never have determined upon so bold a crime, if she had not been quite sure, that after the burning of her letters, no proof could be brought against her."

"That is it!" cried the doctor.

M. Magloire did not conceal his impatience. He said dryly,—

"Unfortunately, gentlemen, it does not depend on you to acquit or condemn M. de Boiscoran. I am not here to convince you, or to be convinced: I came to discuss with M. de Boiscoran's friends our line of conduct, and the basis of our defence."

And M. Magloire was evidently right in this estimate of his duty. He went and leaned against the mantelpiece; and, when the others had taken their seats around him, he began,—

"In the first place, I will admit the allegations made by M. de Boiscoran. He is innocent. He has been the lover of Countess Claudieuse; but he has no proof. This being granted, what is to be done? Shall I advise him to send for the magistrate, and to confess it all?"

No one replied at first. It was only after a long silence that Dr. Seignebos said,—

"That would be very serious."

"Very serious, indeed," repeated the famous lawyer. "Our own feelings give us the measure of what M. Galpin will think. First of all, he, also, will ask for proof, the evidence of a witness, any thing, in fact. And, when Jacques tells him that he has nothing to give but his word, M. Galpin will tell him that he does not speak the truth."

"He might, perhaps, consent to extend the investigation," said M. Seneschal. "He might possibly summon the countess."

M. Magloire nodded, and said,—

"He would certainly summon her. But, then, would she confess? It would be madness to expect that. If she is guilty, she is far too strong-minded to let the truth escape her. She would deny every thing, haughtily, magnificently, and in such a manner as not to leave a shadow of doubt."

"That is only too probable," growled the doctor. "That poor Galpin is not the strongest of men."

"What would be the result of such a step?" asked M. Magloire. "M. de Boiscoran's case would be a hundred times worse; for to his crime would now be added the odium of the meanest, vilest calumny."

M. Folgat was following with the utmost attention. He said,—

"I am very glad to hear my honorable colleague give utterance to that opinion. We must give up all hope of delaying the proceedings, and let M. de Boiscoran go into court at once."

M. de Chandore raised his hands to heaven, as if in sheer despair.

"But Dionysia will die of grief and shame," he exclaimed.

M. Magloire, absorbed in his own views, went on,—

"Well, here we are now before the court at Sauveterre, before a jury composed of people from this district, incapable of prevarication, I am sure, but, unfortunately, under the influence of that public opinion which has long since condemned M. de Boiscoran. The proceedings begin; the judge questions the accused. Will he say what he told me,—that, after having been the lover of the Countess Claudieuse, he had gone to Valpinson to carry her back her letters, and to get his own, and that they are all burnt? Suppose he says so. Immediately then there will arise a storm of indignation; and he will be overwhelmed with curses and with contempt. Well, thereupon, the president of the court uses his discretionary powers, suspends the trial, and sends for the Countess Claudieuse. Since we look upon her as guilty, we must needs endow her with supernatural energy. She had foreseen what is coming, and has read over her part. When summoned, she appears, pale, dressed in black; and a murmur of respectful sympathy greets her at her entrance. You see her before you, don't you? The president explains to her why she has been sent for, and she does not comprehend. She cannot possibly comprehend such an abominable calumny. But when she has comprehended it? Do you see the lofty look by which she crushes Jacques, and the grandeur with which she replies, 'When this man had failed in trying to murder my husband, he tried to disgrace his wife. I intrust to you my honor as a mother and a wife, gentlemen. I shall not answer the infamous charges of this abject calumniator.'"

"But that means the galleys for Jacques," exclaimed M. de Chandore, "or even the scaffold!"

"That would be the maximum, at all events," replied the advocate of Sauveterre. "But the trial goes on; the prosecuting attorney demands an overwhelming punishment; and at last the prisoner's council is called upon to speak. Gentlemen, you were impatient at my persistence. I do not credit, I confess, the statement made by M. de Boiscoran. But my young colleague here does credit it. Well, let him tell us candidly. Would he dare to plead this statement, and assert that the Countess Claudieuse had been Jacques's mistress?"

M. Folgat looked annoyed.

"I don't know," he said in an undertone.

"Well, I know you would not," exclaimed M. Magloire; "and you would be right, for you would risk your reputation without the slightest chance of saving Jacques. Yes, no chance whatever! For after all, let us suppose, what can hardly be even supposed, you should prove that Jacques has told the truth, that he has been the lover of the countess. What would happen then? They arrest the countess. Do they release M. de Boiscoran on that account? Certainly not! They keep him in prison, and say to him. 'This woman has attempted her husband's life; but she had been your mistress, and you are her accomplice.'

"That is the situation, gentlemen!"

M. Magloire had stripped it of all unnecessary comments, of idle conjecture, and all sentimental phraseology, and placed it before them as it had to be looked at, in all its fearful simplicity.

Grandpapa Chandore was terrified. He rose, and said in an almost inaudible voice,—

"Ah, all is over indeed! Innocent, or guilty, Jacques de Boiscoran will be condemned."

M. Magloire made no reply.

"And that is," continued the old gentleman, "what you call justice!"

"Alas!" sighed M. Seneschal, "it is useless to deny it: trials by jury are a lottery."

M. de Chandore, driven nearly to madness by his despair, interrupted him,—

"In other words, Jacques's honor and life depend at this hour on a chance,—on the weather on the day of the trial, or the health of a juror. And if Jacques was the only one! But there is Dionysia's life, gentlemen, my child's life, also at stake. If you strike Jacques, you strike Dionysia!"

M. Folgat could hardly restrain a tear. M. Seneschal, and even the doctor, shuddered at such grief in an old man, who was threatened in all that was dearest to him,—in his one great love upon earth. He had taken the hand of the great advocate of Sauveterre, and, pressing it convulsively, he went on,—

"You will save him, Magloire, won't you? What does it matter whether he be innocent or guilty, since Dionysia loves him? You have saved so many in your life! It is well known the judges cannot resist the weight of your words. You will find means to save a poor, unhappy man who once was your friend."

The eminent lawyer looked cast-down, as if he had been guilty himself. When Dr. Seignebos saw this, he exclaimed,—

"What do you mean, friend Magloire? Are you no longer the man whose marvellous eloquence is the pride of our country? Hold your head up: for shame! Never was a nobler cause intrusted to you."

But he shook his head, and murmured,—

"I have no faith in it; and I cannot plead when my conscience does not furnish the arguments."

And becoming more and more embarrassed, he added,—

"Seignebos was right in saying just now, I am not the man for such a cause. Here all my experience would be of no use. It will be better to intrust it to my young brother here."

For the first time in his life, M. Folgat came here upon a case such as enables a man to rise to eminence, and to open a great future before him. For the first time, he came upon a case in which were united all the elements of supreme interest,—greatness of crime, eminence of victim, character of the accused, mystery, variety of opinions, difficulty of defence, and uncertainty of issue,—one of those causes for which an advocate is filled with enthusiasm, which he seizes upon with all his energies, and in which he shares all the anxiety and all the hopes with his client.

He would readily have given five years' income to be offered the management of this case; but he was, above all, an honest man. He said, therefore,—

"You would not think of abandoning M. de Boiscoran, M. Magloire?"

"You will be more useful to him than I can be," was the reply.

Perhaps M. Folgat was inwardly of the same opinion. Still he said,—

"You have not considered what an effect this would have."

"Oh!"

"What would the public think if they heard all of a sudden that you had withdrawn? 'This affair of M. de Boiscoran must be a very bad one indeed,' they would say, 'that M. Magloire should refuse to plead in it.' And that would be an additional burden laid upon the unfortunate man."

The doctor gave his friend no time to reply.

"Magloire is not at liberty to withdraw," he said, "but he has the right to associate a brother-lawyer with himself. He must remain the advocate and counsel of M. de Boiscoran; but M. Folgat can lend him the assistance of his advice, the support of his youth and his activity, and even of his eloquence."

A passing blush colored the cheeks of the young lawyer.

"I am entirely at M. Magloire's service," he said.

The famous advocate of Sauveterre considered a while. After a few moments he turned to his young colleague, and asked him,—

"Have you any plan? Any idea? What would you do?"

To the astonishment of all, M. Folgat now revealed his true character to some extent. He looked taller, his face brightened up, his eyes shone brightly, and he said in a full, sonorous voice,—a voice which by its metallic ring made all hearts vibrate,—

"First of all, I should go and see M. de Boiscoran. He alone should determine my final decision. But my plan is formed now. I, gentlemen, I have faith, as I told you before. The man whom Miss Dionysia loves cannot be a criminal. What would I do? I would prove the truth of M. de Boiscoran's statement. Can that be done? I hope so. He tells us that there are no proofs or witnesses of his intimacy with the Countess Claudieuse. I am sure he is mistaken. She has shown, he says, extraordinary care and prudence. That may be. But mistrust challenges suspicion; and, when you take the greatest precautions, you are most likely to be watched. You want to hide, and you are discovered. You see nobody; but they see you.

"If I were charged with the defence, I should commence to-morrow a counter-investigation. We have money, the Marquis de Boiscoran has influential connections; and we should have help everywhere. Before forty-eight hours are gone, I should have experienced agents at work. I know Vine Street in Passy: it is a lonely street; but it has eyes, as all streets have. Why should not some of these eyes have noticed the mysterious visits of the countess? My agents would inquire from house to house. Nor would it be necessary to mention names. They would not be charged with a search after the Countess Claudieuse, but after an unknown lady, dressed so and so; and, if they should discover any one who had seen her, and who could identify her, that man would be our first witness.

"In the meantime, I should go in search of this friend of M. de Boiscoran's, this Englishman, whose name he assumed; and the London police would aid me in my efforts. If that Englishman is dead, we would hear of it, and it would be a misfortune. If he is only at the other end of the world, the transatlantic cable enables us to question him, and to be answered in a week.

"I should, at the same time, have sent detectives after that English maid-servant who attended to the house in Vine Street. M. de Boiscoran declares that she has never even caught a glimpse of the countess. I do not believe it. It is out of question that a servant should not wish for the means, and find them, of seeing the face of the woman who comes to see her master.

"And that is not all. There were other people who came to the house in Vine Street. I should examine them one by one,—the gardener and his help, the water-carrier, the upholsterer, the errand-boys of all the merchants. Who can say whether one of them is not in possession of this truth which we are seeking?

"Finally, when a woman has spent so many days in a house, it is almost impossible that she should not have left some traces of her passage behind her. Since then, you will say, there has been the war, and then the commune. Nevertheless, I should examine the ruins, every tree in the garden, every pane in the windows: I should compel the very mirrors that have escaped destruction to give me back the image which they have so often reflected."

"Ah, I call that speaking!" cried the doctor, full of enthusiasm.

The others trembled with excitement. They felt that the struggle was commencing. But, unmindful of the impression he had produced, M. Folgat went on,—

"Here in Sauveterre, the task would be more difficult; but, in case of success, the result, also, would be more decided. I should bring down from Paris one of those keen, subtle detectives who have made an art of their profession, and I should know how to stimulate his vanity. He, of course, would have to know every thing, even the names; but there would be no danger in that. His desire to succeed, the splendor of the reward, even his professional habits, would be our security. He would come down secretly, concealed under whatever disguise would appear to him most useful for his purpose; and he would begin once more, for the benefit of the defence, the investigation carried on by M. Galpin for the benefit of the prosecution. Would he find out any thing?

We can but hope so. I know detectives, who, by the aid of smaller material, have unravelled far deeper mysteries."

Grandpapa Chandore, excellent M. Seneschal, Dr. Seignebos, and even M. Magloire, were literally drinking in the words of the Paris lawyer.

"Is that all, gentlemen?" he continued. "By no means! Thanks to his great experience, Dr. Seignebos had, on the very first day, instinctively guessed who was the most important personage of this mysterious drama."

"Cocoleu!"

"Exactly, Cocoleu. Whether he be actor, confident, or eye-witness, Cocoleu has evidently the key to this mystery. This key we must make every effort to obtain from him. Medical experts have just declared him idiotic; nevertheless, we protest. We claim that the imbecility of this wretch is partly assumed. We maintain that his obstinate silence is a vile imposture. What! he should have intelligence enough to testify against us, and yet not have left enough of it now to explain, or even to repeat his evidence? That is inadmissible. We maintain that he keeps silent now just as he spoke that night,—by order. If his silence was less profitable for the prosecution, they would soon find means to break it. We demand that such means should be employed. We demand that the person who has before been able to loosen his tongue should be sent for, and ordered to try the experiment over again. We call for a new examination by experts: we cannot judge all of a sudden, and in forty-eight hours, what is the true mental condition of a man, especially when that man is suspected of being an impostor. And we require, above all, that these new experts should be qualified by knowledge and experience."

Dr. Seignebos was quivering with excitement. He heard all his own ideas repeated in a concise, energetic manner.

"Yes," he cried, "that is the way to do it! Let me have full power, and in less than a fortnight Cocoleu is unmasked."

Less expansive, the eminent advocate of Sauveterre simply shook hands with M. Folgat, and said,—

"You see, M. de Boiscoran's case ought to be put in your hands."

The young lawyer made no effort to protest. When he began to speak, his determination was already formed.

"Whatever can humanly be done," he replied, "I will do. If I accept the task, I shall devote myself body and soul to it. But I insist upon it, it is understood, and must be publicly announced, that M. Magloire does not withdraw from the case, and that I act only as his junior."

"Agreed," said the old advocate.

"Well. When shall we go and see M. de Boiscoran?"

"To-morrow morning."

"I can, of course, take no steps till I have seen him."

"Yes, but you cannot be admitted, except by a special permission from M. Galpin; and I doubt if we can procure that to-day."

"That is provoking."

"No, since we have our work all cut out for to-day. We have to go over all the papers of the proceedings, which the magistrate has placed in my hands."

Dr. Seignebos was boiling over with impatience. He broke in,—

"Oh, what words! Go to work, Mr. Advocate, to work, I say. Come, shall we go?"

They were leaving the room when M. de Chandore called them back by a gesture. He said,—

"So far, gentlemen, we have thought of Jacques alone. And Dionysia?"

The others looked at him, full of surprise.

"What am I to say if she asks me what the result of M. Magloire's interview with Jacques has been, and why you would say nothing in her presence?"

Dr. Seignebos had confessed it more than once: he was no friend of concealment.

"You will tell her the truth," was his advice.

"What? How can I tell her that Jacques has been the lover of the Countess Claudieuse?"

"She will hear of it sooner or later. Miss Dionysia is a sensible, energetic girl."

"Yes; but Miss Dionysia is as ignorant as a holy angel," broke in M. Folgat eagerly, "and she loves M. de Boiscoran. Why should we trouble the purity of her thoughts and her happiness? Is she not unhappy enough? M. de Boiscoran is no longer kept in close confinement. He will see his betrothed, and, if he thinks proper, he can tell her. He alone has the right to do so. I shall, however, dissuade him. From what I know of Miss Chandore's character, it would be impossible for her to control herself, if she should meet the Countess Claudieuse."

"M. de Chandore ought not to say any thing," said M. Magloire decisively. "It is too much already, to have to intrust the marchioness with the secret; for you must not forget, gentlemen, that the slightest indiscretion would certainly ruin all of M. Folgat's delicate plans."

Thereupon all went out; and M. de Chandore, left alone, said to himself,—

"Yes, they are right; but what am I to say?"

He was thinking it over almost painfully, when a maid came in, and told him that Miss Dionysia wanted to see him.

"I am coming," he said.

And he followed her with heavy steps, and trying to compose his features so as to efface all traces of the terrible emotions through which he had passed. The two aunts had taken Dionysia and the marchioness to the parlor in the upper story. Here M. de Chandore found them all assembled,—the marchioness, pale and overcome, extended in an easy-chair; but Dionysia, walking up and down with burning cheeks and blazing eyes. As soon as he entered, she asked him in a sharp, sad voice,—

"Well? There is no hope, I suppose."

"More hope than ever, on the contrary," he replied, trying to smile.

"Then why did M. De Magloire send us all out?"

The old gentleman had had time to prepare a fib.

"Because M. Magloire had to tell us a piece of bad news. There is no chance of no true bill being found. Jacques will have to appear in court."

The marchioness jumped up like a piece of mechanism, and cried,—

"What! Jacques before the assizes? My son? A Boiscoran?" And she fell back into her chair. Not a muscle in Dionysia's face had moved. She said in a strange tone of voice,—

"I was prepared for something worse. One may avoid the court."

With these words she left the room, shutting the door so violently, that both the Misses Lavarande hastened after her. Now M. de Chandore thought he might speak freely. He stood up before the marchioness, and gave vent to that fearful wrath which had been rising within him for a long time.

"Your son," he cried, "your Jacques, I wish he were dead a thousand times! The wretch who is killing my child, for you see he is killing her."

And, without pity, he told her the whole story of Jacques and the Countess Claudieuse. The marchioness was overcome. She had even ceased to sob, and had not strength enough left to ask him to have pity on her. And, when he had ended, she whispered to herself with an expression of unspeakable suffering,—

"Adultery! Oh, my God! what punishment!"

XVI.

M. Folgat and M. Magloire went to the courthouse; and, as they descended the steep street from M. de Chandore's house, the Paris lawyer said,—

"M. Galpin must fancy himself wonderfully safe in his position, that he should grant the defence permission to see all the papers of the prosecution."

Ordinarily such leave is given only after the court has begun proceedings against the accused, and the presiding judge has questioned him. This looks like crying injustice to the prisoner; and hence arrangements can be made by which the rigor of the law is somewhat mitigated. With the consent of the commonwealth attorney, and upon his responsibility, the magistrate who had carried on the preliminary investigation may inform the accused, or his counsel, by word of mouth, or by a copy of all or of part, of what has happened during the first inquiry. That is what M. Galpin had done.

And on the part of a man who was ever ready to interpret the law in its strictest meaning, and who no more dared proceed without authority for every step than a blind man without his staff,—or on the part of such a man, an enemy, too, of M. de Boiscoran, this permission granted to the defence was full of meaning. But did it really mean what M. Folgat thought it did?

"I am almost sure you are mistaken," said M. Magloire. "I know the good man, having practiced with him for many years. If he were sure of himself, he would be pitiless. If he is kind, he is afraid. This concession is a door which he keeps open, in case of defeat."

The eminent counsel was right. However well convinced M. Galpin might be of Jacques's guilt, he was still very much troubled about his means of defence. Twenty examinations had elicited nothing from his prisoner but protestations of innocence. When he was driven to the wall, he would reply,—

"I shall explain when I have seen my counsel."

This is often the reply of the most stupid scamp, who only wants to gain time. But M. Galpin knew his former friend, and had too high an opinion of his mind, not to fear that there was something serious beneath his obstinate silence.

What was it? A clever falsehood? a cunningly-devised *alibi*? Or witnesses bribed long beforehand?

M. Galpin would have given much to know. And it was for the purpose of finding it out sooner, that he had given the permission. Before he granted it, however, he had conferred with the commonwealth attorney. Excellent M. Daubigeon, whom he found, as usual, admiring the beautiful gilt edging of his beloved books, had treated him badly.

"Do you come for any more signatures?" he had exclaimed. "You shall have them. If you want any thing else, your servant.

"'When the blunder is made, It is too late, I tell thee, to come for advice.'"

However discouraging such a welcome might be, M. Galpin did not give up his purpose. He said in his bitterest tone,—

"You still insist that it is a blunder to do one's duty. Has not a crime been committed? Is it not my duty to find out the author, and to have him punished? Well? Is it my fault if the author of this crime is an old friend of mine, and if I was once upon a time on the point of marrying a relation of his? There is no one in court who doubts M. de Boiscoran's guilt; there is no one who dares blame me: and yet they are all as cold as ice towards me."

"Such is the world," said M. Daubigeon with a face full of irony. "They praise virtue; but they hate it."

"Well, yes! that is so," cried M. Galpin in his turn. "Yes, they blame people who have done what they had not the courage to do. The attorney general has congratulated me, because he judges things from on high and impartially. Here cliques are all-powerful. Even those who ought to encourage and support me, cry out against me. My natural ally, the commonwealth attorney, forsakes me and laughs at me. The president of the court, my immediate superior, said to me this morning with intolerable irony, 'I hardly know any magistrate who would be able as you are to sacrifice his relations and his friends to the interests of truth and justice. You are one of the ancients: you will rise high.'"

His friend could not listen any further. He said,—

"Let us break off there: we shall never understand each other. Is Jacques de Boiscoran innocent, or guilty? I do not know. But I do know that he was the pleasantest man in the world, an admirable

- 277 -

host, a good talker, a scholar, and that he owned the finest editions of Horace and Juvenal that I have ever seen. I liked him. I like him still; and it distresses me to think of him in prison. I know that we had the most pleasant relations with each other, and that now they are broken off. And you, you complain! Am I the ambitious man? Do I want to have my name connected with a world-famous trial? M. de Boiscoran will in all probability be condemned. You ought to be delighted. And still you complain? Why, one cannot have everything. Who ever undertook a great enterprise, and never repented of it?"

After that there was nothing left for M. Galpin but to go away. He did go in a fury, but at the same time determined to profit by the rude truths which M. Daubigeon had told him; for he knew very well that his friend represented in his views nearly the whole community. He was fully prepared to carry out his plan. Immediately after his return, he communicated the papers of the prosecution to the defence, and directed his clerk to show himself as obliging as he could. M. Mechinet was not a little surprised at these orders. He knew his master thoroughly,—this magistrate, whose shadow he had been now for so many years.

"You are afraid, dear sir," he had said to himself.

And as M. Galpin repeated the injunction, adding that the honor of justice required the utmost courtesy when rigor was not to be employed, the old clerk replied very gravely,—

"Oh! be reassured, sir. I shall not be wanting in courtesy."

But, as soon as the magistrate turned his back, Mechinet laughed aloud.

"He would not recommend me to be obliging," he thought, "if he suspected the truth, and knew how far I am devoted to the defence. What a fury he would be in, if he should ever find out that I have betrayed all the secrets of the investigation, that I have carried letters to and from the prisoner, that I have made of Trumence an accomplice, and of Blangin the jailer an agent, that I have helped Miss Dionysia to visit her betrothed in jail!"

For he had done all this four times more than enough to be dismissed from his place, and even to become, at least for some months, one of Blangin's boarders. He shivered all down his back when he thought of this; and he had been furiously angry, when, one evening, his sisters, the devout seamstresses, had taken it into their heads to say to him,—

"Certainly, Mechinet, you are a different man ever since that visit of Miss Chandore."

"Abominable talkers!" he had exclaimed, in a tone of voice which frightened them out of their wits. "Do you want to see me hanged?"

But, if he had these attacks of rage, he felt not a moment's remorse. Miss Dionysia had completely bewitched him; and he judged M. Galpin's conduct as severely as she did.

To be sure, M. Galpin had done nothing contrary to law; but he had violated the spirit of the law. Having once summoned courage to begin proceedings against his friend, he had not been able to remain impartial. Afraid of being charged with timidity, he had exaggerated his severity. And, above all, he had carried on the inquiry solely in the interests of a conviction, as if the crime had been proved, and the prisoner had not protested his innocence.

Now, Mechinet firmly believed in this innocence; and he was fully persuaded that the day on which Jacques de Boiscoran saw his counsel would be the day of his justification. This will show with what eagerness he went to the court-house to wait for M. Magloire.

But at noon the great lawyer had not yet come. He was still consulting with M. de Chandore.

"Could any thing amiss have happened?" thought the clerk.

And his restlessness was so great, that, instead of going home to breakfast with his sisters, he sent an office-boy for a roll and a glass of water. At last, as three o'clock struck, M. Magloire and M. Folgat arrived; and Mechinet saw at once in their faces, that he had been mistaken, and that Jacques had not explained. Still, before M. Magloire, he did not dare inquire.

"Here are the papers," he said simply, putting upon the table an immense box.

Then, drawing M. Folgat aside, he asked,—

"What is the matter, pray?"

The clerk had certainly acted so well, that they could have no secret from him; and he so was fully committed, that there was no danger in relying upon his discretion. Still M. Folgat did not dare to mention the name of the Countess Claudieuse; and he replied evasively,—

"This is the matter: M. de Boiscoran explains fully; but he had no proofs for his statement, and we are busy collecting proofs."

Then he went and sat down by M. Magloire, who was already deep in the papers. With the help of those documents, it was easy to follow step by step M. Galpin's work, to see the efforts he had made, and to comprehend his strategy.

First of all, the two lawyers looked for the papers concerning Cocoleu. They found none. Of the statement of the idiot on the night of the fire, of the efforts made since to obtain from him a repetition of this evidence, of the report of the experts,—of all this there was not a trace to be found.

M. Galpin dropped Cocoleu. He had a right to do so. The prosecution, of course, only keeps those witnesses which it thinks useful, and drops all the others.

"Ah, the scamp is clever!" growled M. Magloire in his disappointment.

It was really very well done. M. Galpin deprived by this step the defence of one of their surest means, of one of those incidents in a trial which are apt to affect the mind of the jury so powerfully.

"We can, however, summon him at any time," said M. Magloire.

They might do so, it is true; but what a difference it would make! If Cocoleu appeared for M. Galpin, he was a witness for the prosecution, and the defence could exclaim with indignation,—

"What! You suspect the prisoner upon the evidence of such a creature?"

But, if he had to be summoned by the defence, he became prisoner's evidence, that is to say, one of those witnesses whom the jury always suspect; and then the prosecution would exclaim,—

"What do you hope for from a poor idiot, whose mental condition is such, that we refused his evidence when it might have been most useful to us?"

"If we have to go into court," murmured M. Folgat, "here is certainly a considerable chance of which we are deprived. The whole character of the case is changed. But, then, how can M. Galpin prove the guilt?"

Oh! in the simplest possible manner. He started from the fact that Count Claudieuse was able to give the precise hour at which the crime was committed. Thence he passed on immediately to the deposition of young Ribot, who had met M. de Boiscoran on his way to Valpinson, crossing the marshes, before the crime, and to that of Gaudry, who had seen him come back from Valpinson through the woods, after the crime. Three other witnesses who had turned up during the investigation confirmed this evidence; and by these means alone, and by comparing the hours, M. Galpin succeeded in proving, almost beyond doubt, that the accused had gone to Valpinson, and nowhere else, and that he had been there at the time the crime was committed.

What was he doing there?

To this question the prosecution replied by the evidence taken on the first day of the inquiry, by the water in which Jacques had washed his hands, the cartridge-case found near the house, and the identity of the shot extracted from the count's wounds with those seized with the gun at Boiscoran.

Every thing was plain, precise, and formidable, admitting of no discussion, no doubt, no suggestion. It looked like a mathematical deduction.

"Whether he be innocent or guilty," said M. Magloire to his young colleague, "Jacques is lost, if we cannot get hold of some evidence against the Countess Claudieuse. And even in that case, even if it should be established that she is guilty, Jacques will always be looked upon as her accomplice."

Nevertheless, they spent a part of the night in going over all the papers carefully, and in studying every point made by the prosecution.

Next morning, about nine o'clock, having had only a few hours' sleep, they went together to the prison.

XVII.

The night before, the jailer of Sauveterre had said to his wife, at supper,—

"I am tired of the life I am leading here. They have paid me for my place, have not they? Well, I mean to go."

"You are a fool!" his wife had replied. "As long as M. de Boiscoran is a prisoner there is a chance of profit. You don't know how rich those Chandores are. You ought to stay."

Like many other husbands, Blangin fancied he was master in his own house.

He remonstrated. He swore to make the ceiling fall down upon him. He demonstrated by the strength of his arm that he was master. But—

But, notwithstanding all this, Mrs. Blangin having decided that he should stay, he did stay. Sitting in front of his jail, and given up to the most dismal presentiments, he was smoking his pipe, when M. Magloire and M. Folgat appeared at the prison, and handed him M. Galpin's permit. He rose as they came in. He was afraid of them, not knowing whether they were in Miss Dionysia's secret or not. He therefore politely doffed his worsted cap, took his pipe from his mouth, and said,—

"Ah! You come to see M. de Boiscoran, gentlemen? I will show you in: just give me time to go for my keys."

M. Magloire held him back.

"First of all," he said, "how is M. de Boiscoran?"

"Only so-so," replied the jailer.

"What is the matter?"

"Why, what is the matter with all prisoners when they see that things are likely to turn out badly for them?"

The two lawyers looked at each other sadly.

It was clear that Blangin thought Jacques guilty, and that was a bad omen. The persons who stand guard over prisoners have generally a very keen scent; and not unfrequently lawyers consult them, very much as an author consults the actors of the theatre on which his piece is to appear.

"Has he told you any thing?" asked M. Folgat.

"Me personally, nothing," replied the jailer.

And shaking his head, he added,—

"But you know we have our experience. When a prisoner has been with his counsel, I almost always go up to see him, and to offer him something,—a little trifle to set him up again. So yesterday, after M. Magloire had been here, I climbed up"—

"And you found M. de Boiscoran sick?"

"I found him in a pitiful condition, gentlemen. He lay on his stomach on his bed, his head in the pillow, and stiff as a corpse. I was some time in his cell before he heard me. I shook my keys, I stamped, I coughed. No use. I became frightened. I went up to him, and took him by the shoulder. 'Eh, sir!' Great God! he leaped up as if shot and, sitting up, he said, 'What to you want?' Of course, I tried to console him, to explain to him that he ought to speak out; that it is rather unpleasant to appear in court, but that people don't die of it; that they even come out of it as white as snow, if they have a good advocate. I might just as well have been singing, 'O sensible woman.' The more I said, the fiercer he looked; and at last he cried, without letting me finish, 'Get out from here! Leave me!'"

He paused a moment to take a whiff at his pipe; but it had gone out: he put it in his pocket, and went on,—

"I might have told him that I had a right to come into the cells whenever I liked, and to stay there as long as it pleases me. But prisoners are like children: you must not worry them. But I opened the wicket, and I remained there, watching him. Ah, gentlemen, I have been here twenty years, and I have seen many desperate men; but I never saw any despair like this young man's. He had jumped up as soon as I turned my back, and he was walking up and down, sobbing aloud. He looked as pale as death; and the big tears were running down his cheeks in torrents."

M. Magloire felt each one of these details like a stab at his heart. His opinion had not materially changed since the day before; but he had had time to reflect, and to reproach himself for his harshness.

"I was at my post for an hour at least," continued the jailer, "when all of a sudden M. de Boiscoran throws himself upon the door, and begins to knock at it with his feet, and to call as loud as he can. I keep him waiting a little while, so he should not know I was so near by, and then I open, pretending to have hurried up ever so fast. As soon as I show myself he says, 'I have the right to receive visitors, have I not? And nobody has been to see me?'— 'No one.'—'Are you sure?'—'Quite sure.' I thought I had killed him. He put his hands to his forehead this way; and then he said, 'No one!—no mother, no betrothed, no friend! Well, it is all over. I am no longer in existence. I am forgotten, abandoned, disowned.' He said this in a voice that would have drawn tears from stones; and I, I suggested to him to write a letter, which I would send to M. de Chandore. But he became furious at once, and cried, 'No, never! Leave me. There is nothing left for me but death.'"

M. Folgat had not uttered a word; but his pallor betrayed his emotions.

"You will understand, gentlemen," Blangin went on, "that I did not feel quite reassured. It is a bad cell that in which M. de Boiscoran is staying. Since I have been at Sauveterre, one man has killed himself in it, and one man has tried to commit suicide. So I called Trumence, a poor vagrant who assists me in the jail; and we arranged it that one of us would always be on guard, never losing the prisoner out of sight for a moment. But it was a useless precaution. At night, when they carried M. de Boiscoran his supper, he was perfectly calm; and he even said he would try to eat something to keep his strength. Poor man! If he has no other strength than what his meal would give him, he won't go far. He had not swallowed four mouthfuls, when he was almost smothered; and Trumence and I at one time thought he would die on our hands: I almost thought it might be fortunate. However, about nine o'clock he was a little better; and he remained all night long at his window."

M. Magloire could stand it no longer.

"Let us go up," he said to his colleague.

They went up. But, as they entered the passage, they noticed Trumence, who was making signs to them to step lightly.

"What is the matter?" they asked in an undertone.

"I believe he is asleep," replied the prisoner. "Poor man! Who knows but he dreams he is free, and in his beautiful chateau?"

M. Folgat went on tiptoe to the wicket. But Jacques had waked up. He had heard steps and voices, and he had just risen. Blangin, therefore, opened the door; and at once M. Magloire said the prisoner,—

"I bring you reenforcements,—M. Folgat, my colleague, who has come down from Paris, with your mother."

Coolly, and without saying a word, M. de Boiscoran bowed.

"I see you are angry with me," continued M. Magloire. "I was too quick yesterday, much too quick."

Jacques shook his head, and said in an icy tone,—

"I was angry; but I have reflected since, and now I thank you for your candor. At least, I know my fate. Innocent though I be, if I go into court, I shall be condemned as an incendiary and a murderer. I shall prefer not going into court at all."

"Poor man! But all hope is not lost."

"Yes. Who would believe me, if you, my friend, cannot believe me?"

"I would," said M. Folgat promptly, "I, who, without knowing you, from the beginning believed in your innocence,—I who, now that I have seen you, adhere to my conviction."

Quicker than thought, M. de Boiscoran had seized the young advocate's hand, and, pressing it convulsively, said,—

"Thanks, oh, thanks for that word alone! I bless you, sir, for the faith you have in me!"

This was the first time that the unfortunate man, since his arrest, felt a ray of hope. Alas! it passed in a second. His eye became dim again; his brow clouded over; and he said in a hoarse voice,—

"Unfortunately, nothing can be done for me now. No doubt M. Magloire has told you my sad history and my statement. I have no proof; or at least, to furnish proof, I would have to enter into details which the court would refuse to admit; or if by a miracle they were admitted, I should be ruined forever by them. They are confidences which cannot be spoken of, secrets which are never betrayed, veils which must not be lifted. It is better to be condemned innocent than to be acquitted infamous and dishonored. Gentlemen, I decline being defended."

What was his desperate purpose that he should have come to such a decision?

His counsel trembled as they thought they guessed it.

"You have no right," said M. Folgat, "to give yourself up thus."

"Why not?"

"Because you are not alone in your trouble, sir. Because you have relations, friends, and"—

A bitter, ironical smile appeared on the lips of Jacques de Boiscoran as he broke in,—

"What do I owe to them, if they have not even the courage to wait for the sentence to be pronounced before they condemn me? Their merciless verdict has actually anticipated that of the jury. It was to an unknown person, to you, M. Folgat, that I had to be indebted for the first expression of sympathy."

"Ah, that is not so," exclaimed M. Magloire, "you know very well."

Jacques did not seem to hear him. He went on,—

"Friends? Oh, yes! I had friends in my days of prosperity. There was M. Galpin and M. Daubigeon: they were my friends. One has become my judge, the most cruel and pitiless of judges; and the other, who is commonwealth attorney, has not even made an effort to come to my assistance. M. Magloire also used to be a friend of mine, and told me a hundred times, that I could count upon him as I count upon myself, and that was my reason to choose him as my counsel; and, when I endeavored to convince him of my innocence, he told me I lied."

Once more the eminent advocate of Sauveterre tried to protest; but it was in vain.

"Relations!" continued Jacques with a voice trembling with indignation—"oh, yes! I have relations, a father and a mother. Where are they when their son, victimized by unheard-of fatality, is struggling in the meshes of a most odious and infamous plot?

"My father stays quietly in Paris, devoted to his pursuits and usual pleasures. My mother has come down to Sauveterre. She is here now; and she has been told that I am at liberty to receive visitors: but in vain. I was hoping for her yesterday; but the wretch who is accused of a crime is no longer her son! She never came. No one came. Henceforth I stand alone in the world; and now you see why I have a right to dispose of myself."

M. Folgat did not think for a moment of discussing the point. It would have been useless. Despair never reasons. He only said,—

"You forget Miss Chandore, sir."

Jacques turned crimson all over, and he murmured, trembling in all his limbs,—

"Dionysia!"

"Yes, Dionysia," said the young advocate. "You forget her courage, her devotion, and all she has done for you. Can you say that she abandons and denies you,—she who set aside all her reserve and her timidity for your sake, and came and spent a whole night in this prison? She was risking nothing less than her maidenly honor; for she might have been discovered or betrayed. She knew that very well, nevertheless she did not hesitate."

"Ah! you are cruel, sir," broke in Jacques.

And pressing the lawyer's arm hard, he went on,—

"And do you not understand that her memory kills me, and that my misery is all the greater as I know but too well what bliss I am losing? Do you not see that I love Dionysia as woman never was loved before? Ah, if my life alone was at stake! I, at least, I have to make amends for a great wrong; but she—Great God, why did I ever come across her path?"

He remained for a moment buried in thought; then he added,—

"And yet she, also, did not come yesterday. Why? Oh! no doubt they have told her all. They have told her how I came to be at Valpinson the night of the crime."

"You are mistaken, Jacques," said M. Magloire. "Miss Chandore knows nothing."

"Is it possible?"

"M. Magloire did not speak in her presence," added M. Folgat; "and we have bound over M. de Chandore to secrecy. I insisted upon it that you alone had the right to tell the truth to Miss Dionysia."

"Then how does she explain it to herself that I am not set free?"

"She cannot explain it."

"Great God! she does not also think I am guilty?"

"If you were to tell her so yourself, she would not believe you."

"And still she never came here yesterday."

"She could not. Although they told her nothing, your mother had to be told. The marchioness was literally thunderstruck. She remained for more than an hour unconscious in Miss Dionysia's arms. When she recovered her consciousness, her first words were for you; but it was then too late to be admitted here."

When M. Folgat mentioned Miss Dionysia's name, he had found the surest, and perhaps the only means to break Jacques's purpose.

"How can I ever sufficiently thank you, sir?" asked the latter.

"By promising me that you will forever abandon that fatal resolve which you had formed," replied the young advocate. "If you were guilty, I should be the first to say, 'Be it so!' and I would furnish you with the means. Suicide would be an expiation. But, as you are innocent, you have no right to kill yourself: suicide would be a confession."

"What am I to do?"

"Defend yourself. Fight."

"Without hope?"

"Yes, even without hope. When you faced the Prussians, did you ever think of blowing out your brains? No! and yet you knew that they were superior in numbers, and would conquer, in all probability. Well, you are once more in face of the enemy; and even if you were certain of being conquered, that is to say, of being condemned, and it was the day before you should have to mount the scaffold, I should still say, 'Fight. You must live on; for up to that hour something may happen which will enable us to discover the guilty one.' And, if no such event should happen, I should repeat, nevertheless, 'You must wait for the executioner in order to protest from the scaffold against the judicial murder, and once more to affirm your innocence.'"

As M. Folgat uttered these words, Jacques had gradually recovered his bearing; and now he said,—

"Upon my honor, sir, I promise you I will hold out to the bitter end."

"Well!" said M. Magloire,—"very well!"

"First of all," replied M. Folgat, "I mean to recommence, for our benefit the investigation which M. Galpin has left incomplete. To-night your mother and I will leave for Paris. I have come to ask you for the necessary information, and for the means to explore your house in Vine Street, to discover the friend whose name you assumed, and the servant who waited upon you."

The bolts were drawn as he said this; and at the open wicket appeared Blangin's rubicund face.

"The Marchioness de Boiscoran," he said, "is in the parlor, and begs you will come down as soon as you have done with these gentlemen."

Jacques turned very pale.

"My mother," he murmured. Then he added, speaking to the jailer,—

"Do not go yet. We have nearly done."

His agitation was too great: he could not master it. He said to the two lawyers,—

"We must stop here for to-day. I cannot think now."

But M. Folgat had declared he would leave for Paris that very night; and he was determined to do so. He said, therefore,—

"Our success depends on the rapidity of our movements. I beg you will let me insist upon your giving me at once the few items of information which I need for my purposes."

Jacques shook his head sadly. He began,—

"The task is out of your power, sir."

"Nevertheless, do what my colleague asks you," urged M. Magloire. Without any further opposition, and, who knows? Perhaps with a secret hope which he would not confess to himself, Jacques informed the young advocate of the most minute details about his relations to the Countess Claudieuse. He told him at what hour she used to come to the house, what roads she took, and how she was most commonly dressed. The keys of the house were at Boiscoran, in a drawer which Jacques described. He had only to ask Anthony for them. Then he mentioned how they might find out what had become of that Englishman whose name he had borrowed. Sir Francis Burnett had a brother in London. Jacques did not know his precise address; but he knew he had important business-relations with India, and had, once upon a time, been cashier in the great house of Gilmour and Benson.

As to the English servant-girl who had for three years attended to his house in Vine Street, Jacques had taken her blindly, upon the recommendation of an agency in the suburbs; and he had had nothing to do with her, except to pay her her wages, and, occasionally, some little gratuity besides. All he could say, and even that he had learned by mere chance, was, that the girl's name was Suky Wood; that she was a native of Folkstone, where her parents kept a sailor's tavern; and that, before coming to France, she had been a chambermaid at the Adelphi in Liverpool.

M. Folgat took careful notes of all he could learn. Then he said,—

"This is more than enough to begin the campaign. Now you must give me the name and address of your tradesmen in Passy."

"You will find a list in a small pocket-book which is in the same drawer with the keys. In the same drawer are also all the deeds and other papers concerning the house. Finally, you might take Anthony with you: he is devoted to me."

"I shall certainly take him, if you permit me," replied the lawyer. Then putting up his notes, he added,—

"I shall not be absent more than three or four days; and, as soon as I return, we will draw up our plan of defence. Till then, my dear client, keep up your courage."

They called Blangin to open the door for them; and, after having shaken hands with Jacques de Boiscoran, M. Folgat and M. Magloire went away.

"Well, are we going down now?" asked the jailer.

But Jacques made no reply.

He had most ardently hoped for his mother's visit; and now, when he was about to see her, he felt assailed by all kinds of vague and sombre apprehensions. The last time he had kissed her was in Paris, in the beautiful parlor of their family mansion. He had left her, his heart swelling with hopes and joy, to go to his Dionysia; and his mother, he remembered distinctly, had said to him, "I shall not see you again till the day before the wedding."

And now she was to see him again, in the parlor of a jail, accused of an abominable crime. And perhaps she was doubtful of his innocence.

"Sir, the marchioness is waiting for you," said the jailer once more. At the man's voice, Jacques trembled.

"I am ready," he replied: "let us go!" And, while descending the stairs, he tried his best to compose his features, and to arm himself with courage and calmness.

"For," he said, "She must not become aware of it, how horrible my position is."

At the foot of the steps, Blangin pointed at a door, and said,—

"That is the parlor. When the marchioness wants to go, please call me."

On the threshold, Jacques paused once more.

The parlor of the jail at Sauveterre is an immense vaulted hall, lighted up by two narrow windows with close, heavy iron gratings. There is no furniture save a coarse bench fastened to the damp, untidy wall; and on this bench, in the full light of the sun, sat, or rather lay, apparently bereft of all strength, the Marchioness of Boiscoran.

When Jacques saw her, he could hardly suppress a cry of horror and grief. Was that really his mother,—that thin old lady with the sallow complexion, the red eyes, and trembling hands?

"O God, O God!" he murmured.

She heard him, for she raised her head; and, when she recognized him, she wanted to rise; but her strength forsook her, and she sank back upon the bench, crying,—

"O Jacques, my child!"

She, also, was terrified when she saw what two months of anguish and sleeplessness had done for Jacques. But he was kneeling at her feet upon the muddy pavement, and said in a barely intelligible voice,—

"Can you pardon me the great grief I cause you?"

She looked at him for a moment with a bewildered air; and then, all of a sudden, she took his head in her two hands, kissed him with passionate vehemence, and said,—

"Will I pardon you? Alas, what have I to pardon? If you were guilty, I should love you still; and you are innocent."

Jacques breathed more freely. In his mother's voice he felt that she, at least, was sure of him.

"And father?" he asked.

There was a faint blush on the pale cheeks of the marchioness.

"I shall see him to-morrow," she replied; "for I leave to-night with M. Folgat."

"What! In this state of weakness?"

"I must."

"Could not father leave his collections for a few days? Why did he not come down? Does he think I am guilty?"

"No; it is just because he is so sure of your innocence, that he remains in Paris. He does not believe you in danger. He insists upon it that justice cannot err."

"I hope so," said Jacques with a forced smile.

Then changing his tone,—

"And Dionysia? Why did she not come with you?"

"Because I would not have it. She knows nothing. It has been agreed upon that the name of the Countess Claudieuse is not to be mentioned in her presence; and I wanted to speak to you about that abominable woman. Jacques, my poor child, where has that unlucky passion brought you!"

He made no reply.

"Did you love her?" asked the marchioness.

"I thought I did."

"And she?"

"Oh, she! God alone knows the secret of that strange heart."

"There is nothing to hope from her, then, no pity, no remorse?"

"Nothing. I have given her up. She has had her revenge. She had forewarned me."

The marchioness sighed.

"I thought so," she said. "Last Sunday, when I knew as yet of nothing, I happened to be close to her at church, and unconsciously admired her profound devotion, the purity of her eye, and the nobility of her manner. Yesterday, when I heard the truth, I shuddered. I felt how formidable a woman must be who can affect such calmness at a time when her lover lies in prison accused of the crime which she has committed."

"Nothing in the world would trouble her, mother."

"Still she ought to tremble; for she must know that you have told us every thing. How can we unmask her?"

But time was passing; and Blangin came to tell the marchioness that she had to withdraw. She went, after having kissed her son once more.

That same evening, according to their arrangement, she left for Paris, accompanied by M. Folgat and old Anthony.

XVIII.

At Sauveterre, everybody, M. de Chandore as much as Jacques himself, blamed the Marquis de Boiscoran. He persisted in remaining in Paris, it is true: but it was certainly not from indifference; for he was dying with anxiety. He had shut himself up, and refused to see even his oldest friends, even his beloved dealers in curiosities. He never went out; the dust accumulated on his collections; and nothing could arouse him from this state of prostration, except a letter from Sauveterre.

Every morning he received three or four,—from the marchioness or M. Folgat, from M. Seneschal or M. Magloire, from M. de Chandore, Dionysia, or even from Dr. Seignebos. Thus he could follow at a distance all the phases, and even the smallest changes, in the proceedings. Only one thing he would not do: he would not come down, however important his coming might be for his son. He did not move.

Once only he had received, through Dionysia's agency, a letter from Jacques himself; and then he ordered his servant to get ready his trunks for the same evening. But at the last moment he had given counter-orders, saying that he had reconsidered, and would not go.

"There is something extraordinary going on in the mind of the marquis," said the servants to each other.

The fact is, he spent his days, and a part of his nights, in his cabinet, half-buried in an arm-chair, resting little, and sleeping still less, insensible to all that went on around him. On his table he had arranged all his letters from Sauveterre in order; and he read and re-read them incessantly, examining the phrases, and trying, ever in vain, to disengage the truth from this mass of details and statements. He was no longer as sure of his son as at first: far from it! Every day had brought him a new doubt; every letter, additional uncertainty. Hence he was all the time a prey to most harassing apprehensions. He put them aside; but they returned, stronger and more irresistible than before like the waves of the rising tide.

He was thus one morning in his cabinet. It was very early yet; but he was more than ever suffering from anxiety, for M. Folgat had written, "To-morrow all uncertainty will end. To-morrow the close confinement will be raised, and M. Jacques will see M. Magloire, the counsel whom he has chosen. We will write immediately."

It was for this news the marquis was waiting now. Twice already he had rung to inquire if the mail had not come yet, when all of a sudden his valet appeared and with a frightened air said,—

"The marchioness. She has just come with Anthony, M. Jacques's own man."

He hardly said so, when the marchioness herself entered, looking even worse than she had done in the prison parlor; for she was overcome by the fatigue of a night spent on the road.

The marquis had started up suddenly. As soon as the servant had left the room, and shut the door again, he said with trembling voice, as if wishing for an answer, and still fearing to hear it,—

"Has any thing unusual happened?"

"Yes."

"Good or bad?"

"Sad."

"Great God! Jacques has not confessed?"

"How could he confess when he is innocent?"

"Then he has explained?"

"As far as I am concerned, and M. Folgat, Dr. Seignebos, and all who know him and love him, yes, but not for the public, for his enemies, or the law. He has explained every thing; but he has no proof."

The mournful features of the marquis settled into still deeper gloom.

"In other words, he has to be believed on his own word?" he asked.

"Don't you believe him?"

"I am not the judge of that, but the jury."

"Well, for the jury he will find proof. M. Folgat, who has come in the same train with me, and whom you will see to-day, hopes to discover proof."

"Proof of what?"

Perhaps the marchioness was not unprepared for such a reception. She expected it, and still she was disconcerted.

"Jacques," she began, "has been the lover of the Countess Claudieuse."

"Ah, ah!" broke in the marquis.

And, in a tone of offensive irony, he added,—

"No doubt another story of adultery; eh?"

The marchioness did not answer. She quietly went on,—

"When the countess heard of Jacques's marriage, and that he abandoned her, she became exasperated, and determined to be avenged."

"And, in order to be avenged, she attempted to murder her husband; eh?"

"She wished to be free."

The Marquis de Boiscoran interrupted his wife with a formidable oath. Then he cried,—

"And that is all Jacques could invent! And to come to such an abortive story—was that the reason of his obstinate silence?"

"You do not let me finish. Our son is the victim of unparalleled coincidences."

"Of course! Unparalleled coincidences! That is what every one of the thousand or two thousand rascals say who are sentenced every year. Do you think they confess? Not they! Ask them, and they will prove to you that they are the victims of fate, of some dark plot, and, finally, of an error of judgment. As if justice could err in these days of ours, after all these preliminary examinations, long inquiries, and careful investigations."

"You will see M. Folgat. He will tell you what hope there is."

"And if all hope fails?"

The marchioness hung her head.

"All would not be lost yet. But then we should have to endure the pain of seeing our son brought up in court."

The tall figure of the old gentleman had once more risen to its full height; his face grew red; and the most appalling wrath flashed from his eyes.

"Jacques brought up in court?" he cried, with a formidable voice. "And you come and tell me that coolly, as if it were a very simple and quite natural matter! And what will happen then, if he is in court? He will be condemned; and a Boiscoran will go to the galleys. But no, that cannot be! I do not say that a Boiscoran may not commit a crime, passion makes us do strange things; but a Boiscoran, when he regains his senses, knows what becomes him to do. Blood washes out all stains. Jacques prefers the executioner; he waits; he is cunning; he means to plead. If he but save his head, he is quite content. A few years at hard labor, I suppose, will be a trifle to him. And that coward should be a Boiscoran: my blood should flow in his veins! Come, come, madam, Jacques is no son of mine."

Crushed as the marchioness had seemed to be till now, she rose under this atrocious insult.

"Sir!" she cried.

But M. de Boiscoran was not in a state to listen to her.

"I know what I am saying," he went on. "I remember every thing, if you have forgotten every thing. Come, let us go back to your past. Remember the time when Jacques was born, and tell me what year it was when M. de Margeril refused to meet me."

Indignation restored to the marchioness her strength. She cried,—

"And you come and tell me this to-day, after thirty years, and God knows under what circumstances!"

"Yes, after thirty years. Eternity might pass over these recollections, and it would not efface them. And, but for these circumstances to which you refer, I should never have said any thing. At the time to which I allude, I had to choose between two evils,—either to be ridiculous, or to be hated. I preferred to keep silence, and not to inquire too far. My happiness was gone; but I wished to save my peace. We have lived together on excellent terms; but there has always been between us this high wall, this suspicion. As long as I was doubtful, I kept silent. But now, when the facts confirm my doubts, I say again, 'Jacques is no son of mine!'"

Overcome with grief, shame, and indignation, the Marchioness de Boiscoran was wringing her hands; then she cried,—

"What a humiliation! What you are saying is too horrible. It is unworthy of you to add this terrible suffering to the martyrdom which I am enduring."

M. de Boiscoran laughed convulsively.

"Have I brought about this catastrophe?"

"Well then yes! One day I was imprudent and indiscreet. I was young; I knew nothing of life; the world worshipped me; and you, my husband, my guide, gave yourself up to your ambition, and left me to myself. I could not foresee the consequences of a very inoffensive piece of coquetry."

"You see, then, now these consequences. After thirty years, I disown the child that bears my name; and I say, that, if he is innocent, he suffers for his mother's sins. Fate would have it that your son should covet his neighbor's wife, and, having taken her, it is but justice that he should die the death of the adulterer."

"But you know very well that I have never forgotten my duty."

"I know nothing."

"You have acknowledged it, because you refused to hear the explanation which would have justified me."

"True, I did shrink from an explanation, which, with your unbearable pride, would necessarily have led to a rupture, and thus to a fearful scandal."

The marchioness might have told her husband, that, by refusing to hear her explanation, he had forfeited all right to utter a reproach; but she felt it would be useless, and thus he went on,—

"All I do know is, that there is somewhere in this world a man whom I wanted to kill. Gossiping people betrayed his name to me. I went to him, and told him that I demanded satisfaction, and that I hoped he would conceal the real reason for our encounter even from our seconds. He refused to give me satisfaction, on the ground that he did not owe me any, that you had been calumniated, and that he would meet me only if I should insult him publicly."

"Well?"

"What could I do after that? Investigate the matter? You had no doubt taken your precautions, and it would have amounted to nothing. Watch you? I should only have demeaned myself uselessly; for you were no doubt on your guard. Should I ask for a divorce? The law afforded me that remedy. I might have dragged you into court, held you up to the sarcasms of my counsel, and exposed you to the jests of your own. I had a right to humble you, to dishonor my name, to proclaim your disgrace, to publish it in the newspapers. Ah, I would have died rather!"

The marchioness seemed to be puzzled.

"That was the explanation of your conduct?"

"Yes, that was my reason for giving up public life, ambitious as I was. That was the reason why I withdrew from the world; for I thought everybody smiled as I passed. That is why I gave up to you the management of our house and the education of your son, why I became a passionate collector, a half-mad original. And you find out only to-day that you have ruined my life?"

There was more compassion than resentment in the manner in which the marchioness looked at her husband.

"You had mentioned to me your unjust suspicions," she replied; "but I felt strong in my innocence, and I was in hope that time and my conduct would efface them."

"Faith once lost never comes back again."

"The fearful idea that you could doubt of your paternity had never even occurred to me."

The marquis shook his head.

"Still it was so," he replied. "I have suffered terribly. I loved Jacques. Yes, in spite of all, in spite of myself, I loved him. Had he not all the qualities which are the pride and the joy of a family? Was he not generous and noble-hearted, open to all lofty sentiments, affectionate, and always anxious to please me? I never had to complain of him. And even lately, during this abominable war, has he not again shown his courage, and valiantly earned the cross which they gave him? At all times, and from all sides, I have been congratulated on his account. They praised his talents and his assiduity. Alas! at the very moment when they told me what a happy father I was, I was the most wretched of men. How many times would I have drawn him to my heart! But immediately that terrible doubt rose within me, if he should not be my son; and I pushed him back, and looked in his features for a trace of another man's features."

His wrath had cooled down, perhaps by its very excess.

He felt a certain tenderness in his heart, and sinking into his chair, and hiding his face in his hands, he murmured,—

"If he should be my son, however; if he should be innocent! Ah, this doubt is intolerable! And I who would not move from here,—I who have done nothing for him,—I might have done every thing at first. It would have been easy for me to obtain a change of venue to free him from this Galpin, formerly his friend, and now his enemy."

M. de Boiscoran was right when he said that his wife's pride was unmanageable. And still, as cruelly wounded as woman well could be, she now suppressed her pride, and, thinking only of her son, remained quite humble. Drawing from her bosom the letter which Jacques had sent to her the day before she left Sauveterre, she handed it to her husband, saying,—

"Will you read what our son says?"

The marquis's hand trembled as he took the letter; and, when he had torn it open, he read,—

"Do you forsake me too, father, when everybody forsakes me? And yet I have never needed your love as much as now. The peril is imminent. Every thing is against me. Never has such a combination of fatal circumstances been seen before. I may not be able to prove my innocence; but you,—you surely cannot think your son guilty of such an absurd and heinous crime! Oh, no! surely not. My mind is made up. I shall fight to the bitter end. To my last breath I shall defend, not my life, but my honor. Ah, if you but knew! But there are things which cannot be written, and which only a father can be told. I beseech you come to me, let me see you, let me hold your hand in mine. Do not refuse this last and greatest comfort to your unhappy son."

The marquis had started up.

"Oh, yes, very unhappy indeed!" he cried.

And, bowing to his wife, he said,—

"I interrupted you. Now, pray tell me all."

Maternal love conquered womanly resentment. Without a shadow of hesitation, and as if nothing had taken place, the marchioness gave her husband the whole of Jacques's statement as he had made it to M. Magloire.

The marquis seemed to be amazed.

"That is unheard of!" he said.

And, when his wife had finished, he added,—

"That was the reason why Jacques was so very angry when you spoke of inviting the Countess Claudieuse, and why he told you, that, if he saw her enter at one door, he would walk out of the other. We did not understand his aversion."

"Alas! it was not aversion. Jacques only obeyed at that time the cunning lessons given him by the countess."

In less than one minute the most contradictory resolutions seemed to flit across the marquis's face. He hesitated, and at last he said,—

"Whatever can be done to make up for my inaction, I will do. I will go to Sauveterre. Jacques must be saved. M. de Margeril is all-powerful. Go to him. I permit it. I beg you will do it."

The eyes of the marchioness filled with tears, hot tears, the first she had shed since the beginning of this scene.

"Do you not see," she asked, "that what you wish me to do is now impossible? Every thing, yes, every thing in the world but that. But Jacques and I—we are innocent. God will have pity on us. M. Folgat will save us."

XIX.

M. Folgat was already at work. He had confidence in his cause, a firm conviction of the innocence of his client, a desire to solve the mystery, a love of battle, and an intense thirst for success: all these motives combined to stimulate the talents of the young advocate, and to increase his activity.

And, above all this, there was a mysterious and indefinable sentiment with which Dionysia had inspired him; for he had succumbed to her charms, like everybody else. It was not love, for he who says love says hope; and he knew perfectly well that altogether and forever Dionysia belonged to Jacques. It was a sweet and all-powerful sentiment, which made him wish to devote himself to her, and to count for something in her life and in her happiness.

It was for her sake that he had sacrificed all his business, and forgotten his clients, in order to stay at Sauveterre. It was for her sake, above all, that he wished to save Jacques.

He had no sooner arrived at the station, and left the Marchioness de Boiscoran in old Anthony's care, than he jumped into a cab, and had himself driven to his house. He had sent a telegram the day before; and his servant was waiting for him. In less than no time he had changed his clothes. Immediately he went back to his carriage, and went in search of the man, who, he thought, was most likely to be able to fathom this mystery.

This was a certain Goudar, who was connected with the police department in some capacity or other, and at all events received an income large enough to make him very comfortable. He was one of those agents for every thing whom the police keep employed for specially delicate operations, which require both tact and keen scent, an intrepidity beyond all doubt, and imperturbable self-possession. M. Folgat had had opportunities of knowing and appreciating him in the famous case of the Mutual Discount Society.

He was instructed to track the cashier who had fled, having a deficit of several millions. Goudar had caught him in Canada, after pursuing him for three months all over America; but, on the day of his arrest, this cashier had in his pocket-book and his trunk only some forty thousand francs.

What had become of the millions?

When he was questioned, he said he had spent them. He had gambled in stocks, he had become unfortunate, etc.

Everybody believed him except Goudar.

Stimulated by the promise of a magnificent reward, he began his campaign once more; and, in less than six weeks, he had gotten hold of sixteen hundred thousand francs which the cashier had deposited in London with a woman of bad character.

The story is well known; but what is not known is the genius, the fertility of resources, and the ingenuity of expedients, which Goudar displayed in obtaining such a success. M. Folgat, however, was fully aware of it; for he had been the counsel of the stockholders of the Mutual Discount Society; and he had vowed, that, if ever the opportunity should come, he would employ this marvellously able man.

Goudar, who was married, and had a child, lived out of the world on the road to Versailles, not far from the fortifications. He occupied with his family a small house which he owned,—a veritable philosopher's home, with a little garden in front, and a vast garden behind, in which he raised vegetables and admirable fruit, and where he kept all kinds of animals.

When M. Folgat stepped out of his carriage before this pleasant home, a young woman of twenty-five or twenty-six, of surpassing beauty, young and fresh, was playing in the front garden with a little girl of three or four years, all milk and roses.

"M. Goudar, madam?" asked M. Folgat, raising his hat.

The young woman blushed slightly, and answered modestly, but without embarrassment, and in a most pleasing voice,—

"My husband is in the garden; and you will find him, if you will walk down this path around the house."

The young man followed the direction, and soon saw his man at a distance. His head covered with an old straw hat, without a coat, and in slippers, with a huge blue apron such as gardeners wear, Goudar had climbed up a ladder, and was busy dropping into a horsehair bag the magnificent Chasselas grapes of his trellises. When he heard the sand grate under the footsteps of the newcomer, he turned his head, and at once said,—

"Why, M. Folgat? Good morning, sir!"

The young advocate was not a little surprised to see himself recognized so instantaneously. He should certainly never have recognized the detective. It was more than three years since they had seen each other; and how often had they seen each other then? Twice, and not an hour each time.

It is true that Goudar was one of those men whom nobody remembers. Of middle height, he was neither stout nor thin, neither dark nor light haired, neither young nor old. A clerk in a passport office would certainly have written him down thus: Forehead, ordinary; nose, ordinary; mouth, ordinary, eyes, neutral color; special marks, none.

It could not be said that he looked stupid; but neither did he look intelligent. Every thing in him was ordinary, indifferent, and undecided. Not one marked feature. He would necessarily pass unobserved, and be forgotten as soon as he had passed.

"You find me busy securing my crops for the winter," he said to M. Folgat. "A pleasant job. However, I am at your service. Let me put these three bunches into their three bags, and I'll come down."

This was the work of an instant; and, as soon as he had reached the ground, he turned round, and asked,—

"Well, and what do you think of my garden?"

And at once he begged M. Folgat to visit his domain, and, with all the enthusiasm of the land-owner, he praised the flavor of his duchess pears, the bright colors of his dahlias, the new arrangements in his poultry-yard, which was full of rabbit-houses, and the beauty of his pond, with its ducks of all colors and all possible varieties.

In his heart, M. Folgat swore at this enthusiasm. What time he was losing! But, when you expect a service from a man, you must, at least, flatter his weak side. He did not spare praise, therefore. He even pulled out his cigar-case, and, still with a view to win the great man's good graces, he offered it to him, saying,—

"Can I offer you one?"

"Thanks! I never smoke," replied Goudar.

And, when he saw the astonishment of the advocate, he explained,—

"At least not at home. I am disposed to think the odor is unpleasant to my wife."

Positively, if M. Folgat had not known the man, he would have taken him for some good and simple retired grocer, inoffensive, and any thing but bright, and, bowing to him politely, he would have taken his leave. But he had seen him at work; and so he followed him obediently to his greenhouse, his melon-house, and his marvellous asparagus-beds.

At last Goudar took his guest to the end of the garden, to a bower in which were some chairs and a table, saying,—

"Now let us sit down, and tell me your business; for I know you did not come solely for the pleasure of seeing my domain."

Goudar was one of those men who have heard in their lives more confessions than ten priests, ten lawyers, and ten doctors all together. You could tell him every thing. Without a moment's hesitation, therefore, and without a break, M. Folgat told him the whole story of Jacques and the Countess Claudieuse. He listened, without saying a word, without moving a muscle in his face. When the lawyer had finished, he simply said,—

"Well?"

"First of all," replied M. Folgat, "I should like to hear your opinion. Do you believe the statement made by M. de Boiscoran?"

"Why not? I have seen much stranger cases than that."

"Then you think, that, in spite of the charges brought against him, we must believe in his innocence?"

"Pardon me, I think nothing at all. Why, you must study a matter before you can have an opinion."

He smiled; and, looking at the young advocate, he said,—

"But why all these preliminaries? What do you want of me?"

"Your assistance to get at the truth."

The detective evidently expected something of the kind. After a minute's reflection, he looked fixedly at M. Folgat, and said,—

"If I understand you correctly, you would like to begin a counter-investigation for the benefit of the defence?"

"Exactly."

"And unknown to the prosecution?"

"Precisely."

"Well, I cannot possibly serve you."

The young advocate knew too well how such things work not to be prepared for a certain amount of resistance; and he had thought of means to overcome it.

"That is not your final decision, my dear Goudar?" he said.

"Pardon me. I am not my own master. I have my duty to fulfil, and my daily occupation."

"You can at any time obtain leave of absence for a month."

"So I might; but they would certainly wonder at such a furlough at headquarters. They would probably have me watched; and, if they found out that I was doing police work for private individuals, they would scold me grievously, and deprive themselves henceforth of my services."

"Oh!"

"There is no 'oh!' about it. They would do what I tell you, and they would be right; for, after all, what would become of us, and what would become of the safety and liberty of us all, if any one could come and use the agents of the police for his private purposes? And what would become of me if I should lose my place?"

"M. de Boiscoran's family is very rich, and they would prove their gratitude magnificently to the man who would save him."

"And if I did not save him? And if, instead of gathering proof of his innocence, I should only meet with more evidence of his guilt?"

The objection was so well founded, that M. Folgat preferred not to discuss it.

"I might," he said, "hand you at once, and as a retainer, a considerable sum, which you could keep, whatever the result might be."

"What sum? A hundred Napoleons? Certainly a hundred Napoleons are not to be despised; but what would they do for me if I were turned out? I have to think of somebody else besides myself. I have a wife and a child; and my whole fortune consists in this little cottage, which is not even entirely paid for. My place is not a gold-mine; but, with the special rewards which I receive, it brings me, good years and bad years, seven or eight thousand francs, and I can lay by two or three thousand."

The young lawyer stopped him by a friendly gesture, and said,—

"If I were to offer you ten thousand francs?"

"A year's income."

"If I offered you fifteen thousand!"

Goudar made no reply; but his eyes spoke.

"It is a most interesting case, this case of M. de Boiscoran," continued M. Folgat, "and such as does not occur often. The man who should expose the emptiness of the accusation would make a great reputation for himself."

"Would he make friends also at the bar?"

"I admit he would not."

The detective shook his head.

"Well, I confess," he said, "I do not work for glory, nor from love of my art. I know very well that vanity is the great motive-power with some of my colleagues; but I am more practical. I have never liked my profession; and, if I continue to practise it, it is because I have not the money to go into any other. It drives my wife to despair, besides: she is only half alive as long as I am away; and she trembles every morning for fear I may be brought home with a knife between my shoulders."

M. Folgat had listened attentively; but at the same time he had pulled out a pocket-book, which looked decidedly plethoric, and placed it on the table.

"With fifteen thousand francs," he said, "a man may do something."

"That is true. There is a piece of land for sale adjoining my garden, which would suit me exactly. Flowers bring a good price in Paris, and that business would please my wife. Fruit, also yields a good profit."

The advocate knew now that he had caught his man.

"Remember, too, my dear Goudar, that, if you succeed, these fifteen thousand francs would only be a part payment. They might, perhaps, double the sum. M. de Boiscoran is the most liberal of men, and he would take pleasure in royally rewarding the man who should have saved him."

As he spoke, he opened the pocket-book, and drew from it fifteen thousand-franc notes, which he spread out on the table.

"To any one but to you," he went on, "I should hesitate to pay such a sum in advance. Another man might take the money, and never trouble himself about the affair. But I know your uprightness; and, if you give me your word in return for the notes, I shall be satisfied. Come, shall it be so?"

The detective was evidently not a little excited; for, self-possessed as he was, he had turned somewhat pale. He hesitated, handled the bank-notes, and then, all of a sudden, said,—

"Wait two minutes."

He got up instantly, and ran towards the house.

"Is he going to consult his wife?" M. Folgat asked himself.

He did so; for the next moment they appeared at the other end of the walk, engaged in a lively discussion. However, the discussion did not last long. Goudar came back to the bower, and said,—

"Agreed! I am your man!"

The advocate was delighted, and shook his hand.

"Thank you!" he cried; "for, with your assistance, I am almost sure of success. Unfortunately, we have no time to lose. When can you go to work?"

"This moment. Give me time to change my costume; and I am at your service. You will have to give me the keys of the house in Passy."

"I have them here in my pocket."

"Well, then let us go there at once; for I must, first of all, reconnoitre the ground. And you shall see if it takes me long to dress."

In less than fifteen minutes he reappeared in a long overcoat, with gloves on, looking, for all the world, like one of those retired grocers who have made a fortune, and settled somewhere outside of the corporation of Paris, displaying their idleness in broad daylight, and repenting forever that they have given up their occupation.

"Let us go," he said to the lawyer.

After having bowed to Mrs. Goudar, who accompanied them with a radiant smile, they got into the carriage, calling out to the driver,—

"Vine Street, Passy, No. 23."

This Vine Street is a curious street, leading nowhere, little known, and so deserted, that the grass grows everywhere. It stretches out long and dreary, is hilly, muddy, scarcely paved, and full of holes, and looks much more like a wretched village lane than like a street belonging to Paris. No shops, only a few homes, but on the right and the left interminable walls, overtopped by lofty trees.

"Ah! the place is well chosen for mysterious rendezvouses," growled Goudar. "Too well chosen, I dare say; for we shall pick up no information here."

The carriage stopped before a small door, in a thick wall, which bore the traces of the two sieges in a number of places.

"Here is No. 23," said the driver; "but I see no house."

It could not be seen from the street; but, when they got in, Mr. Folgat and Goudar saw it, rising in the centre of an immense garden, simple and pretty, with a double porch, a slate roof, and newly-painted blinds.

"Great God!" exclaimed the detective, "what a place for a gardener!"

And M. Folgat felt so keenly the man's ill-concealed desire, that he at once said,—

"If we save M. de Boiscoran, I am sure he will not keep this house."

"Let us go in," cried the detective, in a voice which revealed all his intense desire to succeed.

Unfortunately, Jacques de Boiscoran had spoken but too truly, when he said that no trace was left of former days. Furniture, carpets, all was new; and Goudar and M. Folgat in vain explored the four rooms down stairs, and the four rooms up stairs, the basement, where the kitchen was, and finally the garret.

"We shall find nothing here," declared the detective. "To satisfy my conscience, I shall come and spend an afternoon here; but now we have more important business. Let us go and see the neighbors!"

There are not many neighbors in Vine Street.

A teacher and a nurseryman, a locksmith and a liveryman, five or six owners of houses, and the inevitable keeper of a wine-shop and restaurant, these were the whole population.

"We shall soon make the rounds," said Goudar, after having ordered the coachman to wait for them at the end of the street.

Neither the head master nor his assistants knew any thing. The nurseryman had heard it said that No. 23 belonged to an Englishman; but he had never seen him, and did not even know his name.

The locksmith knew that he was called Francis Burnett. He had done some work for him, for which he had been well paid, and thus he had frequently seen him; but it was so long since, that he did not think he would recognize him.

"We are unlucky," said M. Folgat, after this visit.

The memory of the liveryman was more trustworthy. He said he knew the Englishman of No. 23 very well, having driven him three or four times; and the description he gave of him answered fully to Jacques de Boiscoran. He also remembered that one evening, when the weather was wretched, Sir Burnett had come himself to order a carriage. It was for a lady, who had got in alone, and who had been driven to the Place de la Madeleine. But it was a dark night; the lady wore a thick veil; he had not been able to distinguish her features, and all he could say was that she looked above medium height.

"It is always the same story," said Goudar. "But the wine-merchant ought to be best informed. If I were alone I would breakfast there."

"I shall breakfast with you," said M. Folgat.

- 311 -

They did so, and they did wisely.

The wine-merchant did not know much; but his waiter, who had been with him five or six years, knew Sir Burnett, as everybody called the Englishman, by sight, and was quite well acquainted with the servant-girl, Suky Wood. While he was bringing in breakfast, he told them all he knew.

Suky, he said, was a tall, strapping girl, with hair red enough to set her bonnets on fire, and graceful enough to be mistaken for a heavy dragoon in female disguise. He had often had long talks with her when she came to fetch some ready-made dish, or to buy some beer, of which she was very fond. She told him she was very pleased with her place, as she got plenty of money, and had, so to say, nothing to do, being left alone in the house for nine months in the year. From her the waiter had also learned that Sir Burnett must have another house, and that he came to Vine Street only to receive visits from a lady.

This lady troubled Suky very much. She declared she had never been able to see the end of her nose even, so very cautious was she in all her movements; but she intended to see her in spite of all.

"And you may be sure she managed to do it some time or other," Goudar whispered into M. Folgat's ear.

Finally they learned from this waiter, that Suky had been very intimate with the servant of an old gentleman who lived quite alone in No. 27.

"We must see her," said Goudar.

Luckily the girl's master had just gone out, and she was alone in the house. At first she was a little frightened at being called upon and questioned by two unknown men; but the detective knew how to reassure her very quickly, and, as she was a great talker, she confirmed all the waiter at the restaurant had told them, and added some details.

Suky had been very intimate with her; she had never hesitated to tell her that Burnett was not an Englishman; that his name was not Burnett, and that he was concealing himself in Vine Street under a false name, for the purpose of meeting there his lady-love, who was a grand, fine lady, and marvellously beautiful. Finally, at the outbreak of the war, Suky had told her that she was going back to England to her relations. When they left the old bachelor's house, Goudar said to the young advocate,—

"We have obtained but little information, and the jurymen would pay little attention to it; but there is enough of it to confirm, at least in part, M. de Boiscoran's statement. We can prove that he met a lady here who had the greatest interest in remaining unknown. Was this, as he says, the Countess Claudieuse? We might find this out from Suky; for she has seen her, beyond all doubt. Hence we must hunt up Suky. And now, let us take our carriage, and go to headquarters. You can wait for me at the café near the Palais de Justice. I shall not be away more than a quarter of an hour."

It took him, however, a good hour and a half; M. Folgat was beginning to be troubled, when he at last reappeared, looking very well pleased.

"Waiter, a glass of beer!" he said.

And, sitting down so as to face the advocate, he said,—

"I stayed away rather long; but I did not lose any time. In the first place, I procured a month's leave of absence; then I put my hand upon the very man whom I wanted to send after Sir Burnett and Miss Suky. He is a good fellow, called Barousse, fine like a needle, and speaks English like a native. He demands twenty-five francs a day, his travelling-expenses, and a gratuity of fifteen hundred francs if he succeeds. I have agreed to meet him at six to give him a definite answer. If you accept the conditions, he will leave for England to-night, well drilled by me."

Instead of any answer, M. Folgat drew from his pocket-book a thousand-franc note, and said,—

"Here is something to begin with."

Goudar had finished his beer, and said,—

"Well, then, I must leave you. I am going to hang abut M. de Tassar's house, and make my inquiries. Perhaps I may pick up something there. To-morrow I shall spend my day in searching the house in Vine Street and in questioning all the tradesmen on your list. The day after to-morrow I shall probably have finished here.

So that in four or five days there will arrive in Sauveterre a somebody, who will be myself." And as he got up, he added,—

"For I must save M. de Boiscoran. I will and I must do it. He has too nice a house. Well, we shall see each other at Sauveterre."

It struck four o'clock. M. Folgat left the café immediately after Goudar, and went down the river to University Street. He was anxious to see the marquis and the marchioness.

"The marchioness is resting," said the valet; "but the marquis is in his cabinet."

M. Folgat was shown in, and found him still under the effects of the terrible scene he had undergone in the morning. He had said nothing to his wife that he did not really think; but he was distressed at having said it under such circumstances. And yet he felt a kind of relief; for, to tell the truth, he felt as if the horrible doubts which he had kept secret so many years had vanished as soon as they were spoken out. When he saw M. Folgat, he asked in a sadly-changed voice,—

"Well?"

The young advocate repeated in detail the account given by the marchioness; but he added what the latter had not been able to mention, because she did not know it, the desperate resolution which Jacques had formed. At this revelation the marquis looked utterly overcome.

"The unhappy man!" he cried. "And I accused him of—He thought of killing himself!"

"And we had a great trouble, M. Magloire, and myself," added M. Folgat, "to overcome his resolution, great trouble to make him understand, that never, under any circumstances, ought an innocent man to think of committing suicide."

A big tear rolled down the furrowed cheek of the old gentleman; and he murmured,—

"Ah! I have been cruelly unjust. Poor, unhappy child!"

Then he added aloud,—

"But I shall see him. I have determined to accompany the marchioness to Sauveterre. When will you leave?"

"Nothing keeps me here in Paris. I have done all that could be done, and I might return this evening. But I am really too tired. I think I shall to-morrow take the train at 10.45."

"If you do so, we shall travel in company; you understand? To-morrow at ten o'clock at the Orleans station. We shall reach Sauveterre by midnight."

XX.

When the Marchioness de Boiscoran, on the day of her departure for Paris, had gone to see her son, Dionysia had asked her to let her go with her. She resisted, and the young girl did not insist.

"I see they are trying to conceal something from me," she said simply; "but it does not matter."

And she had taken refuge in the sitting-room; and there, taking her usual seat, as in the happy days when Jacques spent all his evenings by her side, she had remained long hours immovable, looking as if, with her mind's eye, she was following invisible scenes far away.

Grandpapa Chandore and the two aunts were indescribably anxious. They knew their Dionysia, their darling child, better than she knew herself, having nursed and watched her for twenty years. They knew every expression of her face, every gesture, every intonation of voice, and could almost read her thoughts in her features.

"Most assuredly Dionysia is meditating upon something very serious," they said. "She is evidently calculating and preparing for a great resolution."

The old gentleman thought so too, and asked her repeatedly,—

"What are you thinking of, dear child?"

"Of nothing, dear papa," she replied.

"You are sadder than usual: why are you so?"

"Alas! How do I know? Does anybody know why one day we have sunshine in our hearts, and another day dismal clouds?"

But the next day she insisted upon being taken to her seamstresses, and finding Mechinet, the clerk, there, she remained a full half-hour in conference with him. Then, in the evening, when Dr. Seignebos, after a short visit, was leaving the room, she lay in wait for him, and kept him talking a long time at the door. Finally, the day after, she asked once more to be allowed to go and see Jacques. They could no longer refuse her this sad satisfaction; and it was agreed that the older of the two Misses Lavarande, Miss Adelaide, should accompany her.

About two o'clock on that day they knocked at the prison-door, and asked the jailer, who had come to open the door, to let them see Jacques.

"I'll go for him at once, madam," replied Blangin. "In the meantime pray step in here: the parlor is rather damp, and the less you stay in it, the better it will be."

Dionysia did so, or rather, she did a great deal more; for, leaving her aunt down stairs, she drew Mrs. Blangin to the upper room, having something to say to her, as she pretended.

When they came down again, Blangin told them that M. de Boiscoran was waiting for them.

"Come!" said the young girl to her aunt.

But she had not taken ten steps in the long narrow passage which led to the parlor, when she stopped. The damp which fell from the vaulted ceiling like a pall upon her, and the emotions which were agitating her heart, combined to overwhelm her. She tottered, and had to lean against the wall, reeking as it was with wet and with saltpetre.

"O Lord, you are ill!" cried Miss Adelaide.

Dionysia beckoned to her to be silent.

"Oh, it is nothing!" she said. "Be quiet!"

And gathering up all her strength, and putting her little hand upon the old lady's shoulder, she said,—

"My darling aunty, you must render us an immense service. It is all important that I should speak to Jacques alone. It would be very dangerous for us to be overheard. I know they often set spies to listen to prisoners' talk. Do please, dear aunt, remain here in the passage, and give us warning, if anybody should come."

"You do not think of it, dear child. Would it be proper?"

The young girl stopped her again.

"Was it proper when I came and spent a night here? Alas! in our position, every thing is proper that may be useful."

And, as Aunt Lavarande made no reply, she felt sure of her perfect submission, and went on towards the parlor.

"Dionysia!" cried Jacques as soon as she entered,—"Dionysia!"

He was standing in the centre of this mournful hall, looking whiter than the whitewash on the wall, but apparently calm, and almost smiling. The violence with which he controlled himself was horrible. But how could he allow his betrothed to see his despair? Ought he not, on the contrary, do every thing to reassure her?

He came up to her, took her hands in his, and said,—

"Ah, it is so kind in you to come! and yet I have looked for you ever since the morning. I have been watching and waiting, and trembling at every noise. But will you ever forgive me for having made you come to a place like this, untidy and ugly, without the fatal poetry of horror even?"

She looked at him with such obstinate fixedness, that the words expired on his lips.

"Why will you tell me a falsehood?" she said sadly.

"I tell you a falsehood!"

"Yes. Why do you affect this gayety and tranquillity, which are so far from your heart? Have you no longer confidence in me? Do you think I am a child, from whom the truth must be concealed, or so feeble and good for nothing, that I cannot bear my share of your troubles? Do not smile, Jacques; for I know you have no hope."

"You are mistaken, Dionysia, I assure you."

"No, Jacques. They are concealing something from me, I know, and I do not ask you to tell me what it is. I know quite enough. You will have to appear in court."

"I beg your pardon. That question has not yet been decided."

"But it will be decided, and against you."

Jacques knew very well it would be so, and dreaded it; but he still insisted upon playing his part.

"Well," he said, "if I appear in court, I shall be acquitted."

"Are you quite sure of that?"

"I have ninety-nine chances out of a hundred for me."

"There is one, however, against you," cried the young girl. And seizing Jacques's hands, and pressing them with a force of which he would never have suspected her, she added,—

"You have no right to run that one chance."

Jacques trembled in all his limbs. Was it possible? Did he understand her? Did Dionysia herself come and suggest to him that act of supreme despair, from which his counsel had so strongly dissuaded him?

"What do you mean?" he said with trembling voice.

"You must escape."

"Escape?"

"Nothing so easy. I have considered the whole matter thoroughly. The jailers are in our pay. I have just come to an understanding with Blangin's wife. One evening, as soon as night falls, they will open the doors to you. A horse will be ready for you outside of town, and relays have been prepared. In four hours you can reach Rochelle. There, one of those pilot-boats which can stand any storm takes you on board, and carries you to England."

Jacques shook his head.

"That cannot be," he replied. "I am innocent. I cannot abandon all I hold dear,—you, Dionysia."

A deep flush covered the young girl's cheeks. She stammered,—

"I have expressed myself badly. You shall not go alone."

He raised his hands to heaven, as if in utter despair.

"Great God! Thou grantest me this consolation!"

But Dionysia went on speaking in a firmer voice.

"Did you think I would be mean enough to forsake the friend who is betrayed by everybody else? No, no! Grandpapa and my aunts will accompany me, and we will meet you in England. You will change your name, and go across to America; and we will look out, far in the West, for some new country where we can establish ourselves. It won't be France, to be sure. But our country, Jacques, is the country where we are free, where we are beloved, where we are happy."

Jacques de Boiscoran was moved to the last fibre of his innermost heart, and in a kind of ecstasy which did not allow him to keep up any longer his mask of impassive indifference. Was there a man upon earth who could receive a more glorious proof of love and devotion? And from what a woman! From a young girl, who united in herself all the qualities of which a single one makes others proud,—intelligence and grace, high rank and fortune, beauty and angelic purity.

Ah! she did not hesitate like that other one; she did not think of asking for securities before she granted the first favor; she did not make a science of duplicity, nor hypocrisy her only virtue. She gave herself up entirely, and without the slightest reserve.

And all this at the moment when Jacques saw every thing else around him crumbled to pieces, when he was on the very brink of utter despair, just then this happiness came to him, this great and unexpected happiness, which well-nigh broke his heart.

For a moment he could not move, he could not think.

Then all of a sudden, drawing his betrothed to him, pressing her convulsively to his bosom, and covering her hair with a thousand kisses, he cried,—

"I bless you, oh, my darling! I bless you, my well beloved! I shall mourn no longer. Whatever may happen, I have had my share of heavenly bliss."

She thought he consented. Palpitating like the bird in the hand of a child, she drew back, and looking at Jacques with ineffable love and tenderness, she said,—

"Let us fix the day!"

"What day?"

"The day for your flight."

This word alone recalled Jacques to a sense of his fearful position. He was soaring in the supreme heights of the ether, and he was plunged down into the vile mud of reality. His face, radiant with celestial joy, grew dark in an instant, and he said hoarsely,—

"That dream is too beautiful to be realized."

"What do you say?" she stammered.

"I can not, I must not, escape!"

"You refuse me, Jacques?"

He made no reply.

"You refuse me, when I swear to you that I will join you, and share your exile? Do you doubt my word? Do you fear that my grandfather or my aunts might keep me here in spite of myself?"

As this suppliant voice fell upon his ears, Jacques felt as if all his energy abandoned him, and his will was shaken.

"I beseech you, Dionysia," he said, "do not insist, do not deprive me of my courage."

She was evidently suffering agonies. Her eyes shone with unbearable fire. Her dry lips were trembling.

"You will submit to being brought up in court?" she asked.

"Yes!"

"And if you are condemned?"

"I may be, I know."

"This is madness!" cried the young girl.

In her despair she was wringing her hands; and then the words escaped from her lips, almost unconsciously,—

"Great God," she said, "inspire me! How can I bend him? What must I say? Jacques, do you love me no longer? For my sake, if not for your own, I beseech you, let us flee! You escape disgrace; you secure liberty. Can nothing touch you? What do you want? Must I throw myself at your feet?"

And she really let herself fall at his feet.

"Flee!" she repeated again and again. "Oh, flee!"

Like all truly energetic men, Jacques recovered in the very excess of his emotion all his self-possession. Gathering his bewildered thoughts by a great effort of mind, he raised Dionysia, and carried her, almost fainting, to the rough prison bench; then, kneeling down by her side, and taking her hands he said,—

"Dionysia, for pity's sake, come to yourself and listen to me. I am innocent; and to flee would be to confess that I am guilty."

"Ah! what does that matter?"

"Do you think that my escape would stop the trial? No. Although absent, I should still be tried, and found guilty without any opposition: I should be condemned, disgraced, irrevocably dishonored."

"What does it matter?"

Then he felt that such arguments would never bring her back to reason. He rose, therefore, and said in a firm voice,—

"Let me tell you what you do not know. To flee would be easy, I agree. I think, as you do, we could reach England readily enough, and we might even take ship there without trouble. But what then? The cable is faster than the fastest steamer; and, upon landing on American soil, I should, no doubt, be met by agents with orders to arrest me. But suppose even I should escape this first danger. Do you think there is in all this world an asylum for incendiaries and murderers? There is none. At the extreme confines of civilization I should still meet with police-agents and soldiers, who, an extradition treaty in hand, would give me up to the government of my country. If I were alone, I might possibly escape all these dangers. But I should never succeed if I had you near me, and Grandpapa Chandore, and your two aunts."

Dionysia was forcibly struck by these objections, of which she had had no idea. She said nothing.

"Still, suppose we might possibly escape all such dangers. What would our life be! Do you know what it would mean to have to hide and to run incessantly, to have to avoid the looks of every stranger, and to tremble, day by day, at the thought of discovery? With me, Dionysia, your existence would be that of the wife of one of those banditti whom the police are hunting down in his dens. And you ought to know that such a life is so intolerable, that hardened criminals have been unable to endure it, and have given up their life for the boon of a night's quiet sleep."

Big tears were silently rolling down the poor girl's cheeks. She murmured,—

"Perhaps you are right, Jacques. But, O Jacques, if they should condemn you!"

"Well, I should at least have done my duty. I should have met fate, and defended my honor. And, whatever the sentence may be, it will not overthrow me; for, as long as my heart beats within me, I mean to defend myself. And, if I die before I succeed in proving my innocence, I shall leave it to you, Dionysia, to your kindred, and to my friends, to continue the struggle, and to restore my honor."

She was worthy of comprehending and of appreciating such sentiments.

"I was wrong, Jacques," she said, offering him her hand: "you must forgive me."

She had risen, and, after a few moments' hesitation, was about to leave the room, when Jacques retained her, saying,—

"I do not mean to escape; but would not the people who have agreed to favor my evasion be willing to furnish me the means for passing a few hours outside of my prison?"

"I think they would," replied the young girl; "And, if you wish it, I will make sure of it."

"Yes. That might be a last resort."

With these words they parted, exhorting each other to keep up their courage, and promising each other to meet again during the next days.

Dionysia found her poor aunt Lavarande very tired of the long watch; and they hastened home.

"How pale you are!" exclaimed M. de Chandore, when he saw his grand-daughter; "and how red your eyes are! What has happened?"

She told him every thing; and the old gentleman felt chilled to the marrow of his bones, when he found that it had depended on Jacques alone to carry off his grandchild. But he had not done so.

"Ah, he is an honest man!" he said.

And, pressing his lips on Dionysia's brow, he added,—

"And you love him more than ever?"

"Alas!" she replied, "is he not more unhappy than ever?"

XXI.

"Have you heard the news?"

"No: what is it?"

"Dionysia de Chandore has been to see M. de Boiscoran in prison."

"Is it possible?"

"Yes, indeed! Twenty people have seen her come back from there, leaning on the arm of the older Miss Lavarande. She went in at ten minutes past ten, and she did not come out till a quarter-past three."

"Is the young woman mad?"

"And the aunt—what do you think of the aunt?"

"She must be as mad as the niece."

"And M. de Chandore?"

"He must have lost his senses to allow such a scandal. But you know very well, grandfather and aunts never had any will but Dionysia's."

"A nice training!"

"And nice fruits of such an education! After such a scandal, no man will be bold enough to marry her."

Such were the comments on Dionysia's visit to Jacques, when the news became known. It flew at once all over town. The ladies "in society" could not recover from it; for people are exceedingly virtuous at Sauveterre, and hence they claim the right of being exceedingly strict in their judgment. There is no trifling permitted on the score of propriety.

The person who defies public opinion is lost. Now, public opinion was decidedly against Jacques de Boiscoran. He was down, and everybody was ready to kick him.

"Will he get out of it?"

This problem, which was day by day discussed at the "Literary Club," had called forth torrents of eloquence, terrible discussions, and even one or two serious quarrels, one of which had ended in a duel. But nobody asked any longer,—

"Is he innocent?"

Dr. Seignebos's eloquence, the influence of M. Seneschal, and the cunning plots of Mechinet, had all failed.

"Ah, what an interesting trial it will be!" said many people, who were all eagerness to know who would be the presiding judge, in order to ask him for tickets of admission. Day by day the interest in the trial became deeper; and all who were in any way connected with it were watched with great curiosity. Everybody wanted to know what they were doing, what they thought, and what they had said.

They saw in the absence of the Marquis de Boiscoran an additional proof of Jacques's guilt. The continued presence of M. Folgat also created no small wonder. His extreme reserve, which they ascribed to his excessive and ill-placed pride, had made him generally disliked. And now they said,—

"He must have hardly any thing to do in Paris, that he can spend so many months in Sauveterre."

The editor of "The Sauveterre Independent" naturally found the affair a veritable gold-mine for his paper. He forgot his old quarrel with the editor of "The Impartial Journal," whom he accused of Bonapartism, and who retaliated by calling him a Communist. Each day brought, in addition to the usual mention under the "local" head, some article on the "Boiscoran Case." He wrote,—

"The health of Count C., instead of improving, is declining visibly. He used to get up occasionally when he first came to Sauveterre; and now he rarely leaves his bed. The wound in the shoulder, which at first seemed to be the least dangerous, has suddenly become much inflamed, owing to the tropical heat of the last days. At one time gangrene was apprehended, and it was feared that amputation would become necessary. Yesterday Dr. S. seemed to be much disturbed.

"And, as misfortunes never come singly, the youngest daughter of Count C. is very ill. She had the measles at the time of the fire; and the fright, the cold, and the removal, have brought on a relapse, which may be dangerous.

"Amid all these cruel trials, the Countess C. is admirable in her devotion, her courage, and her resignation. Whenever she leaves the bedside of her dear patients to pray at church for them, she is received with the most touching sympathy and the most sincere admiration by the whole population."

"Ah, that wretch Boiscoran!" cried the good people of Sauveterre when they read such an article.

The next day, they found this,—

"We have sent to the hospital to inquire from the lady superior how the poor idiot is, who has taken such a prominent part in the bloody drama at Valpinson. His mental condition remains unchanged since he has been examined by experts. The spark of intelligence which the crime had elicited seems to be extinguished entirely and forever. It is impossible to obtain a word from him. He is, however, not locked up. Inoffensive and gentle, like a poor animal that has lost its master, he wanders mournfully through the courts and gardens of the hospital. Dr. S., who used to take a lively interest in him, hardly ever sees him now.

"It was thought at one time, that C. would be summoned to give evidence in the approaching trial. We are informed by high authority, that such a dramatic scene must not be expected to take place. C. will not appear before the jury."

"Certainly, Cocoleu's deposition must have been an interposition of Providence," said people who were not far from believing that it was a genuine miracle.

The next day the editor took M. Galpin in hand.

"M. G., the eminent magistrate, is very unwell just now, and very naturally so after an investigation of such length and importance as that which preceded the Boiscoran trial. We are told that he only awaits the decree of the court, to ask for a furlough and to go to one of the rural stations of the Pyrenees."

Then came Jacques's turn,—

"M. J. de B. stands his imprisonment better than could be expected. According to direct information, his health is excellent, and his spirits do not seem to have suffered. He reads much, and spends part of the night in preparing his defence, and making notes for his counsel."

Then came, from day to day, smaller items,—

"M. J. de B. is no longer in close confinement."

Or,—

"M. de B. had this morning an interview with his counsel, M. M., the most eminent member of our bar, and M. F., a young but distinguished advocate from Paris. The conference lasted several hours. We abstain from giving details; but our readers will understand the reserve required in the case of an accused who insists upon protesting energetically that he is innocent."

And, again,—

"M. de B. was yesterday visited by his mother."

Or, finally,—

"We hear at the last moment that the Marchioness de B. and M. Folgat have left for Paris. Our correspondent in P. writes us that the decree of the court will not be delayed much longer."

Never had "The Sauveterre Independent" been read with so much interest. And, as everybody endeavored to be better informed than his neighbor, quite a number of idle men had assumed the duty of watching Jacques's friends, and spent their days in trying to find out what was going on at M. de Chandore's house. Thus it came about, that, on the evening of Dionysia's visit to Jacques, the street was full of curious people. Towards half-past ten, they saw M. de Chandore's carriage come out of the courtyard, and draw up at the door. At eleven o'clock M. de Chandore and Dr. Seignebos got in, the coachman whipped the horse, and they drove off.

"Where can they be going?" asked they.

They followed the carriage. The two gentlemen drove to the station. They had received a telegram, and were expecting the return of the marchioness and M. Folgat, accompanied, this time, by the old marquis.

They reached there much too soon. The local branch railway which goes to Sauveterre is not famous for regularity, and still reminds its patrons occasionally of the old habits of stage-coaches, when the driver or the conductor had, at the last moment, to stop to pick up something they had forgotten. At a quarter-past midnight the train, which ought to have been there twenty minutes before, had not yet been signalled. Every thing around was silent and deserted. Through the windows the station-master might be seen fast asleep in his huge leather chair. Clerks and porters all were asleep, stretched out on the benches of the waiting-room. But people are accustomed to such delays at Sauveterre; they are prepared for being kept waiting: and the doctor and M. de Chandore were walking up and down the platform, being neither astonished nor impatient at the irregularity. Nor would they have been much surprised if they had been told that they were closely watched all the time: they knew their good town. Still it was so. Two curious men, more obstinate than the others, had jumped into the omnibus which runs between the station and the town; and now, standing a little aside, they said to each other,—

"I say, what can they be waiting for?"

At last towards one o'clock, a bell rang, and the station seemed to start into life. The station-master opened his door, the porters stretched themselves and rubbed their eyes, oaths were heard, doors slammed, and the large hand-barrows came in sight.

Then a low thunder-like noise came nearer and nearer; and almost instantly a fierce red light at the far end of the track shone out in the dark night like a ball of fire. M. de Chandore and the doctor hastened to the waiting-room.

The train stopped. A door opened, and the marchioness appeared, leaning on M. Folgat's arm. The marquis, a travelling-bag in hand, followed next.

"That was it!" said the volunteer spies, who had flattened their noses against the window-panes.

And, as the train brought no other passengers, they succeeded in making the omnibus conductor start at once, eager as they were to proclaim the arrival of the prisoner's father.

The hour was unfavorable: everybody was asleep; but they did not give up the hope of finding somebody yet at the club. People stay up very late at the club, for there is play going on there, and at times pretty heavy play: you can lose your five hundred francs quite readily there. Thus the indefatigable news-hunters had a fair chance of finding open ears for their great piece of news. And yet, if they had been less eager to spread it, they might have witnessed, perhaps not entirely unmoved, this first interview between M. de Chandore and the Marquis de Boiscoran.

By a natural impulse they had both hastened forward, and shook hands in the most energetic manner. Tears stood in their eyes. They opened their lips to speak; but they said nothing. Besides, there was no need of words between them. That close embrace had told Jacques's father clearly enough what Dionysia's grandfather must have suffered. They remained thus standing motionless, looking at each other, when Dr. Seignebos, who could not be still for any length of time, came up, and asked,—

"The trunks are on the carriage: shall we go?"

They left the station. The night was clear; and on the horizon, above the dark mass of the sleeping town, there rose against the pale-blue sky the two towers of the old castle, which now served as prison to Sauveterre.

"That is the place where my Jacques is kept," murmured the marquis. "There my son is imprisoned, accused of horrible crimes."

"We will get him out of it," said the doctor cheerfully, as he helped the old gentleman into the carriage.

But in vain did he try, during the drive, to rouse, as he called it, the spirits of his companions. His hopes found no echo in their distressed hearts.

M. Folgat inquired after Dionysia, whom he had been surprised not to see at the station. M. de Chandore replied that she had staid at home with the Misses Lavarande, to keep M. Magloire company; and that was all.

There are situations in which it is painful to talk. The marquis had enough to do to suppress the spasmodic sobs which now and then would rise in his throat. He was upset by the thought that he was at Sauveterre. Whatever may be said to the contrary, distance does not weaken our emotions. Shaking hands with M. de Chandore in person had moved him more deeply than all the letters he had received for a month. And when he saw Jacques's prison from afar, he had the first clear notion of the horrible tortures endured by his son. The marchioness was utterly exhausted: she felt as if all the springs in her system were broken.

M. de Chandore trembled when he looked at them, and saw how they all were on the point of succumbing. If they despaired, what could he hope for,—he, who knew how indissolubly Dionysia's fate in life was connected with Jacques?

At length the carriage stopped before his house. The door opened instantly, and the marchioness found herself in Dionysia's arms, and soon after comfortably seated in an easy-chair. The others had followed her. It was past two o'clock; but every minute now was valuable. Arranging his spectacles, Dr. Seignebos said,—

"I propose that we exchange our information. I, for my part, I am still at the same point. But you know my views. I do not give them up. Cocoleu is an impostor, and it shall be proved. I appear to notice him no longer; but, in reality, I watch him more closely than ever."

Dionysia interrupted him, saying,—

"Before any thing is decided, there is one fact which you all ought to know. Listen."

Pale like death, for it cost her a great struggle to reveal thus the secret of her heart, but with a voice full of energy, and an eye full of fire, she told them what she had already confessed to her grandfather; viz., the propositions she had made to Jacques, and his obstinate refusal to accede to them.

"Well done, madame!" said Dr. Seignebos, full of enthusiasm. "Well done! Jacques is very unfortunate, and still he is to be envied."

Dionysia finished her recital. Then, turning with a triumphant air to M. Magloire, she added,—

"After that, is there any one yet who could believe that Jacques is a vile assassin?"

The eminent advocate of Sauveterre was not one of those men who prize their opinions more highly than truth itself.

"I confess," he said, "that, if I were to go and see Jacques to-morrow for the first time, I should not speak to him as I did before."

"And I," exclaimed the Marquis de Boiscoran,—"I declare that I answer for my son as for myself, and I mean to tell him so to-morrow."

Then turning towards his wife, and speaking so low, that she alone could hear him, he added,—

"And I hope you will forgive me those suspicions which now fill me with horror."

But the marchioness had no strength left: she fainted, and had to be removed, accompanied by Dionysia and the Misses Lavarande. As soon as they were out of the room, Dr. Seignebos locked the door, rested his elbow on the chimney, and, taking off his spectacles to wipe them, said to M. Folgat,—

"Now we can speak freely. What news do you bring us?"

XXII.

It had just struck eleven o'clock, when the jailer, Blangin, entered Jacques's cell in great excitement, and said,—

"Sir, your father is down stairs."

The prisoner jumped up, thunderstruck.

The night before he had received a note from M. de Chandore, informing him of the marquis's arrival; and his whole time had since been spent in preparing himself for the interview. How would it be? He had nothing by which to judge. He had therefore determined to be quite reserved. And, whilst he was following Blangin along the dismal passage and down the interminable steps, he was busily composing respectful phrases, and trying to look self-possessed.

But, before he could utter a single word, he was in his father's arms. He felt himself pressed against his heart, and heard him stammer,—

"Jacques, my dear son, my unfortunate child!"

In all his life, long and stormy as it had been, the marquis had not been tried so severely. Drawing Jacques to one of the parlor-windows, and leaning back a little, so as to see him better, he was amazed how he could ever have doubted his son. It seemed to him that he was standing there himself. He recognized his own feature and carriage, his own frank but rather haughty expression, his own clear, bright eye.

Then, suddenly noticing details, he was shocked to see Jacques so much reduced. He found him looking painfully pale, and he actually discovered at the temples more than one silvery hair amid his thick black curls.

"Poor child!" he said. "How you must have suffered!"

"I thought I should lose my senses," replied Jacques simply.

And with a tremor in his voice, he asked,—

"But, dear father, why did you give me no sign of life? Why did you stay away so long?"

The marquis was not unprepared for such a question. But how could he answer it? Could he ever tell Jacques the true secret of his hesitation? Turning his eyes aside, he answered,—

"I hoped I should be able to serve you better by remaining in Paris." But his embarrassment was too evident to escape Jacques.

"You did not doubt your own child, father?" he asked sadly.

"Never!" cried the marquis, "I never doubted a moment. Ask your mother, and she will tell you that it was this proud assurance I felt which kept me from coming down with her. When I heard of what they accused you, I said 'It is absurd!'"

Jacques shook his head, and said,—

"The accusation was absurd; and yet you see what it has brought me to."

Two big tears, which he could no longer retain, burnt in the eyes of the old gentleman.

"You blame me, Jacques," he said. "You blame your father."

There is not a man alive who could see his father shed tears, and not feel his heart melt within him. All the resolutions Jacques had formed vanished in an instant. Pressing his father's hand in his own, he said,—

"No, I do not blame you, father. And still I have no words to tell you how much your absence has added to my sufferings. I thought I was abandoned, disowned."

For the first time since his imprisonment, the unfortunate man found a heart to whom he could confide all the bitterness that overflowed in his own heart. With his mother and with Dionysia, honor forbade him to show despair. The incredulity of M. Magloire had made all confidence impossible; and M. Folgat, although as sympathetic as man could be was, after all, a perfect stranger.

But now he had near him a friend, the dearest and most precious friend that a man can ever have,—his father: now he had nothing to fear.

"Is there a human being in this world," he said, "whose misfortunes equal mine? To be innocent, and not to be able to prove it! To know the guilty one, and not to dare mention the name. Ah! at first I did not take in the whole horror of my situation. I was frightened, to be sure; but I had recovered, thinking that surely justice would not be slow in discovering the truth. Justice! It was my friend Galpin who represented it, and he cared little enough for truth: his only aim was to prove that the man whom he accused was the guilty man. Read the papers, father, and you will see how I have been victimized by the most unheard-of combination of circumstances. Every thing is against me. Never has that mysterious, blind, and absurd power manifested itself so clearly,—that awful power which we call fate.

"First I was kept by a sense of honor from mentioning the name of the Countess Claudieuse, and then by prudence. The first time I mentioned it to M. Magloire, he told me I lied. Then I thought every thing lost. I saw no other end but the court, and, after the trial, the galleys or the scaffold. I wanted to kill myself. My friends made me understand that I did not belong to myself, and that, as long as I had a spark of energy and a ray of intelligence left me, I had no right to dispose of my life."

"Poor, poor child!" said the marquis. "No, you have no such right."

"Yesterday," continued Jacques, "Dionysia came to see me. Do you know what brought her here? She offered to flee with me. Father, that temptation was terrible. Once free, and Dionysia by my side, what cared I for the world? She insisted, like the matchless girl that she is; and look there, there, on the spot where you now stand, she threw herself at my feet, imploring me to flee. I doubt whether I can save my life; but I remain here."

He felt deeply moved, and sank upon the rough bench, hiding his face in his hands, perhaps to conceal his tears.

Suddenly, however, he was seized with one of those attacks of rage which had come to him but too often during his imprisonment, and he exclaimed,—

"But what have I done to deserve such fearful punishment?"

The brow of the marquis suddenly darkened; and he replied solemnly,—

"You have coveted your neighbor's wife, my son."

Jacques shrugged his shoulders. He said,—

"I loved the Countess Claudieuse, and she loved me."

"Adultery is a crime, Jacques."

"A crime? Magloire said the same thing. But, father, do you really think so? Then it is a crime which has nothing appalling about it, to which every thing invites and encourages, of which everybody boasts, and at which the world smiles. The law, it is true, gives the husband the right of life and death; but, if you appeal to the law, it gives the guilty man six months' imprisonment, or makes him pay a few thousand francs."

Ah, if he had known, the unfortunate man!

"Jacques," said the marquis, "the Countess Claudieuse hints, as you say, that one of her daughters, the youngest, is your child?"

"That may be so."

The Marquis de Boiscoran shuddered. Then he exclaimed bitterly,—

"That may be so! You say that carelessly, indifferently, madman! Did you never think of the grief Count Claudieuse would feel if he should learn the truth? And even if he merely suspected it! Can you not comprehend that such a suspicion is quite sufficient to embitter a whole life, to ruin the life of that girl? Have you never told yourself that such a doubt inflicts a more atrocious punishment than any thing you have yet suffered?"

He paused. A few words more, and he would have betrayed his secret. Checking his excitement by an heroic effort, he said,—

"But I did not come here to discuss this question; I came to tell you, that, whatever may happen, your father will stand by you, and that, if you must undergo the disgrace of appearing in court, I will take a seat by your side."

In spite of his own great trouble, Jacques had not been able to avoid seeing his father's unusual excitement and his sudden vehemence. For a second, he had a vague perception of the truth; but, before the suspicion could assume any shape, it had vanished before this promise which his father made, to face by his side the overwhelming humiliation of a judgment in court,—a promise full of divine self-abnegation and paternal love. His gratitude burst forth in the words,—

"Ah, father! I ought to ask your pardon for ever having doubted your heart for a moment."

M. de Boiscoran tried his best to recover his self-possession. At last he said in an earnest voice,—

"Yes, I love you, my son; and still you must not make me out more of a hero than I am. I still hope we may be spared the appearance in court."

"Has any thing new been discovered?"

"M. Folgat has found some traces which justify legitimate hopes, although, as yet, no real success has been achieved."

Jacques looked rather discouraged.

"Traces?" he asked.

"Be patient. They are feeble traces, I admit, and such as could not be produced in court; but from day to day they may become decisive. And already they have had one good effect: they have brought us back M. Magloire."

"O God! Could I really be saved?"

"I shall leave to M. Folgat," continued the marquis, "the satisfaction of telling you the result of his efforts. He can explain their bearing better than I could. And you will not have long to wait; for last night, or rather this morning, when we separated, he and M. Magloire agreed to meet here at the prison, before two o'clock."

A few minutes later a rapid step approached in the passage; and Trumence appeared, the prisoner of whom Blangin had made an assistant, and whom Mechinet had employed to carry Jacques's letters to Dionysia. He was a tall well-made man of twenty-five or six years, whose large mouth and small eyes were perpetually laughing. A vagabond without hearth or home, Trumence had once been a land-owner. At the death of his parents, when he was only eighteen years old, Trumence had come into possession of a house surrounded by a yard, a garden, several acres of land, and a salt meadow; all worth about fifteen thousand francs. Unfortunately the time for the conscription was near. Like many young men of that district, Trumence believed in witchcraft, and had gone to buy a charm, which cost him fifty francs. It consisted of three tamarind-branches gathered on Christmas Eve, and tied together by a magic number of hairs drawn from a dead man's head. Having sewed this charm into his waistcoat, Trumence had gone to town, and, plunging his hand boldly into the urn, had drawn number three. This was unexpected. But as he had a great horror of military service, and, well-made as he was, felt quite sure that he would not be rejected, he determined to employ a chance much more certain to succeed; namely, to borrow money in order to buy a substitute.

As he was a land-owner, he found no difficulty in meeting with an obliging person, who consented to lend him for two years thirty-five hundred francs, in return for a first mortgage on his property. When the papers were signed, and Trumence had the money in his pocket, he set out for Rochefort, where dealers in substitutes abounded; and for the sum of two thousand francs, exclusive of some smaller items, they furnished him a substitute of the best quality.

Delighted with the operation, Trumence was about to return home, when his evil star led him to sup at his inn with a countryman, a former schoolmate, who was now a sailor on board a coal-barge. Of course, countrymen when they meet must drink. They did drink; and, as the sailor very soon scented the twelve hundred francs which remained in Trumence's pockets, he swore that he was going to have a jolly time, and would not return on board his barge as long as there remained a cent in his friend's pocket. So it happened, that, after a fortnight's carouse, the sailor was arrested and put in jail; and Trumence was compelled to borrow five francs from the stage-driver to enable him to get home.

This fortnight was decisive for his life. During these days he had lost all taste for work, and acquired a real passion for taverns where they played with greasy cards. After his return he tried to continue this jolly life; and, to do so, he made more debts. He sold, piece after piece, all he possessed that was salable, down to his mattress and his tools. This was not the way to repay the thirty-five hundred francs which he owed. When pay-day came, the creditor, seeing that his security was diminishing every day, lost no time. Before Trumence was well aware of what was going on, an execution was in the house; his lands were sold; and one fine day he found himself in the street, possessing literally nothing in the world but the wretched clothes on his back.

He might easily have found employment; for he was a good workman, and people were fond of him in spite of all. But he was even more afraid of work than he was fond of drink. Whenever want pressed too hard, he worked a few days; but, as soon as he had earned ten francs, good-by! Off he went, lounging by the road-side, talking with the wagoners, or loafing about the villages, and watching for one of those kind topers, who, rather than drink alone, invite the first-comer. Trumence boasted of being well known all along the coast, and even far into the department. And what was most surprising was that people did not blame him much for his idleness. Good housewives in the country would, it is true, greet him with a "Well, what do you want here, good-for-nothing?" But they would rarely refuse him a bowl of soup or a glass of white wine. His unchanging good-humor, and his obliging disposition, explained this forbearance. This man, who would refuse a well-paid job, was ever ready to lend a hand for nothing. And he was handy at every thing, by land and by water, he called it, so that the farmer whose business was pressing, and the fisherman in his boat who wanted help, appealed alike to Trumence.

The mischief, however, is, that this life of rural beggary, if it has its good days, also has its evil times. On certain days, Trumence could not find either kind-hearted topers or hospitable housewives. Hunger, however, was ever on hand; then he had to become a marauder; dig some potatoes, and cook them in a corner of a wood, or pilfer the orchards. And if he found neither potatoes in the fields, nor apples in the orchards, what could he do but climb a fence, or scale a wall?

Relatively speaking, Trumence was an honest man, and incapable of stealing a piece of money; but vegetables, fruits, chickens—

Thus it had come about that he had been arrested twice, and condemned to several days' imprisonment; and each time he had vowed solemnly that he would never be caught at it again, and that he was going to work hard. And yet he had been caught again.

The poor fellow had told his misfortunes to Jacques; and Jacques, who owed it to him that he could, when still in close confinement, correspond with Dionysia, felt very kindly towards him. Hence, when he saw him come up very respectful, and cap in hand, he asked,—

"What is it, Trumence?"

"Sir," replied the vagrant, "M. Blangin sends you word that the two advocates are coming up to your room."

Once more the marquis embraced his son, saying,—

"Do not keep them waiting, and keep up your courage."

XXIII.

The Marquis de Boiscoran had not been mistaken about M. Magloire. Much shaken by Dionysia's statement, he had been completely overcome by M. Folgat's explanations; and, when he now came to the jail, it was with a determination to prove Jacques's innocence.

"But I doubt very much whether he will ever forgive me for my incredulity," he said to M. Folgat while they were waiting for the prisoner in his cell.

Jacques came in, still deeply moved by the scene with his father. M. Magloire went up to him, and said,—

"I have never been able to conceal my thoughts, Jacques. When I thought you guilty, and felt sure that you accused the Countess Claudieuse falsely, I told you so with almost brutal candor. I have since found out my error, and am now convinced of the truth of your statement: so I come and tell you as frankly, Jacques, I was wrong to have had more faith in the reputation of a woman than in the words of a friend. Will you give me your hand?"

The prisoner grasped his hand with a profusion of joy, and cried,—

"Since you believe in my innocence, others may believe in me too, and my salvation is drawing near."

The melancholy faces of the two advocates told him that he was rejoicing too soon. His features expressed his grief; but he said with a firm voice,—

"Well, I see that the struggle will be a hard one, and that the result is still uncertain. Never mind. You may be sure I will not give way."

In the meantime M. Folgat had spread out on the table all the papers he had brought with him,—copies furnished by Mechinet, and notes taken during his rapid journey.

"First of all, my dear client," he said, "I must inform you of what has been done."

And when he had stated every thing, down to the minutest details of what Goudar and he had done, he said,—

"Let us sum up. We are able to prove three things: 1. That the house in Vine Street belongs to you, and that Sir Francis Burnett, who is known there, and you are one; 2. That you were visited in this house by a lady, who, from all the precautions she took, had powerful reasons to remain unknown; 3. That the visits of this lady took place at certain epochs every year, which coincided precisely with the journeys which the Countess Claudieuse yearly made to Paris."

The great advocate of Sauveterre expressed his assent.

"Yes," he said, "all this is fully established."

"For ourselves, we have another certainty,—that Suky Wood, the servant of the false Sir Francis Burnett, has watched the mysterious lady; that she has seen her, and consequently would know her again."

"True, that appears from the deposition of the girl's friend."

"Consequently, if we discover Suky Wood, the Countess Claudieuse is unmasked."

"If we discover her," said M. Magloire. "And here, unfortunately, we enter into the region of suppositions."

"Suppositions!" said M. Folgat. "Well, call them so; but they are based upon positive facts, and supported by a hundred precedents. Why should we not find this Suky Wood, whose birthplace and family we know, and who has no reason for concealment? Goudar has found very different people; and Goudar is on our side. And you may be sure he will not be asleep. I have held out to him a certain hope which will make him do miracles,—the hope of receiving as a reward, if he succeeds, the house in Vine Street. The stakes are too magnificent: he must win the game,—he who has won so many already. Who knows what he may not have discovered since we left him? Has he not done wonders already?"

"It is marvellous!" cried Jacques, amazed at these results.

Older than M. Folgat and Jacques, the eminent advocate of Sauveterre was less ready to feel such enthusiasm.

"Yes," he said, "it is marvellous; and, if we had time, I would say as you do, 'We shall carry the day!' But there is no time for Goudar's investigations: the sessions are on hand, and it seems to me it would be very difficult to obtain a postponement."

"Besides, I do not wish it to be postponed," said Jacques.

"But"—

"On no account, Magloire, never! What? I should endure three months more of this anguish which tortures me? I could not do it: my strength is exhausted. This uncertainty has been too much for me. I could bear no more suspense."

M. Folgat interrupted him, saying,—

"Do not trouble yourself about that: a postponement is out of the question. On what pretext could we ask for it? The only way would be to introduce an entirely new element in the case. We should have to summon the Countess Claudieuse."

The greatest surprise appeared on Jacques's face.

"Will we not summon her anyhow?" he asked.

"That depends."

"I do not understand you."

"It is very simple, however. If Goudar should succeed, before the trial, in collecting sufficient evidence against her, I should summon her certainly; and then the case would naturally change entirely; the whole proceeding would begin anew; and you would probably appear only as a witness. If, on the contrary, we obtain, before the trial begins, no other proof but what we have now, I shall not mention her name even; for that would, in my opinion, and in M. Magloire's opinion, ruin your cause irrevocably."

"Yes," said the great advocate, "that is my opinion."

Jacques's amazement was boundless.

"Still," he said, "in self-defence, I must, if I am brought up in court, speak of my relations to the Countess Claudieuse."

"No."

"But that is my only explanation."

"If it were credited."

"And you think you can defend me, you think you can save me, without telling the truth?"

M. Folgat shook his head, and said,—

"In court the truth is the last thing to be thought of."

"Oh!"

"Do you think the jury would credit allegations which M. Magloire did not credit? No. Well, then, we had better not speak of them any more, and try to find some explanation which will meet the charges brought against you. Do you think we should be the first to act thus? By no means. There are very few cases in which the prosecution says all it knows, and still fewer in which the defence calls for every thing it might call for. Out of ten criminal trials, there are at least three in which side-issues are raised. What will be the charge in court against you? The substance of the romance which the magistrate has invented in order to prove your guilt. You must meet him with another romance which proves your innocence."

"But the truth."

"Is dependent on probability, my dear client. Ask M. Magloire. The prosecution only asks for probability: hence probability is all the defence has to care for. Human justice is feeble, and limited in its means; it cannot go down to the very bottom of things; it cannot judge of motives, and fathom consciences. It can only judge from appearances, and decide by plausibility; there is hardly a case which has not some unexplored mystery, some undiscovered secret. The truth! Ah! do you think M. Galpin has looked for it? If he did, why did he not summon Cocoleu? But no, as long as he can produce a criminal, who may be responsible for the crime, he is quite content. The truth! Which of us knows the real truth? Your case, M. de Boiscoran, is one of those in which neither the prosecution, nor the defence, nor the accused himself, knows the truth of the matter."

There followed a long silence, so deep a silence, that the step of the sentinel could be heard, who was walking up and down under the prison-windows. M. Folgat had said all he thought proper to say: he feared, in saying more, to assume too great a responsibility. It was, after all, Jacques's life and Jacques's honor which were at stake. He alone, therefore, ought to decide the nature of his defence. If his judgment was too forcibly controlled by his counsel, he would have had a right hereafter to say, "Why did you not leave me free to choose? I should not have been condemned."

To show this very clearly, M. Folgat went on,—

"The advice I give you, my dear client, is, in my eyes, the best; it is the advice I would give my own brother. But, unfortunately, I cannot say it is infallible. You must decide yourself. Whatever you may resolve, I am still at your service."

Jacques made no reply. His elbows resting on the table, his face in his hands, he remained motionless, like a statue, absorbed in his thoughts. What should he do? Should he follow his first impulse, tear the veil aside, and proclaim the truth? That was a doubtful policy, but also, what a triumph if he succeeded!

Should he adopt the views of his counsel, employ subterfuges and falsehoods? That was more certain of success; but to be successful in this way—was that a real victory?

Jacques was in a terrible perplexity. He felt it but too clearly. The decision he must form now would decide his fate. Suddenly he raised his head, and said,—

"What is your advice, M. Magloire?"

The great advocate of Sauveterre frowned angrily; and said, in a somewhat rough tone of voice,—

"I have had the honor to place before your mother all that my young colleague has just told you. M. Folgat has but one fault,—he is too cautious. The physician must not ask what his patient thinks of his remedies: he must prescribe them. It may be that our prescriptions do not meet with success; but, if you do not follow them, you are most assuredly lost."

Jacques hesitated for some minutes longer. These prescriptions, as M. Magloire called them, were painfully repugnant to his chivalrous and open character.

"Would it be worth while," he murmured, "to be acquitted on such terms? Would I really be exculpated by such proceedings? Would not my whole life thereafter be disgraced by suspicions? I should not come out from the trial with a clear acquittal: I should have escaped by a mere chance."

"That would still better than to go, by a clear judgment, to the galleys," said M. Magloire brutally.

This word, "the galleys," made Jacques bound. He rose, walked up and down a few times in his room, and then, placing himself in front of his counsel, said,—

"I put myself in your hands, gentlemen. Tell me what I must do."

Jacques had at least this merit, if he once formed a resolution, he was sure to adhere to it. Calm now, and self-possessed, he sat down, and said, with a melancholy smile,—

"Let us hear the plan of battle."

This plan had been for a month now the one great thought of M. Folgat. All his intelligence, all his sagacity and knowledge of the world, had been brought to bear upon this case, which he had made his own, so to say, by his almost passionate interest. He knew the tactics of the prosecution as well as M. Galpin himself, and he knew its weak and its strong side even better than M. Galpin.

"We shall go on, therefore," he began, "as if there was no such person as the Countess Claudieuse. We know nothing of her. We shall say nothing of the meeting at Valpinson, nor of the burned letters."

"That is settled."

"That being so, we must next look, not for the manner in which we spent our time, but for our purpose in going out the evening of the crime. Ah! If we could suggest a plausible, a very probable purpose, I should almost guarantee our success; for we need not hesitate to say there is the turning-point of the whole case, on which all the discussions will turn."

Jacques did not seem to be fully convinced of this view. He said,—

"You think that possible?"

"Unfortunately, it is but too certain; and, if I say unfortunately, it is because here we have to meet a terrible charge, the most decisive, by all means, that has been raised, one on which M. Galpin has not insisted (he is much too clever for that), but one which, in the hands of the prosecution, may become a terrible weapon."

"I must confess," said Jacques, "I do not very well see"—

"Have you forgotten the letter you wrote to Miss Dionysia the evening of the crime?" broke in M. Magloire.

Jacques looked first at one, and then at the other of his counsel.

"What," he said, "that letter?"

"Overwhelms us, my dear client," said M. Folgat. "Don't you remember it? You told your betrothed in that note, that you would be prevented from enjoying the evening with her by some business of the greatest importance, and which could not be delayed? Thus, you see, you had determined beforehand, and after mature consideration, to spend that evening in doing a certain thing. What was it? 'The murder of Count Claudieuse,' says the prosecution. What can we say?"

"But, I beg your pardon—that letter. Miss Dionysia surely has not handed it over to them?"

"No; but the prosecution is aware of its existence. M. de Chandore and M. Seneschal have spoken of it in the hope of exculpating you, and have even mentioned the contents. And M. Galpin knows it so well, that he had repeatedly mentioned it to you, and you have confessed all that he could desire."

The young advocate looked among his papers; and soon he had found what he wanted.

"Look here," he said, "in your third examination, I find this,—"

"'QUESTION.—You were shortly to marry Miss Chandore?

ANSWER.—Yes.

Q—For some time you had been spending your evenings with her?

A.—Yes, all.

Q.—Except the one of the crime?

A.—Unfortunately.

Q.—Then your betrothed must have wondered at your absence?

A.—No: I had written to her.'"

"Do you hear, Jacques?" cried M. Magloire. "Notice that M. Galpin takes care not to insist. He does not wish to rouse your suspicions. He has got you to confess, and that is enough for him."

But, in the meantime, M. Folgat had found another paper.

"In your sixth examination," he went on, "I have noticed this,—

"'Q.—You left your house with your gun on your shoulder, without any definite aim?

A.—I shall explain that when I have consulted with counsel.

Q.—You need no consultation to tell the truth.

- 345 -

A.—I shall not change my resolution.

Q.—Then you will not tell me where you were between eight and midnight?

A.—I shall answer that question at the same time with the other.

Q.—You must have had very strong reasons to keep you out, as you were expected by your betrothed, Miss Chandore?

A.—I had written to her not to expect me."'

"Ah! M. Galpin is a clever fellow," growled M. Magloire.

"Finally," said M. Folgat, "here is a passage from your last but one examination,—

"'Q.—When you wanted to send anybody to Sauveterre, whom did you usually employ?

A.—The son of one of my tenants, Michael.

Q.—It was he, I suppose, who, on the evening of the crime, carried the letter to Miss Chandore, in which you told her not to expect you?

A.—Yes.

Q.—You pretended you would be kept by some important business?

A.—That is the usual pretext.

Q.—But in your case it was no pretext. Where had you to go? and where did you go?

A.—As long as I have not seen counsel I shall say nothing.

Q.—Have a care: the system of negation and concealment is dangerous.

A.—I know it, and I accept the consequences."'

Jacques was dumfounded. And necessarily every accused person is equally surprised when he hears what he has stated in the examination. There is not one who does not exclaim,—

"What, I said that? Never!"

He has said it, and there is no denying it; for there it is written, and signed by himself. How could he ever say so?

Ah! that is the point. However clever a man may be, he cannot for many months keep all his faculties on the stretch, and all his energy up to its full power. He has his hours of prostration and his hours of hope, his attacks of despair and his moments of courage; and the impassive magistrate takes advantage of them all. Innocent or guilty, no prisoner can cope with him. However powerful his memory may be, how can he recall an answer which he may have given weeks and weeks before? The magistrate, however, remembers it; and twenty times, if need be, he brings it up again. And as the small snowflake may become an irresistible avalanche, so an insignificant word, uttered at haphazard, forgotten, then recalled, commented upon, and enlarged may become crushing evidence.

Jacques now experienced this. These questions had been put to him so skilfully, and at such long intervals of time, that he had totally forgotten them; and yet now, when he recalled his answers, he had to acknowledge that he had confessed his purpose to devote that evening to some business of great importance.

"That is fearful!" he cried.

And, overcome by the terrible reality of M. Folgat's apprehension, he added,—

"How can we get out of that?"

"I told you," replied M. Folgat, "we must find some plausible explanation."

"I am sure I am incapable of that."

The young lawyer seemed to reflect a moment, and then he said,—

"You have been a prisoner while I have been free. For a month now I have thought this matter over."

"Ah!"

"Where was your wedding to be?"

"At my house at Boiscoran."

"Where was the religious ceremony to take place?"

"At the church at Brechy."

"Have you ever spoken of that to the priest?"

"Several times. One day especially, when we discussed it in a pleasant way, he said jestingly to me, 'I shall have you, after all in my confessional.'"

M. Folgat almost trembled with satisfaction, and Jacques saw it.

"Then the priest at Brechy was your friend?"

"An intimate friend. He sometimes came to dine with me quite unceremoniously, and I never passed him without shaking hands with him."

The young lawyer's joy was growing perceptibly.

"Well," he said, "my explanation is becoming quite plausible. Just hear what I have positively ascertained to be the fact. In the time from nine to eleven o'clock, on the night of the crime, there was not a soul at the parsonage in Brechy. The priest was dining with M. Besson, at his house; and his servant had gone out to meet him with a lantern."

"I understand," said M. Magloire.

"Why should you not have gone to see the priest at Brechy, my dear client? In the first place, you had to arrange the details of the ceremony with him; then, as he is your friend, and a man of experience, and a priest, you wanted to ask him for his advice before taking so grave a step, and, finally, you intended to fulfil that religious duty of which he spoke, and which you were rather reluctant to comply with."

"Well said!" approved the eminent lawyer of Sauveterre,—"very well said!"

"So, you see, my dear client, it was for the purpose of consulting the priest at Brechy that you deprived yourself of the pleasure of spending the evening with your betrothed. Now let us see how that answers the allegations of the prosecution. They ask you why you took to the marshes. Why? Because it was the shortest way, and you were afraid of finding the priest in bed. Nothing more natural;

for it is well known that the excellent man is in the habit of going to bed at nine o'clock. Still you had put yourself out in vain; for, when you knocked at the door of the parsonage, nobody came to open."

Here M. Magloire interrupted his colleague, saying,—

"So far, all is very well. But now there comes a very great improbability. No one would think of going through the forest of Rochepommier in order to return from Brechy to Boiscoran. If you knew the country"—

"I know it; for I have carefully explored it. And the proof of it is, that, having foreseen the objection, I have found an answer. While M. de Boiscoran knocked at the door, a little peasant-girl passed by, and told him that she had just met the priest at a place called the Marshalls' Cross-roads. As the parsonage stands quite isolated, at the end of the village, such an incident is very probable. As for the priest, chance led me to learn this: precisely at the hour at which M. de Boiscoran would have been at Brechy, a priest passed the Marshalls' Cross-roads; and this priest, whom I have seen, belongs to the next parish. He also dined at M. Besson's, and had just been sent for to attend a dying woman. The little girl, therefore, did not tell a story; she only made a mistake."

"Excellent!" said M. Magloire.

"Still," continued M. Folgat, "after this information, what did M. de Boiscoran do? He went on; and, hoping every moment to meet the priest, he walked as far as the forest of Rochepommier. Finding, at last, that the peasant-girl had—purposely or not—led him astray, he determined to return to Boiscoran through the woods. But he was in very bad humor at having thus lost an evening which he might have spent with his betrothed; and this made him swear and curse, as the witness Gaudry has testified."

The famous lawyer of Sauveterre shook his head.

"That is ingenious, I admit; and I confess, in all humility, that I could not have suggested any thing as good. But—for there is a but—your story sins by its very simplicity. The prosecution will say, 'If that is the truth, why did not M. de Boiscoran say so at once? And what need was there to consult his counsel?'"

M. Folgat showed in his face that he was making a great effort to meet the objection. After a while, he replied,—

"I know but too well that that is the weak spot in our armor,—a very weak spot, too; for it is quite clear, that, if M. de Boiscoran had given this explanation on the day of his arrest, he would have been released instantly. But what better can be found? What else can be found? However, this is only a rough sketch of my plan, and I have never put it into words yet till now. With your assistance, M. Magloire, with the aid of Mechinet, to whom I am already indebted for very valuable information, with the aid of all our friends, in fine, I cannot help hoping that I may be able to improve my plan by adding some mysterious secret which may help to explain M. de Boiscoran's reticence. I thought, at one time, of calling in politics, and to pretend, that, on account of the peculiar views of which he is suspected, M. de Boiscoran preferred keeping his relations with the priest at Brechy a secret."

"Oh, that would have been most unfortunate!" broke in M. Magloire. "We are not only religious at Sauveterre, we are devout, my good colleague,—excessively devout."

"And I have given up that idea."

Jacques, who had till now kept silent and motionless, now raised himself suddenly to his full height, and cried, in a voice of concentrated rage,—

"Is it not too bad, is it not atrocious, that we should be compelled to concoct a falsehood? And I am innocent! What more could be done if I were a murderer?"

Jacques was perfectly right: it was monstrous that he should be absolutely forced to conceal the truth. But his counsel took no notice of his indignation: they were too deeply absorbed in examining minutely their system of defence.

"Let us go on to the other points of the accusation," said M. Magloire.

"If my version is accepted," replied M. Folgat, "the rest follows as a matter of course. But will they accept it? On the day on which he was arrested, M. de Boiscoran, trying to find an excuse for having been out that night, has said that he had gone to see his wood-merchant at Brechy. That was a disastrous imprudence. And here is the real danger. As to the rest, that amounts to nothing. There is the water in which M. de Boiscoran washed his hands when he came home, and in which they have found traces of burnt paper. We have only to modify the facts very slightly to explain that. We have only to state that M. de Boiscoran is a passionate smoker: that is well known. He had taken with him a goodly supply of cigarettes when he set out for Brechy; but he had taken no matches. And that is a fact. We can furnish proof, we can produce witnesses, we had no matches; for we had forgotten our match-box, the day before, at M. de Chandore's,—the box which we always carry about on our person, which everybody knows, and which is still lying on the mantelpiece in Miss Dionysia's little boudoir. Well, having no matches, we found that we could go no farther without a smoke. We had gone quite far already; and the question was, Shall we go on without smoking, or return? No need of either! There was our gun; and we knew very well what sportsmen do under such circumstances. We took the shot out of one of our cartridges, and, in setting the powder on fire, we lighted a piece of paper. This is an operation in which you cannot help blackening your fingers. As we had to repeat it several times, our hands were very much soiled and very black, and the nails full of little fragments of burnt paper."

"Ah! now you are right," exclaimed M. Magloire. "Well done!"

His young colleague became more and more animated; and always employing the profession "we," which his brethren affect, he went on,—

"This water, which you dwell upon so much, is the clearest evidence of our innocence. If we had been an incendiary, we should certainly have poured it out as hurriedly as the murderer tries to wash out the blood-stains on his clothes, which betray him."

"Very well," said M. Magloire again approvingly.

"And your other charges," continued M. Folgat, as if he were standing in court, and addressing the jury,—"your other charges have all the same weight. Our letter to Miss Dionysia—why do you refer to that? Because, you say, it proves our premeditation. Ah! there I hold you. Are we really so stupid and bereft of common sense? That is not our reputation. What! we premeditate a crime, and we do not say to ourselves that we shall certainly be convicted unless we prepare an *alibi!* What! we leave home with the fixed purpose of killing a man, and we load our gun with small-shot! Really, you make the defence too easy; for your charges do not stand being examined."

It was Jacques's turn, this time, to testify his approbation.

"That is," he said, "what I have told Galpin over and over again; and he never had any thing to say in reply. We must insist on that point."

M. Folgat was consulting his notes.

"I now come to a very important circumstance, and one which I should, at the trial, make a decisive question, if it should be favorable to our side. Your valet, my dear client,—your old Anthony,—told me that he had cleaned and washed your breech-loader the night before the crime."

"Great God!" exclaimed Jacques.

"Well, I see you appreciate the importance of the fact. Between that cleaning and the time when you set a cartridge on fire, in order to burn the letters of the Countess Claudieuse, did you fire your gun? If you did, we must say nothing more about it. If you did not, one of the barrels of the breech-loader must be clean, and then you are safe."

For more than a minute, Jacques remained silent, trying to recall the facts; at last he replied,—

"It seems to me, I am sure, I fired at a rabbit on the morning of the fatal day."

M. Magloire looked disappointed.

"Fate again!" he said.

"Oh, wait!" cried Jacques. "I am quite sure, at all events, that I killed that rabbit at the first shot. Consequently, I can have fouled only one barrel of the gun. If I have used the same barrel at Valpinson, to get a light, I am safe. With a double gun, one almost instinctively first uses the right-hand barrel."

M. Magloire's face grew darker.

"Never mind," he said, "we cannot possibly make an argument upon such an uncertain chance,—a chance which, in case of error, would almost fatally turn against us. But at the trial, when they show you the gun, examine it, so that you can tell me how that matter stands."

Thus they had sketched the outlines of their plan of defence. There remained nothing now but to perfect the details; and to this task the two lawyers were devoting themselves still, when Blangin, the jailer, called to them through the wicket, that the doors of the prison were about to be closed.

"Five minutes more, my good Blangin!" cried Jacques.

And drawing his two friends aside, as far from the wicket as he could, he said to them in a low and distressed voice,—

"A thought has occurred to me, gentlemen, which I think I ought to mention to you. It cannot be but that the Countess Claudieuse must be suffering terribly since I am in prison. However, sure she may be of having left no trace behind her that could betray her, she must tremble at the idea that I may, after all, tell the truth in self-defence. She would deny, I know, and she is so sure of her prestige, that she knows my accusation would not injure her marvellous reputation. Nevertheless, she cannot but shrink from the scandal. Who knows if she might not give us the means to escape from the trial, to avoid such exposure? Why might not one of you gentleman make the attempt?"

M. Folgat was a man of quick resolution.

"I will try, if you will give me a line of introduction."

Jacque immediately sat down, and wrote,—

"I have told my counsel, M. Folgat, every thing. Save me, and I swear to you eternal silence. Will you let me perish, Genevieve, when you know I am innocent?

"JACQUES." "Is that enough?" he asked, handing the lawyer the note.

"Yes; and I promise you I will see the Countess Claudieuse within the next forty-eight hours."

Blangin was becoming impatient; and the two advocates had to leave the prison. As they crossed the New-Market Square, they noticed, not far from them, a wandering musician, who was followed by a number of boys and girls.

It was a kind of minstrel, dressed in a sort of garment which was no longer an overcoat and had not yet assumed the shape of a shortcoat. He was strumming on a wretched fiddle; but his voice was good, and the ballad he sang had the full flavor of the local accent:—

> *"In the spring, mother Redbreast*
>
> *Made her nest in the bushes,*
>
> *The good lady!*
>
> *Made her nest in the bushes,*
>
> *The good lady!"*

Instinctively M. Folgat was fumbling in his pocket for a few cents, when the musician came up to him, held out his hat as if to ask alms, and said,—

"You do not recognize me?"

The advocate started.

"You here!" he said.

"Yes, I myself. I came this morning. I was watching for you; for I must see you this evening at nine o'clock. Come and open the little garden-gate at M. de Chandore's for me."

And, taking up his fiddle again, he wandered off listlessly, singing with his clear voice,—

> *"And a few, a few weeks later,*
>
> *She had a wee, a wee bit birdy."*

XXIV.

The great lawyer of Sauveterre had been far more astonished at the unexpected and extraordinary meeting than M. Folgat. As soon as the wandering minstrel had left them, he asked his young colleague,—

"You know that individual?"

"That individual," replied M. Folgat, "is none other than the agent whose services I have engaged, and whom I mentioned to you."

"Goudar?"

"Yes, Goudar."

"And did you not recognize him?"

The young advocate smiled.

"Not until he spoke," he replied. "The Goudar whom I know is tall, thin, beardless, and wears his hair cut like a brush. This street-musician is low, bearded, and has long, smooth hair falling down his back. How could I recognize my man in that vagabond costume, with a violin in his hand, and a provincial song set to music?"

M. Magloire smiled too, as he said,—

"What are, after all, professional actors in comparison with these men! Here is one who pretends having reached Sauveterre only this morning, and who knows the country as well as Trumence himself. He has not been here twelve hours, and he speaks already of M. de Chandore's little garden-gate."

"Oh! I can explain that circumstance now, although, at first, it surprised me very much. When I told Goudar the whole story, I no doubt mentioned the little gate in connection with Mechinet."

Whilst they were chatting thus, they had reached the upper end of National Street. Here they stopped; and M. Magloire said,—

"One word before we part. Are you quite resolved to see the Countess Claudieuse?"

"I have promised."

"What do you propose telling her?"

"I do not know. That depends upon how she receives me."

"As far as I know her, she will, upon looking at the note, merely order you out."

"Who knows! At all events, I shall not have to reproach myself for having shrunk from a step which in my heart I thought it my duty to take."

"Whatever may happen, be prudent, and do not allow yourself to get angry. Remember that a scene with her would compel us to change our whole line of defence, and that that is the only one which promises any success."

"Oh, do not fear!"

Thereupon, shaking hands once more, they parted, M. Magloire returning to his house, and M. Folgat going up the street. It struck half-past five, and the young advocate hurried on for fear of being too late. He found them waiting for him to go to dinner; but, as he entered the room, he forgot all his excuses in his painful surprise at the mournful and dejected appearance of the prisoner's friends and relatives.

"Have we any bad news?" he asked with a hesitating voice.

"The worst we had to fear," replied the Marquis de Boiscoran. "We had all foreseen it; and still, as you see, it has surprised us all, like a clap of thunder."

The young lawyer beat his forehead, and cried,—

"The court has ordered the trial!"

The marquis only bent his head, as if his voice, had failed him to answer the question.

"It is still a great secret," said Dionysia; "and we only know it, thanks to the indiscretion of our kind, our devoted Mechinet. Jacques will have to appear before the Assizes."

She was interrupted by a servant, who entered to announce that dinner was on the table.

They all went into the dining-room; but the last event made it well-nigh impossible for them to eat. Dionysia alone, deriving from feverish excitement an amazing energy, aided M. Folgat in keeping up the conversation. From her the young advocate learned that Count Claudieuse was decidedly worse, and that he would have received, in the day, the last sacrament, but for the decided opposition of Dr. Seignebos, who had declared that the slightest excitement might kill his patient.

"And if he dies," said M. de Chandore, "that is the finishing stroke. Public opinion, already incensed against Jacques, will become implacable."

However, the meal came to an end; and M. Folgat went up to Dionysia, saying,—

"I must beg of you, madam, to trust me with the key to the little garden-gate."

She looked at him quite astonished.

"I have to see a detective secretly, who has promised me his assistance."

"Is he here?"

"He came this morning."

When Dionysia had handed him the key, M. Folgat hastened to reach the end of the garden; and, at the third stroke of nine o'clock, the minstrel of the New-Market Square, Goudar, pushed the little gate, and, his violin under his arm, slipped into the garden.

"A day lost!" he exclaimed, without thinking of saluting the young lawyer,—"a whole day; for I could do nothing till I had seen you."

He seemed to be so angry, that M. Folgat tried to soothe him.

"Let me first of all compliment you on your disguise," he said. But Goudar did not seem to be open to praise.

"What would a detective be worth if he could not disguise himself! A great merit, forsooth! And I tell you, I hate it! But I could not think of coming to Sauveterre in my own person, a detective. Ugh! Everybody would have run away; and what a pack of lies they would have told me! So I had to assume that hideous masquerade. To think that I once took six months' lessons from a music-teacher merely to fit myself for that character! A wandering musician, you see, can go anywhere, and nobody is surprised; he goes about the streets, or he travels along the high-road; he enters into yards, and slips into houses; he asks alms: and in so doing, he accosts everybody, speaks to them, follows them. And as to my precious dialect, you must know I have been down here once for half a year, hunting up counterfeiters; and, if you don't catch a provincial accent in six months, you don't deserve belonging to the police. And I do belong to it, to the great distress of my wife, and to my own disgust."

"If your ambition is really what you say, my dear, Goudar," said M. Folgat, interrupting him, "you may be able to leave your profession very soon—if you succeed in saving M. de Boiscoran."

"He would give me his house in Vine Street?"

"With all his heart!"

The detective looked up, and repeated slowly,—

"The house in Vine Street, the paradise of this world. An immense garden, a soil of marvellous beauty. And what an exposure! There are walls there on which I could raise finer peaches than they have at Montreuil, and richer Chasselas than those of Fontainebleau!"

"Did you find any thing there?" asked M. Folgat.

Goudar, thus recalled to business, looked angry again.

"Nothing at all," he replied. "Nor did I learn any thing from the tradesmen. I am no further advanced than I was the first day."

"Let us hope you will have more luck here."

"I hope so; but I need your assistance to commence operations. I must see Dr. Seignebos, and Mechinet the clerk. Ask them to meet me at the place I shall assign in a note which I will send them."

"I will tell them."

"Now, if you want my *incognito* to be respected, you must get me a permit from the mayor, for Goudar, street-musician. I keep my name, because here nobody knows me. But I must have the permit this evening. Wherever I might present myself, asking for a bed, they would call for my papers."

"Wait here for a quarter of an hour, there is a bench," said M. Folgat, "and I'll go at once to the mayor."

A quarter of an hour later, Goudar had his permit in his pocket, and went to take lodgings at the Red Lamb, the worst tavern in all Sauveterre.

When a painful and inevitable duty is to be performed, the true character of a man is apt to appear in its true light. Some people postpone it as long as they can, and delay, like those pious persons who keep the biggest sin for the end of their confession: others, on the contrary, are in a hurry to be relieved of their anxiety, and make an end of it as soon as they can. M. Folgat belonged to this latter class.

Next morning he woke up at daylight, and said to himself,—

"I will call upon the Countess Claudieuse this morning."

At eight o'clock, he left the house, dressed more carefully than usual, and told the servant that he did not wish to be waited for if he should not be back for breakfast.

He went first to the court-house, hoping to meet the clerk there. He was not disappointed. The waiting-rooms were quite deserted yet; but Mechinet was already at work in his office, writing with the feverish haste of a man who has to pay for a piece of property that he wants to call his own.

When he saw Folgat enter, he rose, and said at once,—

"You have heard the decision of the court?"

"Yes, thanks to your kindness; and I must confess it has not surprised me. What do they think of it here?"

"Everybody expects a condemnation."

"Well, we shall see!" said the young advocate.

And, lowering his voice, he added,—

"But I came for another purpose. The agent whom I expected has come, and he wishes to see you. He will write to you to make an appointment, and I hope you will consent."

"Certainly, with all my heart," replied the clerk. "And God grant that he may succeed in extricating M. de Boiscoran from his difficulties, even if it were only to take the conceit out of my master."

"Ah! is M. Galpin so triumphant?"

"Without the slightest reserve. He sees his old friend already at the galleys. He has received another letter of congratulation from the attorney general, and came here yesterday, when the court had adjourned, to read it to any one who would listen. Everybody, of course, complimented him, except the president, who turned his back upon him, and the commonwealth attorney, who told him in Latin that he was selling the bear's skin before he had killed him."

In the meantime steps were heard coming down the passages; and M. Folgat said hurriedly,—

"One more suggestion. Goudar desires to remain unknown. Do not speak of him to any living soul, and especially show no surprise at the costume in which you see him."

The noise of a door which was opened interrupted him. One of the judges entered, who, after having bowed very civilly, asked the clerk a number of questions about a case which was to come on the same day.

"Good-bye, M. Mechinet," said the young advocate.

And his next visit was to Dr. Seignebos. When he rang the bell, a servant came to the door, and said,—

"The doctor is gone out; but he will be back directly, and has told me to beg you to wait for him in his study."

Such an evidence of perfect trust was unheard of. No one was ever allowed to remain alone in his sanctuary. It was an immense room, quite full of most varied objects, which at a glance revealed the opinions, tastes, and predilections of the owner. The first thing to strike the visitor as he entered was an admirable bust of Bichat, flanked on either side by smaller busts of Robespierre and

Rousseau. A clock of the time of Louis XIV. stood between the windows, and marked the seconds with a noise which sounded like the rattling of old iron. One whole side was filled with books of all kinds, unbound or bound, in a way which would have set M. Daubigeon laughing very heartily. A huge cupboard adapted for collections of plants bespoke a passing fancy for botany; while an electric machine recalled the time when the doctor believed in cures by electricity.

On the table in the centre of the room vast piles of books betrayed the doctor's recent studies. All the authors who have spoken of insanity or idiocy were there, from Apostolides to Tardien. M. Folgat was still looking around when Dr. Seignebos entered, always like a bombshell, but far more cheerful than usual.

"I knew I should find you here!" he cried still in the door. "You come to ask me to meet Goudar."

The young advocate started, and said, all amazed,—

"Who can have told you?"

"Goudar himself. I like that man. I am sure no one will suspect me of having a fancy for any thing that is connected with the police. I have had too much to do all my life with spies and that ilk. But your man might almost reconcile me with that department."

"When did you see him?"

"This morning at seven. He was so prodigiously tired of losing his time in his garret at the Red Lamb, that it occurred to him to pretend illness, and to send for me. I went, and found a kind of street-minstrel, who seemed to me to be perfectly well. But, as soon as we were alone, he told me all about it, asking me my opinion, and telling me his ideas. M. Folgat, that man Goudar is very clever: I tell you so; and we understand each other perfectly."

"Has he told you what he proposes to do?"

"Nearly so. But he has not authorized me to speak of it. Have patience; let him go to work, wait, and you will see if old Seignebos has a keen scent."

Saying this with an air of sublime conceit, he took off his spectacles, and set to work wiping them industriously.

"Well, I will wait," said the young advocate. "And, since that makes an end to my business here, I beg you will let me speak to you of another matter. M. de Boiscoran has charged me with a message to the Countess Claudieuse."

"The deuce!"

"And to try to obtain from her the means for our discharge."

"Do you expect she will do it?"

M. Folgat could hardly retain an impatient gesture.

"I have accepted the mission," he said dryly, "and I mean to carry it out."

"I understand, my dear sir. But you will not see the countess. The count is very ill. She does not leave his bedside, and does not even receive her most intimate friends."

"And still I must see her. I must at any hazard place a note which my client has confided to me, in her own hands. And look here, doctor, I mean to be frank with you. It was exactly because I foresaw there would be difficulties, that I came to you to ask your assistance in overcoming or avoiding them."

"To me?"

"Are you not the count's physician?"

"Ten thousand devils!" cried Dr. Seignebos. "You do not mince matters, you lawyers!"

And then speaking in a lower tone, and replying apparently to his own objections rather than to M. Folgat, he said,—

"Certainly, I attend Count Claudieuse, whose illness, by the way, upsets all my theories, and defies all my experience: but for that very reason I can do nothing. Our profession has certain rules which cannot be infringed upon without compromising the whole medical profession."

"But it is a question of life and death with Jacques, sir, with a friend."

"And a fellow Republican, to be sure. But I cannot help you without abusing the confidence of the Countess Claudieuse."

"Ah, sir! Has not that woman committed a crime for which M. de Boiscoran, though innocent, will be arraigned in court?"

"I think so; but still"—

He reflected a moment, and then suddenly snatched up his broad-brimmed hat, drew it over his head, and cried,—

"In fact, so much the worse for her! There are sacred interests which override every thing. Come!"

XXV.

Count Claudieuse and his wife had installed themselves, the day after the fire, in Mautrec Street. The house which the mayor had taken for them had been for more than a century in the possession of the great Julias family, and is still considered one of the finest and most magnificent mansions in Sauveterre.

In less than ten minutes Dr. Seignebos and M. Folgat had reached the house. From the street, nothing was visible but a tall wall, as old as the castle, according to the claims of archaeologists, and covered all over with a mass of wild flowers. In this wall there is a huge entrance-gate with folding-doors. During the day one-half is opened, and a light, low open-work railing put in, which rings a bell as soon as it is pushed open.

You then cross a large garden, in which a dozen statues, covered with green moss, are falling to pieces on their pedestals, overshadowed by magnificent old linden-trees. The house has only two stories. A large hall extends from end to end of the lower story; and at the end a wide staircase with stone steps and a superb iron railing leads up stairs. When they entered the hall, Dr. Seignebos opened a door on the right hand.

"Step in here and wait," he said to M. Folgat. "I will go up stairs and see the count, whose room is in the second story, and I will send you the countess."

The young advocate did as he was bid, and found himself in a large room, brilliantly lighted up by three tall windows that went down to the ground, and looked out upon the garden. This room must have been superb formerly. The walls were wainscoted with arabesques and lines in gold. The ceiling was painted, and represented a number of fat little angels sporting in a sky full of golden stars.

But time had passed its destroying hand over all this splendor of the past age, had half effaced the paintings, tarnished the gold of the arabesques, and faded the blue of the ceiling and the rosy little loves. Nor was the furniture calculated to make compensation for this decay. The windows had no curtains. On the mantelpiece stood a worn-out clock and half-broken candelabra; then, here and there, pieces of furniture that would not match, such as had been rescued from the fire at Valpinson,—chairs, sofas, arm-chairs, and a round table, all battered and blackened by the flames.

But M. Folgat paid little attention to these details. He only thought of the grave step on which he was venturing, and which he now only looked at in its full strangeness and extreme boldness. Perhaps he would have fled at the last moment if he could have done so; and he was only able by a supreme effort to control his excitement.

At last he heard a rapid, light step in the hall; and almost immediately the Countess Claudieuse appeared. He recognized her at once, such as Jacques had described her to him, calm, serious, and serene, as if her soul were soaring high above all human passions. Far from diminishing her exquisite beauty, the terrible events of the last months had only surrounded her, as it were, with a divine halo. She had fallen off a little, however. And the dark semicircle under her eyes, and the disorder of her hair, betrayed the fatigue and the anxiety of the long nights which she had spent by her husband's bedside.

As M. Folgat was bowing, she asked,—

"You are M. de Boiscoran's counsel?"

"Yes, madam," replied the young advocate.

"The doctor tells me you wish to speak to me."

"Yes, madam."

With a queenly air, she pointed to a chair, and, sitting down herself, she said,—

"I hear, sir."

M. Folgat began with beating heart, but a firm voice,—

"I ought, first of all, madam, to state to you my client's true position."

"That is useless, sir. I know."

"You know, madam, that he has been summoned to trial, and that he may be condemned?"

She shook her head with a painful movement, and said very softly,—

"I know, sir, that Count Claudieuse has been the victim of a most infamous attempt at murder; that he is still in danger, and that, unless God works a miracle, I shall soon be without a husband, and my children without a father."

"But M. de Boiscoran is innocent, madam."

The features of the countess assumed an expression of profound surprise; and, looking fixedly at M. Folgat, she said,—

"And who, then, is the murderer?"

Ah! It cost the young advocate no small effort to prevent his lips from uttering the fatal word, "You," prompted by his indignant conscience. But he thought of the success of his mission; and, instead of replying, he said,—

"To a prisoner, madam, to an unfortunate man on the eve of judgment, an advocate is a confessor, to whom he tells every thing. I must add that the counsel of the accused is like a priest: he must forget the secrets which have been confided to him."

"I do not understand, sir."

"My client, madam, had a very simple means to prove his innocence. He had only to tell the truth. He has preferred risking his own honor rather than to betray the honor of another person."

The countess looked impatient, and broke in, saying,—

"My moments are counted, sir. May I beg you will be more explicit?"

But M. Folgat had gone as far as he well could go.

"I am desired by M. de Boiscoran, madam, to hand you a letter."

The Countess Claudieuse seemed to be overwhelmed with surprise.

"To me?" she said. "On what ground?"

Without saying a word, M. Folgat drew Jacques's letter from his portfolio, and handed it to her.

"Here it is!" he said.

She took it with a perfectly steady hand, and opened it slowly. But, as soon as she had run her eye over it, she rose, turned crimson in her face, and said with flaming eyes,—

"Do you know, sir, what this letter contains?"

"Yes."

"Do you know that M. de Boiscoran dares call me by my first name, Genevieve, as my husband does, and my father?"

The decisive moment had come, and M. Folgat had all his self-possession.

"M. de Boiscoran, madame, claims that he used to call you so in former days,—in Vine Street,—in days when you called him Jacques."

The countess seemed to be utterly bewildered.

"But that is sheer infamy, sir," she stammered. "What! M. de Boiscoran should have dared tell you that I, the countess Claudieuse, have been his—mistress?"

"He certainly said so, madam; and he affirms, that a few moments before the fire broke out, he was near you, and that, if his hands were blackened, it was because he had burned your letters and his."

She rose at these words, and said in a penetrating voice,—

"And you could believe that,—you? Ah! M. de Boiscoran's other crimes are nothing in comparison with this! He is not satisfied with having burnt our house, and ruined us: he means to dishonor us. He is not satisfied with having murdered my husband: he must ruin the honor of his wife also."

She spoke so loud, that her voice must have been distinctly heard in the vestibule.

"Lower, madam, I pray you speak lower," said M. Folgat.

She cast upon him a crushing glance; and, raising her voice still higher, she went on,—

"Yes, I understand very well that you are afraid of being heard. But I—what have I to fear? I could wish the whole world to hear us, and to judge between us. Lower, you say? Why should I speak less loud? Do you think that if Count Claudieuse were not on his death-bed, this letter would not have long since been in his hands? Ah, he would soon have satisfaction for such an infamous letter, he! But I, a poor woman! I have never seen so clearly that the world thinks my husband is lost already, and that I am alone in this world, without a protector, without friends."

"But, madam, M. de Boiscoran pledges himself to the most perfect secrecy."

"Secrecy in what? In your cowardly insults, your abominable plots, of which this, no doubt, is but a beginning?"

M. Folgat turned livid under this insult.

"Ah, take care, madam," he said in a hoarse voice: "we have proof, absolute, overwhelming proof."

The countess stopped him by an imperious gesture, and with the haughtiest disdain, grief, and wrath, she said,—

"Well, then, produce your proof. Go, hasten, act as you like. We shall see if the vile calumnies of an incendiary can stain the pure reputation of an honest woman. We shall see if a single speck of this mud in which you wallow can reach up to me."

And, throwing Jacques's letter at M. Folgat's feet, she went to the door.

"Madam," said M. Folgat once more,—"madam!"

She did not even condescend to turn round: she disappeared, leaving him standing in the middle of the room, so overcome with amazement, that he could not collect his thoughts. Fortunately Dr. Seignebos came in.

"Upon my word!" he said, "I never thought the countess would take my treachery so coolly. When she came out from you just now, she asked me, in the same tone as every day, how I had found her husband, and what was to be done. I told her"—

But the rest of the sentence remained unspoken: the doctor had become aware of M. Folgat's utter consternation.

"Why, what on earth is the matter?" he asked.

The young advocate looked at him with an utterly bewildered air.

"This is the matter: I ask myself whether I am awake or dreaming. This is the matter: that, if this woman is guilty, she possesses an audacity beyond all belief."

"How, if? Have you changed your mind about her guilt?"

M. Folgat looked altogether disheartened.

"Ah!" he said, "I hardly know myself. Do you not see that I have lost my head, that I do not know what to think, and what to believe?"

"Oh!"

"Yes, indeed! And yet, doctor, I am not a simpleton. I have now been pleading five years in criminal courts: I have had to dive down into the lowest depths of society; I have seen strange things, and met with exceptional specimens, and heard fabulous stories"—

It was the doctor's turn, now, to be amazed; and he actually forgot to trouble his gold spectacles.

"Why? What did the countess say?" he asked.

"I might tell you every word," replied M. Folgat, "and you would be none the wiser. You ought to have been here, and seen her, and heard her! What a woman! Not a muscle in her face was moving; her eye remained limpid and clear; no emotion was felt in her voice. And with what an air she defied me! But come, doctor, let us be gone!"

They went out, and had already gone about a third down the long avenue in the garden, when they saw the oldest daughter of the countess coming towards them, on her way to the house, accompanied by her governess. Dr. Seignebos stopped, and pressing the arm of the young advocate, and bending over to him, he whispered into his ear,—

"Mind!" he said. "You know the truth is in the lips of children."

"What do you expect?" murmured M. Folgat.

"To settle a doubtful point. Hush! Let me manage it."

By this time the little girl had come up to them. It was a very graceful girl of eight or nine years, light haired, with large blue eyes, tall for her age, and displaying all the intelligence of a young girl, without her timidity.

"How are you, little Martha?" said the doctor to her in his gentlest voice, which was very soft when he chose.

"Good-morning, gentlemen!" she replied with a nice little courtesy.

Dr. Seignebos bent down to kiss her rosy cheeks, and them, looking at her, he said,—

"You look sad, Martha?"

"Yes, because papa and little sister are sick," she replied with a deep sigh.

"And also because you miss Valpinson?"

"Oh, yes!"

"Still it is very pretty here, and you have a large garden to play in."

She shook her head, and, lowering her voice, she said,—

"It is certainly very pretty here; but—I am afraid."

"And of what, little one?"

She pointed to the statues, and all shuddering, she said,—

"In the evening, when it grows dark, I fancy they are moving. I think I see people hiding behind the trees, like the man who wanted to kill papa."

"You ought to drive away those ugly notions, Miss Martha," said M. Folgat.

But Dr. Seignebos did not allow him to go on.

"What, Martha? I did not know you were so timid. I thought, on the contrary, you were very brave. Your papa told me the night of the fire you were not afraid of any thing."

"Papa was right."

"And yet, when you were aroused by the flames, it must have been terrible."

"Oh! it was not the flames which waked me, doctor."

"Still the fire had broken out."

"I was not asleep at that time, doctor. I had been roused by the slamming of the door, which mamma had closed very noisily when she came in."

One and the same presentiment made M. Folgat tremble and the doctor.

"You must be mistaken, Martha," the doctor went on. "Your mamma had not come back at the time of the fire."

"Oh, yes, sir!"

"No, you are mistaken."

The little girl drew herself up with that solemn air which children are apt to assume when their statements are doubted. She said,—

"I am quite sure of what I say, and I remember every thing perfectly. I had been put to bed at the usual hour, and, as I was very tired with playing, I had fallen asleep at once. While I was asleep, mamma had gone out; but her coming back waked me up. As soon as she came in, she bent over little sister's bed, and looked at her for a moment so sadly, that I thought I should cry. Then she went, and sat down by the window; and from my bed, where I lay silently watching her, I saw the tears running down her cheeks, when all of a sudden a shot was fired."

M. Folgat and Dr. Seignebos looked anxiously at each other.

"Then, my little one," insisted Dr. Seignebos, "you are quite sure your mamma was in your room when the first shot was fired?"

"Certainly, doctor. And mamma, when she heard it, rose up straight, and lowered her head, like one who listens. Almost immediately, the second shot was fired. Mamma raised her hands to heaven, and cried out, 'Great God!' And then she went out, running fast."

Never was a smile more false than that which Dr. Seignebos forced himself to retain on his lips while the little girl was telling her story.

"You have dreamed all that, Martha," he said.

The governess here interposed, saying,—

"The young lady has not dreamed it, sir. I, also, heard the shots fired; and I had just opened the door of my room to hear what was going on, when I saw madame cross the landing swiftly, and rush down stairs.

"Oh! I do not doubt it," said the doctor, in the most indifferent tone he could command: "the circumstance is very trifling."

But the little girl was bent on finishing her story.

"When mamma had left," she went on, "I became frightened, and raised myself on my bed to listen. Soon I heard a noise which I did not know,—cracking and snapping of wood, and then cries at a distance. I got more frightened, jumped down, and ran to open the door. But I nearly fell down, there was such a cloud of smoke and sparks. Still I did not lose my head. I waked my little sister, and tried to get on the staircase, when Cocoleu rushed in like a madman, and took us both out."

"Martha," called a voice from the house, "Martha!"

The child cut short her story, and said,—

"Mamma is calling me."

And, dropping again her nice little courtesy, she said,—

"Good-by, gentlemen!"

Martha had disappeared; and Dr. Seignebos and M. Folgat, still standing on the same spot, looked at each other in utter distress.

"We have nothing more to do here," said M. Folgat.

"No, indeed! Let us go back and make haste; for perhaps they are waiting for me. You must breakfast with me."

They went away very much disheartened, and so absorbed in their defeat, that they forgot to return the salutations with which they were greeted in the street,—a circumstance carefully noticed by several watchful observers.

When the doctor reached home, he said to his servant,—

"This gentleman will breakfast with me. Give us a bottle of medis."

And, when he had shown the advocate into his study, he asked,—

"And now what do you think of your adventure?"

M. Folgat looked completely undone.

"I cannot understand it," he murmured.

"Could it be possible that the countess should have tutored the child to say what she told us?"

"No."

"And her governess?"

"Still less. A woman of that character trusts nobody. She struggles; she triumphs or succumbs alone."

"Then the child and the governess have told us the truth?"

"I am convinced of that."

"So am I. Then she had no share in the murder of her husband?"

"Alas!"

M. Folgat did not notice that his "Alas!" was received by Dr. Seignebos with an air of triumph. He had taken off his spectacles, and, wiping them vigorously, he said,—

"If the countess is innocent, Jacques must be guilty, you think? Jacques must have deceived us all, then?"

M. Folgat shook his head.

- 372 -

"I pray you, doctor, do not press me just now. Give me time to collect my thoughts. I am bewildered by all these conjectures. No, I am sure M. de Boiscoran has not told a falsehood, and the countess has been his mistress. No, he has not deceived us; and on the night of the crime he really had an interview with the countess. Did not Martha tell us that her mother had gone out? And where could she have gone, except to meet M. de Boiscoran?"

He paused a moment.

"Oh, come, come!" said the physician, "you need not be afraid of me."

"Well, it might possibly be, that, after the countess had left M. de Boiscoran, Fate might have stepped in. Jacques has told us how the letters which he was burning had suddenly blazed up, and with such violence that he was frightened. Who can tell whether some burning fragments may not have set a straw-rick on fire? You can judge yourself. On the point of leaving the place, M. de Boiscoran sees this beginning of a fire. He hastens to put it out. His efforts are unsuccessful. The fire increases step by step: it lights up the whole front of the chateau. At that moment Count Claudieuse comes out. Jacques thinks he has been watched and detected; he sees his marriage broken off, his life ruined, his happiness destroyed; he loses his head, aims, fires, and flees instantly. And thus you explain his missing the count, and also this fact which seemed to preclude the idea of premeditated murder, that the gun was loaded with small-shot."

"Great God!" cried the doctor.

"What, what have I said?"

"Take care never to repeat that! The suggestion you make is so fearfully plausible, that, if it becomes known, no one will ever believe you when you tell the real truth."

"The truth? Then you think I am mistaken?"

"Most assuredly."

Then fixing his spectacles on his nose, Dr. Seignebos added,—

"I never could admit that the countess should have fired at her husband. I now see that I was right. She has not committed the crime directly; but she has done it indirectly."

"Oh!"

"She would not be the first woman who has done so. What I imagine is this: the countess had made up her mind, and arranged her plan, before meeting Jacques. The murderer was already at his post. If she had succeeded in winning Jacques back, her accomplice would have put away his gun, and quietly gone to bed. As she could not induce Jacques to give up his marriage, she made a sign, and the fire was lighted, and the count was shot."

The young advocate did not seem to be fully convinced.

"In that case, there would have been premeditation," he objected; "and how, then, came the gun to be loaded with small-shot?"

"The accomplice had not sense enough to know better."

Although he saw very well the doctor's drift, M. Folgat started up,—

"What?" he said, "always Cocoleu?"

Dr. Seignebos tapped his forehead with the end of his finger, and replied,—

"When an idea has once made its way in there, it remains fixed. Yes, the countess has an accomplice; and that accomplice is Cocoleu; and, if he has no sense, you see the wretched idiot at least carries his devotion and his discretion very far."

"If what you say is true, doctor, we shall never get the key of this affair; for Cocoleu will never confess."

"Don't swear to that. There is a way."

He was interrupted by the sudden entrance of his servant.

"Sir," said the latter, "there is a gendarme below who brings you a man who has to be sent to the hospital at once."

"Show them up," said the doctor.

- 374 -

"And, while the servant was gone to do his bidding, the doctor said,—

"And here is the way. Now mind!"

A heavy step was heard shaking the stairs; and almost immediately a gendarme appeared, who in one hand held a violin, and with the other aided a poor creature, who seemed unable to walk alone.

"Goudar!" was on M. Folgat's lips.

It was Goudar, really, but in what a state! His clothes muddy, and torn, pale, with haggard eyes, his beard and his lips covered with a white foam.

"The story is this," said the gendarme. "This individual was playing the fiddle in the court of the barrack, and we were looking out of the window, when all of a sudden he fell on the ground, rolled about, twisted and writhed, while he uttered fearful howls, and foamed like a mad dog. We picked him up; and I bring him to you."

"Leave us alone with him," said the physician.

The gendarme went out; and, as soon as the door was shut, Goudar cried with a voice full of intense disgust,—

"What a profession! Just look at me! What a disgrace if my wife should see me in this state! Phew!"

And, pulling a handkerchief from his pocket, he wiped his face, and drew from his mouth a small piece of soap.

"But the point is," said the doctor, "that you have played the epileptic so well, that the gendarmes have been taken in."

"A fine trick indeed, and very creditable."

"An excellent trick, since you can now quite safely go to the hospital. They will put you in the same ward with Cocoleu, and I shall come and see you every morning. You are free to act now."

"Never mind me," said the detective. "I have my plan."

Then turning to M. Folgat, he added,—

"I am a prisoner now; but I have taken my precautions. The agent whom I have sent to England will report to you. I have, besides, to ask a favor at your hands. I have written to my wife to send her letters to you: you can send them to me by the doctor. And now I am ready to become Cocoleu's companion, and I mean to earn the house in Vine Street."

Dr. Seignebos signed an order of admission. He recalled the gendarme; and, after having praised his kindness, he asked him to take "that poor devil" to the hospital. When he was alone once more with M. Folgat, he said,—

"Now, my dear friend, let us consult. Shall we speak of what Martha has told us and of Goudar's plan. I think not; for M. Galpin is watching us; and, if a mere suspicion of what is going on reaches the prosecution, all is lost. Let us content ourselves, then, with reporting to Jacques your interview with the countess; and as to the rest, Silence!"

XXVI.

Like all very clever men, Dr. Seignebos made the mistake of thinking other people as cunning as he was himself. M. Galpin was, of course, watching him, but by no means with the energy which one would have expected from so ambitious a man. He had, of course, been the first to be notified that the case was to be tried in open court, and from that moment he felt relieved of all anxiety.

As to remorse, he had none. He did not even regret any thing. He did not think of it, that the prisoner who was thus to be tried had once been his friend,—a friend of whom he was proud, whose hospitality he had enjoyed, and whose favor he had eagerly sought in his matrimonial aspirations. No. He only saw one thing,—that he had engaged in a dangerous affair, on which his whole future was depending, and that he was going to win triumphantly.

Evidently his responsibility was by no means gone; but his zeal in preparing the case for trial was no longer required. He need not appear at the trial. Whatever must be the result, he thought he should escape the blame, which he should surely have incurred if no true bill had been found. He did not disguise it from himself that he should be looked at askance by all Sauveterre, that his social relations were well-nigh broken off, and that no one would henceforth heartily shake hands with him. But that gave him no concern. Sauveterre, a miserable little town of five thousand inhabitants! He hoped with certainty he would not remain there long; and a brilliant preferment would amply repay him for his courage, and relieve him from all foolish reproaches.

Besides, once in the large city to which he would be promoted, he could hope that distance would aid in attenuating and even effacing the impression made by his conduct. All that would be remembered after a time would be his reputation as one of those famous judges, who, according to the stereotyped phrase, "sacrifice every thing to the sacred interests of justice, who put inflexible duty high above all the considerations that trouble and disturb the vulgar mind, and whose heart is like a rock, against which all human passions are helplessly broken to pieces."

With such a reputation, with his knowledge of the world, and his eagerness to succeed, opportunities would not be wanting to put himself forward, to make himself known, to become useful, indispensable even. He saw himself already on the highest rungs of the official ladder. He was a judge in Bordeaux, in Lyons, in Paris itself!

With such rose-colored dreams he fell asleep at night. The next morning, as he crossed the streets, his carriage haughtier and stiffer than ever, his firmly-closed lips, and the cold and severe look of his eyes, told the curious observers that there must be something new.

"M. de Boiscoran's case must be very bad indeed," they said, "or M. Galpin would not look so very proud."

He went first to the commonwealth attorney. The truth is, he was still smarting under the severe reproaches of M. Daubigeon, and he thought he would enjoy his revenge now. He found the old book-worm, as usual, among his beloved books, and in worse humor than ever. He ignored it, handed him a number of papers to sign; and when his business was over, and while he was carefully replacing the documents in his bag with his monogram on the outside, he added with an air of indifference,—

"Well, my dear sir, you have heard the decision of the court? Which of us was right?"

M. Daubigeon shrugged his shoulders, and said angrily,—

"Of course I am nothing but an old fool, a maniac: I give it up; and I say, like Horace's man,—

> *'Stultum me fateor, liceat concedere vires*
>
> *Atque etiam insanum.'"*

"You are joking. But what would have happened if I had listened to you?"

"I don't care to know."

"M. de Boiscoran would none the less have been sent to a jury."

"May be."

"Anybody else would have collected the proofs of his guilt just as well as I."

"That is a question."

"And I should have injured my reputation very seriously; for they would have called me one of those timid magistrates who are frightened at a nothing."

"That is as good a reputation as some others," broke in the commonwealth attorney.

He had vowed he would answer only in monosyllables; but his anger made him forget his oath. He added in a very severe tone,—

"Another man would not have been bent exclusively upon proving that M. de Boiscoran was guilty."

"I certainly have proved it."

"Another man would have tried to solve the mystery."

"But I have solved it, I should think."

M. Daubigeon bowed ironically, and said,—

"I congratulate you. It must be delightful to know the secret of all things, only you may be mistaken. You are an excellent hand at such investigations; but I am an older man than you in the profession. The more I think in this case, the less I understand it. If you know every thing so perfectly well, I wish you would tell me what could have been the motive for the crime, for, after all, we do not run the risk of losing our head without some very powerful and tangible purpose. Where was Jacques's interest? You will tell me he hated Count Claudieuse. But is that an answer. Come, go for a moment to your own conscience. But stop! No one likes to do that."

M. Galpin was beginning to regret that he had ever come. He had hoped to find M. Daubigeon quite penitent, and here he was worse than ever.

"The Court of Inquiry has felt no such scruples," he said dryly.

"No; but the jury may feel some. They are, occasionally, men of sense."

"The jury will condemn M. de Boiscoran without hesitation."

"I would not swear to that."

"You would if you knew who will plead."

"Oh!"

"The prosecution will employ M. Gransiere!"

"Oh, oh!"

"You will not deny that he is a first-class man?"

The magistrate was evidently becoming angry; his ears reddened up; and in the same proportion M. Daubigeon regained his calmness.

"God forbid that I should deny M. Gransiere's eloquence. He is a powerful speaker, and rarely misses his man. But then, you know, cases are like books: they have their luck or ill luck. Jacques will be well defended."

"I am not afraid of M. Magloire."

"But Mr. Folgat?"

"A young man with no weight. I should be far more afraid of M. Lachant."

"Do you know the plan of the defence?"

This was evidently the place where the shoe pinched; but M. Galpin took care not to let it be seen, and replied,—

"I do not. But that does not matter. M. de Boiscoran's friends at first thought of making capital out of Cocoleu; but they have given that up. I am sure of that! The police-agent whom I have charged to keep his eyes on the idiot tells me that Dr. Seignebos does not trouble himself about the man any more."

M. Daubigeon smiled sarcastically, and said, much more for the purpose of teasing his visitor than because he believed it himself,—

"Take care! do not trust appearances. You have to do with very clever people. I always told you Cocoleu is probably the mainspring of the whole case. The very fact that M. Gransiere will speak ought to make you tremble. If he should not succeed, he would, of course, blame you, and never forgive you in all his life. Now, you know he may fail. 'There is many a slip between the cup and the lip.'

"And I am disposed to think with Villon,—

'Nothing is so certain as uncertain things.'"

M. Galpin could tell very well that he should gain nothing by prolonging the discussion, and so he said,—

"Happen what may, I shall always know that my conscience supports me."

Then he made great haste to take leave, lest an answer should come from M. Daubigeon. He went out; and as he descended the stairs, he said to himself,—

"It is losing time to reason with that old fogy who sees in the events of the day only so many opportunities for quotations."

But he struggled in vain against his own feelings; he had lost his self-confidence. M. Daubigeon had revealed to him a new danger which he had not foreseen. And what a danger!—the resentment of one of the most eminent men of the French bar, one of those bitter, bilious men who never forgive. M. Galpin had, no doubt, thought of the possibility of failure, that is to say, of an acquittal; but he had never considered the consequences of such a check.

Who would have to pay for it? The prosecuting attorney first and foremost, because, in France, the prosecuting attorney makes the accusation a personal matter, and considers himself insulted and humiliated, if he misses his man.

Now, what would happen in such a case?

M. Gransiere, no doubt, would hold him responsible. He would say,—

"I had to draw my arguments from your part of the work. I did not obtain a condemnation, because your work was imperfect. A man like myself ought not to be exposed to such an humiliation, and, least of all, in a case which is sure to create an immense sensation. You do not understand your business."

Such words were a public disgrace. Instead of the hoped-for promotion, they would bring him an order to go into exile, to Corsica, or to Algiers.

M. Galpin shuddered at the idea. He saw himself buried under the ruins of his castles in Spain. And, unluckily, he went once more over all the papers of the investigation, analyzing the evidence he had, like a soldier, who, on the eve of a battle, furbishes up his arms. However, he only found one objection, the same which M. Daubigeon had made,—what interest could Jacques have had in committing so great a crime?

"There," he said, "is evidently the weak part of the armor; and I would do well to point it out to M. Gransiere. Jacques's counsel are capable of making that the turning-point of their plea."

And, in spite of all he had said to M. Daubigeon, he was very much afraid of the counsel for the defence. He knew perfectly well the prestige which M. Magloire derived from his integrity and disinterestedness. It was no secret to him, that a cause which M. Magloire espoused was at once considered a good cause. They said of him,—

"He may be mistaken; but whatever he says he believes." He could not but have a powerful influence, therefore, not on judges who came into court with well-established opinions, but with jurymen who are under the influence of the moment, and may be carried off by the eloquence of a speech. It is true, M. Magloire did not possess that burning eloquence which thrills a crowd, but M. Folgat had it, and in an uncommon degree. M. Galpin had made inquiries; and one of his Paris friends had written to him,—

"Mistrust Folgat. He is a far more dangerous logician than Lachant, and possesses the same skill in troubling the consciences of jurymen, in moving them, drawing tears from them, and forcing them into an acquittal. Mind, especially, any incidents that may happen during the trial; for he has always some kind of surprise in reserve."

"These are my adversaries," thought M. Galpin. "What surprise, I wonder, is there in store for me? Have they really given up all idea of using Cocoleu?"

He had no reason for mistrusting his agent; and yet his apprehensions became so serious, that he went out of his way to look in at the hospital. The lady superior received him, as a matter of course, with all the signs of profound respect; and, when he inquired about Cocoleu, she added,—

"Would you like to see him?"

"I confess I should be very glad to do so."

"Come with me, then."

She took him into the garden, and there asked a gardener,—

"Where is the idiot?"

The man put his spade into the ground; and, with that affected reverence which characterizes all persons employed in a convent, he answered,—

"The idiot is down there in the middle avenue, mother, in his usual place, you know, which nothing will induce him to leave."

M. Galpin and the lady superior found him there. They had taken off the rags which he wore when he was admitted, and put him into the hospital-dress, which was a large gray coat and a cotton cap. He did not look any more intelligent for that; but he was less repulsive. He was seated on the ground, playing with the gravel.

"Well, my boy," asked M. Galpin, "how do you like this?"

He raised his inane face, and fixed his dull eye on the lady superior; but he made no reply.

"Would you like to go back to Valpinson?" asked the lawyer again. He shuddered, but did not open his lips.

"Look here," said M. Galpin, "answer me, and I'll give you a ten-cent piece."

No: Cocoleu was at his play again.

"That is the way he is always," declared the lady superior. "Since he is here, no one has ever gotten a word out of him. Promises, threats, nothing has any effect. One day I thought I would try an experiment; and, instead of letting him have his breakfast, I said to him, 'You shall have nothing to eat till you say, "I am hungry."'" At the end of twenty-four hours I had to let him have his pittance; for he would have starved himself sooner than utter a word."

"What does Dr. Seignebos think of him?"

"The doctor does not want to hear his name mentioned," replied the lady superior.

And, raising her eyes to heaven, she added,—

"And that is a clear proof, that, but for the direct intervention of Providence, the poor creature would never have denounced the crime which he had witnessed."

Immediately, however, she returned to earthly things, and asked,—

"But will you not relieve us soon of this poor idiot, who is a heavy charge on our hospital? Why not send him back to his village, where he found his support before? We have quite a number of sick and poor, and very little room."

"We must wait, sister, till M. de Boiscoran's trial is finished," replied the magistrate.

The lady superior looked resigned, and said,—

"That is what the mayor told me, and it is very provoking, I must say: however, they have allowed me to turn him out of the room which they had given him at first. I have sent him to the Insane Ward. That is the name we give to a few little rooms, enclosed by a wall, where we keep the poor insane, who are sent to us provisionally."

Here she was interrupted by the janitor of the hospital, who came up, bowing.

"What do you want?" she asked.

Vaudevin, the janitor, handed her a note.

"A man brought by a gendarme," he replied. "Immediately to be admitted."

The lady superior read the note, signed by Dr. Seignebos.

"Epileptic," she said, "and somewhat idiotic: as if we wanted any more! And a stranger into the bargain! Really Dr. Seignebos is too yielding. Why does he not send all these people to their own parish to be taken care of?"

And, with a very elastic step for her age, she went to the parlor, followed by M. Galpin and the janitor. They had put the new patient in there, and, sunk upon a bench, he looked the picture of utter idiocy. After having looked at him for a minute, she said,—

"Put him in the Insane Ward: he can keep Cocoleu company. And let the sister know at the drug-room. But no, I will go myself. You will excuse me, sir."

And then she left the room. M. Galpin was much comforted.

"There is no danger here," he said to himself. "And if M. Folgat counts upon any incident during the trial, Cocoleu, at all events, will not furnish it to him."

XXVII.

At the same hour when the magistrate left the hospital, Dr. Seignebos and M. Folgat parted, after a frugal breakfast,—the one to visit his patients, the other to go to the prison. The young advocate was very much troubled. He hung his head as he went down the street; and the diplomatic citizens who compared his dejected appearance with the victorious air of M. Galpin came to the conclusion that Jacques de Boiscoran was irrevocably lost.

At that moment M. Folgat was almost of their opinion. He had to pass through one of those attacks of discouragement, to which the most energetic men succumb at times, when they are bent upon pursuing an uncertain end which they ardently desire.

The declarations made by little Martha and the governess had literally overwhelmed him. Just when he thought he had the end of the thread in his hand, the tangle had become worse than ever. And so it had been from the commencement. At every step he took, the problem had become more complicated than ever. At every effort he made, the darkness, instead of being dispelled, had become deeper. Not that he as yet doubted Jacques's innocence. No! The suspicion which for a moment had flashed through his mind had passed away instantly. He admitted, with Dr. Seignebos, the possibility that there was an accomplice, and that it was Cocoleu, in all probability, who had been charged with the execution of the crime. But how could that fact be made useful to the defence? He saw no way.

Goudar was an able man; and the manner in which he had introduced himself into the hospital and Cocoleu's company indicated a master. But however cunning he was, however experienced in all the tricks of his profession, how could he ever hope to make a man confess who intrenched himself behind the rampart of feigned imbecility? If he had only had an abundance of time before him! But the days were counted, and he would have to hurry his measures.

"I feel like giving it up," thought the young lawyer.

In the meantime he had reached the prison. He felt the necessity of concealing his anxiety. While Blangin went before him through the long passages, rattling his keys, he endeavored to give to his features an expression of hopeful confidence.

"At last you come!" cried Jacques.

He had evidently suffered terribly since the day before. A feverish restlessness had disordered his features, and reddened his eyes. He was shaking with nervous tremor. Still he waited till the jailer had shut the door; and then he asked hoarsely,—

"What did she say?"

M. Folgat gave him a minute account of his mission, quoting the words of the countess almost literally.

"That is just like her!" exclaimed the prisoner. "I think I can hear her! What a woman! To defy me in this way!"

And in his anger he wrung his hands till they nearly bled.

"You see," said the young advocate, "there is no use in trying to get outside of our circle of defence. Any new effort would be useless."

"No!" replied Jacques. "No, I shall not stop there!"

And after a few moments' reflection,—if he can be said to have been able to reflect,—he said,—

"I hope you will pardon me, my dear sir, for having exposed you to such insults. I ought to have foreseen it, or, rather, I did foresee it. I knew that was not the way to begin the battle. But I was a coward, I was afraid, I drew back, fool that I was! As if I had not known that we shall at any rate have to come to the last extremity! Well, I am ready now, and I shall do it!"

"What do you mean to do?"

"I shall go and see the Countess Claudieuse. I shall tell her"—

"Oh!"

"You do not think she will deny it to my face? When I once have her under my eye, I shall make her confess the crime of which I am accused."

M. Folgat had promised Dr. Seignebos not to mention what Martha and her governess had said; but he felt no longer bound to conceal it.

"And if the countess should not be guilty?" he asked.

"Who, then, could be guilty?"

"If she had an accomplice?"

"Well, she will tell me who it is. I will insist upon it, I will make her tell. I will not be disgraced. I am innocent, I will not go to the galleys!"

To try and make Jacques listen to reason would have been madness just now.

"Have a care," said the young lawyer. "Our defence is difficult enough already; do not make it still more so."

"I shall be careful."

"A scene might ruin us irrevocably."

"Be not afraid!"

M. Folgat said nothing more. He thought he could guess by what means Jacques would try to get out of prison. But he did not ask him about the details, because his position as his counsel made it his duty not to know, or, at least, to seem not to know, certain things.

"Now, my dear sir," said the prisoner, "you will render me a service, will you not?"

"What is it?"

"I want to know as accurately as possible how the house in which the countess lives is arranged."

Without saying a word, M. Folgat took out a sheet of paper, and drew on it a plan of the house, as far as he knew,—of the garden, the entrance-hall, and the sitting-room.

"And the count's room," asked Jacques, "where is that?"

"In the upper story."

"You are sure he cannot get up?"

"Dr. Seignebos told me so."

The prisoner seemed to be delighted.

"Then all is right," he said, "and I have only to ask you, my dear counsel, to tell Miss Dionysia that I must see her to-day, as soon as possible. I wish her to come accompanied by one of her aunts only. And, I beseech you, make haste."

M. Folgat did hasten; so that, twenty minutes later, he was at the young lady's house. She was in her chamber. He sent word to her that he wished to see her; and, as soon as she heard that Jacques wanted her, she said simply,—

"I am ready to go."

And, calling one of the Misses Lavarande, she told her,—

"Come, Aunt Elizabeth, be quick. Take your hat and your shawl. I am going out, and you are going with me."

The prisoner counted so fully upon the promptness of his betrothed, that he had already gone down into the parlor when she arrived at the prison, quite out of breath from having walked so fast. He took her hands, and, pressing them to his lips, he said,—

"Oh, my darling! how shall I ever thank you for your sublime fidelity in my misfortune? If I escape, my whole life will not suffice to prove my gratitude."

But he tried to master his emotion, and turning to Aunt Elizabeth, he said,—

"Will you pardon me if I beg you to render me once more the service you have done me before? It is all important that no one should hear what I am going to say to Dionysia. I know I am watched."

Accustomed to passive obedience, the good lady left the room without daring to make the slightest remark, and went to keep watch in the passage. Dionysia was very much surprised; but Jacques did not give her time to utter a word. He said at once,—

"You told me in this very place, that, if I wished to escape, Blangin would furnish me the means, did you not?"

The young girl drew back, and stammered with an air of utter bewilderment,—

"You do not want to flee?"

"Never! Under no circumstances! But you ought to remember, that, while resisting all your arguments, I told you, that perhaps, some day or other, I might require a few hours of liberty."

"I remember."

"I begged you to sound the jailer on that point."

"I did so. For money he will always be ready to do your bidding."

Jacques seemed to breathe more freely.

"Well, then," he said again, "the time has come. To-morrow I shall have to be away all the evening. I shall like to leave about nine; and I shall be back at midnight."

Dionysia stopped him.

"Wait," she said; "I want to call Blangin's wife."

The household of the jailer of Sauveterre was like many others. The husband was brutal, imperious, and tyrannical: he talked loud and positively, and thus made it appear that he was the master. The wife was humble, submissive, apparently resigned, and always ready to obey; but in reality she ruled by intelligence, as he ruled by main force. When the husband had promised any thing, the consent of the wife had still to be obtained; but, when the wife undertook to do any thing, the husband was bound through her. Dionysia, therefore, knew very well that she would have first to win over the wife. Mrs. Blangin came up in haste, her mouth full of hypocritical assurances of good will, vowing that she was heart and soul at her dear mistress's command, recalling with delight the happy days when she was in M. de Chandore's service, and regretting forevermore.

"I know," the young girl cut her short, "you are attached to me. But listen!"

And then she promptly explained to her what she wanted; while Jacques, standing a little aside in the shade, watched the impression on the woman's face. Gradually she raised her head; and, when Dionysia had finished, she said in a very different tone,—

"I understand perfectly, and, if I were the master, I should say, 'All right!' But Blangin is master of the jail. Well, he is not bad; but he insists upon doing his duty. We have nothing but our place to live upon."

"Have I not paid you as much as your place is worth?"

"Oh, I know you do not mind paying."

"You had promised me to speak to your husband about this matter."

"I have done so; but"—

"I would give as much as I did before."

"In gold?"

"Well, be it so, in gold."

A flash of covetousness broke forth from under the thick brows of the jailer's wife; but, quite self-possessed, she went on,—

"In that case, my man will probably consent. I will go and put him right, and then you can talk to him."

She went out hastily, and, as soon as she had disappeared, Jacques asked Dionysia,—

"How much have you paid Blangin so far?"

"Seventeen thousand francs."

"These people are robbing you outrageously."

"Ah, what does the money matter? I wish we were both of us ruined, if you were but free."

But it had not taken the wife long to persuade the husband. Blangin's heavy steps were heard in the passage; and almost immediately, he entered, cap in hand, looking obsequious and restless.

"My wife has told me every thing," he said, "and I consent. Only we must understand each other. This is no trifle you are asking for."

Jacques interrupted him, and said,—

"Let us not exaggerate the matter. I do not mean to escape: I only want to leave for a time. I shall come back, I give you my word of honor."

"Upon my life, that is not what troubles me. If the question was only to let you run off altogether, I should open the doors wide, and say, 'Good-by!' A prisoner who runs away—that happens every day; but a prisoner who leaves for a few hours, and comes back again—Suppose anybody were to see you in town? Or if any one came and wanted to see you while you are gone? Or if they saw you come back again? What should I say? I am quite ready to be turned off for negligence. I have been paid for that. But to be tried as an accomplice, and to be put into jail myself. Stop! That is not what I mean to do."

This was evidently but a preface.

"Oh! why lose so many words?" asked Dionysia. "Explain yourself clearly."

"Well, M. de Boiscoran cannot leave by the gate. At tattoo, at eight o'clock, the soldiers on guard at this season of the year go inside the prison, and until *reveille* in the morning, or, in others words, till five o'clock, I can neither open nor shut the gates without calling the sergeant in command of the post."

"Did he want to extort more money? Did he make the difficulties out greater than they really were?"

"After all," said Jacques, "if you consent, there must be a way."

The jailer could dissemble no longer: he came out with it bluntly.

"If the thing is to be done, you must get out as if you were escaping in good earnest. The wall between the two towers is, to my knowledge, at one place not over two feet thick; and on the other side, where there are nothing but bare grounds and the old ramparts, they never put a sentinel. I will get you a crowbar and a pickaxe, and you make a hole in the wall."

Jacques shrugged his shoulders.

"And the next day," he said, "when I am back, how will you explain that hole?"

Blangin smiled.

"Be sure," he replied, "I won't say the rats did it. I have thought of that too. At the same time with you, another prisoner will run off, who will not come back."

"What prisoner?"

"Trumence, to be sure. He will be delighted to get away, and he will help you in making the hole in the wall. You must make your bargain with him, but, of course, without letting him know that I

- 391 -

know any thing. In this way, happen what may, I shall not be in danger."

The plan was really a good one; only Blangin ought not to have claimed the honor of inventing it: the idea came from his wife.

"Well," replied Jacques, "that is settled. Get me the pickaxe and the crowbar, show me the place where we must make the hole, and I will take charge of Trumence. To-morrow you shall have the money."

He was on the point of following the jailer, when Dionysia held him back; and, lifting up her beautiful eyes to him, she said in a tremor,—

"You see, Jacques, I have not hesitated to dare every thing in order to procure you a few house of liberty. May I not know what you are going to do in that time?"

And, as he made no reply, she repeated,—

"Where are you going?"

A rush of blood colored the face of the unfortunate man; and he said in an embarrassed voice,—

"I beseech you, Dionysia, do not insist upon my telling you. Permit me to keep this secret, the only one I have ever kept from you."

Two tears trembled for a moment in the long lashes of the young girl, and then silently rolled down her cheeks.

"I understand you," she stammered. "I understand but too well. Although I know so little of life, I had a presentiment, as soon as I saw that they were hiding something from me. Now I cannot doubt any longer. You will go to see a woman to-morrow"—

"Dionysia," Jacques said with folded hands,—"Dionysia, I beseech you!"

She did not hear him. Gently shaking her heard, she went on,—

"A woman whom you have loved, or whom you love still, at whose feet you have probably murmured the same words which you whispered at my feet. How could you think of her in the midst of all your anxieties? She cannot love you, I am sure. Why did she not come to you when she found that you were in prison, and falsely accused of an abominable crime?"

Jacques cold bear it no longer.

"Great God!" he cried, "I would a thousand times rather tell you every thing than allow such a suspicion to remain in your heart! Listen, and forgive me."

But she stopped him, putting her hand on his lips, and saying, all in a tremor,—

"No, I do not wish to know any thing,—nothing at all. I believe in you. Only you must remember that you are every thing to me,—hope, life, happiness. If you should have deceived me, I know but too well—poor me!—that I would not cease loving you; but I should not have long to suffer."

Overcome with grief and affection, Jacques repeated,—

"Dionysia, Dionysia, my darling, let me confess to you who this woman is, and why I must see her."

"No," she interrupted him, "no! Do what your conscience bids you do. I believe in you."

And instead of offering to let him kiss her forehead, as usual, she hurried off with her Aunt Elizabeth, and that so quickly, that, when he rushed after her, he only saw, as it were, a shadow at the end of the long passage.

Never until this moment had Jacques found it in his heart really to hate the Countess Claudieuse with that blind and furious hatred which dreams of nothing but vengeance. Many a time, no doubt, he had cursed her in the solitude of his prison; but even when he was most furious against her, a feeling of pity had risen in his heart for her whom he had once loved so dearly; for he did not disguise it to himself, he had once loved her to distraction. Even in his prison he trembled, as he thought of some of his first meetings with her, as he saw before his mind's eye her features swimming in voluptuous languor, as he heard the silvery ring of her voice, or inhaled the perfume she loved ever to have about her. She had exposed him to the danger of losing his position, his future, his honor even; and he still felt inclined to forgive her. But now she threatened him with the loss of his betrothed, the loss of that pure and chaste love which burnt in Dionysia's heart, and he could not endure that.

"I will spare her no longer," he cried, mad with wrath. "I will hesitate no longer. I have not the right to do so; for I am bound to defend Dionysia!"

He was more than ever determined to risk that adventure on the next day, feeling quite sure now that his courage would not fail him.

It was Trumence to-night—perhaps by the jailer's skilful management—who was ordered to take the prisoner back to his cell, and, according to the jail-dictionary, to "curl him up" there. He called him in, and at once plainly told him what he expected him to do. Upon Blangin's assurance, he expected the vagabond would jump at the mere idea of escaping from jail. But by no means. Trumence's smiling features grew dark; and, scratching himself behind the ear furiously, he replied,—

"You see—excuse me, I don't want to run away at all."

Jacques was amazed. If Trumence refused his cooperation he could not go out, or, at least, he would have to wait.

"Are you in earnest, Trumence?" he asked.

"Certainly I am, my dear sir. Here, you see, I am not so badly off: I have a good bed, I have two meals a day, I have nothing to do, and I pick up now and then, from one man or another, a few cents to buy me a pinch of tobacco or a glass of wine."

"But your liberty?"

"Well, I shall get that too. I have committed no crime. I may have gotten over a wall into an orchard; but people are not hanged for that. I have consulted M. Magloire, and he told me precisely how I stand. They will try me in a police-court, and they will give me three or four months. Well, that is not so very bad. But, if I run away, they put the gendarmes on my track; they bring me back here; and then I know how they will treat me. Besides, to break jail is a grave offence."

How could he overcome such wise conclusions and such excellent reasons? Jacques was very much troubled.

"Why should the gendarmes take you again?" he asked.

"Because they are gendarmes, my dear sir. And then, that is not all. If it were spring, I should say at once, 'I am your man.' But we have autumn now; we are going to have bad weather; work will be scarce."

Although an incurable idler, Trumence had always a good deal to say about work.

"You won't help them in the vintage?" asked Jacques.

The vagabond looked almost repenting.

"To be sure, the vintage must have commenced," he said.

"Well?"

"But that only lasts a fortnight, and then comes winter. And winter is no man's friend: it's my enemy. I know I have been without a place to lie down when it has been freezing to split stones, and the snow was a foot deep. Oh! here they have stoves, and the Board gives very warm clothes."

"Yes; but there are no merry evenings here, Trumence, eh? None of those merry evenings, when the hot wine goes round, and you tell the girls all sorts of stories, while you are shelling peas, or shucking corn?"

"Oh! I know. I do enjoy those evenings. But the cold! Where should I go when I have not a cent?"

That was exactly where Jacques wanted to lead him.

"I have money," he said.

"I know you have."

"You do not think I would let you go off with empty pockets? I would give you any thing you may ask."

"Really?" cried the vagrant.

And looking at Jacques with a mingled expression of hope, surprise, and delight, he added,—

"You see I should want a good deal. Winter is long. I should want—let me see, I should want fifty Napoleons!"

"You shall have a hundred," said Jacques.

Trumence's eyes began to dance. He probably had a vision of those irresistible taverns at Rochefort, where he had led such a merry life. But he could not believe such happiness to be real.

"You are not making fun of me?" he asked timidly.

"Do you want the whole sum at once?" replied Jacques. "Wait."

He drew from the drawer in his table a thousand-franc note. But, at the sight of the note, the vagrant drew back the hand which he had promptly stretched out to take the money.

"Oh! that kind? No! I know what that paper is worth: I have had some of them myself. But what could I do with one of them now? It would not be worth more to me than a leaf of a tree; for, at the first place I should want it changed, they would arrest me."

"That is easily remedied. By to-morrow I shall have gold, or small notes, so you can have your choice."

This time Trumence clapped his hands in great joy.

"Give me some of one kind, and some of the other," he said, "and I am your man! Hurrah for liberty! Where is that wall that we are to go through?"

"I will show you to-morrow; and till then, Trumence, silence."

It was only the next day that Blangin showed Jacques the place where the wall had least thickness. It was in a kind of cellar, where nobody ever came, and where cast-off tools were stored away.

"In order that you may not be interrupted," said the jailer, "I will ask two of my comrades to dine with me, and I shall invite the sergeant on duty. They will enjoy themselves, and never think of the prisoners. My wife will keep a sharp lookout; and, if any of the rounds should come this way, she would warn you, and quick, quick, you would be back in your room."

All was settled; and, as soon as night came, Jacques and Trumence, taking a candle with them, slipped down into the cellar, and went to work. It was a hard task to get through this old wall, and Jacques would never have been able to accomplish it alone. The thickness was even less than what Blangin had stated it to be;

but the hardness was far beyond expectation. Our fathers built well. In course of time the cement had become one with the stone, and acquired the same hardness. It was as if they had attacked a block of granite. The vagrant had, fortunately, a strong arm; and, in spite of the precautions which they had to take to prevent being heard, he had, in less than an hour, made a hole through which a man could pass. He put his head in; and, after a moment's examination, he said,—

"All right! The night is dark, and the place is deserted. Upon my word, I will risk it!"

He went through; Jacques followed; and instinctively they hastened towards a place where several trees made a dark shadow. Once there, Jacques handed Trumence a package of five-franc notes, and said,—

"Add this to the hundred Napoleons I have given you before. Thank you: you are a good fellow, and, if I get out of my trouble, I will not forget you. And now let us part. Make haste, be careful, and good luck!"

After these words he went off rapidly. But Trumence did not march off in the opposite direction, as had been agreed upon.

"Anyhow," said the poor vagrant to himself, "this is a curious story about the poor gentleman. Where on earth can he be going?"

And, curiosity getting the better of prudence, he followed him.

XXVIII.

Jacques de Boiscoran went straight to Mautrec Street. But he knew with what horror he was looked upon by the population; and in order to avoid being recognized, and perhaps arrested, he did not take the most direct route, nor did he choose the more frequented streets. He went a long way around, and well-nigh lost himself in the winding, dark lanes of the old town. He walked along in Feverish haste, turning aside from the rare passers-by, pulling his felt hat down over his eyes, and, for still greater safety, holding his handkerchief over his face. It was nearly half-past nine when he at last reached the house inhabited by Count and Countess Claudieuse. The little gate had been taken out, and the great doors were closed.

Never mind! Jacques had his plan. He rang the bell.

A maid, who did not know him, came to the door.

"Is the Countess Claudieuse in?" he asked.

"The countess does not see anybody," replied the girl. "She is sitting up with the count, who is very ill to-night."

"But I must see her."

"Impossible."

"Tell her that a gentleman who has been sent by M. Galpin desires to see her for a moment. It is the Boiscoran affair."

"Why did you not say so at once?" said the servant. "Come in." And forgetting, in her hurry, to close the gates again, she went before Jacques through the garden, showed him into the vestibule, and then opened the parlor-door, saying,—

"Will you please go in here and sit down, while I go to tell the countess?"

After lighting one of the candles on the mantelpiece, she went out. So far, every thing had gone well for Jacques, and even better than he could have expected. Nothing remained now to be done, except to prevent the countess from going back and escaping, as soon as she should have recognized Jacques. Fortunately the parlor-door opened into the room. He went and put himself behind the open half, and waited there.

For twenty-four hours he had prepared himself for this interview, and arranged in his head the very words he would use. But now, at the last moment, all his ideas flew away, like dry leaves under the breath of a tempest. His heart was beating with such violence, that he thought it filled the whole room with the noise. He imagined he was cool, and, in fact, he possessed that lucidity which gives to certain acts of madmen an appearance of sense.

He was surprised at being kept waiting so long, when, at last, light steps, and the rustling of a dress, warned him that the countess was coming.

She came in, dressed in a long, dark, undress robe, and took a few steps into the room, astonished at not seeing the person who was waiting for her.

It was exactly as Jacques had foreseen.

He pushed to, violently, the open half of the door; and, placing himself before her, he said,—

"We are alone!"

She turned round at the noise, and cried,—

"Jacques!"

And terrified, as if she had seen a ghost, she looked all around, hoping to see a way out. One of the tall windows of the room, which went down to the ground, was half open, and she rushed towards it; but Jacques anticipated her, and said,—

"Do not attempt to escape; for I swear I should pursue you into your husband's room, to the foot of his bed."

She looked at him as if she did not comprehend.

"You," she stammered,—"you here!"

"Yes," he replied, "I am here. You are astonished, are you? You said to yourself, 'He is in prison, well kept under lock and key: I can sleep in peace. No evidence can be found. He will not speak. I have committed the crime, and he will be punished for it. I am guilty; but I shall escape. He is innocent, and he is lost.' You thought it was all settled? Well, no, it is not. I am here!"

An expression of unspeakable horror contracted the beautiful features of the countess. She said,—

"This is monstrous!"

"Monstrous indeed!"

"Murderer! Incendiary!"

He burst out laughing, a strident, convulsive, terrible laughter.

"And you," he said, "you call me so?"

By one great effort the Countess Claudieuse recovered her energy.

"Yes," she replied, "yes, I do! You cannot deny your crime to me. I know, I know the motives which the judges do not even guess. You thought I would carry out my threats, and you were frightened. When I left you in such haste, you said to yourself, 'It is all over: she will tell her husband.' And then you kindled that fire in order to draw my husband out of the house, you incendiary! And then you fired at my husband, you murderer!"

He was still laughing.

"And that is your plan?" he broke in. "Who do you think will believe such an absurd story? Our letters were burnt; and, if you deny having been my mistress, I can just as well deny having been your lover. And, besides, would the exposure do me any harm? You know very well it would not. You are perfectly aware, that, as society is with us, the same thing which disgraces a woman rather raises a man in the estimate of the world. And as to my being afraid of Count Claudieuse, it is well known that I am afraid of nobody. At the time when we were concealing our love in the house in Vine Street, yes, at that time, I might have been afraid of your husband; for he might have surprised us there, the code in one hand, a revolver in the other, and have availed himself of that stupid and savage law which makes the husband the judge of his own case, and the executor of the sentence which he himself pronounces. But setting aside such a case, the case of being taken in the act, which allows a man to kill like a dog another man, who can not or will not defend himself, what did I care for Count Claudieuse? What did I care for your threats or for his hatred?" He said these words with perfect calmness, but with that cold, cutting tone which is as sharp as a sword, and with that positiveness which enters irresistibly into the mind. The countess was tottering, and stammered almost inaudibly,—

"Who would imagine such a thing? Is it possible?"

Then, suddenly raising her head, she said,—

"But I am losing my senses. If you are innocent, who, then, could be the guilty man?"

Jacques seized her hands almost madly, and pressing them painfully, and bending over her so closely that she felt his hot breath like a flame touching her face, he hissed into her ear,—

"You, wretched creature, you!"

And then pushing her from him with such violence that she fell into a chair, he continued,—

"You, who wanted to be a widow in order to prevent me from breaking the chains in which you held me. At our last meeting, when I thought you were crushed by grief, and felt overcome by your hypocritical tears, I was weak enough, I was stupid enough, to say that I married Dionysia only because you were not free. Then you cried, 'O God, how happy I am that that idea did not occur to me before!' What idea was that, Genevieve? Come, answer me and confess, that it occurred to you too soon after all, since you have carried it out?"

And repeating with crushing irony the words just uttered by the countess, he said,—

"If you are innocent, who, then, would be the guilty man?"

Quite beside herself, she sprang up from her chair, and casting at Jacques one of those glances which seem to enter through our eyes into the very heart of our hearts, she asked,—

"Is it really possible that you have not committed this abominable crime?"

He shrugged his shoulders.

"But then," she repeated, almost panting, "is it true, can it really be true, that you think I have committed it?"

"Perhaps you have only ordered it to be committed."

With a wild gesture she raised her arms to heaven, and cried in a heart-rending voice,—

"O God, O God! He believes it! he really believes it!"

There followed great silence, dismal, formidable silence, such as in nature follows the crash of the thunderbolt.

Standing face to face, Jacques and the Countess Claudieuse looked at each other madly, feeling that the fatal hour in their lives had come at last.

Each felt a growing, a sure conviction of the other. There was no need of explanations. They had been misled by appearances: they acknowledged it; they were sure of it.

And this discovery was so fearful, so overwhelming, that neither thought of who the real guilty one might be.

"What is to be done?" asked the countess.

"The truth must be told," replied Jacques.

"Which?"

"That I have been your lover; that I went to Valpinson by appointment with you; that the cartridge-case which was found there was used by me to get fire; that my blackened hands were soiled by the half-burnt fragment of our letters, which I had tried to scatter."

"Never!" cried the countess.

Jacques's face turned crimson, as he said with an accent of merciless severity,—

"It shall be told! I will have it so, and it must be done!"

The countess seemed to be furious.

"Never!" she cried again, "never!"

And with convulsive haste she added,—

"Do you not see that the truth cannot possibly be told. They would never believe in our innocence. They would only look upon us as accomplices."

"Never mind. I am not willing to die."

"Say that you will not die alone."

"Be it so."

"To confess every thing would never save you, but would most assuredly ruin me. Is that what you want? Would your fate appear less cruel to you, if there were two victims instead of one?"

He stopped her by a threatening gesture, and cried,—

"Are you always the same? I am sinking, I am drowning; and she calculates, she bargains! And she said she loved me!"

"Jacques!" broke in the countess.

And drawing close up to him, she said,—

"Ah! I calculate, I bargain? Well, listen. Yes, it is true. I did value my reputation as an honest woman more highly, a thousand times more, than my life; but, above my life and my reputation, I valued you. You are drowning, you say. Well, then, let us flee. One word from you, and I leave all,—honor, country, family, husband, children. Say one word, and I follow you without turning my head, without a regret, without a remorse."

Her whole body was shivering from head to foot; her bosom rose and fell; her eyes shone with unbearable brilliancy.

Thanks to the violence of her action, her dress, put on in great haste, had opened, and her dishevelled hair flowed in golden masses over her bosom and her shoulders, which matched the purest marble in their dazzling whiteness.

And in a voice trembling with pent-up passion, now sweet and soft like a tender caress, and now deep and sonorous like a bell, she went on,—

"What keeps us? Since you have escaped from prison, the greatest difficulty is overcome. I thought at first of taking our girl, your girl, Jacques; but she is very ill; and besides a child might betray us. If we go alone, they will never overtake us. We will have money enough, I am sure, Jacques. We will flee to those distant countries which appear in books of travels in such fairy-like beauty. There, unknown, forgotten, unnoticed, our life will be one unbroken enjoyment. You will never again say that I bargain. I will be yours, entirely, and solely yours, body and soul, your wife, your slave."

She threw her head back, and with half-closed eyes, bending with her whole person toward him, she said in melting tones,—

"Say, Jacques, will you? Jacques!"

He pushed her aside with a fierce gesture. It seemed to him almost a sacrilege that she also, like Dionysia, should propose to him to flee.

"Rather the galleys!" he cried.

She turned deadly pale; a spasm of rage convulsed her features; and drawing back, stiff and stern, she said,—

"What else do you want?"

"Your help to save me," he replied.

"At the risk of ruining myself?"

He made no reply.

Then she, who had just now been all humility, raised herself to her full height, and in a tone of bitterest sarcasm said slowly,—

"In other words, you want me to sacrifice myself, and at the same time all my family. For your sake? Yes, but even more for Miss Chandore's sake. And you think that it is quite a simple thing. I am the past to you, satiety, disgust: she is the future to you, desire, happiness. And you think it quite natural that the old love should make a footstool of her love and her honor for the new love? You think little of my being disgraced, provided she be honored; of my weeping bitterly, if she but smile? Well, no, no! it is madness in you to come and ask me to save you, so that you may throw yourself into the arms of another. It is madness, when in order to tear you from Dionysia, I am ready to ruin myself, provided only that you be lost to her forever."

"Wretch!" cried Jacques.

She looked at him with a mocking air, and her eyes beamed with infernal audacity.

"You do not know me yet," she cried. "Go, speak, denounce me! M. Folgat no doubt has told you how I can deny and defend myself."

Maddened by indignation, and excited to a point where reason loses its power over us, Jacques de Boiscoran moved with uplifted hand towards the countess, when suddenly a voice said,—

"Do not strike that woman!"

Jacques and the countess turned round, and uttered, both at the same instant, the same kind of sharp, terrible cry, which must have been heard a great distance.

In the frame of the door stood Count Claudieuse, a revolver in his hand, and ready to fire.

He looked as pale as a ghost; and the white flannel dressing-gown which he had hastily thrown around him hung like a pall around his lean limbs. The first cry uttered by the countess had been heard by him on the bed on which he lay apparently dying. A terrible presentiment had seized him. He had risen from his bed, and, dragging himself slowly along, holding painfully to the balusters, he had come down.

"I have heard all," he said, casting crushing looks at both the guilty ones.

The countess uttered a deep, hoarse sigh, and sank into a chair. But Jacques drew himself up, and said,—

"I have insulted you terribly, sir. Avenge yourself."

The count shrugged his shoulders.

"Great God! You would allow me to be condemned for a crime which I have not committed. Ah, that would be the meanest cowardice."

The count was so feeble that he had to lean against the door-post.

"Would it be cowardly?" he asked. "Then, what do you call the act of that miserable man who meanly, disgracefully robs another man of his wife, and palms off his own children upon him? It is true you are neither an incendiary nor an assassin. But what is fire in my house in comparison with the ruin of all my faith? What are the wounds in my body in comparison with that wound in my heart, which never can heal? I leave you to the court, sir."

Jacques was terrified; he saw the abyss opening before him that was to swallow him up.

"Rather death," he cried,—"death."

And, baring his breast, he said,—

"But why do you not fire, sir? Why do you not fire? Are you afraid of blood? Shoot! I have been the lover of your wife: your youngest daughter is my child."

The count lowered his weapon.

"The courts of justice are more certain," he said. "You have robbed me of my honor: now I want yours. And, if you cannot be condemned without it, I shall say, I shall swear, that I recognized you. You shall go to the galleys, M. de Boiscoran."

He was on the point of coming forward; but his strength was exhausted, and he fell forward, face downward, and arms outstretched.

Overcome with horror, half mad, Jacques fled.

XXIX.

M. Folgat had just risen. Standing before his mirror, hung up to one of the windows in his room, he had just finished shaving himself, when the door was thrown open violently, and old Anthony appeared quite beside himself.

"Ah, sir, what a terrible thing!"

"What?"

"Run away, disappeared!"

"Who?"

"Master Jacques!"

The surprise was so great, that M. Folgat nearly let his razor drop: he said, however, peremptorily,—

"That is false!"

"Alas, sir," replied the old servant, "everybody is full of it in town. All the details are known. I have just seen a man who says he met master last night, about eleven o'clock, running like a madman down National Street."

"That is absurd."

"I have only told Miss Dionysia so far, and she sent me to you. You ought to go and make inquiry."

The advice was not needed. Wiping his face hastily, the young advocate went to dress at once. He was ready in a moment; and, having run down the stairs, he was crossing the passage when he heard somebody call his name. He turned round, and saw Dionysia making him a sign to come into the boudoir in which she was usually sitting. He did so.

Dionysia and the young advocate alone knew what a desperate venture Jacques had undertaken the night before. They had not said a word about it to each other; but each had noticed the preoccupation of the other. All the evening M. Folgat had not spoken ten words, and Dionysia had, immediately after dinner, gone up to her own room.

"Well?" she asked.

"The report, madam, must be false," replied the advocate.

"Who knows?"

"His evasion would be a confession of his crime. It is only the guilty who try to escape; and M. de Boiscoran is innocent. You can rest quite assured, madam, it is not so. I pray you be quiet."

Who would not have pitied the poor girl at that moment? She was as white as her collar, and trembled violently. Big tears ran over her eyes; and at each word a violent sob rose in her throat.

"You know where Jacques went last night?" she asked again.

"Yes."

She turned her head a little aside, and went on, in a hardly audible voice,—

"He went to see once more a person whose influence over him is, probably, all powerful. It may be that she has upset him, stunned him. Might she not have prevailed upon him to escape from the disgrace of appearing in court, charged with such a crime?"

"No, madam, no!"

"This person has always been Jacques's evil genius. She loves him, I am sure. She must have been incensed at the idea of his becoming my husband. Perhaps, in order to induce him to flee, she has fled with him."

"Ah! do not be afraid, madam: the Countess Claudieuse is incapable of such devotion."

Dionysia threw herself back in utter amazement; and, raising her wide-open eyes to the young advocate, she said with an air of stupefaction,—

"The Countess Claudieuse?"

M. Folgat saw his indiscretion. He had been under the impression that Jacques had told his betrothed every thing; and her very manner of speaking had confirmed him in his conviction.

"Ah, it is the Countess Claudieuse," she went on,—"that lady whom all revere as if she were a saint. And I, who only the other day marvelled at her fervor in praying,—I who pitied her with all my heart,—I—Ah! I now see what they were hiding from me."

Distressed by the blunder which he had committed, the young advocate said,—

"I shall never forgive myself, madam, for having mentioned that name in your presence."

She smiled sadly.

"Perhaps you have rendered me a great service, sir. But, I pray, go and see what the truth is about this report."

M. Folgat had not walked down half the street, when he became aware that something extraordinary must really have happened. The whole town was in uproar. People stood at their doors, talking. Groups here and there were engaged in lively discussions.

Hastening his steps, he was just turning into National Street, when he was stopped by three or four gentlemen, whose acquaintance he had, in some way or other, been forced to make since he was at Sauveterre.

"Well, sir?" said one of these amiable friends, "your client, it seems, is running about nicely."

"I do not understand," replied M. Folgat in a tone of ice.

"Why? Don't you know your client has run off?"

"Are you quite sure of that?"

"Certainly. The wife of a workman whom I employ was the person through whom the escape became known. She had gone on the old ramparts to cut grass there for her goat; and, when she came to the prison wall, she saw a big hole had been made there. She gave at once the alarm; the guard came up; and they reported the matter immediately to the commonwealth attorney."

For M. Folgat the evidence was not satisfactory yet. He asked,—

"Well? And M. de Boiscoran?"

"Cannot be found. Ah, I tell you, it is just as I say. I know it from a friend who heard it from a clerk at the mayor's office. Blangin the jailer, they say, is seriously implicated."

"I hope soon to see you again," said the young advocate, and left him abruptly.

The gentleman seemed to be very grievously offended at such treatment; but the young advocate paid no attention to him, and rapidly crossed the New-Market Square.

He was become apprehensive. He did not fear an evasion, but thought there might have occurred some fearful catastrophe. A hundred persons, at least, were assembled around the prison-doors, standing there with open mouths and eager eyes; and the sentinels had much trouble in keeping them back.

M. Folgat made his way through the crowd, and went in.

In the court-yard he found the commonwealth attorney, the chief of police, the captain of the gendarmes, M. Seneschal, and, finally, M. Galpin, all standing before the janitor's lodge in animated discussion. The magistrate looked paler than ever, and was, as they called it in Sauveterre, in bull-dog humor. There was reason for it.

He had been informed as promptly as M. Folgat, and had, with equal promptness, dressed, and hastened to the prison. And all along his way, unmistakable evidence had proved to him that public opinion was fiercely roused against the accused, but that it was as deeply excited against himself.

On all sides he had been greeted by ironical salutations, mocking smiles, and even expressions of condolence at the loss of his prisoner. Two men, whom he suspected of being in close relations with Dr. Seignebos, had even murmured, as he passed by them,—

"Cheated, Mr. Bloodhound."

He was the first to notice the young advocate, and at once said to him,—

"Well, sir, do you come for news?"

But M. Folgat was not the man to be taken in twice the same day. Concealing his apprehensions under the most punctilious politeness, he replied,—

"I have heard all kinds of reports; but they do not affect me. M. de Boiscoran has too much confidence in the excellency of his cause and the justice of his country to think of escaping. I only came to confer with him."

"And you are right!" exclaimed M. Daubigeon. "M. de Boiscoran is in his cell, utterly unaware of all the rumors that are afloat. It was Trumence who has run off,—Trumence, the light-footed. He was kept in prison for form's sake only, and helped the keeper as a kind of assistant jailer. He it is who has made a hole in the wall, and escaped, thinking, no doubt, that the heavens are a better roof than the finest jail."

A little distance behind the group stood Blangin, the jailer, affecting a contrite and distressed air.

"Take the counsel to the prisoner Boiscoran," said M. Galpin dryly, fearing, perhaps, that M. Daubigeon might regale the public with all the bitter epigrams with which he persecuted him privately. The jailer bowed to the ground, and obeyed the order; but, as soon as he was alone with M. Folgat in the porch of the building, he blew up his cheek, and then tapped it, saying,—

"Cheated all around."

Then he burst out laughing. The young advocate pretended not to understand him. It was but prudent that he should appear ignorant of what had happened the night before, and thus avoid all suspicion of a complicity which substantially did not exist.

"And still," Blangin went on, "this is not the end of it yet. The gendarmes are all out. If they should catch my poor Trumence! That man is such a fool, the most stupid judge would worm his secret out of him in five minutes. And then, who would be in a bad box?"

M. Folgat still made no reply; but the other did not seem to mind that much. He continued,—

"I only want to do one thing, and that is to give up my keys as soon as possible. I am tired of this profession of jailer. Besides, I shall not be able to stay here much longer. This escape has put a flea into the ear of the authorities, and they are going to give me an assistant, a former police sergeant, who is as bad as a watchdog. Ah! the good days of M. de Boiscoran are over: no more stolen visits, no more promenades. He is to be watched day and night."

Blangin had stopped at the foot of the staircase to give all these explanations.

"Let us go up," he said now, as M. Folgat showed signs of growing impatience.

He found Jacques lying on his bed, all dressed; and at the first glance he saw that a great misfortune had happened.

"One more hope gone?" he asked.

The prisoner raised himself up with difficulty, and sat up on the side of his bed; then he replied in a voice of utter despair,—

"I am lost, and this time hopelessly."

"Oh!"

"Just listen!"

The young advocate could not help shuddering as he heard the account given by Jacques of what had happened the night before. And when it was finished, he said,—

"You are right. If Count Claudieuse carries out his threat, it may be a condemnation."

"It must be a condemnation, you mean. Well, you need not doubt. He will carry out his threat."

And shaking his head with an air of desolation, he added,—

"And the most formidable part of it is this: I cannot blame him for doing it. The jealousy of husbands is often nothing more than self-love. When they find they have been deceived, their vanity is offended; but their heart remains whole. But in this case it is very different. He not only loved his wife, he worshipped her. She was his happiness, life itself. When I took her from him, I robbed him of all he had,—yes, of all! I never knew what adultery meant till I saw him overcome with shame and rage. He was left without any thing in a moment. His wife had a lover: his favorite daughter was not his own! I suffer terribly; but it is nothing, I am sure, in comparison with what he suffers. And you expect, that, holding a weapon in his hand, he should not use it? It is a treacherous, dishonest weapon, to be sure; but have I been frank and honest? It would be a mean, ignoble vengeance, you will say; but what was the offence? In his place, I dare say, I should do as he does."

M. Folgat was thunderstruck.

"But after that," he asked, "when you left the house?"

Jacques passed his hand mechanically over his forehead, as if to gather his thoughts, and then went on,—

"After that I fled precipitately, like a man who has committed a crime. The garden-door was open, and I rushed out. I could not tell you with certainty in what direction I ran, through what streets I passed. I had but one fixed idea,—to get away from that house as quickly and as far as possible. I did not know what I was doing. I went, I went. When I came to myself, I was many miles away from Sauveterre, on the road to Boiscoran. The instinct of the animal within me had guided me on the familiar way to my house. At the first moment I could not comprehend how I had gotten there. I felt like a drunkard whose head is filled with the vapors of alcohol, and who, when he is roused, tries to remember what has happened during his intoxication. Alas! I recalled the fearful reality but too soon. I knew that I ought to go back to prison, that it was an absolute necessity; and yet I felt at times so weary, so exhausted, that I was afraid I should not be able to get back. Still I did reach the prison. Blangin was waiting for me, all anxiety; for it was nearly two o'clock. He helped me to get up here. I threw myself, all dressed as I was, on my bed, and I fell fast asleep in an instant. But my sleep was a miserable sleep, broken by terrible dreams, in which I saw myself chained to the galleys, or mounting the scaffold with a priest by my side; and even at this moment I hardly know whether I am awake or asleep, and whether I am not still suffering under a fearful nightmare."

M. Folgat could hardly conceal a tear. He murmured,—

"Poor man!"

"Oh, yes, poor man indeed!" repeated Jacques. "Why did I not follow my first inspiration last night when I found myself on the high-road. I should have gone on to Boiscoran, I should have gone up stairs to my room, and there I should have blown out my brains. I should then suffer no more."

Was he once more giving himself up to that fatal idea of suicide?

"And your parents," said M. Folgat.

"My parents! And do you think they will survive my condemnation?"

"And Miss Chandore?"

He shuddered, and said fiercely,—

"Ah! it is for her sake first of all that I ought to make an end of it. Poor Dionysia! Certainly she would grieve terribly when she heard of my suicide. But she is not twenty yet. My memory would soon fade in her heart; and weeks growing into months, and months into years, she would find comfort. To live means to forget."

"No! You cannot really think what you are saying!" broke in M. Folgat. "You know very well that she—she would never forget you!"

A tear appeared in the eyes of the unfortunate man, and he said in a half-smothered voice,—

"You are right. I believe to strike me down means to strike her down also. But do you think what life would be after a condemnation? Can you imagine what her sensations would be, if day after day she had to say to herself, 'He whom alone I love upon earth is at the galleys, mixed up with the lowest of criminals, disgraced for life, dishonored.' Ah! death is a thousand times preferable."

"Jacques, M. de Boiscoran, do you forget that you have given me your word of honor?"

"The proof that I have not forgotten it is that you see me here. But, never mind, the day is not very far off when you will see me so wretched that you yourself will be the first to put a weapon into my hands."

But the young advocate was one of those men whom difficulties only excite and stimulate, instead of discouraging. He had already recovered somewhat from the first great shock, and he said,—

"Before you throw down your hand, wait, at least, till the game is lost. You are not sentenced yet. Far from it! You are innocent, and there is divine justice. Who tells us that Count Claudieuse will really give evidence? We do not even know whether he has not, at this moment, drawn his last breath upon earth!"

Jacques leaped up as if in a spasm, and turning deadly pale, exclaimed,—

"Ah, don't say that! That fatal thought has already occurred to me, that perhaps he did not rise again last night. Would to God that that be not so! for then I should but too surely be an assassin. He was my first thought when I awoke. I thought of sending out to make inquiries. But I did not dare do it."

M. Folgat felt his heart oppressed with most painful anxiety, like the prisoner himself. Hence he said at once,—

"We cannot remain in this uncertainty. We can do nothing as long as the count's fate is unknown to us; for on his fate depends ours. Allow me to leave you now. I will let you know as soon as I hear any thing positive. And, above all, keep up your courage, whatever may happen."

The young advocate was sure of finding reliable information at Dr. Seignebos's house. He hastened there; and, as soon as he entered, the physician cried,—

"Ah, there you are coming at last! I give up twenty of my worst patients to see you, and you keep me waiting forever. I was sure you would come. What happened last night at Count Claudieuse's house?"

"Then you know"—

"I know nothing. I have seen the results; but I do not know the cause. The result was this: last night, about eleven o'clock, I had just gone to bed, tired to death, when, all of a sudden, somebody rings my bell as if he were determined to break it. I do not like people to perform so violently at my door; and I was getting up to let the man know my mind, when Count Claudieuse's servant rushed in, pushing my own servant unceremoniously aside, and cried out to me to come instantly, as his master had just died."

"Great God!"

"That is what I said, because, although I knew the count was very ill, I did not think he was so near death."

"Then, he is really dead?"

"Not at all. But, if you interrupt me continually, I shall never be able to tell you."

And taking off his spectacles, wiping them, and putting them on again, he went on,—

"I was dressed in an instant, and in a few minutes I was at the house. They asked me to go into the sitting-room down stairs. There I found, to my great amazement, Count Claudieuse, lying on a sofa. He was pale and stiff, his features fearfully distorted, and on his forehead a slight wound, from which a slender thread of blood was trickling down. Upon my word I thought it was all over."

"And the countess?"

"The countess was kneeling by her husband; and, with the help of her women, she was trying to resuscitate him by rubbing him, and putting hot napkins on his chest. But for these wise precautions she would be a widow at this moment; whilst, as it is, he may live a long time yet. This precious count has a wonderful tenacity of life. We, four of us, then took him and carried him up stairs, and put him to bed, after having carefully warmed it first. He soon began to move; he opened his eyes; and a quarter of an hour later he had recovered his consciousness, and spoke readily, though with a somewhat feeble voice. Then, of course, I asked what had happened, and for the first time in my life I saw the marvellous self-possession of the countess forsake her. She stammered pitifully, looking at her husband with a most frightened air, as if she wished to read in his eyes what she should say. He undertook to answer me; but he, also was evidently very much embarrassed. He said, that being left alone, and feeling better than usual, he had taken it into his head to try his strength. He had risen, put on his dressing-gown, and gone down stairs; but, in the act of entering the room, he had become dizzy, and had fallen so unfortunately as to hurt his forehead against the sharp corner of a table. I affected to believe it, and said, 'You have done a very imprudent thing, and you must not do it again.' Then he looked at his wife in a very singular way, and replied, 'Oh! you can be sure I shall not commit another imprudence. I want too much to get well. I have never wished it so much as now.'"

M. Folgat was on the point of replying; but the doctor closed his lips with his hand, and said,—

"Wait, I have not done yet."

And, manipulating his spectacles most assiduously, he added,—

"I was just going home, when suddenly a chambermaid came in with a frightened air to tell the countess that her older daughter, little Martha, whom you know, had just been seized with terrible convulsions. Of course I went to see her, and found her suffering from a truly fearful nervous attack. It was only with great difficulty I could quiet her; and when I thought she had recovered, suspecting that there might be some connection between her attack and the accident that had befallen her father, I said in the most paternal tone I could assume, 'Now my child, you must tell me what was the matter.' She hesitated a while, and then she said, 'I was frightened.'—'Frightened at what, my darling?' She raised herself on her bed, trying to consult her mother's eyes; but I had placed myself between them, so that she could not see them. When I repeated my question, she said, 'Well, you see, I had just gone to bed, when I heard the bell ring. I got up, and went to the window to see who could be coming so late. I saw the servant go and open the door, a candlestick in her hand, and come back to the house, followed by a gentleman, whom I did not know.' The countess interrupted her here, saying, 'It was a messenger from the court, who had been sent to me with an urgent letter.' But I pretended not to hear her; and, turning still to Martha, I asked again, 'And it was this gentleman who frightened you so?'—'Oh, no!'—'What then?' Out of the corner of my eye I was watching the countess. She seemed to be terribly embarrassed. Still she did not dare to stop her daughter. 'Well, doctor,' said the little girl, 'no sooner had the gentleman gone into the house than I saw one of the statues under the trees there come down from its pedestal, move on, and glide very quietly along the avenue of lime-trees.'"

M. Folgat trembled.

"Do you remember, doctor," he said, "the day we were questioning little Martha, she said she was terribly frightened by the statutes in the garden?"

"Yes, indeed!" replied the doctor. "But wait a while. The countess promptly interrupted her daughter, saying to me, 'But, dear doctor, you ought to forbid the child to have such notions in her head. At Valpinson she never was afraid, and even at night, quite alone, and without a light, all over the house. But here she is frightened at every thing; and, as soon as night comes, she fancies the garden is full of ghosts. You are too big now, Martha, to think that statues, which are made of stone, can come to life, and walk about.' The child was shuddering.

"'The other times, mamma,' she said, 'I was not quite sure; but this time I am sure. I wanted to go away from the window, and I could not do it. It was too strong for me: so that I saw it all, saw it perfectly. I saw the statue, the ghost, come up the avenue slowly and cautiously, and then place itself behind the last tree, the one that is nearest to the parlor window. Then I heard a loud cry, then nothing more. The ghost remained all the time behind the tree, and I saw all it did: it turned to the left and the right; it drew itself up; and it crouched down. Then, all of a sudden, two terrible cries; but, O mamma, such cries! Then the ghost raised one arm, this way, and all of a sudden it was gone; but almost the same moment another one came out, and then disappeared, too.'"

M. Folgat was utterly overcome with amazement.

"Oh, these ghosts!" he said.

"You suspect them, do you? I suspected them at once. Still I pretended to turn Martha's whole story into a joke, and tried to explain to her how the darkness made us liable to have all kinds of optical illusions; so that when I left, and a servant was sent with a candle to light me on my way, the countess was quite sure that I had no suspicion. I had none; but I had more than that. As soon as I entered the garden, therefore, I dropped a piece of money which I had kept in my hand for the purpose. Of course I set to work looking for it at the foot of the tree nearest to the parlor-window, while the servant helped with his candle. Well, M. Folgat, I can assure you that it was not a ghost that had been walking about under the trees; and, if the footmarks which I found there were made by a statue, that statue must have enormous feet, and wear huge iron-shod shoes."

The young advocate was prepared for this. He said,—

"There is no doubt: the scene had a witness."

XXX.

"What scene? What witness? That is what I wanted to hear from you, and why I was waiting so impatiently for you," said Dr. Seignebos to M. Folgat. "I have seen and stated the results: now it is for you to give me the cause."

Nevertheless, he did not seem to be in the least surprised by what the young advocate told him of Jacques's desperate enterprise, and of the tragic result. As soon as he had heard it all, he exclaimed,—

"I thought so: yes, upon my word! By racking my brains all night long, I had very nearly guessed the whole story. And who, in Jacques's place, would not have been desirous to make one last effort? But certainly fate is against him."

"Who knows?" said M. Folgat. And, without giving the doctor time to reply, he went on,—

"In what are our chances worse than they were before? In no way. We can to-day, just as well as we could yesterday, lay our hands upon those proofs which we know do exist, and which would save us. Who tells us that at this moment Sir Francis Burnett and Suky Wood may not have been found? Is your confidence in Goudar shaken?"

"Oh, as to that, not at all! I saw him this morning at the hospital, when I paid my usual visit; and he found an opportunity to tell me that he was almost certain of success."

"Well?"

"I am persuaded Cocoleu will speak. But will he speak in time? That is the question. Ah, if we had but a month's time, I should say Jacques is safe. But our hours are counted, you know. The court will be held next week. I am told the presiding judge has already arrived, and M. Gransiere has engaged rooms at the hotel. What do you mean to do if nothing new occurs in the meantime?"

"M. Magloire and I will obstinately adhere to our plan of defence."

"And if Count Claudieuse keeps his promise, and declares that he recognized Jacques in the act of firing at him?"

"We shall say he is mistaken."

"And Jacques will be condemned."

"Well," said the young advocate.

And lowering his voice, as if he did not wish to be overheard, he added,—

"Only the sentence will not be a fatal sentence. Ah, do not interrupt me, doctor, and upon your life, upon Jacques's life, do not say a word of what I am going to tell you. A suspicion which should cross M. Galpin's mind would destroy my last hope; for it would give him an opportunity of correcting a blunder which he has committed, and which justifies me in saying to you, 'Even if the count should give evidence, even if sentence should be passed, nothing would be lost yet.'"

He had become animated; and his accent and his gestures made you feel that he was sure of himself.

"No," he repeated, "nothing would be lost; and then we should have time before us, while waiting for a second trial, to hunt up our witnesses, and to force Cocoleu to tell the truth. Let the count say what he chooses, I like it all the better: I shall thus be relieved of my last scruples. It seemed to me odious to betray the countess, because I thought the most cruelly punished would be the count. But, if the count attacks us, we are on the defence; and public opinion will be on our side. More than that, they will admire us for having sacrificed our honor to a woman's honor, and for having allowed ourselves to be condemned rather than to give up the name of her who has given herself to us."

The physician did not seem to be convinced; but the young advocate paid no attention. He went on,—

"No, our success in a second trial would be almost certain. The scene in Mautrec Street has been seen by a witness: his iron-shod shoes have left, as you say, their marks under the linden-trees nearest to the parlor-window, and little Martha has watched his movements. Who can this witness be unless it is Trumence? Well, we shall lay hands upon him. He was standing so that he could see every thing, and hear every word. He will tell what he saw and what he heard. He will tell how Count Claudieuse called out to M. de Boiscoran, 'No, I do not want to kill you! I have a surer vengeance than that: you shall go to the galleys.'"

Dr. Seignebos sadly shook his head as he said,—

"I hope your expectations may be realized, my dear sir."

But they came again for the doctor the third time to-day. Shaking hands with the young advocate, he parted with his young friend, who after a short visit to M. Magloire, whom he thought it his duty to keep well informed of all that was going on, hastened to the house of M. de Chandore. As soon as he looked into Dionysia's face, he knew that he had nothing to tell her; that she knew all the facts, and how unjust her suspicions had been.

"What did I tell you, madam?" he said very modestly.

She blushed, ashamed at having let him see the secret doubts which had troubled her so sorely, and, instead of replying, she said,—

"There are some letters for you, M. Folgat. They have carried them up stairs to your room."

He found two letters,—one from Mrs. Goudar, the other from the agent who had been sent to England.

The former was of no importance. Mrs. Goudar only asked him to send a note, which she enclosed, to her husband.

The second, on the other hand, was of the very greatest interest. The agent wrote,—

"Not without great difficulties, and especially not without a heavy outlay of money, I have at length discovered Sir Francis Burnett's brother in London, the former cashier of the house of Gilmour and Benson.

"Our Sir Francis is not dead. He was sent by his father to Madras, to attend to very important financial matters, and is expected back by the next mail steamer. We shall be informed of his arrival on the very day on which he lands.

"I have had less trouble in discovering Suky Wood's family. They are people very well off, who keep a sailor's tavern in Folkstone. They had news from their daughter about three weeks ago; but, although they profess to be very much attached to her, they could not tell me accurately where she was just now. All they know is, that she has gone to Jersey to act as barmaid in a public house.

"But that is enough for me. The island is not very large; and I know it quite well, having once before followed a notary public there, who had run off with the money of his clients. You may consider Suky as safe.

"When you receive this letter, I shall be on my way to Jersey.

"Send me money there to the Golden Apple Hotel, where I propose to lodge. Life is amazingly dear in London; and I have very little left of the sum you gave me on parting."

Thus, in this direction, at least, every thing was going well.

Quite elated by this first success, M. Folgat put a thousand-franc note into an envelope, directed it as desired, and sent it at once to the post-office. Then he asked M. de Chandore to lend him his carriage, and went out to Boiscoran.

He wanted to see Michael, the tenant's son, who had been so prompt in finding Cocoleu, and in bringing him into town. He found him, fortunately, just coming home, bringing in a cart loaded with straw; and, taking him aside, he asked him,—

"Will you render M. de Boiscoran a great service?"

"What must I do?" replied the young man in a tone of voice which said, better than all protestations could have done, that he was ready to do any thing.

"Do you know Trumence?"

"The former basket-weaver of Tremblade?"

"Exactly."

"Upon my word, don't I know him? He has stolen apples enough from me, the scamp! But I don't blame him so much, after all; for he is a good fellow, in spite of that."

"He was in prison at Sauveterre."

"Yes, I know; he had broken down a gate near Brechy and"—

"Well, he has escaped."

"Ah, the scamp!"

"And we must find him again. They have put the gendarmes on his track; but will they catch him?"

Michael burst out laughing.

"Never in his life!" he said. "Trumence will make his way to Oleron, where he has friends; the gendarmes will be after him in vain."

M. Folgat slapped Michael amicably on the shoulder, and said,—

"But you, if you choose? Oh! do not look angry at me. We do not want to have him arrested. All I want you to do is to hand him a letter from me, and to bring me back his answer."

"If that is all, then I am your man. Just give me time to change my clothes, and to let father know, and I am off."

Thus M. Folgat began, as far as in him lay, to prepare for future action, trying to counteract all the cunning measures of the prosecution by such combinations as were suggested to him by his experience and his genius.

Did it follow from this, that his faith in ultimate success was strong enough to make him speak of it to his most reliable friends, even, say to Dr. Seignebos, to M. Magloire, or to good M. Mechinet?

No; for, bearing all the responsibility on his own shoulders, he had carefully weighed the contrary chances of the terrible game in which he proposed to engage, and in which the stakes were the honor and the life of a man. He knew, better than anybody else, that a mere nothing might destroy all his plans, and that Jacques's fate was dependent on the most trivial accident.

Like a great general on the eve of a battle, he managed to control his feelings, affecting, for the benefit of others, a confidence which he did not really feel, and allowing no feature of his face to betray the great anxiety which generally kept him awake more than half the night.

And certainly it required a character of marvellous strength to remain impassive and resolute under such circumstances.

Everybody around him was in despair, and gave up all hope.

The house of M. de Chandore, once so full of life and merriment, had become as silent and sombre as a tomb.

The last two months had made of M. de Chandore an old man in good earnest. His tall figure had begun to stoop, and he looked bent and broken. He walked with difficulty, and his hands began to tremble.

The Marquis de Boiscoran had been hit even harder. He, who only a few weeks before looked robust and hearty, now appeared almost decrepit. He did not eat, so to say, and did not sleep. He became frightfully thin. It gave him pain to utter a word.

As to the marchioness, the very sources of life seemed to have been sapped within her. She had had to hear M. Magloire say that Jacques's safety would have been put beyond all doubt if they had succeeded in obtaining a change of venue, or an adjournment of the trial. And it was her fault that such a change had not been applied for. That thought was death to her. She had hardly strength enough left to drag herself every day as far as the jail to see her son.

The two Misses Lavarande had to bear all the practical difficulties arising from this sore trial: they went and came, looking as pale as ghosts, whispering in a low voice, and walking on tiptoe, as if there had been a death in the house.

Dionysia alone showed greater energy as the troubles increased. She did not indulge in much hope.

"I know Jacques will be condemned," she said to M. Folgat. But she said, also, that despair belonged to criminals only, and that the fatal mistake for which Jacques was likely to suffer ought to inspire his friends with nothing but indignation and thirst for vengeance.

And, while her grandfather and the Marquis de Boiscoran went out as little as possible, she took pains to show herself in town, astonishing the ladies "in good society" by the way in which she received their false expressions of sympathy. But it was evident that she was only held up by a kind of feverish excitement, which gave to her cheeks their bright color, to her eyes their brilliancy, and to her voice its clear, silvery ring. Ah! for her sake mainly, M. Folgat longed to end this uncertainty which is so much more painful than the greatest misfortune.

The time was drawing near.

As Dr. Seignebos had announced, the president of the tribunal, M. Domini, had already arrived in Sauveterre.

He was one of those men whose character is an honor to the bench, full of the dignity of his profession, but not thinking himself infallible, firm without useless rigor, cold and still kind-hearted, having no other mistress but Justice, and knowing no other ambition but that of establishing the truth.

He had examined Jacques, as he was bound to do; but the examination had been, as it always is, a mere formality, and had led to no result.

The next step was the selection of a jury.

The jurymen had already begun to arrive from all parts of the department. They lodged at the Hotel de France, where they took their meals in common in the large back dining-room, which is always specially reserved for their use.

In the afternoon one might see them, looking grave and thoughtful, take a walk on the New-Market Square, or on the old ramparts.

M. Gransiere, also, had arrived. But he kept strictly in retirement in his room at the Hotel de la Poste, where M. Galpin every day spent several hours in close conference with him.

"It seems," said Mechinet in confidence to M. Folgat,—"it seems they are preparing an overwhelming charge."

The day after, Dionysia opened "The Sauveterre Independent," and found in it an announcement of the cases set down for each day,—

MONDAY..... Fraudulent bankruptcy, defalcation, forgery.

TUESDAY.... Murder, theft.

WEDNESDAY.. Infanticide, domestic theft.

THURSDAY... Incendiarism, and attempted assassination

(case of M. de Boiscoran).

This was, therefore, the great day on which the good people of Sauveterre expected to enjoy the most delightful emotions. Hence there was an immense pressure brought to bear upon all the principal members of the court to obtain tickets of admission. People who, the night before, had refused to speak to M. Galpin, would stop him the next day in the street, and beg him to give them a ticket, not for themselves, but for "their lady." Finally, the unheard-of fact became known, that tickets were openly sold for money! One family had actually the incomprehensible courage to write to the Marquis de Boiscoran for three tickets, promising, in return, "by their attitude in court" to contribute to the acquittal of the accused.

In the midst of all these rumors, the city was suddenly startled by a list of subscriptions in behalf of the families of the unfortunate firemen who had perished in the fire at Valpinson.

Who had started this paper? M. Seneschal tried in vain to discover the hand that had struck this blow. The secret of this treacherous trick was well kept. But it was a most atrocious trick to revive thus, on the eve of the trial, such mournful memories and such bitter hatred.

"That man Galpin had a hand in it," said Dr. Seignebos, grinding his teeth. "And to think that he may, after all, be triumphant! Ah, why did not Goudar commence his experiment a little sooner?"

For Goudar, while assuring everybody of certain success, asked for time. To disarm the mistrust of an idiot like Cocoleu was not the work of a day or a week. He declared, that, if he should be overhasty, he would most assuredly ruin every thing.

Otherwise, nothing new occurred.

Count Claudieuse was getting rather better.

The agent in Jersey had telegraphed that he was on Suky's track; that he would certainly catch her, but that he could not say when.

Michael, finally, had in vain searched the whole district, and been all over Oleron; no one had been able to give him any news of Trumence.

Thus, on the day when the session began, a council was held, in which all of Jacques's friends took part; and here it was resolved that his counsel would not mention the name of the Countess Claudieuse, and would, even if the count should offer to give evidence, adhere to the plan of defence suggested by M. Folgat.

Alas! the chances of success seemed hourly to diminish; for the jury, very much against the usual experience, appeared to be excessively severe. The bankrupt was sentenced to twenty years' hard labor. The man accused of murder could not even obtain the plea of "extenuating circumstances," and was sentenced to death.

This was on Wednesday.

It was decided that M. de Chandore and the Marquis and the Marchioness de Boiscoran should attend the trial. They wanted to spare Dionysia the terrible excitement; but she declared that, in that case, she should go alone to the court-house; and thus they were forced to submit to her will.

Thanks to an order from M. Domini, M. Folgat and M. Magloire could spend the evening with Jacques in order to determine all the details, and to agree upon certain replies to be given.

Jacques looked excessively pale, but was quite composed. And when his counsel left him, saying,—

"Keep up your courage and hope," he replied,—

"Hope I have none; but courage—I assure you, I have courage!"

XXXI.

At last, in his dark cell, Jacques de Boiscoran saw the day break that was to decide his fate.

He was to be tried to-day.

The occasion was, of course, too good to be neglected by "The Sauveterre Independent." Although a morning paper, it published, "in view of the gravity of the circumstances," an evening edition, which a dozen newsboys cried out in the streets up to mid-night. And this was what it said,—

ASSIZES AT SAUVETERRE. THURSDAY, 23.

Presiding Judge.—M. DOMINI.

ASSASSINATION! INCENDIARISM!

[Special Correspondence of the Independent.]

Whence this unusual commotion, this uproar, this great excitement, in our peaceful city? Whence these gatherings of our public squares, these groups in front of all the houses! Whence this restlessness on all faces, this anxiety in all eyes?

The reason is, that to-day this terrible Valpinson case will be brought up in court, after having for so many weeks now agitated our people.

To-day this man who is charged with such fearful crimes is to be tried.

Hence all steps are eagerly turned towards the court-house: the people all hurry, and rush in the same direction.

The court-house! Long before daylight it was surrounded by an eager multitude, which the constables and the gendarmes could only with difficulty keep within bounds.

They press and crowd and push. Coarse words fly to and fro. From words they pass to gestures, from gestures to blows. A row is imminent. Women cry, men swear, and two peasants from Brechy are arrested on the spot.

It is well known that there will be few only, happy enough to get in. The great square would not contain all these curious people, who have gathered here from all parts of the district: how should the court-room be able to hold them?

And still our authorities, always anxious to please their constituents, who have bestowed their confidence upon them, have resorted to heroic measures. They have had two partition walls taken down, so that a part of the great hall is added to the court-room proper.

M. Lautier, the city architect, who is a good judge in such matters, assures us that this immense hall will accommodate twelve hundred persons.

But what are twelve hundred persons?

Long before the hour fixed for the opening of the court, every thing is full to overflowing. A pin might be thrown into the room, and it could not fall to the ground.

Not an inch of space is lost. All around, along the wall men are standing in close ranks. On both sides of the platform, chairs have been put, which are occupied by a large number of our first ladies in good society, not only of Sauveterre, however, but also of the neighborhood and even other cites. Some of them appear in magnificent toilettes.

A thousand reports are current, a thousand conjectures are formed, which we shall take care not to report. Why should we?

Let us say, however, that the accused has not availed himself of his right to reject a certain number of jurymen. He has accepted all the names which were drawn by lot, and which the prosecuting attorney did not object to.

We obtained this information from an attorney, a friend of ours; and, just as he had told us all about it, a great noise rose at the door, which was followed by rapid moving of chairs, and half-smothered exclamations.

It was the family of the accused, who had come in, and now occupied the seats assigned them close by the platform.

The Marquis de Boiscoran had on his arm Miss Chandore, who wore with great grace and dignity a dark gray dress, trimmed with cherry-colored ribbons. M. de Chandore escorted the Marchioness de Boiscoran. The marquis and the baron looked cold and reserved. The mother of the accused appears utterly overcome. Miss Chandore, on the contrary, is lively, does not seem in the least concerned, and returns with a bright smile the few greetings she receives from various parts of the court-room.

But soon they are no longer an object of curiosity.

The attention of all is now directed towards a large table standing before the judges, and on which may be seen a number of articles covered by large red cloth.

These are the articles to be used in evidence.

In the meantime it strikes eleven o'clock. The sheriff's officers move about the room, seeing that every thing is in order.

Then a small door opens on the left, and the counsel for the defence enter.

Our readers know who they are. One is M. Magloire, the ornament of our bar; the other, an advocate from the capital, M. Folgat, quite young, but already famous.

M. Magloire looks as he does on his best days, and smilingly converses with the mayor of Sauveterre; while M. Folgat opens his blue bag, and consults his papers.

Half-past eleven!

An usher announces,—

The court.

M. Domini takes the chair. M. Gransiere occupies the seat of the prosecuting attorney.

Behind them the jurymen sit down, looking grave and solemn.

Everybody rises, everybody strains his eyes to see, and stands on tiptoe. Some persons in the back rows even get upon their chairs.

The president has ordered the prisoner to be brought in.

He appears.

He is dressed in black, and with great elegance. It is noticed that he wears in his buttonhole the ribbon of the Legion of Honor.

He looks pale; but his eye is clear and open, full of confidence, yet not defiant. His carriage is proud, though melancholy.

He has hardly taken his seat when a gentleman passes over three rows of chairs, and, in spite of the officers of the court, succeeds in shaking hands with him. It is Dr. Seignebos.

The president orders the sheriff to proclaim silence; and, after having reminded the audience that all expressions of approbation or disapprobation are strictly prohibited, he turns to the accused, and asks him,—

"Tell me your first names, your family name, your age, your profession, and your domicile."

The accused replies,—

"Louis Trivulce Jacques de Boiscoran, twenty-seven years, land-owner, residing at Boiscoran, district of Sauveterre."

"Sit down, and listen to the charges which are brought against you."

The clerk, M. Mechinet, thereupon reads the charges, which, in their terrible simplicity, cause a shudder to pass through the whole audience.

We shall not repeat them here, as all the incidents which they relate are well known to our readers.

[Examination of the Accused.]

PRESIDENT.—Accused, rise and answer clearly. During the preliminary investigation, you have refused to answer several questions. Now the matter must be cleared up. And I am bound to tell you it is to your interest to answer frankly.

ACCUSED.—No one desires more than I do that the truth be known. I am ready to answer.

P.—Why were you so reticent in your first examination?

A.—I though it important for my interests to answer only in court.

P.—You have heard of what crimes you are accused?

A.—I am innocent. And, first of all, I beg you will allow me to say one thing. The crime committed at Valpinson is an atrocious, cowardly crime; but it is at the same time an absurdly stupid crime, more like the unconscious act of a madman. Now, I have always been looked upon as not lacking exactly in intelligence.

P.—That is a discussion.

A.—Still, Mr. President—

P.—Hereafter you shall have full liberty to state your argument. For the present you must be content to answer the questions which I shall ask you.

A.—I submit.

P.—Were you not soon to be married?

At this question all eyes are turned towards Miss Chandore, who blushes till she is as red as a poppy, but does not cast down her eyes.

A.—(In a low voice.) Yes.

P.—Did you not write to your betrothed a few hours before the crime was committed?

A.—Yes, sir; and I sent her my letter by the son of one of my tenants, Michael.

P.—What did you write to her?

- 431 -

A.—That important business would prevent me from spending the evening with her.

P.—What was that business?

At the moment when the accused opened his lips to reply, the president stopped him by a gesture, and said,—

P.—Take care! You were asked this question during the preliminary investigation, and you replied that you had to go to Brechy to see your wood-merchant.

A.—I did indeed make that reply on the spur of the moment. It was not exact.

P.—Why did you tell a falsehood?

A.—(After an expression of indignation, which was noticed by all.) I could not believe that I was in danger. It seemed to me impossible that I should be reached by an accusation, which nevertheless, has brought me into this court. Hence I did not deem it necessary to make my private affairs public.

P.—But you very soon found out that you were in danger?

A.—Yes, I did.

P.—Why did you not tell the truth then?

A.—Because the magistrate who carried on the investigation had been too intimate a friend of mine to inspire me with confidence.

P.—Explain yourself more fully.

A.—I must ask leave to say no more. I might, in speaking of M. Galpin, be found to be wanting in moderation.

A low murmur accompanies this reply made by the accused.

P.—Such murmurs are improper, and I remind the audience of the respect due to the court.

M. Gransiere, the prosecuting attorney, rises,—

"We cannot tolerate such recriminations against a magistrate who has done his duty nobly, and in spite of the pain it caused him. If the accused had well-founded objections to the magistrate, why did he not make them known? He cannot plead ignorance: he knows the law, he is a lawyer himself. His counsel, moreover, are men of experience."

M. Magloire replies, in his seat,—

"We were of the opinion that the accused ought to ask for a change of venue. He declined to follow our advice, being confident, as he said, that his cause was a good one."

M. Gransiere, resuming his seat,—

"The jury will judge of this plea."

P.—(To the accused.) And now are you ready to tell the truth with regard to that business which prevented you from spending the evening with your betrothed?

A.—Yes, sir. My wedding was to take place at the church in Brechy, and I had to make my arrangements with the priest about the ceremony. I had, besides, to fulfil certain religious duties. The priest at Brechy, who is a friend of mine, will tell you, that, although no day had been fixed, it had been agreed upon between us that I should come to confession on one of the evenings of the week since he insisted upon it.

The audience, which had been expecting some very exciting revelations, seemed to be much disappointed; and ironical laughter was heard in various directions.

P.—(In a severe tone of voice.) This laughter is indecent and objectionable. Sheriff, take out the persons who presume to laugh. And once more I give notice, that, at the first disturbance, I shall order the room to be cleared.

Then, turning again to the accused, he said,—

P.—Go on!

A.—I went therefore to the priest at Brechy, that evening: unluckily there was no one at home at the parsonage when I got there. I was ringing the third or fourth time in vain, when a little peasant-girl came by, who told me that she had just met the priest at the Marshalls' Cross-roads. I thought at once I would go and meet him, and went in that direction. But I walked more than four miles without meeting him. I thought the girl must have been mistaken, and went home again.

P.—Is that your explanation?

A.—Yes.

P.—And you think it a plausible one?

A.—I have promised to say not what is plausible, but what is true. I may confess, however, that, precisely because the explanation is so simple, I did not venture at first to give it. And yet if no crime had been committed, and I had said the day after, "Yesterday I went to see the priest at Brechy, and did not find him," who would have seen any thing unnatural in my statement?

P.—And, in order to fulfil so simple a duty, you chose a roundabout way, which is not only troublesome, but actually dangerous, right across the swamps?

A.—I chose the shortest way.

P.—Then, why were you so frightened upon meeting young Ribot at the Seille Canal?

A.—I was not frightened, but simply surprised, as one is apt to be when suddenly meeting a man where no one is expected. And, if I was surprised, young Ribot was not less so.

P.—You see that you hoped to meet no one?

A.—Pardon me, I did not say so. To expect is not the same as to hope.

P.—Why, then did you take such pains to explain your being there?

A.—I gave no explanations. Young Ribot first told me, laughingly, where he was going, and then I told him that I was going to Brechy.

P.—You told him, also, that you were going through the marshes to shoot birds, and, at the same time you showed him your gun?

A.—That may be. But is that any proof against me? I think just the contrary. If I had had such criminal intentions as the prosecution suggests, I should certainly have gone back after meeting people, knowing that I was exposed to great danger. But I was only going to see my friend, the priest.

P.—And for such a visit you took your gun?

A.—My land lies in the woods and marshes, and there was not a day when I did not bag a rabbit or a waterfowl. Everybody in the neighborhood will tell you that I never went out without a gun.

P.—And on your return, why did you go through the forest of Rochepommier?

A.—Because, from the place where I was on the road, it was probably the shortest way to Boiscoran. I say probably, because just then I did not think much about that. A man who is taking a walk would be very much embarrassed, in the majority of cases, if he had to give a precise account why he took one road rather than another.

P.—You were seen in the forest by a woodcutter, called Gaudry?

A.—So I was told by the magistrate.

P.—That witness deposes that you were in a state of great excitement. You were tearing leaves from the branches, you were talking loud.

A.—I certainly was very much vexed at having lost my evening, and particularly vexed at having relied on the little peasant-girl. It is quite likely that I might have exclaimed, as I walked along, "Plague upon my friend, the priest, who goes and dines in town!" or some such words.

There was a smile in the assembly, but not such as to attract the president's attention.

P.—You know that the priest of Brechy was dining out that day?

M. Magloire rose, and said,—

"It is through us, sir, that the accused has found out this fact. When he told us how he had spent the evening, we went to see the priest at Brechy, who told us how it came about that neither he nor his old servant was at the parsonage. At our request the priest has been summoned. We shall also produce another priest, who at that time passed the Marshalls' Cross-roads, and was the one whom the little girl had seen."

Having made a sign to counsel to sit down again, the president once more turns to the accused.

P.—The woman Courtois who met you deposes that you looked very curious. You did not speak to her: you were in great haste to escape from her.

A.—The night was much too dark for the woman to see my face. She asked me to render her a slight service, and I did so. I did not speak to her, because I had nothing to say to her. I did not leave her suddenly, but only got ahead of her, because her ass walked very slowly.

At a sign from the president, the ushers raise the red cloth which cover the objects on the table.

Great curiosity is manifested by the whole audience; and all rise, and stretch their necks to see better. On the table are displayed clothes, a pair of velveteen trousers, a shooting-jacket of maroon-colored velveteen, an old straw hat, and a pair of dun-colored leather boots. By their side lie a double-barrelled gun, packages of cartridges, two bowls filled with small-shot, and, finally, a large china basin, with a dark sediment at the bottom.

P.—(Showing these objects to the accused.) Are those the clothes which you wore the evening of the crime?

A.—Yes, sir.

P.—A curious costume in which to visit a venerable ecclesiastic, and to perform religious duties.

A.—The priest at Brechy was my friend. Our intimacy will explain, even if it does not justify, the liberty I took.

P.—Do you also recognize this basin? The water has been allowed to evaporate, and the residue alone remains there on the bottom.

A.—It is true, that, when the magistrate appeared at my house, he found there the basin full of dark water, which was thick with half-burnt *debris*. He asked me about this water, and I did not hesitate a moment to tell him that I had washed my hands in it the evening before, after my return home.

Is it not evident, that if I had been guilty, my first effort would have been to put every evidence of my crime out of the way? And yet this circumstance is looked upon as the strongest evidence of my guilt, and the prosecution produces it as the most serious charge against me.

P.—It is very strong and serious indeed.

A.—Well, nothing can be more easily explained than that. I am a great smoker. When I left home the evening of the crime, I took cigars in abundance; but, when I was about to light one, I found that I had no matches.

M. Magloire rises, and says,—

"And I wish to point out that this is not one of those explanations which are invented, after the fact, to meet the necessities of a doubtful case. We have absolute and overwhelming proof of it. M. de Boiscoran did not have the little match-box which he usually carries about him, at that time, because he had left it at M. de Chandore's house, on the mantelpiece, where I have seen it, and where it still is."

P.—That is sufficient, M. Magloire. Let the defendant go on.

A.—I wanted to smoke; and so I resorted to the usual expedient, which all sportsmen know. I tore open one of my cartridges, put, instead of the lead, a piece of paper inside, and set it on fire.

P.—And thus you get a light?

A.—Not always, but certainly in one case out of three.

P.—And the operation blackens the hands?

A.—Not the operation itself. But, when I had lit my cigar, I could not throw away the burning paper as it was: I might have kindled a regular fire.

P.—In the marshes?

A.—But, sir, I smoked five or six cigars during the evening, which means that I had to repeat the operation a dozen times at least, and in different places,—in the woods and on the high-road. Each time I quenched the fire with my fingers; and, as the powder is always greasy, my hands naturally became soon as black as those of a charcoal-burner.

The accused gives this explanation in a perfectly natural but still rather excited manner, which seems to make a great impression.

P.—Let us go on to your gun. Do you recognize it?

A.—Yes, sir. May I look at it?

P.—Yes.

The accused takes up the gun with feverish eagerness, snaps the two cocks, and puts one of his fingers inside the barrels.

He turns crimson, and, bending down to his counsel, says a few words to them so quickly and so low, that they do not reach us.

P.—What is the matter?

M. MAGLOIRE.—(Rising.) A fact has become patent which at once establishes the innocence of M. de Boiscoran. By providential intercession, his servant Anthony had cleaned the gun two days before the day of the crime. It appears now that one of the barrels is still clean, and in good condition. Hence it cannot be M. de Boiscoran who has fired twice at Count Claudieuse.

During this time the accused has gone up to the table on which the objects are lying. He wraps his handkerchief around the ramrod, slips it into one of the barrels, draws it out again, and shows that it is hardly soiled.

The whole audience is in a state of great excitement.

P.—Do the same thing to the other barrel.

The accused does it. The handkerchief remains clean.

P.—You see, and still you have told us that you had burnt, perhaps, a dozen cartridges to light your cigars. But the prosecution had foreseen this objection, and they are prepared to meet it. Sheriff, bring in the witness, Maucroy.

Our readers all know this gentleman, whose beautiful collection of weapons, sporting-articles, and fishing-tackle, is one of the ornaments of our great Square. He is dressed up, and without hesitation takes the required oath.

P.—Repeat your deposition with regard to this gun.

WITNESS.—It is an excellent gun, and very costly: such guns are not made in France, where people are too economical.

At this answer the whole audience laughs. M. Maucroy is not exactly famous for cheap bargains. Even some of the jurymen can hardly control their laughter.

P.—Never mind your reflections on that object. Tell us only what you know about the peculiarities of this gun.

WITNESS.—Well, thanks to a peculiar arrangement of the cartridges, and thanks, also, to the special nature of the fulminating material, the barrels hardly ever become foul.

A.—(Eagerly.) You are mistaken, sir. I have myself cleaned my gun frequently; and I have, just on the contrary, found the barrels extremely foul.

WITNESS.—Because you had fired too often. But I mean to say that you can use up two or three cartridges without a trace being left in the barrels.

A.—I deny that positively.

P.—(To witness.) And if a dozen cartridges were burnt?

WITNESS.—Oh, then, the barrels would be very foul.

P.—Examine the barrels, and tell us what you see.

WITNESS.—(After a minute examination.) I declare that two cartridges cannot have been used since the gun was cleaned.

P.—(To the accused.) Well, what becomes of that dozen cartridges which you have used up to light your cigars, and which had blackened your hands so badly?

M. MAGLOIRE.—The question is too serious to be left entirely in the hands of a single witness.

THE PROSECUTING ATTORNEY.—We only desire the truth. It is easy to make an experiment.

WITNESS.—Oh, certainly!

P.—Let it be done.

Witness puts a cartridge into each barrel, and goes to the window to explode them. The sudden explosion is followed by the screams of several ladies.

WITNESS.—(Returning, and showing that the barrels are no more foul than they were before.) Well, you see I was right.

P.—(To the accused.) You see this circumstance on which you relied so securely, so far from helping you, only proves that your explanation of the blackened state of your hands was a falsehood.

Upon the president's order, witness is taken out, and the examination of the accused is continued.

P.—What were your relations with Count Claudieuse?

A.—We had no intercourse with each other.

P.—But it was known all over the country that you hated him?

A.—That is a mistake. I declare, upon my honor, that I always looked upon him as the best and most honorable of men.

P.—There, at least, you agree with all who knew him. Still you are at law with him?

A.—I have inherited that suit from my uncle, together with his fortune. I carried it on, but very quietly. I asked for nothing better than a compromise.

P.—And, when Count Claudieuse refused, you were incensed?

A.—No.

P.—You were so irritated against him, that you once actually aimed your gun at him. At another time you said, "He will not leave me alone till I put a ball into him." Do not deny! You will hear what the witnesses say.

Thereupon, the accused resumes his place. He looks as confident as ever, and carries his head high. He has entirely overcome any feeling of discouragement, and converses with his counsel in the most composed manner.

There can be no doubt, that, at this stage of the proceedings, public opinion is on his side. He has won the good-will even of those who came there strongly prejudiced. No one can help being impressed by his proud but mournful expression of fate; and all are touched by the extreme simplicity of his answers.

Although the discussion about the gun has not turned out to his advantage, it does not seem to have injured him. People are eagerly discussing the question of the fouling of guns. A number of incredulous persons, whom the experiment has not convinced, maintain that M. Maucroy has been too rash in his statements. Others express surprise at the reserve shown by counsel,—less by that of M. Folgat, who is unknown here, than by that of M. Magloire, who usually allows no opportunity to escape, but is sure to profit by the smallest incident.

The proceedings are not exactly suspended; but there is a pause, whilst the ushers cover the articles on the table once more with red cloth, and, after several comings and goings, roll a large arm-chair in front of the judge's seat.

At last one of the ushers comes up to the president, and whispers something into his ear.

The president only nods his head.

When the usher has left the room, M. Domini says,—

"We shall now proceed to hear the witnesses, and we propose to begin with Count Claudieuse. Although seriously indisposed, he has preferred to appear in court."

At these words Dr. Seignebos is seen to start up, as if he wished to address the court; but one of his friends, sitting by him, pulls him down by his coat. M. Folgat makes a sign to him, and he sits down again.

P.—Sheriff, bring in Count Claudieuse.

[Examination of Witnesses.]

The small door through which the armorer Maucroy had been admitted opens once more, and Count Claudieuse enters. Supported and almost carried by his man-servant.

He is greeted by a murmur of sympathetic pity. He is frightfully thin; and his features look as haggard as if he were about to give up the ghost. The whole vitality of his system seems to have centred in his eyes, which shine with extraordinary brilliancy.

He takes the oath in an almost inaudible voice.

But the silence is so deep, that when the president asks him the usual question, "Do you swear to tell the whole truth?" and he answers, "I swear," the words are distinctly heard all over the court-room.

P.—(Very kindly.) We are very much obliged to you, sir, for the effort which you have made. That chair has been brought in for you: please sit down.

COUNT CLAUDIEUSE.—I thank you, sir; but I am strong enough to stand.

P.—Please tell us, then, what you know of the attempt made on your life.

C.C.—It might have been eleven o'clock: I had gone to bed a little while before, and blown out my light. I was in that half state which is neither waking nor sleeping, when I saw my room lighted up by a dazzling glare. I saw it was fire. I jumped out of bed, and, only lightly dressed, rushed down the stairs. I found some difficulty in opening the outer door, which I had locked myself. At last I succeeded. But I had no sooner put my foot outside than I felt a terrible pain in my right side, and at the same time I heard an explosion of fire-arms. Instinctively I rushed towards the place from which the shot seemed to have been fired; but, before I had taken three steps, I was struck once more in my shoulder, and fell down unconscious.

P.—How long a time was there between the first and the second shots?

C.C.—Almost three or four seconds.

P.—Was that time enough to distinguish the murderer?

C.C.—Yes; and I saw him run from behind a wood-pile, where he had been lying in ambush, and escape into the country.

P.—You can tell us, no doubt, how he was dressed?

C.C.—Certainly. He had on a pair of light gray trousers, a dark coat, and a large straw hat.

At a sign from the president, and in the midst of the most profound silence, the ushers remove the red cloth from the table.

P.—(Pointing at the clothes of the accused.) Does the costume which you describe correspond with those cloths?

C.C.—Of course; for they are the same.

P.—Then you must have recognized the murderer.

C.C.—The fire was so large at that time, that it was as bright as daylight. I recognized M. Jacques de Boiscoran.

There was, probably, in the whole vast audience assembled under that roof, not a heart that was not seized with unspeakable anguish when these crushing words were uttered.

We were so fully prepared for them, that we could watch the accused closely.

Not a muscle in his face seemed to move. His counsel showed as little any signs of surprise or emotion.

Like ourselves, the president also, and the prosecuting attorney, had been watching the accused and his counsel. Did they expect a protest, an answer, any thing at all? Perhaps they did.

But, as nothing came, the president continued, turning to witness,—

P.—Your declaration is a very serious one, sir.

C.C.—I know its weight.

P.—It is entirely different from your first deposition made before the investigating magistrate.

C.C.—It is.

P.—When you were examined a few hours after the crime, you declared that you had not recognized the murderer. More than that, when M. de Boiscoran's name was mentioned, you seemed to be indignant of such a suspicion, and almost became surety yourself for his innocence.

C.C.—That was contrary to truth. I felt a very natural sense of commiseration, and tried to save a man who belonged to a highly esteemed family from disgraceful punishment.

P.—But now?

C.C.—Now I see that I was wrong, and that the law ought to have its course. And this is my reason for coming here,—although afflicted by a disease which never spares, and on the point of appearing before God—in order to tell you M. de Boiscoran is guilty. I recognized him.

P.—(To the accused.) Do you hear?

The accused rises and says,—

A.—By all that is dear and sacred to me in the world, I swear that I am innocent. Count Claudieuse says he is about to appear before God: I appeal to the justice of God.

Sobs well-nigh drown the voice of the accused. The Marchioness de Boiscoran is overcome by a nervous attack. She is carried out stiff and inanimate; and Dr. Seignebos and Miss Chandore hasten after her.

A.—(To Count Claudieuse.) You have killed my mother!

Certainly, all who had hoped for scenes of thrilling interest were not disappointed. Everybody looks overcome with excitement. Tears appear in the eyes of almost all the ladies.

And yet those who watch the glances which are exchanged between M. de Boiscoran and Count Claudieuse cannot help asking themselves, if there is not something else between these two men, besides what the trial has made known. We cannot explain to ourselves these singular answers given to the president's questions, nor does any one understand the silence observed by M. de Boiscoran's counsel. Do they abandon their client? No; for we see them go up to him, shake hands with him, and lavish upon him every sign of friendly consolation and encouragement.

We may even be permitted to say, that, to all appearances, the president himself and the prosecuting attorney were, for a moment, perfectly overcome with surprise. At all events, we thought so at the moment.

But the president continues,—

P.—I have but just been asking the accused, count, whether there was any ground of enmity between you.

C.C.—(In a steadily declining voice.) I know no other ground except our lawsuit about a little stream of water.

P.—Has not the accused once threatened to fire at you?

C.C.—Yes; but I did not think he was in earnest, and I never resented the matter.

P. Do you persist in your declaration?

C.C.—I do. And once more, upon my oath, I declare solemnly that I recognized, in such a manner as to prevent any possible mistake, M. Jacques Boiscoran.

It was evidently time that Count Claudieuse should end his evidence. He begins to totter; his eyes close; his head rolls from side to side; and two ushers have to come to his assistance to enable him, with the help of his own servant, to leave the room.

Is the Countess Claudieuse to be called next?

It was thought so; but it was not so. The countess being kept by the bedside of one of her daughters, who is most dangerously ill, will not be called at all; and the clerk of the court is ordered to read her deposition.

Although her description of the terrible event is very graphic, it contains no new facts, and will remain without influence on the proceedings.

The next witness is Ribot.

This is a fine handsome countryman, a regular village cock, with a pink-and-blue cravat around his neck, and a huge gold chain dangling from his watch-pocket. He seems to be very proud of his appearance and looks around with an air of the most perfect self-satisfaction.

In the same way he relates his meeting with the accused in a tone of great importance. He knows every thing and explains every thing. With a little encouragement he would, no doubt, declare that the accused had confided to him all his plans of incendiarism and murder. His answers are almost all received with great hilarity, which bring down upon the audience another and very severe reprimand from the president.

The witness Gaudry, who succeeds him, is a small, wretched-looking man, with a false and timid eye, who exhausts himself in bows and scrapes. Quite different from Ribot, he seems to have forgotten every thing. It is evident he is afraid of committing himself. He praises the count; but he does not speak the less well of M. de Boiscoran. He assures the court of his profound respect for them all,—for the ladies and gentlemen present, for everybody, in fine.

The woman Courtois, who comes next, evidently wishes she were a thousand miles away. The president has to make the very greatest efforts to obtain, word by word, her evidence, which, after all, amounts to next to nothing.

Then follow two farmers from Brechy, who have been present at the violent altercation which ended in M. de Boiscoran's aiming with his gun at Count Claudieuse.

Their account, interrupted by numberless parentheses, is very obscure. One of the counsel of the defendant requests them to be more explicit; and thereupon they become utterly unintelligible. Besides, they contradict each other. One has looked upon the act of the accused as a mere jest: the other has looked upon it so seriously as to throw himself between the two men, in order to prevent M. de Boiscoran from killing his adversary then and there.

Once more the accused protests, energetically, he never hated Count Claudieuse: there was no reason why he should hate him.

The obstinate peasant insists upon it that a lawsuit is always a sufficient reason for hating a man. And thereupon he undertakes to explain the lawsuit, and how Count Claudieuse, by stopping the water of the Seille, overflowed M. de Boiscoran's meadows.

The president at last stops the discussion, and orders another witness to be brought in.

This man swears he has heard M. de Boiscoran say, that, sooner or later, he would put a ball into Count Claudieuse. He adds, that the accused is a terrible man, who threatened to shoot people upon the slightest provocation. And, to support his evidence, he states that once before, to the knowledge of the whole country, M. de Boiscoran has fired at a man.

The accused undertakes to explain this. A scamp, who he thinks was no one else but the witness on the stand, came every night and stole his tenants' fruit and vegetables. One night he kept watch, and gave him a load of salt. He does not know whether he hit him. At all events, the thief never complained, and thus was never found out.

The next witness is a constable from Brechy. He deposes that once Count Claudieuse, by stopping up the waters of the little stream, the Seille, had caused M. de Boiscoran a loss of twenty thousand weight of first-rate hay. He confesses that such a bad neighbor would certainly have exasperated him.

The prosecuting attorney does not deny the fact, but adds, that Count Claudieuse offered to pay damages. M. de Boiscoran had refused with insulting haughtiness.

The accused replies, that he had refused upon the advice of his lawyer, but that he had not used insulting words.

Next appeared the witnesses summoned by the defence.

The first is the excellent priest from Brechy. He confirms the statement of the accused. He was dining, the evening of the crime, at the house of M. de Besson; his servant had come for him; and the parsonage was deserted. He states that he had really arranged with M. de Boiscoran that the latter should come some evening of that week to fulfil the religious duties which the church requires before it allows a marriage to be consecrated. He has known Jacques de Boiscoran from a child, and knows no better and no more honorable man. In his opinion, that hatred, of which so much has been said, never had any existence. He cannot believe, and does not believe, that the accused is guilty.

The second witness is the priest of an adjoining parish. He states, that, between nine and ten o'clock, he was on the road, near the Marshalls' Cross-roads. The night was quite dark. He is of the same size as the priest at Brechy; and the little girl might very well have taken him for the latter, thus misleading M. de Boiscoran.

Three other witnesses are introduced; and then, as neither the accused nor his counsel have any thing to add, the prosecuting attorney begins his speech.

[The Charge.]

M. Gransiere's eloquence is so widely known, and so justly appreciated, that we need not refer to it here. We will only say that he surpassed himself in this charge, which, for more than an hour, held the large assembly in anxious and breathless suspense, and caused all hearts to vibrate with the most intense excitement.

He commences with a description of Valpinson, "this poetic and charming residence, where the noble old trees of Rochepommier are mirrored in the crystal waves of the Seille.

"There," he went on to say,—"there lived the Count and the Countess Claudieuse,—he one of those noblemen of a past age who worshipped honor, and were devoted to duty; she one of those women who are the glory of their sex, and the perfect model of all domestic virtues.

"Heaven had blessed their union, and given them two children, to whom they were tenderly attached. Fortune smiled upon their wise efforts. Esteemed by all, cherished, and revered, they lived happy, and might have counted upon long years of prosperity.

"But no. Hate was hovering over them.

"One evening, a fatal glare arouses the count. He rushes out; he hears the report of a gun. He hears it a second time, and he sinks down, bathed in his blood. The countess also is alarmed by the explosion, and hastens to the spot: she stumbles; she sees the lifeless body of her husband, and sinks unconscious to the ground.

"Are the children also to perish? No. Providence watches. A flash of intelligence pierces the night of an insane man, who rushes through the flames, and snatches the children from the fire that was already threatening their couch.

"Their lives are saved; but the fire continues its destructive march.

"At the sound of the terrible fire-bell, all the inhabitants of the neighboring villages hurry to the spot. But there is no one to direct their efforts; there are no engines; and they can do nothing.

"But all of a sudden a distant rumbling sound revives hope in their hearts. They know the fire-engines are coming. They come; they reach the spot; and whatever men can do is done at once.

"But great God! What mean those cries of horror which suddenly rise on all sides? The roof of the house is falling, and buries under its ruins two men, the most zealous and most courageous of all the zealous and courageous men,—Bolton the drummer, who had just now summoned his neighbors to come to the rescue, and Guillebault, a father with five children.

"High above the crash and the hissing of flames rise their heart-rending cries. They call for help. Will they be allowed to perish? A gendarme rushes forward, and with him a farmer from Brechy. But their heroism is useless: the monster keeps its prey. The two men also are apparently doomed; and only by unheard-of efforts, and at great peril of life, can they be rescued from the furnace. But they are so grievously wounded, that they will remain infirm for the rest of their lives, compelled to appeal to public charity for their subsistence."

Then the prosecuting attorney proceeds to paint the whole of the disaster at Valpinson in the sombrest colors, and with all the resources of his well-known eloquence. He describes the Countess Claudieuse as she kneels by the side of her dying husband, while the crowd is eagerly pressing around the wounded man and struggling with the flames for the charred remains of the unfortunate firemen. With increasing vehemence, he says next,—

"And during all this time what becomes of the author of these fearful misdeeds? When his hatred is gratified, he flees through the wood, and returns to his home. Remorse, there is none. As soon as he reaches the house, he eats, drinks, smokes his cigar. His position in the country is such, and the precautionary measures he had taken appear to him so well chosen, that he thinks he is above suspicion. He is calm. He feels so perfectly safe, that he neglects the commonest precautions, and does not even take the trouble of pouring out the water in which he has washed his hands, blackened as they are by the fire he has just kindled.

"He forgets that Providence whose torch on great occasions illumines and guides human justice.

"And how, indeed, could the law ever have expected to find the guilty man in one of the most magnificent chateaux of the country but for a direct intervention of Providence?

"For the incendiary, the assassin, was actually there, at the Chateau Boiscoran.

"And let no one come and tell us that the past life of Jacques de Boiscoran is such as to protect him against the formidable charges that are brought against him. We know his past life.

"A perfect model of those idle young men who spend in riotous living a fortune painfully amassed by their fathers, Jacques de Boiscoran had not even a profession. Useless to society, a burden to himself, he passed through life like a ship without rudder and without compass, indulging in all kinds of unhealthy fashions in order to spend the hours that were weighing heavily upon him.

"And yet he was ambitious; but his ambition lay in the direction of those dangerous and wicked intrigues which inevitably lead men to crime.

"Hence we see him mixed up with all those sterile and wanton party movements which discredit our days, uttering over and over again hollow phrases in condemnation of all that is noble and sacred, appealing to the most execrable passions of the multitude"—

M. MAGLOIRE.—If this is a political affair, we ought to be informed beforehand.

ATTORNEY-GENERAL.—There is no question of politics here. We speak of the life of a man who has been an apostle of strife.

M. MAGLOIRE.—Does the attorney-general fancy he is preaching peace?

PRESIDENT.—I request counsel for the defence not to interrupt.

ATTORNEY-GENERAL.—And it is in this ambition of the accused that we must look for a key to that terrible hatred which has led him to commit such crimes. That lawsuit about a stream of water is a matter of comparatively little importance. But Jacques de Boiscoran was preparing to become a candidate for election.

A.—I never dreamed of it.

ATTORNEY-GENERAL.—(Not noticing the interruption.) He did not say so; but his friends said it for him, and went about everywhere, repeating that by his position, his wealth, and his opinions, he was the man best worthy of the votes of Republicans. And he would have had an excellent chance, if there had not stood between him and the object of his desires Count Claudieuse, who had already more than once succeeded in defeating similar plots.

M. MAGLOIRE.—(Warmly.) Do you refer to me?

ATTORNEY-GENERAL.—I allude to no one.

M. MAGLOIRE.—You might just as well say at once, that my friends as well as myself are all M. de Boiscoran's accomplices; and that we have employed him to rid us of a formidable adversary.

ATTORNEY-GENERAL.—(Continues.) Gentlemen, this is the real motive of the crime. Hence that hatred which the accused soon is unable to conceal any longer, which overflows in invectives, which breaks forth in threats of death, and which actually carries him so far that he points his gun at Count Claudieuse.

The attorney-general next passes on to examine the charges, which, he declares, are overwhelming and irrefutable. Then he goes on,—

"But what need is there of such questions after the crushing evidence of Count Claudieuse? You have heard it,—on the point of appearing before God!

"His first impulse was to follow the generous nature of his heart, and to pardon the man who had attempted his life. He desired to save him; but, as he felt death come nearer, he saw that he had no right to shield a criminal from the sword of justice: he remembered that there were other victims beside himself.

"And then, rising from his bed of agony, he dragged himself here into court, in order to tell you. 'That is the man! By the light of the fire which he had kindled, I saw him and recognized him. He is the man!'

"And could you hesitate after such evidence? No! I can not and will not believe it. After such crimes, society expects that justice should be done,—justice in the name of Count Claudieuse on his deathbed,—justice in the name of the dead,—justice in the name of Bolton's mother, and of Guillebault's widow and her five children."

A murmur of approbation accompanied the last words of M. Gransiere, and continued for some time after he had concluded. There is not a woman in the whole assembly who does not shed tears.

P.—The counsel for the defence.

[Pleading.]

As M. Magloire had so far alone taken an active part in the defence, it was generally believed that he would speak. But it was not so. M. Folgat rises.

Our court-house here in Sauveterre has at various times reechoed the words of almost all our great masters of forensic eloquence. We have heard Berryer, Dufaure, Jules Favre, and others; but, even after these illustrious orators, M. Folgat still succeeds in astonishing and moving us deeply.

We can, of course, report here only a few of his phrases; and we must utterly abandon all hope of giving an idea of his proud and disdainful attitude, his admirable manner, full of authority, and especially of his full, rich voice, which found its way into every heart.

"To defend certain men against certain charges," he began, "would be to insult them. They cannot be touched. To the portrait drawn by the prosecuting attorney, I shall simply oppose the answer given by the venerable priest of Brechy. What did he tell you? M. de Boiscoran is the best and most honorable of men. There is the truth; they wish to make him out a political intriguant. He had, it is true, a desire to be useful to his country. But, while others debated, he acted. The Sauveterre Volunteers will tell you to what passions he appealed before the enemy, and by what intrigues he won the cross which Chausy himself fastened to his breast. He wanted power, you say. No: he wished for happiness. You speak of a letter written by him, the evening of the crime, to his betrothed. I challenge you to read it. It covers four pages: before you have read two, you will be forced to abandon the case."

Then the young advocate repeats the evidence given by the accused; and really, under the influence of his eloquence, the charges seem to fall to the ground, and to be utterly annihilated.

"And now," he went on, "what other evidence remains there? The evidence given by Count Claudieuse. It is crushing, you say. I say it is singular. What! here is a witness who sees his last hour drawing nigh, and who yet waits for the last minute of his life before he speaks. And you think that is natural! You pretend that it was generosity which made him keep silent. I, I ask you how the most cruel enemy could have acted more atrociously?

"'Never was a case clearer,' says the prosecution. On the contrary, I maintain that never was a case more obscure; and that, so far from fathoming the secret of the whole affair, the prosecution has not found out the first word of it."

M. Folgat takes his seat, and the sheriff's officers have to interfere to prevent applause from breaking out. If the vote had been taken at that moment, M. de Boiscoran would have been acquitted.

But the proceedings are suspended for fifteen minutes; and in the meantime the lamps are lit, for night begins to fall.

When the president resumes his chair, the attorney-general claims his right to speak.

"I shall not reply as I had at first proposed. Count Claudieuse is about to pay with his life for the effort which he has made to place his evidence before you. He could not even be carried home. He is perhaps at this very moment drawing his last breath upon earth in the adjoining room."

The counsel for the defence do not desire to address the jury; and, as the accused also declares that he has nothing more to say, the president sums up, and the jurymen withdrew to their room to deliberate.

The heat is overwhelming, the restraint almost unbearable; and all faces bear the marks of oppressive fatigue; but nobody thinks of leaving the house. A thousand contradictory reports circulate through the excited crowd. Some say that Count Claudieuse has died; others, on the contrary, report him better, and add that he has sent for the priest from Brechy.

At last, a few minutes after nine o'clock, the jury reappears.

Jacques de Boiscoran is declared guilty, and, on the score of extenuating circumstances, sentenced to twenty years' penal labor.

THIRD PART

COCOLEU

I.

Thus M. Galpin triumphed, and M. Gransiere had reason to be proud of his eloquence. Jacques de Boiscoran had been found guilty.

But he looked calm, and even haughty, as the president, M. Domini, pronounced the terrible sentence, a thousand times braver at that moment than the man who, facing the squad of soldiers from whom he is to receive death, refuses to have his eyes bandaged, and himself gives the word of command with a firm voice.

That very morning, a few moments before the beginning of the trial, he had said to Dionysia,—

"I know what is in store for me; but I am innocent. They shall not see me turn pale, nor hear me ask for mercy."

And, gathering up all the energy of which the human heart is capable, he had made a supreme effort at the decisive moment, and kept his word.

Turning quietly to his counsel at the moment when the last words of the president were lost among the din of the crowd, he said,—

"Did I not tell you that the day would come when you yourself would be the first to put a weapon into my hands?"

M. Folgat rose promptly.

He showed neither the anger nor the disappointment of an advocate who has just had a cause which he knew to be just.

"That day has not come yet," he replied. "Remember your promise. As long as there remains a ray of hope, we shall fight.

Now we have much more than mere hope at this moment. In less than a month, in a week, perhaps to-morrow, we shall have our revenge."

The unfortunate man shook his head.

"I shall nevertheless have undergone the disgrace of a condemnation," he murmured.

The taking the ribbon of the Legion of Honor from his buttonhole, he handed it to M. Folgat, saying—

"Keep this in memory of me, and if I never regain the right to wear it"—

In the meantime, however, the gendarmes, whose duty it was to guard the prisoner, had risen; and the sergeant said to Jacques,—

"We must go, sir. Come, come! You need not despair. You need not lose courage. All is not over yet. There is still the appeal for you, and then the petition for pardon, not to speak of what may happen, and cannot be foreseen."

M. Folgat was allowed to accompany the prisoner, and was getting ready to do so; but the latter said, with a pained voice,—

"No, my friend, please leave me alone. Others have more need of your presence than I have. Dionysia, my poor father, my mother. Go to them. Tell them that the horror of my condemnation lies in the thought of them. May they forgive me for the affliction which I cause them, and for the disgrace of having me for their son, for her betrothed!"

Then, pressing the hands of his counsel, he added,—

"And you, my friends, how shall I ever express to you my gratitude? Ah! if incomparable talents, and matchless zeal and ability, had sufficed, I know I should be free. But instead of that"—he pointed at the little door through which he was to pass, and said in a heartrending tone,—

"Instead of that, there is the door to the galleys. Henceforth"—

A sob cut short his words. His strength was exhausted; for if there are, so to say, no limits to the power of endurance of the spirit, the energy of the body has its bounds. Refusing the arm which the sergeant offered him, he rushed out of the room.

M. Magloire was well-nigh beside himself with grief.

"Ah! why could we not save him?" he said to his young colleague. "Let them come and speak to me again of the power of conviction. But we must not stay here: let us go!"

They threw themselves into the crowd, which was slowly dispersing, all palpitating yet with the excitement of the day.

A strange reaction was already beginning to set in,—a reaction perfectly illogic, and yet intelligible, and by no means rare under similar circumstances.

Jacques de Boiscoran, an object of general execration as long as he was only suspected, regained the sympathy of all the moment he was condemned. It was as if the fatal sentence had wiped out the horror of the crime. He was pitied; his fate was deplored; and as they thought of his family, his mother, and his betrothed, they almost cursed the severity of the judges.

Besides, even the least observant among those present had been struck by the singular course which the proceedings had taken. There was not one, probably, in that vast assembly who did not feel that there was a mysterious and unexplored side of the case, which neither the prosecution nor the defence had chosen to approach. Why had Cocoleu been mentioned only once, and then quite incidentally? He was an idiot, to be sure; but it was nevertheless through his evidence alone that suspicions had been aroused against M. de Boiscoran. Why had he not been summoned either by the prosecution or by the defence?

The evidence given by Count Claudieuse, also, although apparently so conclusive at the moment, was now severely criticised.

The most indulgent said,—

"That was not well done. That was a trick. Why did he not speak out before? People do not wait for a man to be down before they strike him."

Others added,—

"And did you notice how M. de Boiscoran and Count Claudieuse looked at each other? Did you hear what they said to each other? One might have sworn that there was something else, something very different from a mere lawsuit, between them."

And on all sides people repeated,—

"At all events, M. Folgat is right. The whole matter is far from being cleared up. The jury was long before they agreed. Perhaps M. de Boiscoran would have been acquitted, if, at the last moment, M. Gransiere had not announced the impending death of Count Claudieuse in the adjoining room."

M. Magloire and M. Folgat listened to all these remarks, as they heard them in the crowd here and there, with great satisfaction; for in spite of all the assertions of magistrates and judges, in spite of all the thundering condemnations against the practice, public opinion will find an echo in the court-room; and, more frequently than we think, public opinion does dictate the verdict of the jury.

"And now," said M. Magloire to his young colleague, "now we can be content. I know Sauveterre by heart. I tell you public opinion is henceforth on our side."

By dint of perseverance they made their way, at last, out through the narrow door of the court-room, when one of the ushers stopped them.

"They wish to see you," said the man.

"Who?"

"The family of the prisoner. Poor people! They are all in there, in M. Mechinet's office. M. Daubigeon told me to keep it for them. The Marchioness de Boiscoran also was carried there when she was taken ill in the court-room."

He accompanied the two gentlemen, while telling them this, to the end of the hall; then he opened a door, and said,—

"They are in there," and withdrew discreetly.

There, in an easy-chair, with closed eyes, and half-open lips, lay Jacques's mother. Her livid pallor and her stiff limbs made her look like a dead person; but, from time to time, spasms shook her whole body, from head to foot. M. de Chandore stood on one side, and the marquis, her husband, on the other, watching her with mournful eyes and in perfect silence. They had been thunderstruck; and, from the moment when the fatal sentence fell upon their ears, neither of them had uttered a word.

Dionysia alone seemed to have preserved the faculty of reasoning and moving. But her face was deep purple; her dry eyes shone with a painful light; and her body shook as with fever. As soon as the two advocates appeared, she cried,—

"And you call this human justice?"

And, as they were silent, she added,—

"Here is Jacques condemned to penal labor; that is to say, he is judicially dishonored, lost, disgraced, forever cut off from human society. He is innocent; but that does not matter. His best friends will know him no longer: no hand will touch his hand hereafter; and even those who were most proud of his affection will pretend to have forgotten his name."

"I understand your grief but too well, madam," said M. Magloire.

"My grief is not as great as my indignation," she broke in. "Jacques must be avenged, and he shall be avenged! I am only twenty, and he is not thirty yet: there is a whole life before us which we can devote to the work of his rehabilitation; for I do not mean to abandon him. I! His undeserved misfortunes make him a thousand times dearer to me, and almost sacred. I was his betrothed this morning: this evening I am his wife. His condemnation was our nuptial benediction. And if it is true, as grandpapa says, that the law prohibits a prisoner to marry the woman he loves, well, I will be his without marriage."

Dionysia spoke all this aloud, so loud that it seemed she wanted all the earth to hear what she was saying.

"Ah! let me reassure you by a single word, madam," said M. Folgat. "We have not yet come to that. The sentence is not final."

The Marquis de Boiscoran and M. de Chandore started.

"What do you mean?"

"An oversight which M. Galpin has committed makes the whole proceeding null and void. You will ask how a man of his character, so painstaking and so formal, should have made such a blunder. Probably because he was blinded by passion. Why had nobody noticed this oversight? Because fate owed us this compensation. There can be no question about the matter. The defect is a defect of form; and the law provides expressly for the case. The sentence must be declared void, and we shall have another trial."

"And you never told us anything of that?" asked Dionysia.

"We hardly dared to think of it," replied M. Magloire. "It was one of those secrets which we dare not confide to our own pillow. Remember, that, in the course of the proceedings, the error might have been corrected at any time. Now it is too late. We have time before us; and the conduct of Count Claudieuse relieves us from all restraint of delicacy. The veil shall be torn now."

The door opened violently, interrupting his words. Dr. Seignebos entered, red with anger, and darting fiery glances from under his gold spectacles.

"Count Claudieuse?" M. Folgat asked eagerly.

"Is next door," replied the doctor. "They have had him down on a mattress, and his wife is by his side. What a profession ours is! Here is a man, a wretch, whom I should be most happy to strangle with my own hands; and I am compelled to do all I can to recall him to life: I must lavish my attentions upon him, and seek every means to relieve his sufferings."

"Is he any better?"

"Not at all! Unless a special miracle should be performed in his behalf, he will leave the court-house only feet forward, and that in twenty-four hours. I have not concealed it from the countess; and I have told her, that, if she wishes her husband to die in peace with Heaven, she has but just time to send for a priest."

"And has she sent for one?"

"Not at all! She told me her husband would be terrified by the appearance of a priest, and that would hasten his end. Even when the good priest from Brechy came of his own accord, she sent him off unceremoniously."

"Ah the miserable woman!" cried Dionysia.

And, after a moment's reflection, she added,—

"And yet that may be our salvation. Yes, certainly. Why should I hesitate? Wait for me here: I am coming back."

She hurried out. Her grandpapa was about to follow her; but M. Folgat stopped him.

"Let her do it," he said,—"let her do it!"

It had just struck ten o'clock. The court-house, just now as full and as noisy as a bee-hive, was silent and deserted. In the immense hall, badly lighted by a smoking lamp, there were only two men to be seen. One was the priest from Brechy, who was praying on his knees close to a door; and the other was the watchman, who was slowly walking up and down, and whose steps resounded there as in a church.

Dionysia went straight up to the latter.

"Where is Count Claudieuse?" she asked.

"There, madam," replied the man, pointing at the door before which the priest was praying,—"there, in the private office of the commonwealth attorney."

"Who is with him?"

"His wife, madam, and a servant."

"Well, go in and tell the Countess Claudieuse,—but so that her husband does not hear you,—that Miss Chandore desires to see her a few moments."

The watchman made no objection, and went in. But, when he came back, he said to the young girl,—

"Madam, the countess sends word that she cannot leave her husband, who is very low."

She stopped him by an impatient gesture, and said,—

"Never mind! Go back and tell the countess, that, if she does not come out, I shall go in this moment; that, if it must be, I shall force my way in; that I shall call for help; that nothing will keep me. I must absolutely see her."

"But, madam"—

"Go! Don't you see that it is a question of life and death?"

There was such authority in her voice, that the watchman no longer hesitated. He went in once more, and reappeared a moment after.

"Go in," he said to the young girl.

She went in, and found herself in a little anteroom which preceded the office of the commonwealth attorney. A large lamp illuminated the room. The door leading to the room in which the count was lying was closed.

In the centre of the room stood the Countess Claudieuse. All these successive blows had not broken her indomitable energy. She looked pale, but calm.

"Since you insist upon it, madam," she began, "I come to tell you myself that I cannot listen to you. Are you not aware that I am standing between two open graves,—that of my poor girl, who is dying at my house, and that of my husband, who is breathing his last in there?"

She made a motion as if she were about to retire; but Dionysia stopped her by a threatening look, and said with a trembling voice,—

"If you go back into that room where your husband is, I shall go back with you, and I shall speak before him. I shall ask you right before him, how you dare order a priest away from his bedside at the moment of death, and whether, after having robbed him of all his happiness in life, you mean to make him unhappy in all eternity."

Instinctively the countess drew back.

"I do not understand you," she said.

"Yes, you do understand me, madam. Why will you deny it? Do you not see that I know every thing, and that I have guessed what you have not told me? Jacques was your lover; and your husband has had his revenge."

"Ah!" cried the countess, "that is too much; that is too much!"

"And you have permitted it," Dionysia went on with breathless haste; "and you did not come, and cry out in open court that your husband was a false witness! What a woman you must be! You do not mind it, that your love carries a poor unfortunate man to the galleys. You mean to live on with this thought in your heart, that the man whom you love is innocent, and nevertheless, disgraced forever, and cut off from human society. A priest might induce the count to retract his statement, you know very well; and hence you refuse to let the priest from Brechy come to his bedside. And what is the end and aim of all your crimes? To save your false reputation as an honest woman. Ah! that is miserable; that is mean; that is infamous!"

The countess was roused at last. What all M. Folgat's skill and ability had not been able to accomplish, Dionysia obtained in an instant by the force of her passion. Throwing aside her mask, the countess exclaimed with a perfect burst of rage,—

"Well, then, no, no! I have not acted so, and permitted all this to happen, because I care for my reputation. My reputation!—what does it matter? It was only a week ago, when Jacques had succeeded in escaping from prison, I offered to flee with him. He had only to say a word, and I should have given up my family, my children, my country, every thing, for him. He answered, 'Rather the galleys!'"

In the midst of all her fearful sufferings, Dionysia's heart filled with unspeakable happiness as she heard these words. Ah! now she could no longer doubt Jacques.

"He has condemned himself, you see," continued the countess. "I was quite willing to ruin myself for him, but certainly not for another woman."

"And that other woman—no doubt you mean me!"

"Yes!—you for whose sake he abandoned me,—you whom he was going to marry,—you with whom he hoped to enjoy long happy years, and a happiness not furtive and sinful like ours, but a legitimate, honest happiness."

Tears were trembling in Dionysia's eyes. She was beloved: she thought of what she must suffer who was not beloved.

"And yet I should have been generous," she murmured. The countess broke out into a fierce, savage laugh.

"And the proof of it is," said the young girl, "that I came to offer you a bargain."

"A bargain?"

"Yes. Save Jacques, and, by all that is sacred to me in the world, I promise I will enter a convent: I will disappear, and you shall never hear my name any more."

Intense astonishment seized the countess, and she looked at Dionysia with a glance full of doubt and mistrust. Such devotion seemed to her too sublime not to conceal some snare.

"You would really do that?" she asked.

"Unhesitatingly."

"You would make a great sacrifice for my benefit?"

"For yours? No, madam, for Jacques's."

"You love him very dearly, do you?"

"I love him dearly enough to prefer his happiness to my own a thousand times over. Even if I were buried in the depths of a convent, I should still have the consolation of knowing that he owed his rehabilitation to me; and I should suffer less in knowing that he belonged to another than that he was innocent, and yet condemned."

But, in proportion as the young girl thus confirmed her sincerity, the brow of the countess grew darker and sterner, and passing blushes mantled her cheek. At last she said with haughty irony,—

"Admirable!"

"Madam!"

"You condescend to give up M. de Boiscoran. Will that make him love me? You know very well he will not. You know that he loves you alone. Heroism with such conditions is easy enough. What have you to fear? Buried in a convent, he will love you only all the more ardently, and he will execrate me all the more fervently."

"He shall never know any thing of our bargain!"

"Ah! What does that matter? He will guess it, if you do not tell him. No: I know what awaits me. I have felt it now for two years,—this agony of seeing him becoming daily more detached from me. What have I not done to keep him near me! How I have stooped to meanness, to falsehood, to keep him a single day longer, perhaps a single hour! But all was useless. I was a burden to him. He loved me no longer; and my love became to him a heavier load than the cannon-ball which they will fasten to his chains at the galleys."

Dionysia shuddered.

"That is horrible!" she murmured.

"Horrible! Yes, but true. You look amazed. That is because you have as yet only seen the morning dawn of your love: wait for the dark evening, and you will understand me. Is not the story of all of us women the same! I have seen Jacques at my feet as you see him at yours: the vows he swears to you, he once swore to me; and he swore them to me with the same voice, tremulous with passion, and with the same burning glances. But you think you will be his wife, and I never was. What does that matter? What does he tell you? That he will love you forever, because his love is under the protection of God and of men. He told me, precisely because our love was not thus protected, that we should be united by indissoluble bonds,—bonds stronger than all others. You have his promise: so had I. And the proof of it is that I gave him every thing,—my honor and the honor of my family, and that I would have given him still more, if there had been any more to give. And now to be betrayed, forsaken, despised, to sink lower and lower, until at last I must become the object of your pity! To have fallen so low, that you should dare come and offer me to give up Jacques for my benefit! Ah, that is maddening! And I should let the vengeance I hold in my hands slip from me at your bidding! I should be stupid enough, blind enough, to allow myself to be touched by your hypocritical tears! I should secure your happiness by the sacrifice of my reputation! No, madam, cherish no such hope!"

Her voice expired in her throat in a kind of toneless rattle. She walked up and down a few times in the room. Then she placed herself straight before Dionysia, and, looking fixedly into her eyes, she asked,—

"Who suggested to you this plan of coming here, this supreme insult which you tried to inflict upon me?"

Dionysia was seized with unspeakable horror, and hardly found heart to reply.

"No one," she murmured.

"M. Folgat?"

"Knows nothing of it."

"And Jacques?"

"I have not seen him. The thought occurred to me quite suddenly, like an inspiration on high. When Dr. Seignebos told me that you had refused to admit the priest from Brechy, I said to myself, 'This is the last misfortune, and the greatest of them all! If Count Claudieuse dies without retracting, Jacques can never be fully restored, whatever may happen hereafter, not even if his innocence should be established.' Then I made up my mind to come to you. Ah! it was a hard task. But I was in hopes I might touch your heart, or that you might be moved by the greatness of my sacrifice."

The countess was really moved. There is no heart absolutely bad, as there is none altogether good. As she listened to Dionysia's passionate entreaty, her resolution began to grow weaker.

"Would it be such a great sacrifice?" she asked.

Tears sprang to the eyes of the poor young girl.

"Alas!" she said, "I offer you my life. I know very well you will not be long jealous of me."

She was interrupted by groans, which seemed to come from the room in which the count was lying.

The countess half-opened the door; and immediately a feeble, and yet imperious voice was heard calling out,—

"Genevieve, I say, Genevieve!"

"I am coming, my dear, in a moment," replied the countess.

"What security can you give me," she said, in a hard and stern voice, after having closed the door again,—"what security do you give me, that if Jacques's innocence were established, and he reinstated, you would not forget your promises?"

"Ah, madam! How or upon what do you want me to swear that I am ready to disappear. Choose your own securities, and I will do whatever you require."

Then, sinking down on her knees, before the countess, she went on,—

"Here I am at your feet, madam, humble and suppliant,—I whom you accuse of a desire to insult you. Have pity on Jacques! Ah! if you loved him as much as I do, you would not hesitate."

The countess raised her suddenly and quickly, and holding her hands in her own, looked at her for more than a minute without saying a word, but with heaving bosom and trembling lips. At last she asked in a voice which was so deeply affected, that it was hardly intelligible.

"What do you want me to do?"

"Induce Count Claudieuse to retract."

The countess shook her head.

"It would be useless to try. You do not know the count. He is a man of iron. You might tear his flesh inch by inch with hot iron pincers, and he would not take back one of his words. You cannot conceive what he has suffered, nor the depth of the hatred, the rage, and the thirst of vengeance, which have accumulated in his heart. It was to torture me that he brought me here to his bedside. Only five minutes ago he told me that he died content, since Jacques was declared guilty, and condemned through his evidence."

She was conquered: her energy was exhausted, and tears came to her eyes.

"He has been so cruelly tried!" she went on. "He loved me to distraction; he loved nothing in the world but me. And I—Ah, if we could know, if we could foresee! No, I shall never be able to induce him to retract."

Dionysia almost forgot her own great grief.

"Nor do I expect you to obtain that favor," she said very gently.

"Who, then?"

"The priest from Brechy. He will surely find words to shake even the firmest resolution. He can speak in the name of that God, who, even on the cross, forgave those who crucified Him."

One moment longer the countess hesitated; and then, overcoming finally the last rebellious impulses of her pride, she said,—

"Well, I will call the priest."

"And I, madam, I swear I will keep my promise."

But the countess stopped her, and said, making a supreme effort over herself,—

"No: I shall try to save Jacques without making conditions. Let him be yours. He loves you, and you were ready to sacrifice your life for his sake. He forsakes me; but I sacrifice my honor to him. Farewell!"

And hastening to the door, while Dionysia returned to her friends, she summoned the priest from Brechy.

II.

M. Daubigeon, the commonwealth attorney, learned that morning from his chief clerk what had happened, and how the proceedings in the Boiscoran case were necessarily null and void on account of a fatal error in form. The counsel of the defence had lost no time, and, after spending the whole night in consultation, had early that morning presented their application for a new trial to the court.

The commonwealth attorney took no pains to conceal his satisfaction.

"Now," he cried, "this will worry my friend Galpin, and clip his wings considerably; and yet I had called his attention to the lines of Horace, in which he speaks of Phaeton's sad fate, and says,—

'Terret ambustus Phaeton avaras Spes.'

But he would not listen to me, forgetting, that, without prudence, force is a danger. And there he is now, in great difficulty, I am sure."

And at once he made haste to dress, and to go and see M. Galpin in order to hear all the details accurately, as he told his clerk, but, in reality, in order to enjoy to his heart's content the discomfiture of the ambitious magistrate.

He found him furious, and ready to tear his hair.

"I am disgraced," he repeated: "I am ruined; I am lost. All my prospects, all my hopes, are gone. I shall never be forgiven for such an oversight."

To look at M. Daubigeon, you would have thought he was sincerely distressed.

"Is it really true," he said with an air of assumed pity,—"is it really true, what they tell me, that this unlucky mistake was made by you?"

"By me? Yes, indeed! I forgot those wretched details which a scholar knows by heart. Can you understand that? And to say that no one noticed my inconceivable blindness! Neither the first court of inquiry, nor the attorney-general himself, nor the presiding judge, ever said a word about it. It is my fate. And that is to be the result of my labors. Everybody, no doubt, said, 'Oh! M. Galpin has the case in hand; he knows all about it: no need to look after the matter when such a man has taken hold of it.' And here I am. Oh! I might kill myself."

"It is all the more fortunate," replied M. Daubigeon, "that yesterday the case was hanging on a thread."

The magistrate gnashed his teeth, and replied,—

"Yes, on a thread, thanks to M. Domini! whose weakness I cannot comprehend, and who did not know at all, or who was not willing to know, how to make the most of the evidence. But it was

M. Gransiere's fault quite as much. What had he to do with politics to drag them into the affair? And whom did he want to hit? No one else but M. Magloire, the man whom everybody respects in the whole district, and who had three warm personal friends among the jurymen. I foresaw it, and I told him where he would get into trouble. But there are people who will not listen. M. Gransiere wants to be elected himself. It is a fancy, a monomania of our day: everybody wants to be a deputy. I wish Heaven would confound all ambitious men!"

For the first time in his life, and no doubt for the last time also, the commonwealth attorney rejoiced at the misfortune of others. Taking savage pleasure in turning the dagger in his poor friend's wounds, he said,—

"No doubt M. Folgat's speech had something to do with it."

"Nothing at all."

"He was brilliantly successful."

"He took them by surprise. It was nothing but a big voice, and grand, rolling sentences."

"But still"—

"And what did he say, after all? That the prosecution did not know the real secret of the case. That is absurd!"

"The new judges may not think so, however."

"We shall see."

"This time M. de Boiscoran's defence will be very different. He will spare nobody. He is down now, and cannot fall any lower."

"That may be. But he also risks having a less indulgent jury, and not getting off with twenty years."

"What do his counsel say?"

"I do not know. But I have just sent my clerk to find out; and, if you choose to wait"—

M. Daubigeon did wait, and he did well; for M. Mechinet came in very soon after, with a long face for the world, but inwardly delighted.

"Well?" asked M. Galpin eagerly.

He shook his head, and said in a melancholy tone of voice,—

"I have never seen any thing like this. How fickle public opinion is, after all! Day before yesterday M. de Boiscoran could not have passed through the town without being mobbed. If he should show himself to-day, they would carry him in triumph. He has been condemned, and now he is a martyr. It is known already that the sentence is void, and they are delighted. My sisters have just told me that the ladies in good society propose to give to the Marchioness de Boiscoran and to Miss Chandore some public evidence of their sympathy. The members of the bar will give M. Folgat a public dinner."

"Why that is monstrous!" cried M. Galpin.

"Well," said M. Daubigeon, "'the opinions of men are more fickle and changeable than the waves of the sea.'"

But, interrupting the quotation, M. Galpin asked his clerk,—

"Well, what else?"

"I went to hand M. Gransiere the letter which you gave me for him"—

"What did he say?"

"I found him in consultation with the president, M. Domini. He took the letter, glanced at it rapidly, and told me in his most icy tone, 'Very well!' To tell the truth, I thought, that, in spite of his stiff and grand air, he was in reality furious."

The magistrate looked utterly in despair.

"I can't stand it," he said sighing. "These men whose veins have no blood in them, but poison, never forgive."

"Day before yesterday you thought very highly of him."

"Day before yesterday he did not look upon me as the cause of a great misfortune for him."

M. Mechinet went on quite eagerly,—

"After leaving M. Gransiere, I went to the court-house, and there I head the great piece of news which has set all the town agog. Count Claudieuse is dead."

M. Daubigeon and M. Galpin looked at each other, and exclaimed in the same breath,—

"Great God! Is that so?"

"He breathed his last this morning, at two or three minutes before six o'clock. I saw his body in the private room of the attorney-general. The priest from Brechy was there, and two other priests from his parish. They were waiting for a bier to have him carried to his house."

"Poor man!" murmured M. Daubigeon.

"But I heard a great deal more," Mechinet said, "from the watchman who was on guard last night. He told me that when the trial was over, and it became known that Count Claudieuse was likely to die, the priest from Brechy came there, and asked to be allowed to offer him the last consolations of his church. The countess refused to let him come to the bedside of her husband. The watchman was amazed at this; and just then Miss Chandore suddenly appeared, and sent word to the countess that she wanted to speak to her."

"Is it possible?"

"Quite certain. They remained together for more than a quarter of an hour. What did they say? The watchman told me he was dying with curiosity to know; but he could hear nothing, because there was the priest from Brechy, all the while, kneeling before the door, and praying. When they parted, they looked terribly excited. Then the countess immediately called in the priest, and he stayed with the count till he died."

M. Daubigeon and M. Galpin had not yet recovered from their amazement at this account, when somebody knocked timidly at the door.

"Come in!" cried Mechinet.

The door opened, and the sergeant of gendarmes appeared.

"I have been sent here by the attorney-general," he said; "and the servant told me you were up here. We have just caught Trumence."

"That man who had escaped from jail?"

"Yes. We were about to carry him back there, when he told us that he had a secret to reveal, a very important, urgent secret, concerning the condemned prisoner, Boiscoran."

"Trumence?"

"Yes. Then we carried him to the court-house, and I came for orders."

"Run and say that I am coming to see him!" cried M. Daubigeon. "Make haste! I am coming after you."

But the gendarme, a model of obedience, had not waited so long: he was already down stairs.

"I must leave you, Galpin," said M. Daubigeon, very much excited. "You heard what the man said. We must know what that means at once."

But the magistrate was not less excited.

"You permit me to accompany you, I hope?" he asked.

He had a right to do so.

"Certainly," replied the commonwealth attorney. "But make haste!"

The recommendation was not needed. M. Galpin had already put on his boots. He now slipped his overcoat over his home dress, as he was; and off they went.

Mechinet followed the two gentlemen as they hastened down the street; and the good people of Sauveterre, always on the lookout, were not a little scandalized at seeing their well-known magistrate, M. Galpin, in his home costume,—he who generally was most scrupulously precise in his dress.

Standing on their door-steps, they said to each other,—

"Something very important must have happened. Just look at these gentlemen!"

The fact was, they were walking so fast, that people might well wonder; and they did not say a word all the way.

But, ere they reached the court-house, they were forced to stop; for some four or five hundred people were filling the court, crowding on the steps, and actually pressing against the doors.

Immediately all became silent; hats were raised; the crowd parted; and a passage was opened.

On the porch appeared the priest from Brechy, and two other priests.

Behind them came attendants from the hospital, who bore a bier covered with black cloth; and beneath the cloth the outlines of a human body could be seen.

The women began to cry; and those who had room enough knelt down.

"Poor countess!" murmured one of them. "Here is her husband dead, and they say one of her daughters is dying at home."

But M. Daubigeon, the magistrate, and Mechinet were too preoccupied with their own interests to think of stopping for more reliable news. The way was open: they went in, and hastened to the clerk's office, where the gendarmes had taken Trumence, and now were guarding him.

He rose as soon as he recognized the gentlemen, and respectfully took off his cap. It was really Trumence; but the good-for-nothing vagrant did not present his usual careless appearance. He looked pale, and was evidently very much excited.

"Well," said M. Daubigeon, "so you have allowed yourself to be retaken?"

"Beg pardon, judge," replied the poor fellow, "I was not retaken. I came of my own accord."

"Involuntarily, you mean?"

"Quite by my own free will! Just ask the sergeant."

The sergeant stepped forward, touched his cap, and reported,—

"That is the naked truth. Trumence came himself to our barrack, and said, 'I surrender as a prisoner. I wish to speak to the commonwealth attorney, and give importance evidence.'"

The vagabond drew himself up proudly,—

"You see, sir, that I did not lie. While these gentlemen were galloping all over the country in search of me, I was snugly ensconced in a garret at the Red Lamb, and did not think of coming out from there till I should be entirely forgotten."

"Yes; but people who lodge at the Red Lamb have to pay, and you had no money."

Trumence very quietly drew from his pocket a handful of Napoleons, and of five-and-twenty-franc notes, and showed them.

"You see that I had the wherewithal to pay for my room," he said. "But I surrendered, because, after all, I am an honest man, and I would rather suffer some trouble myself than see an innocent gentleman go to the galleys."

"M. de Boiscoran?"

"Yes. He is innocent! I know it; I am sure of it; and I can prove it. And, if he will not tell, I will tell,—tell every thing!"

M. Daubigeon and M. Galpin were utterly astounded.

"Explain yourself," they both said in the same breath.

But the vagrant shook his head, pointing at the gendarmes; and, as a man who is quite cognizant of all the formalities of the law, he replied,—

"But it is a great secret; and, when one confesses, one does not like anybody else to hear it but the priest. Besides, I should like my deposition to be taken down in writing."

Upon a sign made by M. Galpin, the gendarmes withdrew; and Mechinet took his seat at a table, with a blank sheet of paper before him.

"Now we can talk," said Trumence: "that's the way I like it. I was not thinking myself of running away. I was pretty well off in jail; winter is coming, I had not a cent; and I knew, that, if I were retaken, I should fare rather badly. But M. Jacques de Boiscoran had a notion to spend a night outside."

"Mind what you are saying," M. Galpin broke in severely. "You cannot play with the law, and go off unpunished."

"May I die if I do not tell the truth!" cried Trumence. "M. Jacques has spent a whole night out of jail."

The magistrate trembled.

"What a story that is!" he said again.

"I have my proof," replied Trumence coldly, "and you shall hear. Well, as he wanted to leave, M. Jacques came to me, and we agreed, that in consideration of a certain sum of money which he has paid me, and of which you have seen just now all that is left, I should make a hole in the wall, and that I should run off altogether, while he was to come back when he had done his business."

"And the jailer?" asked M. Daubigeon.

Like a true peasant of his promise, Trumence was far too cunning to expose Blangin unnecessarily. Assuming, therefore, the whole responsibility of the evasion, he replied,—

"The jailer saw nothing. We had no use for him. Was not I, so to say, under-jailer? Had not I been charged by you yourself, M. Galpin, with keeping watch over M. Jacques? Was it not I who opened and locked his door, who took him to the parlor, and brought him back again?"

That was the exact truth.

"Go on!" said M. Galpin harshly.

"Well," said Trumence, "every thing was done as agreed upon. One evening, about nine o'clock, I make my hole in the wall, and here we are, M. Jacques and I, on the ramparts. There he slips a package of banknotes into my hand, and tells me to run for it, while he goes about his business. I thought he was innocent then; but you see I should not exactly have gone through the fire for him as yet. I said to myself, that perhaps he was making fun of me, and that, once on the wing, he would not be such a fool as to go back into the cage. This made me curious, as he was going off, to see

- 476 -

which way he was going,—and there I was, following him close upon his heels!"

The magistrate and the commonwealth attorney, accustomed as they both were, by the nature of their profession, to conceal their feelings, could hardly restrain now,—one, the hope trembling within him, and the other, the vague apprehensions which began to fill his heart.

Mechinet, who knew already all that was coming, laughed in his sleeve while his pen was flying rapidly over the paper.

"He was afraid he might be recognized," continued the vagrant, "and so M. Jacques had been running ever so fast, keeping close to the wall, and choosing the narrowest lanes. Fortunately, I have a pair of very good legs. He goes through Sauveterre like a race-horse; and, when he reaches Mautrec Street, he begins to ring the bell at a large gate."

"At Count Claudieuse's house!"

"I know now what house it was; but I did not know then. Well, he rings. A servant comes and opens. He speaks to her, and immediately she invites him in, and that so eagerly, that she forgets to close the gate again."

M. Daubigeon stopped him by a gesture.

"Wait!" he said.

And, taking up a blank form, he filled it up, rang the bell, and said to an usher of the court who had hastened in, giving him the printed paper,—

"I want this to be taken immediately. Make haste; and not a word!"

Then Trumence was directed to go on; and he said,—

"There I was, standing in the middle of the street, feeling like a fool. I thought I had nothing left me but to go and use my legs: that was safest for me. But that wretched, half-open gate attracted me. I said to myself, 'If you go in, and they catch you, they will think you have come to steal, and you'll have to pay for it.' That was true; but the temptation was too strong for me. My curiosity broke my heart, so to say, and, 'Come what may, I'll risk it,' I said. I push the huge gate just wide enough to let me in, and here I am in a large garden. It was pitch dark; but, quite at the bottom of the garden, three windows in the lower story of the house were lighted up. I had ventured too far now to go back. So I went on, creeping along stealthily, until I reached a tree, against which I pressed closely, about the length of my arm from one of the windows, which belonged to a beautiful parlor. I look—and I see whom? M. de Boiscoran. As there were no curtains to the windows, I could see as well as I can see you. His face looked terrible. I was asking myself for whom he could be waiting there, when I saw him hiding behind the open door of the room, like a man who is lying in wait for somebody, with evil intentions. This troubled me very much; but the next moment a lady came in. Instantly M. Jacques shuts the door behind her; the lady turns round, sees him, and wants to run, uttering at the same time a loud cry. That lady was the Countess Claudieuse!"

He looked as if he wished to pause to watch the effect of his revelation. But Mechinet was so impatient, that he forgot the modest character of his duty, and said hastily,—

"Go on; go on!"

"One of the windows was half open," continued the vagrant, "and thus I could hear almost as well as I saw. I crouched down on all-fours and kept my head on a level with the ground, so as not to lose a word. Oh, it was fearful! At the first word I understood it all: M. Jacques and the Countess Claudieuse had been lovers."

"This is madness!" cried M. Galpin.

"Well, I tell you I was amazed. The Countess Claudieuse—such a pious lady! But I have ears; don't you think I have? M. Jacques reminded her of the night of the crime, how they had been together a few minutes before the fire broke out, as they had agreed some days before to meet near Valpinson at that very time. At this meeting they had burnt their love-letters, and M. Jacques had blackened his fingers badly in burning them."

"Did you really hear that?" asked M. Daubigeon.

"As I hear you, sir."

"Write it down, Mechinet," said the commonwealth attorney with great eagerness,—"write that down carefully."

The clerk was sure to do it.

"What surprised me most," continued Trumence, "was, that the countess seemed to consider M. Jacques guilty, and he thought she was. Each accused the other of the crime. She said, 'You attempted the life of my husband, because you were afraid of him!' And he said, 'You wanted to kill him, so as to be free, and to prevent my marriage!'"

M. Galpin had sunk into a chair: he stammered,—

"Did anybody ever hear such a thing?"

"However, they explained; and at last they found out that they were both of them innocent. Then M. Jacques entreated the countess to save him; and she replied that she would certainly not save him at the expense of her reputation, and so enable him, as soon as he was free once more, to marry Miss Chandore. Then he said to her, 'Well, then I must tell all;' and she, 'You will not be believed. I shall deny it all, and you have no proof!' In his despair, he reproached her bitterly, and said she had never loved him at all. Then she swore she loved him more than ever; and that, as he was free now, she was ready to abandon every thing, and to escape with him to some foreign country. And she conjured him to flee, in a voice which moved my heart, with loving words such as I have never heard before in my life, and with looks which seemed to be burning fire. What a woman! I did not think he could possibly resist. And yet he did resist; and, perfectly beside himself with anger, he cried, 'Rather the galleys!' Then she laughed, mocking him, and saying, 'Very well, you shall go to the galleys!'"

Although Trumence entered into many details, it was quite evident that he kept back many things.

Still M. Daubigeon did not dare question him, for fear of breaking the thread of his account.

"But that was nothing at all," said the vagrant. "While M. Jacques and the countess were quarrelling in this way, I saw the door of the parlor suddenly open as if by itself, and a phantom appear in it, dressed in a funeral pall. It was Count Claudieuse himself. His face looked terrible; and he had a revolver in his hand. He was leaning against the side of the door; and he listened while his wife and M. Jacques were talking of their former love-affairs. At certain words, he would raise his pistol as if to fire; then he would lower it again, and go on listening. It was so awful, I had not a dry thread on my body. It was very hard not to cry out to M. Jacques and the countess, 'You poor people, don't you see that the count is there?' But they saw nothing; for they were both beside themselves with rage and despair: and at last M. Jacques actually raised his hand to strike the countess. 'Do not strike that woman!' suddenly said the count. They turn round; they see him, and utter a fearful cry. The countess fell on a chair as if she were dead. I was thunderstruck. I never in my life saw a man behave so beautifully as M. Jacques did at that moment. Instead of trying to escape, he opened his coat, and baring his breast, he said to the husband, 'Fire! You are in your right!' The count, however, laughed contemptuously, and said, 'The court will avenge me!'—'You know very well that I am innocent.'—'All the better.'—'It would be infamous to let me be condemned.'—'I shall do more than that. To make your condemnation sure, I shall say that I recognized you.' The count was going to step forward, as he said this; but he was dying. Great God, what a man! He fell forward, lying at full-length on the floor. Then I got frightened, and ran away."

By a very great effort only could the commonwealth attorney control his intense excitement. His voice, however, betrayed him as he asked Trumence, after a solemn pause,—

"Why did you not come and tell us all that at once?"

The vagabond shook his head, and said,—

"I meant to do so; but I was afraid. You ought to understand what I mean. I was afraid I might be punished very severely for having run off."

"Your silence has led the court to commit a grievous mistake."

"I had no idea M. Jacques would be found guilty. Big people like him, who can pay great lawyers, always get out of trouble. Besides, I did not think Count Claudieuse would carry out his threat. To be betrayed by one's wife is hard; but to send an innocent man to the galleys"—

"Still you see"—

"Ah, if I could have foreseen! My intentions were good; and I assure you, although I did not come at once to denounce the whole thing, I was firmly resolved to make a clean breast of it if M. Jacques should get into trouble. And the proof of it is, that instead of running off, and going far away, I very quietly lay concealed at the Red Lamb, waiting for the sentence to be published. As soon as I heard what was done last night, I did not lose an hour, and surrendered at once to the gendarmes."

In the meantime, M. Galpin had overcome his first amazement, and now broke out furiously,—

"This man is an impostor. The money he showed us was paid him to bear false witness. How can we credit his story?"

"We must investigate the matter," replied M. Daubigeon. He rang the bell; and, when the usher came in, he asked,—

"Have you done what I told you?"

"Yes, sir," replied the man. "M. de Boiscoran and the servant of Count Claudieuse are here."

"Bring in the woman: when I ring, show M. de Boiscoran in."

This woman was a big country-girl, plain of face, and square of figure. She seemed to be very much excited, and looked crimson in her face.

"Do you remember," asked M. Daubigeon, "that one night last week a man came to your house, and asked to see your mistress?"

"Oh, yes!" replied the honest girl. "I did not want to let him in at first; but he said he came from the court, and then I let him in."

"Would you recognize him?"

"Certainly."

The commonwealth attorney rang again; the door opened, and Jacques came in, his face full of amazement and wonder.

"That is the man!" cried the servant.

"May I know?" asked the unfortunate man.

"Not yet!" replied M. Daubigeon. "Go back, and be of good hope!"

But Jacques remained standing where he was, like a man who has suddenly been overcome, looking all around with amazed eyes, and evidently unable to comprehend.

How could he have comprehended what was going on?

They had taken him out of his cell without warning; they had carried him to the court-house; and here he was confronted with Trumence, whom he thought he should never see again, and with the servant of the Countess Claudieuse.

M. Galpin looked the picture of consternation; and M. Daubigeon, radiant with delight, bade him be of good hope.

Hopeful of what? How? To what purpose?

And Mechinet made him all kinds of signs.

The usher who had brought him in had actually to take him out.

Immediately the commonwealth attorney turned again to the servant-girl and said,—

"Now, my good girl, can you tell me if any thing special happened in connection with this gentleman's visit at your house?"

"There was a great quarrel between him and master and mistress."

"Were you present?"

"No. But I am quite certain of what I say."

"How so?"

"Well, I will tell you. When I went up stairs to tell the countess that there was a gentleman below who came from the courts, she was in a great hurry to go down, and told me to stay with the count, my master. Of course, I did what she said. But no sooner was she down than I heard a loud cry. Master, who had looked all in a stupor, heard it too: he raised himself on his pillow, and asked me where my mistress was. I told him, and he was just settling down to try and fall asleep again, when the sound of loud voices

- 482 -

came up to us. 'That is very singular,' said master. I offered to go down and see what was the matter: but he told me sharply not to stir an inch. And, when the voices became louder and louder, he said, 'I will go down myself. Give me my dressing-gown.'

"Sick as he was, exhausted, and almost on his deathbed, it was very imprudent in him, and might easily have cost him his life. I ventured to speak to him; but he swore at me, and told me to hush, and to do what he ordered me to do.

"The count—God be merciful to his soul!—was a very good man, certainly; but he was a terrible man also, and when he got angry, and talked in a certain way, everybody in the house began to tremble, even mistress.

"I obeyed, therefore, and did what he wanted. Poor man! He was so weak he could hardly stand up, and had to hold on to a chair while I helped him just to hang his dressing-gown over his shoulders.

"Then I asked him if he would not let me help him down. But looking at me with awful eyes, he said, 'You will do me the favor to stay here, and, whatever may happen, if you dare so much as open the door while I am away, you shall not stay another hour in my service.'

"Then he went out, holding on to the wall; and I remained alone in the chamber, all trembling, and feeling as sick as if I had known that a great misfortune was coming upon us.

"However, I heard nothing more for a time; and as the minutes passed away, I was just beginning to reproach myself for having been so foolishly alarmed, when I heard two cries; but, O sir! two such fearful, sharp cries, that I felt cold shivers running all over me.

"As I did not dare leave the room, I put my ear to the door, and I heard distinctly the count's voice, as he was quarrelling with another gentleman. But I could not catch a single word, and only made out that they were angry about a very serious matter.

"All of a sudden, a great but dull noise, like that of the fall of a heavy body, then another awful cry, I had not a drop of blood left in my veins at that moment.

"Fortunately, the other servants, who had gone to bed, had heard something. They had gotten up, and were now coming down the passage.

"I left the room at all hazards, and went down stairs with the others, and there we found my mistress fainting in an armchair, and my master stretched out at full-length, lying on the floor like a dead man."

"What did I say?" cried Trumence.

But the commonwealth attorney made him a sign to keep quiet; and, turning again to the girl, he asked,—

"And the visitor?"

"He was gone, sir. He had vanished."

"What did you do then?"

"We raised up the count: we carried him up stairs and laid him on his bed. Then we brought mistress round again; and the valet went in haste to fetch Dr. Seignebos."

"What said the countess when she recovered her consciousness?"

"Nothing. Mistress looked like a person who has been knocked in the head."

"Was there any thing else?"

"Oh, yes, sir!"

"What?"

"The oldest of the young ladies, Miss Martha, was seized with terrible convulsions."

"How was that?"

"Why, I only know what miss told us herself."

"Let us hear what she said."

"Ah! It is a very singular story. When this gentleman whom I have just seen here rang the bell at our gate, Miss Martha, who had already gone to bed, got up again, and went to the window to see who it was. She saw me go and open, with a candle in my hand,

and come back again with the gentleman behind me. She was just going to bed again, when she thought she saw one of the statues in the garden move, and walk right off. We told her it could not be so; but she did not mind us. She told us over and over again that she was quite sure that she saw that statue come up the avenue, and take a place behind the tree which is nearest to the parlor-window."

Trumence looked triumphant.

"That was I!" he cried.

The girl looked at him, and said, only moderately surprised,—

"That may very well be."

"What do you know about it?" asked M. Daubigeon.

"I know it must have been a man who had stolen into the garden, and who had frightened Miss Martha so terribly, because Dr. Seignebos dropped, in going out, a five-franc piece just at the foot of that tree, where miss said she had seen the man standing. The valet who showed the doctor out helped him look for his money; and, as they sought with the candle, they saw the footprints of a man who wore iron-shod shoes."

"The marks of my shoes!" broke in Trumence again; and sitting down, and raising his legs, he said to the magistrate,—

"Just look at my shoes, and you will see there is no lack of iron nails!"

But there was no need for such evidence; and he was told,—

"Never mind that! We believe you."

"And you, my good girl," said M. Daubigeon again, "can you tell us, if, after these occurrences, Count Claudieuse had any explanation with your mistress?"

"No, I do not know. Only I saw that the count and the countess were no longer as they used to be with each other."

That was all she knew. She was asked to sign her deposition; and then M. Daubigeon told her she might go.

Then, turning to Trumence, he said,—

"You will be taken to jail now. But you are an honest man, and you need not give yourself any trouble. Go now."

The magistrate and the commonwealth attorney remained alone now, since, of course, a clerk counts for nothing.

"Well," said M. Daubigeon, "what do you think of that?"

M. Galpin was dumfounded.

"It is enough to make one mad," he murmured.

"Do you begin to see how that M. Folgat was right when he said the case was far from being so clear as you pretended?"

"Ah! who would not have been deceived as I was? You yourself, at one time at least, were of my opinion. And yet, if the Countess Claudieuse and M. de Boiscoran are both innocent, who is the guilty one?"

"That is what we shall know very soon; for I am determined I will not allow myself a moment's rest till I have found out the truth of the whole matter. How fortunate it was that this fatal error in form should have made the sentence null and void!"

He was so much excited, that he forgot his never-failing quotations. Turning to the clerk, he said,—

"But we must not lose a minute. Put your legs into active motion, my dear Mechinet, and run and ask M. Folgat to come here. I will wait for him here."

III.

When Dionysia, after leaving the Countess Claudieuse, came back to Jacques's parents and his friends, she said, radiant with hope,—

"Now victory is on our side!"

Her grandfather and the Marquis de Boiscoran urged her to explain; but she refused to say any thing, and only later, towards evening, she confessed to M. Folgat what she had done with the countess, and that it was more than probable that the count would, before he died, retract his evidence.

"That alone would save Jacques," said the young advocate.

But his hope only encouraged him to make still greater efforts; and, all overcome as he was by his labors and emotions of the trial, he spent the night in Grandpapa Chandore's study, preparing with M. Magloire the application they proposed to make for a new trial.

They finished only when it was already broad daylight: so he did not care to go to bed, and installed himself in a large easy-chair for the purpose of getting a few hours' rest.

He had, however, not slept more than an hour, when old Anthony roused him to tell him that there was an unknown man down stairs who asked to see him instantly.

M. Folgat rubbed his eyes, and at once went down: in the passage he found himself face to face with a man of some fifty years, of rather suspicious appearance, who wore his mustache and his chin-beard, and was dressed in a tight coat and large trousers, such as old soldiers affect.

"You are M. Folgat?" asked this man.

"Yes."

"Well, I—I am the agent whom friend Goudar sent to England."

The young lawyer started, and asked,—

"Since when are you here?"

"Since this morning, by express. Twenty-four hours too late, I know; for I bought a newspaper at the station. M. de Boiscoran has been found guilty. And yet I swear I did not lose a minute; and I have well earned the gratuity which I was promised in case of success."

"You have been successful, have you?"

"Of course. Did I not tell you in my letter from Jersey that I was sure of success?"

"You have found Suky?"

"Twenty-four hours after I wrote to you,—in a public-house at Bonly Bay. She would not come, the wretch!"

"You have brought her, however?"

"Of course. She is at the Hotel de France, where I have left her till I could come and see you."

"Does she know any thing?"

"Every thing."

"Make haste and bring her here."

From the time when M. Folgat first hoped for this recovery of the servant-girl, he had made up his mind to make the most of her evidence.

He had slipped a portrait of the Countess Claudieuse into an album of Dionysia's, amidst some thirty photographs. He now went for this album, and had just put it upon the centre-table in the parlor when the agent came back with his captive.

She was a tall, stout woman of some forty years, with hard features, masculine manners, and dressed, as all common English-women are, with great pretensions to fashion.

When M. Folgat questioned her, she answered in very fair, intelligible French, which was only marred by her strong English accent,—

"I stayed four years at the house in Vine Street; and I should be there still, but for the war. As soon as I entered upon my duties, I became aware that I was put in charge of a house in which two lovers had their meetings. I was not exactly pleased, because, you know, we have our self-respect; but it was a good place. I had very little to do, and so I staid. However, my master mistrusted me: I saw that very clearly. When a meeting was to take place, my master sent me on some errand to Versailles, to Saint Germain, or even to Orleans. This hurt me so much, that I determined I would find out what they tried so hard to conceal from me. It was not very difficult; and the very next week I knew that my master was no more Sir Francis Burnett than I was; and that he had borrowed the name from a friend of his."

"How did you go about to find it out?"

"Oh! very simply. One day, when my master went away on foot, I followed him, and saw him go into a house in University Street. Before the house opposite, some servants were standing and talking. I asked them who the gentleman was; and they told me it was the son of the Marquis de Boiscoran."

"So much for the master; but the lady."

Suky Wood smiled.

"As for the lady," she replied, "I did the same thing to find her out. It cost me, however, a great deal more time and a great deal more patience, because she took the very greatest precautions; and I lost more than one afternoon in watching her. But, the more she tried to hide, the more I was curious to know, as a matter of course. At last, one evening when she left the house in her carriage, I took a cab and followed her. I traced her thus to her house; and next morning I talked to the servants there, and they told me that she was a lady who lived in the province, but came every year to Paris to spend a month with her parents, and that her name was Countess Claudieuse."

And Jacques had imagined and strongly maintained that Suky would not know any thing, in fact, could not know any thing!

"But did you ever see this lady?" asked M. Folgat.

"As well as I see you."

"Would you recognize her?"

"Among thousands."

"And if you saw her portrait?"

"I should know it at once."

M. Folgat handed her the album.

"Well, look for her," he said.

She had found the likeness in a moment.

"Here she is!" cried Suky, putting her finger on the photograph.

There was no doubt any longer.

"But now, Miss Suky," said the young advocate, "you will have to repeat all that before a magistrate."

"I will do so with pleasure. It is the truth."

"If that is so, they will send for you at your lodgings, and you will please stay there till you are called. You need not trouble yourself about any thing. You shall have whatever you want, and they will pay you your wages as if you were in service."

M. Folgat had not time to say more; for Dr. Seignebos rushed in like a tempest, and cried out at the top of his voice,—

"Victory! We are victorious now! Great Victory!"

But he could not speak before Suky and the agent. They were sent off; and, as soon as they had left the room, he said to M. Folgat,—

"I am just from the hospital. I have seen Goudar. He had done it. He had made Cocoleu talk."

"And what does he say?"

"Well, exactly what I knew he would say, as soon as they could loose his tongue. But you will hear it all; for it is not enough that Cocoleu should confess it to Goudar: there must be witnesses present to certify to the confessions of the wretch."

"He will not talk before witnesses."

"He must not see them: they can be concealed. The place is admirably adapted for such a purpose."

"But how, if Cocoleu refuses to talk after the witnesses have been introduced?"

"He will not. Goudar has found out a way to make him talk whenever he wants it. Ah! that man is a clever man, and understands his business thoroughly. Have you full confidence in him?"

"Oh, entire!"

"Well, he says he is sure he will succeed. 'Come to-day,' he said to me, 'between one and two, with M. Folgat, the commonwealth attorney, and M. Galpin: put yourself where I will show you, and then let me go to work.' Then he showed me the place where he wants us to remain, and told me how we should let him know when we are all ready."

M. Folgat did not hesitate.

"We have not a moment to lose. Let me go at once to the court-house."

But they were hardly in the passage when they were met by Mechinet, who came running up out of breath, and half mad with delight.

"M. Daubigeon sends me to say you must come to him at once. Great news! Great news!"

And immediately he told them in a few words what had happened in the morning,—Trumence's statement, and the deposition of the maid of Countess Claudieuse.

"Ah, now we are safe!" cried Dr. Seignebos.

M. Folgat was pale with excitement. Still he proposed,—

"Let us tell the marquis and Miss Dionysia what is going on before we leave the house."

"No," said the doctor, "no! Let us wait till every thing is quite safe. Let us go quick; let us go at once."

They were right to make haste. The magistrate and the commonwealth attorney were waiting for them with the greatest impatience. As soon as they came into the small room of the clerk's office, M. Daubigeon cried,—

"Well, I suppose Mechinet has told you all?"

"Yes," replied M. Folgat; "but we have some information of which you have heard as yet nothing."

Then he told them that Suky Wood had arrived, and what she had given in as evidence.

M. Galpin had sunk into a chair, completely crushed by the weight of so many proofs of his misapprehension of the case. There he sat without saying a word, without moving a muscle. But M. Daubigeon was radiant.

"Most assuredly," he cried, "Jacques must be innocent!"

"Most assuredly he is innocent!" said Dr. Seignebos; "and the proof of it is, that I know who is guilty."

"Oh!"

"And you will know too, if you will take the trouble of following me, with M. Galpin, to the hospital."

It was just striking one; and not one of them all had eaten any thing that morning. But they had no time to think of breakfast.

Without a shadow of hesitation, M. Daubigeon turned to M. Galpin, and said,—

"Will you come, Galpin?"

The poor magistrate rose mechanically, after the manner of an automaton, and they went out, creating no small sensation among the good people of Sauveterre, when they appeared thus all in a group.

M. Daubigeon spoke first to the lady superior of the hospital; and, when he had explained to her what their purpose was in coming there, she raised her eyes heavenward, and said with a sigh of resignation,—

"Well, gentlemen, do as you like, and I hope you will be successful; for it is a sore trial for us poor sisters to have these continual visitations in the name of the law."

"Please follow me, then, to the Insane Ward, gentlemen," said the doctor.

They call the Insane Ward at the Sauveterre hospital a small, low building, with a sanded court in front, and a tall wall around the whole. The building is divided into six cells, each of which has two doors,—one opening into the court, and the other an outside door for the assistants and servants.

It was to one of these latter doors that Dr. Seignebos led his friends. And after having recommended to them the most perfect silence, so as not to rouse Cocoleu's suspicions, he invited them into one of the cells, in which the door leading into the court had been closed. There was, however, a little grated window in the upper part of the door, so that they could, without being seen, both see and hear all that was said and done in the court reserved for the use of the insane.

Not two yards from the little window, Goudar and Cocoleu were sitting on a wooden bench in the bright sunlight.

By long study and a great effort of will, Goudar had succeeded in giving to his face a most perfect expression of stupidity: even the people belonging to the hospital thought he was more idiotic than the other.

He held in his hand his violin, which the doctor had ordered to be left to him; and he accompanied himself with a few notes, as he repeated the same familiar song which he had sung on the New-Market Square when he first accosted M. Folgat.

Cocoleu, a large piece of bread-and-butter in one hand, and a big clasp-knife in the other, was finishing his meal.

But this music delighted him so intensely, that he actually forgot to eat, and, with hanging lip and half-closed eyes, rocked himself to and fro, keeping time with the measure.

"They look hideous!" M. Folgat could not keep from whispering. In the meantime Goudar, warned by the preconcerted signal, had finished his song. He bent over, and drew from under the bench an enormous bottle, from which he seemed to draw a considerable quantity of something pleasant.

Then he passed it to Cocoleu, who likewise began to pull, eagerly and long, and with an expression of idiotic beatitude. Then patting his stomach with his hands, he said,—

"That's—that's—that's—good!"

M. Daubigeon whispered into Dr. Seignebos's ear,—

"Ah, I begin to see! I notice from Cocoleu's eyes, that this practice with the bottle must have been going on for some time already. Cocoleu is drunk."

Goudar again took up his violin and repeated his song.

"I—I—want—want to—to drink!" stammered Cocoleu.

Goudar kept him waiting a little while, and then handed him the bottle. The idiot threw back his head, and drank till he had lost his breath. Then Goudar asked,—

"Ah! you did not have such good wine to drink at Valpinson?"

"Oh, yes!" replied Cocoleu.

"But as much as you wanted?"

"Yes. Quite—enough."

And, laughing with some difficulty, he stammered, and stuttered out,—

"I got—got into the cellar through one of the windows; and I drank—drank through—through a—a straw."

"You must be sorry you are no longer there?"

"Oh, yes!"

"But, if you were so well off at Valpinson, why did you set it on fire?"

The witnesses of the strange scene crowded to the little window of the cell, and held their breath with eager expectation.

"I wanted to burn some fagots only, to make the count come out. It was not my fault, if the whole house got on fire."

"And why did you want to kill the count?"

"Because I wanted the great lady to marry M. de Boiscoran."

"Ah! She told you to do it, did she?"

"Oh, no! But she cried so much; and then she told me she would be so happy if her husband were dead. And she was always good to Cocoleu; and the count was always bad; and so I shot him."

"Well! But why, then, did you say it was M. de Boiscoran who shot the count?"

"They said at first it was me. I did not like that. I would rather they should cut off his head than mine."

He shuddered as he said this, so that Goudar, afraid of having gone rather too fast, took up his violin, and gave him a verse of his song to quiet him. Then accompanying his words still now and then with a few notes, and after having allowed Cocoleu to caress his bottle once more, he asked again,—

"Where did you get a gun?"

"I—I had taken it from the count to shoot birds: and I—I have it still—still. It is hid in the hole where Michael found me."

Poor Dr. Seignebos could not stand it any longer. He suddenly pushed open the door, and, rushing into the court, he cried,—

"Bravo, Goudar! Well done!"

At the noise, Cocoleu had started up. He evidently understood it all; for terror drove the fumes of the wine out of his mind in an instant, and he looked frightened to death.

"Ah, you scoundrel!" he howled.

And, throwing himself upon Goudar, he plunged his knife twice into him.

The movement was so rapid and so sudden, that it had been impossible to prevent it. Pushing M. Folgat violently back as he tried to disarm him, Cocoleu leaped into a corner of the court, and there, looking like a wild beast driven to bay, his eyes bloodshot, his mouth foaming, he threatened with his formidable knife to kill any one who should come near him.

At the cries of M. Daubigeon and M. Galpin, the assistants in the hospital came rushing in. The struggle, however, would probably have been a long one, notwithstanding their numbers, if one of the keepers had not, with great presence of mind, climbed up to the top of the wall, and caught the arm of the wretch in a noose. By these means he was thrown down in a moment, disarmed, and rendered harmless.

"You—you may—may do—do what you—you choose; I—I won't say—say another w-w-word!"

In the meantime, poor Dr. Seignebos, who had unwillingly caused the catastrophe, was distressed beyond measure; still he hastened to the assistance of Goudar, who lay insensible on the sand of the court. The two wounds which the detective had received were quite serious, but not fatal, or even very dangerous, as the knife had been turned aside by the ribs. He was at once carried into one of the private rooms of the hospital, and soon recovered his consciousness.

When he saw all four of the gentlemen bending anxiously over his bed, he murmured with a mournful smile,—

"Well, was I not right when I said that my profession is a rascally profession?"

"But you are at liberty now to give it up," replied M. Folgat, "provided always a certain house in Vine Street should not prove too small for your ambition."

The pale face of the detective recovered its color for a moment.

"Will they really give it to me?" he asked.

"Since you have discovered the real criminal, and handed him over to justice."

"Well, then, I will bless these wounds: I feel that I shall be up again in a fortnight. Give me quick pen and ink, that I may write my resignation immediately, and tell my wife the good news."

He was interrupted by the entrance of one of the officers of the court, who, walking up to the commonwealth attorney, said to him respectfully,—

"Sir, the priest from Brechy is waiting for you at your office."

"I am coming directly," replied M. Daubigeon.

And, turning to his companions, he said,—

"Let us go, gentlemen."

The priest was waiting, and rose quickly from his chair when he saw M. Daubigeon enter, accompanied by M. Galpin, M. Folgat, and Dr. Seignebos.

"Perhaps you wish to speak to me alone, sir?" asked M. Daubigeon.

"No, sir," replied the old priest, "no! The words of reparation which have been intrusted to me must be uttered publicly." And handing him a letter, he added,—

"Read this. Please read it aloud."

The commonwealth attorney tore the envelope with a tremulous hand, an then read,—

"Being about to die as a Christian, as I have lived as a Christian, I owe it to myself, I owe it to God whom I have offended, and I owe it to those men whom I have deceived, to declare the truth.

"Actuated by hatred, I have been guilty of giving false evidence in court, and of stating wrongfully that M. de Boiscoran is the man who shot at me, and that I recognized him in the act.

"I did not only not recognize him, but I know that he is innocent. I am sure of it; and I swear it by all I hold sacred in this world which I am about to leave, and in that world in which I must appear before my sovereign Judge.

"May M. de Boiscoran pardon me as I pardon myself.

"TRIVULCE COUNT CLAUDIEUSE."

"Poor man!" murmured M. Folgat.

The priest at once went on,—

"You see, gentlemen, Count Claudieuse withdraws his charge unconditionally. He asks for nothing in return: he only wants the truth to be established. And yet I beg leave to express the last wishes of a dying man. I beseech you, in the new trial, to make no mention of the name of the countess."

Tears were seen in all eyes.

"You may rest assured, reverend father," said M. Daubigeon, "that Count Claudieuse's last wishes shall be attended to. The name of the countess shall not appear. There will be no need for it. The secret of her wrongs shall be religiously kept by those who know it."

It was four o'clock now.

An hour later there arrived at the court-house a gendarme and Michael, the son of the Boiscoran tenant, who had been sent out to ascertain if Cocoleu's statement was true. They brought back the gun which the wretch had used, and which he had concealed in that den which he had dug out for himself in the forest of Rochepommier, and where Michael had discovered him the day after the crime.

Henceforth Jacques's innocence was as clear as daylight; and although he had to bear the burden of his sentence till the judgment was declared void, it was decided, with the consent of the president of the court, M. Domini, and the active cooperation of M. Gransiere, that he should be set free that same evening.

M. Folgat and M. Magloire were charged with the pleasant duty of informing the prisoner of this happy news. They found him walking up and down in his cell like a madman, devoured by unspeakable anguish, and not knowing what to make of the words of hope which M. Daubigeon had spoken to him in the morning.

He was hopeful, it is true; and yet when he was told that he was safe, that he was free, he sank, an inert mass, into a chair, being less able to bear joy than sorrow.

But such emotions are not apt to last long. A few moments later, and Jacques de Boiscoran, arm in arm with his counsel, left his prison, in which he had for several months suffered all that an honest man can suffer. He had paid a fearful penalty for what, in the eyes of so many men, is but a trifling wrong.

When they reached the street in which the Chandores lived, M. Folgat said to his client,—

"They do not expect you, I am sure. Go slowly, while I go ahead to prepare them."

He found Jacques's parents and friends assembled in the parlor, suffering great anxiety; for they had not been able to ascertain if there were any truth in the vague rumors which had reached them.

The young advocate employed the utmost caution in preparing them for the truth; but at the first words Dionysia asked,—

"Where is Jacques?"

Jacques was kneeling at her feet, overcome with gratitude and love.

V.

The next day the funeral of Count Claudieuse took place. His youngest daughter was buried at the same time; and in the evening the Countess left Sauveterre, to make her home henceforth with her father in Paris.

In the proper course of the law, the sentence which condemned Jacques was declared null and void; and Cocoleu, found guilty of having committed the crime at Valpinson, was sentenced to hard labor for life.

A month later Jacques de Boiscoran was married at the church in Brechy to Dionysia de Chandore. The witnesses for the bridegroom were M. Magloire and Dr. Seignebos; the witnesses for the bride, M. Folgat and M. Daubigeon.

Even the excellent commonwealth attorney laid aside on that day some of his usual gravity. He continually repeated,—

> *"Nunc est bibendum, nunc pede libero*
>
> *Pulsanda tellus."*

And he really did drink his glass of wine, and opened the ball with the bride.

M. Galpin, who was sent to Algiers, was not present at the wedding. But M. Mechinet was there, quite brilliant, and, thanks to Jacques, free from all pecuniary troubles.

The two Blangins, husband and wife, have well-nigh spent the whole of the large sums of money which they extorted from Dionysia. Trumence, private bailiff at Boiscoran, is the terror of all vagrants.

And Goudar, in his garden and nursery, sells the finest peaches in Paris.

Lightning Source UK Ltd.
Milton Keynes UK
UKHW040623221118
332785UK00001B/145/P